Declan O'Duinne

The Saga of Roland Inness
Book 6

Wayne Grant

For Phyllis and Don

Contents

NORTHERN IRELAND
1196

Tir Eoghain

Antrim

Castle
Carrickfergus

Tullyhogue

River Blackwater

Lough
Neagh

O'Duinne Rask

River Lagan

Down

River Bann

Armagh
Abbey

Down Abbey

Connacht

Meath

Irish Sea

Dublin

Leinster

N
W   E
S

Names and Places

~

Cenél Eoghain	The clans of central Ulster. Descendants of Niall of the Nine Hostages.
Clan	Extended family or kinship group.
Ford on the Lagan	Site of modern-day Belfast.
Ford on the Bann	Site near modern Portadown.
Levies	Troops drafted into service
Sept	Subgroup of a larger clan.
Tandragee	Site of fictional battle near modern Tandragee.
Tir Eoghain	Central Ulster, covering modern Counties Tyrone and Derry. Held sway over County Armagh. Home of the Cenél Eoghain clans.
Tullyhogue	Hill northeast of Dungannon where the O'Neill chiefs were inaugurated.
Ulster	One of the four ancient Kingdoms of Ireland, taking up the northern quarter of the island.

Declan O'Duinne

Prologue

April, 1196 AD—Tandragee, Ulster

*H*ugh O'Neill lurched to his right, dodging the sword thrust aimed at his throat. The razor-sharp blade slid along his hide-covered shield, digging a furrow but drawing no blood. The man who lunged at him stumbled forward, off balance, into the gap in the Irish line. It was a fatal mistake.

O'Neill pivoted back to his left and brought his axe down behind the Englishman's steel helmet. The blow did not penetrate the mail coif there, but the force of it broke the man's neck. He fell face-down into the bloody, churned-up muck at O'Neill's feet and did not stir. He would be one of the few English knights slain this day.

The stocky Irishman slid left, straddling the Englishman's corpse and hooking the blade of his axe over the rim of an enemy shield. Leaning back, he dragged the shield forward and down. Its owner tried desperately to rip his arm free of the straps but the forward pressure held him secure. The man was an Irish auxiliary who fought for the English and had no mail to protect him. A quick sword thrust by one of O'Neill's warriors pierced him just above the heart.

O'Neill looked down his line. For two hours they had pressed the English hard. Again and again he had led his men along the southern slope of the broad valley to strike the enemy left flank. Here the lines were manned by Irish levies from Antrim and Down who fought by choice or necessity for Sir John de Courcy, the Englishman who ruled the eastern third of

1

Ulster. The Irish lines were stiffened by English knights clad from head to toe in chain mail.

De Courcy's attack had been a surprise and by the time the clans of the Cenél Eoghain had gathered to oppose him he'd crossed the River Bann with seven hundred men and had reached a place the locals called Tandragee, only twelve miles from the sacred abbey town of Armagh. For the clans, Armagh was more than an abbey and village perched on a hill. The church atop that hill was the mother church of all Ireland, founded by Saint Patrick himself when first he brought Christianity to the island. To lose Armagh would be a grievous blow, not only to the Cenél Eoghain who controlled the region, but to the Irish church as well.

And so the clans had gathered.

Outnumbered, de Courcy had pulled his men back to higher ground and dared the Irish to attack. And attack they had. Three times O'Neill watched his men break through the enemy ranks only to be thrown back by the English knights de Courcy had positioned just behind his lines. Now, as the afternoon drew on, the hillside was littered with the bodies of Irishmen on both sides—too many were men of the O'Neill clans, *his men.* They were dying for a king's folly and his own damned pride!

There was no time to think on that now as the English and their Irish levies gave ground slowly up the hill. His men pressed in on them, their war cries mixing with the clash of steel on steel, screams of pain and pleas to God. Then, above the din, Hugh heard a sound he dreaded. It was the piercing note of a hunting horn, the signal to retreat. It came from far off to his left, down on the valley floor. He prayed it was a mistake, but the horn sounded three more times.

O'Neill cursed. He had feared this, had argued against attacking the English on open ground, had begged the King to wait, but Muirchertach Mac Lochlainn had overruled him. This was not O'Neill's first battle against the English and meeting them in the open like this seldom ended well.

He'd pleaded with Mac Lochlainn to fall back to higher ground and let the English attack him there, but the King had refused, openly hinting that O'Neill and his clans had no stomach for a fight. That had stung his pride. And so he'd allowed himself to be goaded into joining a frontal attack against these English invaders. He'd been a fool.

This time would be different.

That's what the King had said. *This time*, they would march into battle against the English bearing the holiest of relics from Armagh—the bell of Saint Patrick. The venerable saint would not fail them. *This time*, God would give them the victory and they would drive the accursed English back into the sea!

Saint Patrick's bell.

Hugh well understood the power this sacred artefact had over the hearts of men. His own clansmen had fallen to their knees in the dawn as Eamon Maelchallain, hereditary Keeper of the bell, paraded the relic before them. To the Irish, Saint Patrick's bell was more than a symbol of Christian faith. It stood for ancient customs passed down in Ulster since the time of Niall of the Nine Hostages, traditions that made the Irish who they were.

The bell itself was not visible, shielded inside a beautifully crafted shrine of bronze and gold that had dazzled in the early morning light. As the shrine passed along the Irish lines, men crossed themselves and arose, sure in their hearts of victory. Hugh had knelt and crossed himself with the others, but doubted that God picked sides in these fights, or that a bell, no matter how sacred, would decide the outcome.

Now, all of his doubts and forebodings came back to him, as down in the valley, he heard another desperate blast from the hunting horn. The Mac Lochlainn clans held the line there, so the signal must have come from the King himself. He edged back behind his own line to see what was happening below and the sight made his stomach clench.

The English heavy cavalry had ripped a gaping hole in the Irish lines on the valley floor and a rout was on. Riders on their big, English-bred warhorses, surged through the gap in the line and fell on the Mac Lochlainn men like a pack of wolves. Their deadly blades rose and fell, glinting in the late afternoon sun. Men went down like wheat before the scythe.

He saw that his own chieftains had heard the horn and were following the orders he'd given them before launching their first

3

charge against the English positions. All along the O'Neill shield wall, men began to back away slowly, edging up the slope toward the thick woods that crowned the southern lip of the valley. He'd ordered their horses picketed on the far side of those woods. Once into the trees, they could break contact with the enemy and, God willing, flee the field without being cut to pieces. It was the only wise decision he'd made this day.

O'Neill looked back toward the valley floor and saw the King's banner fall in the dust. Desperate Irish warriors encircled the Keeper of St Patrick's bell, but to no avail. The English knights rode them under. Eamon Maelchallain fell along with the rest.

O'Neill watched, aghast, as a tall knight, clad in shimmering mail and a white tunic, dismounted from a magnificent white warhorse, and wrenched the bell from its dead Keeper's hands. He'd seen this man before, on other fields of battle. As Sir John de Courcy lifted Patrick's bell in triumph over his head, the leader of Clan O'Neill turned away in disgust.

"Damn the English and damn all Mac Lochlainns!" he cursed and backed away toward the safety of the trees.

***

Finbar Mac Cormaic dabbed a cool cloth on his master's forehead and was pleased to see the man had drifted off to sleep. Cathal O'Duinne had been brought in half-dead and senseless the night before with a deep gash along his rib cage. It had taken his men two days to carry O'Duinne from the field of battle beyond Armagh to his rath in the valley of the Blackwater River and the clan chieftain had lost a lot of blood.

Finbar had gasped when he'd seen his old friend's chalk-white pallor and went to work immediately trying to save him. He'd cleaned and stitched up the wound with practiced skill, but knew that the rest was in God's hands. If Cathal managed to survive the loss of blood and if the wound did not fester, he might yet live. Finbar prayed that he would, but dreaded the news he would have to give his master when he came back to his senses.

For Cathal O'Duinne had lost much more than blood at the fight at Tandragee and it would be Finbar who would have to break the bad tidings to him. Cathal's oldest son, Fagan, had been slain outright, an arrow in his heart, and Keiran, his younger, lay in the next room, racked with fever and missing his right hand, sliced cleanly off by an English broadsword.

All through the night, Finbar had moved between the two wounded men. Near dawn, Keiran's fever abated a little and he took a sip of water. The young warrior looked up at his father's old counsellor with red-rimmed eyes and held up the bandaged stump where his sword hand had been.

"Finbar," he managed to croak, "ye should've let it bleed."

Finbar grimaced. When they'd dragged Keiran in, the stump of his wrist had already been cauterized with a hot blade, but it still bled. He'd used all of his skill to stop the young man's blood loss, binding up the wound with honey and linen. He'd changed the dressing three times through the night and had thanked God when the wound began to clot. Now he realized that the loss of the lad's hand was not the only wound that would need to be treated. He shook his head.

"If yer t' die, Keiran, it'll be God's doin' and none of my own," the older man said sternly. "Ye must be strong. We've lost yer brother and yer father lies in the next room, closer to death than yerself. If, God forbid, he leaves us, the clan will look to you in the days ahead, lad."

Keiran lifted his head from the cot, his eyes brimming with tears.

"They must look elsewhere," he said bitterly, "for I cannot even hold a sword!"

Finbar sighed. Keiran had always lived in the shadow of his older brother, Fagan, and had long ago accepted his lot. The oldest O'Duinne son had been handsome and charismatic and had made no secret of his ambition to succeed his father. Few would have challenged that succession, though Finbar had his doubts about Fagan. Unlike his father who was steady and prudent, the son had been notably rash and hot-headed. Now he was dead and that no longer mattered.

Finbar looked back at Keiran who had fallen back on his cot, his eyes tightly closed. Keiran had been an honest and earnest boy and more than a little clever, but he'd always suffered from

5

crippling doubts and those had not been eased by the dominance of his older brother. Finbar shook his head. With Fagan gone, Keiran could have stepped out of the shadows and made a better clan chief than his dead brother, but this wound…. He knew the stump would heal but would Keiran's spirit?

Finbar slipped quietly out of the room and returned to look in on Cathal. The chieftain seemed to be sleeping, but his breathing was rapid. Finbar touched the wounded man's forehead. It was hot, a sign of infection, though the wound still looked clean. It would now depend on the strength of Cathal O'Duinne's constitution whether he lived or died. Finbar knew that his master was as tough as boot leather and had taken many wounds in his life, but Cathal was no longer young. The man had seen close to fifty summers. Perhaps this would be his last.

So much of Finbar's own life had been bound up with the life of his clan chief. Though he was older by three years than Cathal, they had been boyhood friends. Cathal's father was chieftain of the O'Duinne sept in those days and from an early age, Cathal had shown all the qualities of a leader. He could ride like he'd been born in the saddle and out-wrestle boys who were years older. He was brave and strong and good-natured, though sometimes impulsive. Cathal O'Duinne was all the things that Finbar Mac Cormaic had never been.

As a boy with a spindly frame, Finbar had shown no promise as a warrior and, while not averse to hard work, had displayed little aptitude for herding or farming. As these were the principle occupations men were expected to fill in the sept, his prospects had been limited. But while he was not particularly strong or especially brave, he was clever—very clever. And it was this that set the course of his life.

By age seven, Finbar's active mind took in everything around him in the sept and beyond. He could look at the sun and predict when the cattle would be moved to summer pastures and when the salmon would appear in the rivers. He knew where to find the best stones for the slings used to bring down hares and birds. He knew which of the sept's mothers might hand out sweet morsels to begging boys and which would chase the same boys with a switch. By the age of twelve, he ofttimes heard news from beyond the borders of Tir Eoghain before the men of the sept did.

These talents did not endear Finbar to other boys who found him strange. They mercilessly bullied him until Cathal O'Duinne intervened. Cathal could not abide abusing the weak and took the skinny older boy under his wing. But what began as an act of mercy grew into true friendship. The son of the sept chieftain did not find Finbar's talents strange or frightening. He found them useful. Many a boyhood adventure, and not a few brilliant jests, were launched by Finbar's clever mind and that cemented the bond between them.

Years later, when Cathal became the leader of the O'Duinnes, he had bound Finbar to him by oath. For twenty years thereafter, Finbar Mac Cormaic served as Cathal's closest advisor. It was a role that did not make him popular, but Cathal would not hear a word spoken against his old friend.

Weary beyond words, Finbar turned at last to go, but then Cathal croaked at him from the bed.

"My sons. Finbar, have my sons come to me."

Finbar hung his head. He wanted to lie to the man, to cozen him until he had some of his strength back, but in over forty years of friendship, he had never done such a thing and could not change the habits of a lifetime.

"My lord...Cathal...they cannot come. Fagan was slain in the battle with the English. He is buried on the hill next to your wife."

Finbar heard a half groan, half sob come from the bed.

"Keiran?"

"He lies in the next room, Cathal. Gravely wounded, like yourself, but alive."

Cathal swung his legs off the bed and tried to rise, but fell forward on his hands and knees. Finbar shouted for help and a servant hurried in. Together they lifted the man back onto his bed. Cathal's eyes were slightly mad now and as Finbar started to draw back he sat up and grasped the old man's robe with a gnarled and scarred hand, pulling his old counsellor close.

"I am dying," he gasped, and slumped back onto the bed. The madness drained from his eyes and he looked at Finbar with supplication.

"My sons…Finbar, my sons."

***

Finbar stepped out of the wounded man's chamber and into the common room of the large round house that dominated the walled rath. He found a bench and slumped down. He had not slept in a day and a half and was bone tired. His chin was on his chest and he considered how grey his beard had become.

I'm old, he thought.

He tried to clear his mind. There were important decisions to be made. The clans of the Cenél Eoghain had taken a terrible beating east of Armagh. Many clan chiefs had been killed or wounded and their holiest treasure, the bell of Saint Patrick had been taken from them. Muirchertach Mac Lochlainn, King of Tir Eoghain, had fallen at Tandragee and the men of the Mac Lochlainn clans, fighting on the valley floor, had suffered grievous losses.

Only Hugh O'Neill's skilful fighting retreat into thick woods had saved the O'Neill clans from the same fate, though their losses had been considerable. Word had reached Finbar earlier in the day that Conor, the dead king's son, was laying claim to the throne. The young Mac Lochlainn was calling for a council to be convened at Armagh in just over a fortnight to ratify his right to lead the Cenél Eoghain and rule over Tir Eoghain.

But that right was sure to be challenged. For there were two royal lines within the clans of the Cenél Eoghain—the Mac Lochlainns and the O'Neills. For three hundred years, the kings of Tir Eoghain had come from one of these royal clans, but for the last hundred of those years, only a Mac Lochlainn had ruled.

Hugh O'Neill had made it clear that he would make his own claim to the kingship at the coming council and expected all of the O'Neill septs to stand behind him. Some of these septs, like the O'Cahans and the O'Hagans were large and powerful clans themselves. The O'Duinne clan was a small sept, but was well known for its steadfast support of the O'Neills across uncounted generations. Now that loyalty was about to be tested like never before and the O'Duinnes had no leader capable of standing with Hugh at the council!

Finbar sighed and wished, for the thousandth time, that Maeve O'Duinne were still alive. Cathal's wife had been as smart and steady as her husband and always listened to Finbar's counsel, though she had not always agreed with it. Maeve could have taken up the leadership of the clan until Cathal or Keiran recovered. But she had been gone for over twenty years now, dying as she gave birth to Cathal's youngest son. He missed her still.

Finbar stroked his long beard. To fail the O'Neills at this critical time would forever diminish the standing of the O'Duinnes within the clan. Perhaps Cathal could restore that standing once he recovered, but what if he died? That would truly be a disaster for the sept and for Finbar personally. His unflinching loyalty to Cathal had made him few friends within the extended O'Duinne sept.

I wouldn't last a week, he thought.

He got unsteadily to his feet. He needed sleep, but that would have to wait. An idea had started to nag at him—something that hovered just out of his recollection. He knew from long experience to pay attention to such things. He closed his eyes and tried to clear his mind. And...there it was.

Maeve.

Of course! Sweet Maeve, dying in childbirth. There was *another* O'Duinne heir out there, the youngest of them all. It was a desperate idea, but with Cathal feverish and hovering near death, he could not stake all on the damaged and despairing Keiran. To rely on that thin reed to save the sept's position—and his own—was folly.

He must find the youngest O'Duinne brother.

***

"What?"

Finbar's wife looked at him as though he had lost his mind.

"I said I go to fetch Cathal's son, woman. Now help me find my traveling cloak."

He tried to sound commanding, but that voice rarely worked with his wife. She turned on him, hands on hips.

9

"That boy was taken off to England ten years ago, Finbar. How will you find him and bring him home? You can barely drive a cow into the rath."

"Nevertheless, I will go."

Finbar's wife groaned in frustration.

"Even if you can find your way to England, husband, it's a very big place. Bigger than all Ireland I'm told. How will you find the boy in such a place?"

"You give me too little credit, my dear. I'm a man of no great strength of limb, but when my mind is set on a thing I will see it done. I will ride to the sea and take ship for England. The man who took the boy was from the west of that country as I recall. He was a man of some consequence and if he still lives, there will be those who know of him. I will find that man and when I do, I will find Cathal's son."

"Oh, I give credit when it's due, Finbar Mac Cormaic, but you yourself told me the man who took the lad was a Norman knight. Men of that ilk are born to war and anyone long in such a man's company is most likely dead."

"Nevertheless, I will go."

His wife stamped her foot in frustration.

"I forbid you!" she commanded. "Who will tend to our master if you are off wandering, lost in England?"

"You will, wife. You are as good a leech as I."

"But…"

Finbar raised an open palm to silence her.

"I am not yours to command, my dear. I am Cathal O'Duinne's man to the end and will do what I must to serve him."

Finbar's wife glared at him, ready with an angry retort, but bit back the words. When Finbar's mind was set, there was little chance of changing it.

"Very well, Finbar. Do what you will. You are a foolish old man, but I love you and will pray for yer safe return."

Finbar smiled at her. They'd been together for near fifteen years and she had been a better wife than he had deserved. He walked across the small room they shared and kissed her on the cheek.

"Now help me pack."

She nodded and sniffed, but rummaged around and pulled a leather sack from beneath the sleeping platform and stuffed in his one change of clothes and a few other items that might be useful on a long trip. As she helped him prepare, he turned his attention back to the journey ahead.

He was vague as to exactly where England lay, but knew it was far to the east and across the sea. He had never travelled farther from home than Armagh, which was little more than two leagues away—hardly more than a day's walk.

"De Laval." He said the name out loud.

That had been the Norman's name. He would go to the west of England and look for de Laval there. When he found the Norman, he would find the missing son.

He would find Declan O'Duinne.

The Lost Son

Brother Cyril whistled quietly to himself as he strolled along Barn Lane, which ran just inside the north wall of Chester and up to Northgate Street. He'd made his final stop of the evening at the Holy Goose, one of the finer taverns in the city, and found not a one of his men in their cups. That, and the pleasant evening air of mid-April, had put him in a cheerful mood.

When he had first found his way to Chester two years before, he'd been adrift, a monk in search of penance for murdering a man. Ivar Longbeard, one of the last of the Viking raiders, had killed Cyril's family and taken him as slave from Northumbria. Shipwrecked with his captor on a black sand beach in distant Thule, he'd cut Ivar's throat while the man lay senseless and shoved the body into the sea. Half-dead, he'd been found by Ivar's family and nursed back to health.

To save himself, Cyril had posed as a priest and they'd shown him great kindness, never knowing he'd killed their kinsman. It was their kindness as much as the murder itself that troubled his conscience. In time, he'd sailed back to Britain and taken Holy orders, but still felt he had not fully cleansed his soul of guilt.

He'd travelled across England looking for redemption and found it in Chester. There he had come upon a man face-down in a gutter. The man was trying to rise, but between the ale and a missing arm, he kept slipping back into the muck. Cyril pulled him out and, draping the man's one good arm over his shoulder, helped him stumble back to a barracks near the centre of town. That had been his introduction to the famed Invalid Company and to his new calling.

Like most in England, he had heard of the Invalids and their heroic exploits in the late civil war between Prince John and the forces loyal to King Richard, but what he had found in Chester was at odds with the tales and songs he'd heard of these men. With the war done, the Invalids had reverted to drunkards and brawlers and disturbers of the peace. For a monk in search of a penance, the Invalids were, literally, a Godsend.

Without being invited, he began patrolling the seamier quarters of the town and helping these damaged men to their beds before the cock crowed at dawn. He had wiped the filth from their faces and interceded for them with the Bishop when their outrages became intolerable. It was a burden that suited him. And the Invalids, at first scornful, had come to love the skinny little monk who looked after them and did not judge. They had delighted in proclaiming him their chaplain and he had felt honoured by their trust. Now, for the first time in years, he was fully at peace with himself—and so he whistled.

He was about to turn south on Northgate Street and make his way back to his own little nook in the Invalids' barracks when he saw an old man stumbling along Barn Lane as though lost, or more likely drunk. He crossed over the lane and approached the man.

"Grandfather, you look lost," he called out cheerily.

The old man's head came up sharply as he saw this stranger approach. It was dark, but Cyril could see the man straighten himself, though the effort left the poor fellow swaying a bit from side to side. He'd seen men do this many times as they prepared to make a slurring defence of their sobriety, but as the monk came near, he smelled no drink on the man's breath and the eyes sunk beneath grey brows were sharp and unclouded by ale. No, this man was weary to the bone, not drunk.

"Can I help you, friend?" Cyril asked gently.

The man reached out and grasped the sleeve of the monk's rough brown robe and began to speak haltingly, but with urgency in his voice.

"Aye, Aye, I…"

13

Cyril leaned forward. Those old, sharp eyes never left the monk's own as the words tumbled out in a rush. He spoke in Gaelic, a language Cyril knew a little, but the words came too fast for the monk to follow. Among them, though, was a name very familiar to Brother Cyril.

De Laval.

***

"Roger! Please take care. The boy isn't a rag doll!"

Sir Roger de Laval did not look up at his wife, but spoke to the boy instead, as he stopped bouncing the child on his knee.

"Grandmother says I should stop, Rolf. What do you think?"

The boy began to bounce himself up and down on the big man's knee and his eyes, grey-green like his mother's, begged to resume their game. Sir Roger smiled, setting his knee back in motion as little Rolf grinned. He might be only a year and a half old, but he liked this game and had no fear that the big man would drop him. Sir Roger smiled up at Lady Catherine.

"See, Cathy? He likes it and he's a sturdy little thing."

The knight suddenly straightened his bouncing leg, pitching the boy backwards. Rolf squealed with delight as his "horse" collapsed under him. The sudden drop was the whole point of the game and he knew the strong hands that held his pudgy little wrists would not let him fall.

"Roger, really!" said Lady Catherine. "Don't let Millie see you doing that!"

Sir Roger laughed.

"She can hardly object, Cathy. As you may recall, I played the very same game with her when she was a babe!"

"And he never dropped me once, Mother."

Sir Roger and Lady Catherine looked up to see that their daughter had entered the great hall at Shipbrook.

At his mother's voice, Rolf Inness turned and shouted with glee.

"Horsey!"

Millicent Inness had to smile. She had vague memories of playing "horsey" with the big man who now held her little son. Seeing the two of them together like this touched her heart. They'd travelled to Shipbrook after the spring barley had been planted on the Danish steads up near the Weaver River, but would be leaving on the morrow to return to Danesford. The thought left her a bit wistful.

She loved Shipbrook like a favourite old shoe. She'd grown up here and it had been a happy childhood. As she watched her parents dote on her firstborn, she felt a lump in her throat. She missed them and knew they felt the same about her. But Danesford was her life now and she would not trade that.

"Rolf, let's watch for your father," she said holding out her arms. Roland had ridden out with Declan O'Duinne at first light to join his friend on his daily patrol along the border. It was past noon now and they were due back soon. Sir Roger let the child slide down his legs till his feet touched the floor. The boy toddled over and let himself be scooped up in Millicent's arms. Just then, one of Shipbrook's men-at-arms entered the hall.

"My lord, beggin' yer pardon…and the ladies as well. That monk—the one with the Invalid Company—he's at the gate. Wants to speak to ye, my lord."

Sir Roger raised a quizzical eyebrow, but rose. He crossed to the open door of the hall and descended the steps to the cobbled courtyard. Millicent, with the boy on her hip, followed him. Near the gate, they saw three men who had just dismounted. A thin cloud of dust from the road still hung in the air from their passage. She recognized Jamie Finch, her old friend from their days together in London, and had met the monk, Brother Cyril, once before. But she did not know the rather frail old man with them.

As she followed Sir Roger across the courtyard, she noticed the stranger was watching them keenly or, more precisely, watching her father. He did not take his eyes off the big knight as they approached.

"Welcome to Shipbrook!" Sir Roger greeted them. "Master Finch, I see you are fully fit once more."

Jamie Finch grinned sheepishly and flexed his left arm freely. It had been broken when Haakon the Black knocked him from the wall during the Invalid Company's desperate defence of the fortress at Deganwy.

15

"Aye, my lord! Good as new, I reckon."

Sir Roger grinned back and turned to Brother Cyril.

"And you, friar, I see you've grown no thicker since last we met. I thought most churchmen grew plump over time."

Brother Cyril laughed.

"It seems nothing sticks to my bones, my lord, no matter what I consume. Perhaps someday."

Sir Roger turned to the last of the newcomers. The man was old and a bit unsteady on his feet, but there was something vaguely familiar in his lined face.

"Sir, I am Sir Roger de Laval. You are welcome here at Shipbrook. Have we met?"

"Oh, we *have* met," the old man said in Gaelic, a language Sir Roger understood a little. "Ye right near slew my master back in Tir Eoghain!"

Sir Roger's smile faded.

Tir Eoghain. The English called it Tyrone and it was a place he'd tried to forget.

"I fought many men in Ireland, sir, all now dead to the best of my knowledge" he said flatly.

The old man gave a sly smile.

"All save one, yer lordship. All save Cathal O'Duinne."

***

The guard on watch at the north wall sent word of the patrol's approach and by the time Declan and Roland led the men through the gate and into Shipbrook, a delegation was waiting in the courtyard. Roland turned to Declan as he dismounted.

"Quite the welcoming party," he said with half a smile. "Wonder what we've done?"

Declan scanned the familiar faces, Sir Roger, Millie, Finch, Brother Cyril—and one stranger. He looked for some clue as to why this reception, but could find none.

"I don't know," he said as he climbed out of his saddle, "but we'll soon find out."

He beat the dust from his breeches as he crossed the courtyard and started to make a jest in greeting, but saw the solemn looks on the faces of the waiting group and held his tongue.

Trouble, he thought.

Instinctively he turned toward the one stranger in the group. Something about the shape of the shoulders and the cant of the head brought back an old memory. He stared hard at the old man with the grey beard who stood beside Sir Roger and blinked.

"Bless me," he said quietly. "Finbar, is that you?"

***

"I must go with him," Roland said, as he threw a hooded cloak into his kit.

"Of course, you must," said Millicent.

"Ireland's a dangerous place, I've heard. He shouldn't go alone."

"Very dangerous," Millicent agreed.

"He can take care of himself, I know, but someone will need to watch his back!" Roland said, his voice rising just a bit.

Millicent fixed Roland with eyes that always seemed to see right through him.

"Who are you trying to convince, husband? Not me I hope! What little I know of Ireland frightens me, but Declan's sire is wounded and may be dying. He *must* go, and there are only two men I'd trust to bring him back safely. It cannot be Father, so it must be you."

Roland gave her a rueful smile. The Earl of Chester had been summoned to Brittany the month before by the King and Ranulf had charged Sir Roger with seeing to the security of Chester in his absence. The Lord of Shipbrook had spent much of April in the walled city and hated the duty, but would not shirk it. Sir Roger could not go to Ireland. That left Roland.

There had been a heated discussion earlier in the afternoon as to who else should accompany Declan and Finbar back to their homeland. Roland had offered to detail a score of the best men from the Invalid Company for an armed escort and there would have been no shortage of volunteers, but Declan had rejected that notion.

"We'd be askin' fer trouble. The English barons control the eastern half of Ireland and every port there. I doubt they'd stand idly by while a score of armed men rode across their territory and into the lands still held by the Irish," he'd said.

In the end, he'd asked for only one man from the Invalids to join him, Brother Cyril.

"The Irish put great stock in priests," he said, by way of explanation. "There's an abbey or priory on every other hilltop or river bend in Ireland. Having a priest along may smooth our way."

No one, including Brother Cyril, had objected to the choice. On their foray into Wales, the skinny churchman had proven to be tougher than he looked and not altogether harmless if things came to blows. Roland had insisted from the start that he must go and Declan had not argued with his friend. He'd volunteered without consulting Millicent, but given her fondness for Declan, he'd guessed she wouldn't protest. And, of course, she hadn't.

He took Millicent by the wrist and pulled her close to him. It had been two years since he'd returned from the bloody campaign in Wales that had put Prince Llywelyn on the throne of Gwynedd. Those two years had been a time of blissful peace in Cheshire. It had been a time to build, a time to turn the earth and plant, a time to watch the crops and his new son grow.

He did not miss the fighting, but knew that the days of peace were always numbered. Like the men of Shipbrook, he and his Danes patrolled the northern borders of Cheshire and did not allow their swords to rust or their longbows to lay idle. He was a farmer at heart, but a warrior by trade.

"By God you are a soldier's wife, Millie," he said and nuzzled her cheek.

"I am that." she said and giggled a little as his beard tickled her. "Just see I don't become a soldier's widow. Now, my father is waiting for us in the hall. He wants to impart some words of wisdom before we sup. Go fetch your friend. I'll meet you there."

***

Declan sat on his cot and looked around the simple quarters he called home. The room took up most of the floor above the

18

barracks that housed Shipbrook's men-at-arms and had once belonged to Sir Alwyn Madawc. Sir Alwyn had been Master of the Sword at Shipbrook when first Declan came to this little fortress by the River Dee as a boy of twelve. Alwyn had taught him most of what Declan knew about fighting and not a little of what he knew about life. He stilled missed the burly Welshman, dead these five years.

Now he was Shipbrook's Master of the Sword. It was a position he had never aspired to or imagined for himself, but Sir Roger had insisted. He'd been knighted by Richard the Lionheart, but when Sir Roger de Laval entrusted him with the security of Shipbrook and the Welsh borderlands, that was the greater honour in his eyes.

He rose from his cot and looked out the small window that opened onto the cobbled courtyard. The sun was setting over the west wall, turning high clouds to pink. Below, he saw Roland crossing the courtyard in his direction and felt a knot in the pit of his stomach.

Roland was like a brother to him—nay, more than a brother. As squires they had survived the death and pestilence of the Holy Land together and as knights they had fought side by side through civil wars in England and Wales. They'd kept no secrets from each other—save one.

He heard Roland's footsteps on the stairs and opened the door.

"Ready?" Roland asked cheerily.

Declan beckoned him inside and closed the door behind him.

"For supper, yes. As for Ireland, I know I must go, but I confess—I don't want to."

Roland stared at him, confused.

"Rest easy," he said, "I'm going with you and will watch your back."

Declan shook his head.

"I've no doubt of that, Roland, but it's not my back that troubles me."

Roland laid a hand on his shoulder.

"Then what, Dec?

"It's my father. If he lives, I doubt it will be a welcome reunion for either of us."

Roland stood speechless for a moment.

"How can that be, Dec? You've never said an unkind word about your sire."

"Aye. I was ashamed to speak ill of my own father, even to you. Ye recall the tale I've always told—the one where I was chosen by my father to be squire to a noble Norman knight who had bested him in honourable combat?"

"I remember it well," said Roland. "You told it to me the day we first met on the road to York. It was the first time I'd ever heard of a Norman with any decency in him."

"Well, the part of the story about the noble Norman was true enough," Declan said. "Sir Roger is a noble man in spirit as much as in title, but the part about my father…that was a lie."

"How so?"

"The man was not fighting off a Norman invasion of his homeland. There was no great battle. He had stolen a dozen cows and was caught before he could get clean away."

Roland shook his head.

"Well there was a fight against Normans, if not a great battle, and did you not tell me that cow theft in Ireland was considered an honourable pursuit?"

"Aye, that's true enough, though after chasing Welsh cow thieves all these years, I see it a bit differently now. But it's not the theft of cows that troubles me."

"What then?"

"Cathal O'Duinne gave me away to a complete stranger, Roland. I was twelve years old. What father does that?"

***

Together they made their way to the great hall and found that Millie and Brother Cyril were there ahead of them, as was Rhys Madawc, Sir Roger's squire.

Sir Roger was sitting by the hearth with a small carving knife in his hand, slicing wood shavings from an elm branch into a neat little pile on the floor. He looked up as Roland and Declan entered and motioned them to a wooden bench opposite him where Brother Cyril and Rhys had already found places. Millicent was curled up on a small couch nearby.

The big Norman knight took a moment to inspect the stick he had been whittling, then put it aside and spoke to Declan.

"How fares your friend Finbar?"

Declan shrugged.

"He's all wrung out, my lord. We talked a little, but Lady Catherine shooed me out so he could rest. I think he'll need to regain some of his strength if we are to leave on the morrow. You all heard his message and he did not add much to that when we spoke. There was a great battle. The Irish were routed. My eldest brother was slain in the fight and my other brother and my father were gravely wounded. Keiran lost a hand I'm told, but should live. My father...some think he will die, though Finbar thinks he will not go so easily. It has been a disaster for my clan and for our people, my lord."

"And reason enough for you to return home," said Sir Roger. "Things are quiet here. Baldric can manage the patrols until yer return and it will be good training for young Rhys," he said, nodding toward the Welsh boy.

Declan managed a wan smile at that. As Sir Roger's Master of the Sword, patrolling the borderland was his primary duty, but there had been little to show from the patrols of late. The raids of Welsh cattle thieves into Cheshire had mostly petered out since Prince Llywelyn gained the throne of Gwynedd and made it known that the Earl of Chester was his ally. There could hardly be a better time for him to be absent from Shipbrook.

"I'm sure the border will be in good hands, with Baldric and young Rhys keeping watch, my lord," he said and laid a hand on the stocky squire's shoulder. A sheepish grin played across the boy's face. It was no secret that Rhys regarded Sir Declan with something close to awe, and all knew of Declan's fondness for the lad.

"I've no doubt," Sir Roger replied. "So you must concern yerself with Ireland now. When Finbar regains some of his strength, you must draw him out on how things stand there. Ireland is never stable and that old man strikes me as one who sees and hears much. He might keep you from doing something stupid."

Declan shot a quick glance at Roland who was smiling. "Don't do anything stupid," was advice Sir Roger had been giving the two since they were squires.

"My recollection of Finbar," said Declan, "is he oft times had news before anyone else—and sometimes took pleasure from hinting at events we knew naught of. It used to irritate my father. I'll squeeze what I can out of him."

"Good! I know Ireland's your birthplace, Declan, but you were but a boy when ye left and much has happened there since then."

"True enough, my lord. What with Mohammedans and Welshmen and Flemings to fight, I've been a bit preoccupied with English matters. I've heard little news of home. Finbar tells me our people, the Cenél Eoghain clans, still rule in Tir Eoghain, but they are divided."

Declan leaned over and spoke to Roland and Cyril.

"The English tie themselves in knots pronouncing simple Irish names like Tir Eoghain," he said with a shake of his head. "They call the place Tyrone, but by any name, it appears there is new trouble brewing there, or so says Finbar."

"What trouble?" Cyril asked.

"Trouble much like we had here not so long ago," Declan said, "family members fighting over a throne. But in Ireland it's not brothers, it's distant cousins. For hundreds of years, the Kings of Tyrone have all come from the Mac Lochlainn clan or the O'Neill clan. Finbar says our last king, Muirchertach Mac Lochlainn ordered the attack on the English a fortnight ago that took my brother's life and many others. The King himself was killed for his trouble and his army scattered. His son now claims the throne."

"These O'Neills you spoke of—they believe they can do better?" asked Sir Roger.

"Aye, my lord. My clan shares the blood of the O'Neills and has stood with that clan since long before any man's memory. Finbar says the leader of the O'Neills is a man of courage and sound judgement. There is to be a council held ten days from now and all expect O'Neill to challenge the old King's son for leadership of the Cenél Eoghain."

Sir Roger grunted.

"Such a challenge usually ends in blood and, while the Irish cut each other's throats, the English make ready to pick up the pieces! I spent a year at war in Ireland and did not care for it much. The place seemed much like England in the years after the Conqueror landed at Hastings. Back then, King William offered great tracts of land to his followers—if they could take it by the sword and hold it. So every ambitious second son in Normandy, one of my ancestors among them, crossed the Channel and spread across the land like a swarm of locust. And everywhere they took the land and they held it! The Saxons were brave folk, but could not—or would not—adapt to Norman tactics. Soon enough, there were dirt mounds with timber palisades rising up like boils from Dover to York and the Saxons were dispossessed."

Roland and Declan exchanged glances. They had never heard the big Norman speak of his own folk in this way. Sir Roger saw the look and shrugged.

"I do not condemn my people. These are just the facts. All men are ambitious. Normans took the land from the Saxons and the Saxons took it from the Britons and the Britons, no doubt, took it from someone who held it before them. Normans, Danes, Saxons, Romans—on it goes. And so it has gone these past thirty years in Ireland. When I left that island ten years ago, there were a dozen kings in the lands not already taken by the English, which is worse than having no king at all. And in the English lands, I saw the mottes rising by the fords and crossroads."

Declan shook his head.

"Change does not come easy to the Irish, my lord. I've been taught to fight in the Norman fashion by experts, you and Sir Alwyn principal among them. I've seen the worth of mail and heavy cavalry and fortifications. But the Irish favour the axe and the lance and go unarmoured into battle. They ride horses with no saddles or stirrups and thus, cannot fight as the Normans do while mounted. Their hill forts are weak compared to the Norman mottes. Even with their freedom at stake, I think they will not change."

"Neither did the Saxons," Sir Roger said flatly. "And now they must make way when a Norman passes by. But nothing lasts forever. The Normans are no more interested in change than the Saxons or the Irish and why should they be? They've conquered half of Europe! But one day someone will find a way to beat them. I've long thought that the crooked stick your friend is so skilled with might be that way," he said, nodding toward Roland. "We saw what the Danes and their longbows did to heavy cavalry at Towcester."

Both young knights nodded at that. The Danish bowmen had decimated Prince John's Flemish mercenaries on that bloody field.

"But for now," the big man continued, "the Normans hold the advantage in Ireland and, as always, they are ambitious. There are three Norman barons in the country you must take note of. Our friend Earl William Marshall holds title to Leinster in the south, though he is occupied these days fighting for Richard in France. Lord Walter de Lacy rules Meath in the centre. I knew de Lacy's father, but he met with an unfortunate end and his son, Walter, inherited his lands. Him, I do not know."

"Unfortunate end, my lord?" asked Declan.

Sir Roger winced.

"Very. The man had his head lopped off by an Irishman with an axe while inspecting his new castle at Durrow. Did it with one blow I'm told and got clean away."

"As I say," Declan added dryly, "the Irish favour the axe."

"And, of course, there is Sir John de Courcy," Sir Roger continued. "Him I know all too well."

Declan's head came up at the mention of this name.

"De Courcy has plagued the Cenél Eoghain since I was a babe!" he said, "and he plagues them still. Finbar says it was de Courcy who led the English at the battle where my father and brothers fell."

"I'm not surprised," Sir Roger said. "There is not a bolder, more dangerous man in Christendom than John de Courcy.

With but a score of knights and three hundred foot, he carved out a huge domain in the north of the island and has held it for twenty years. There is much to admire about the man, but much to despise as well."

Sir Roger stopped and scooped up the wood shavings from the floor and tossed them into the fire, sending red and yellow sparks swirling up the chimney.

"De Courcy was the most pious man I've ever seen—and that includes churchmen," he said nodding toward Brother Cyril. "He could spend an entire morning grovelling on his knees, confessing his sinfulness and seeking God's forgiveness, then ride out in the afternoon to burn a village to the ground. He is ruthless and ambitious. I've heard he has taken upon himself the title "Prince of Ulster" these days."

Declan turned to Roland and Brother Cyril.

"Ulster is the name of the ancient kingdom that once covered all of the north of Ireland. That kingdom had split into three by the time the English arrived. Tir Connell is in the far northwest of Ulster, Tyrone covers the middle third of that old kingdom and de Courcy rules the eastern third. His new title suggests he wants it all."

Sir Roger nodded.

"If King Richard were not preoccupied in France, he might take umbrage with de Courcy's use of the royal title of 'prince' and I'm certain it doesn't sit well with our own Prince John! But for now, there are none to challenge whatever de Courcy chooses to do in his domain."

Sir Roger paused, casting back into his memory for any useful information on this Prince of Ulster.

"I've mentioned that the man is pious. He has little regard for the Irish, but holds an odd fascination with your Irish saint, Patrick. The saint is buried at Down near where de Courcy won his first victory in Ulster. I was told he believes the saint ordained his triumph and he's given lavishly to an abbey dedicated to Patrick at Down. Of course he threw out the Irish monks there in favour of proper English brethren—Benedictines from Saint Werburg's abbey right here in Chester."

Brother Cyril spoke now for the first time.

"Few know that Patrick was not Irish. He was an Englishman, taken as a slave to Ireland as a youth. He escaped, took holy vows, then returned to convert those who had enslaved him."

Sir Roger's eyes widened at that.

"Perhaps that explains de Courcy's fascination with the saint. He would appreciate the story of an Englishman bringing truth and salvation to the benighted Irish. He believes he is doing that himself! I only served under the man briefly, but that was enough to take his measure. Within a fortnight, I had seen enough of John de Courcy. So I rode south to Dublin and took ship back home to England.

"With your new squire," Declan added.

"Aye, I reckon you were about twelve years of age then. I'd always been too poor to employ a squire and scarce knew what to do with you."

"You knew enough to have me muck out the stall for Bucephalus," Declan said with a grin.

"That's true enough," said Sir Roger. "You know I owe my acquisition of a squire to de Courcy. In the brief time I served him he ordered me across the River Bann to bring back some cows he claimed had been taken from his land. We tracked the herd for two days west of the Bann and found it not far from another river to the west, the name of which I do not recall."

"It was the Blackwater, my lord," Declan said quietly.

"Aye, that's it. We came upon the herd not far from that river, but your father and his men...*contested* our right to the cows and so there was a fight."

Sir Roger paused, gathering his thoughts.

"Well, it wasn't much of a fight. We outnumbered the Irish lads and, as always, were better armed and wore mail. Declan's sire had neither armour nor shield, but he had an axe and knew well how to use it. He killed two of our men before my sword fetched up beside his helmet and laid him low. After that, the rest of his band fled, leaving me with a herd of skittish cows and your unconscious sire," he said, nodding to Declan.

"I remember that day," said Declan. "Men rode into our rath and sounded the alarm. Some said my father was dead. None

26

seemed ready to go back to his aid, so Finbar gathered my brothers and went to find him. They told me to stay home, but I would not."

"I'd sent my lads back east toward the Bann with the herd," Sir Roger continued, "but I could not leave this man lying there injured on the ground, so I stayed with him. About then, you and yer brothers arrived on the scene and challenged me, though I could see the two older boys had no real stomach for a fight. But you, young Declan, you pushed your way to the front with one of those long-handled axes in yer hand," the big knight said. "I might have had to kill you had another man not held ye back."

Roland glanced over at Declan, who looked uneasy. This was a part of the story he hadn't heard before.

"That was Finbar," said Declan, "and I did want to kill you, my lord."

"I trust the feeling passed,"

Declan smiled wanly.

"In time, my lord. In time."

"A moment after Finbar saved your neck," Sir Roger continued, "yer sire sat up all of a sudden and ordered ye all to lower yer axes. He looked about and saw his cows gone and me sittin' there alone by his side. To this day, I don't know what possessed him to offer you up as my squire. Perhaps he felt a position as squire to a Norman knight was a promotion from being the youngest of three brothers. He never said, though I'm sure he had his reasons. To that point, I had never taken a squire, but there was something about you that persuaded me that I should have one. You wanted no part of it as I recall."

Declan smiled sheepishly.

"I recall protesting rather loudly, but Father would have none of it," he said. "He told me to go and I went."

"You sulked all the way to Dublin, I believe, but you were the only thing of value I came out of Ireland with."

Sir Roger rose and tossed his whittled stick into the hearth.

"I've no more wisdom to give ye, lads. Just see that you get yerself safe back to Shipbrook…back home."

Declan rose, his eyes going moist.

"Be assured, my lord—I am your man and Shipbrook is my home. I'll be back."

***

Declan was mounted on a long-legged chestnut mare in the cobbled courtyard of Shipbrook as the sun made it over the eastern rampart. Beside him, Roland patted the neck of The Grey, his big steady gelding, as they prepared to depart. Millicent appeared at the top of the short steps that led up to main hall of the little fort. She held young Rolf lightly on one flared hip as the boy squirmed around to see what all the excitement was about. Declan was the child's Godfather and took that duty seriously, though hardly sombrely. For a moment Millie paused at the top of the steps to take in the scene. Declan leaned forward from his saddle.

"Rolf! Come see me, lad!"

Millie smiled and came down the steps toward him.

Declan recalled the first time his friend and fellow squire had met his wife-to-be on those very steps. That night he'd warned Roland that Millicent de Laval was hard on squires and it had not been a lie. The little lady of Shipbrook had made both boys the butt of her jests, but time had changed them all in seven years. Millie de Laval had proven herself to be as smart as her formidable mother and as brave as her renowned father. He'd seen Roland fall under her spell and it had worried him, but it need not have. He'd discovered that she was equally smitten with his friend. Together, the three had shared enough adventure to last a lifetime and now…now, Millie was a mother and Roland a father. In truth, he envied them both.

When Millie reached him, the little boy held out his chubby arms and the Irish knight scooped him up, sitting him astride the horse's neck. Rolf delighted himself by tugging on the palfrey's mane and laughing. After a time, Roland led The Grey over to where Declan had started to tickle his little son. He held out his arms and Rolf lunged toward him, having no fear that strong hands would let him fall.

"He moves like that monkey creature we saw in the market at Acre!" Declan said with a laugh.

"Aye," said Roland as he caught the boy. "One day I'll have to teach him to look about before he leaps!"

They'd named the boy Rolf after Roland's father, murdered by William de Ferrers seven years ago. Millie had made the choice, and that had touched Roland.

"We'll have another and name him Roger," he'd promised at the time.

"And if it's a girl?" Millie had asked.

"I think Catherine would do nicely," Roland had replied.

Behind him Brother Cyril and Finbar Mac Cormaic had already mounted. A night's rest had revived the old Irishman who seemed eager to get started on his journey home. Millie, who had been watching her son passed between his Godfather and father, held out her arms and Roland tumbled the boy into his mother's embrace.

It was time.

"Say farewell to your sire, Rolf," she urged. The little boy turned and stared at Roland with big eyes.

"Bye," he announced proudly.

"And bye to you, son," Roland said with a smile. Then he turned serious. "Do what Mother says while I am gone."

Rolf nodded solemnly and Roland turned to Millie.

"It's time to go, love," he said, slipping an arm around her waist and kissing her hard on the lips. "Look for me before Midsummer."

She stood on tiptoes and kissed him back. They had said their private farewells the night before.

"We'll be waiting," she said.

Roland mounted The Grey as Declan raised a hand in farewell to Sir Roger and Lady Catherine. Together, they rode out of Shipbrook.

The Trosc

Domnall O'Byrne cast his eyes over the deck of his small trading cog and out to the broadening estuary of the River Dee. From long experience, he had timed his departure from Chester's Shipgate to catch the turning of the tide from flood to ebb. With half-reefed sails for steerage, he let the current carry his vessel, the *Trosc,* downriver and out to the Irish Sea.

It was a passage O'Byrne had made many times before, bringing woollen cloth from the millers of Chester and slate from the Welsh quarries to eager buyers in the Irish ports of Waterford, Dublin and Carrickfergus. With fair weather for the crossing and a hold full of valuable trade goods, he could not help feeling well-satisfied with this particular voyage, but he cautioned himself to remain vigilant. The Irish Sea was no place to let down one's guard.

But for the moment, the western horizon showed nothing but blue sky and empty sea. With no hazards in view, O'Byrne turned his attention to his four passengers gathered near the bow. While he was happy with the wool and the slate in the hold of his vessel, he was less so with these men. They were a curious lot. By their weapons and their bearing, two were obviously fighting men. In his eleven years as master of the *Trosc*, he had transported many such from England to Ireland. As always, he felt a twinge of guilt at the thought.

He knew that men such as these were, bit by bit, imposing English rule over much of his homeland. While he was honest enough to admit that the new English overlords were hardly worse than the petty Irish kings they had replaced, it still rankled that foreigners held such sway. If the Irish were to be poorly ruled, let it by their own kind! But a man had to make a living, no matter who ruled and these men had paid their fare from Chester to his first stop at Carrickfergus in good silver. If he did not take the English coin, another shipmaster surely would.

The business of transporting fighting men to Ireland had grown particularly lucrative over the past two years. With the return of King Richard from captivity and the failure of Prince John's revolt against his brother, peace had descended on England like a balm. That led fighting men to look elsewhere for employment. Many joined in the Lionheart's new war against Philip of France, but a large number of Englishmen found there was more profit to be made in the constant warfare in Ireland. And so it would seem with these two soldiers, were it not for the monk and the old man who travelled with them.

The friar was thin and wore the brown robes of an Augustinian. He'd kept up an animated conversation with the two armed men in the group as they made their way down the Dee. Monks were common enough passengers in recent years as the church of Rome, through the English church, busily worked to "reform" the Irish church. Encouraged by the Pope, there had been a flood of English priests and prelates making this crossing to help bring the Irish into the light. O'Byrne sneered at the thought.

After the fall of Rome, it had been the church in *Ireland* that had kept the flame of Christianity alive while barbarians stabled their horses in the holy places of the eternal city. Now, the Italian Pope and his lackeys in the English church thought to instruct the church of Saint Patrick on the proper worship of God. If anything, O'Byrne resented the English priests more than the warriors. It was as though the English could not be satisfied with Irish lands—they wanted Ireland's soul as well!

The fourth member of this odd group sat on a bale of woollen cloth and seemed to doze as the others talked freely. This man had seen many a summer and seemed ill-suited for a long journey, but O'Byrne had noticed the man's eyes as he boarded the *Trosc*. They weren't the rheumy eyes of a doddering old man. They were like the eyes of an osprey—taking in everything.

Two fighting men, a monk and a grandfather. All in all, it was a strange traveling party, but they had paid well and without complaint. He was about to turn his attention elsewhere when he saw one of the warriors turn and make his way across the deck toward him. The man was built sturdily with long russet hair tied off in the back. He wore a broadsword at his hip and moved with an easy grace across the deck, despite the roll and pitch of the *Trosc*. Declan O'Duinne approached the man at the helm with a grin.

"Master O'Byrne, it looks like we have fair sailing ahead!"

O'Byrne shrugged.

"We'll see once we strike the bay," he said brusquely.

Declan dropped his grin.

"If the winds are good, how long to port?"

O'Byrne glanced up at his rigging. The wind was picking up as they neared the mouth of the Dee and it would soon be time to unreef the big square sail.

"Wouldn't count on the wind holdin'," he said, "but if it does we should see land by dawn and if it's clear enough to steer by the stars tonight, we might be near enough to Carrickfergus to drop anchor by late morning."

***

"Master O'Byrne is no Master Sparks," muttered Declan as he returned to the group. Master Henry Sparks had sailed them safely to and from the Holy Land aboard his cog, the *Sprite,* and had never failed to be in a good humour, even when fighting off Moors and Berbers at the Pillars of Hercules. "He's Irish and I don't believe he thinks much of us."

Brother Cyril looked back at the man at the steering oar.

"You can hardly blame him. To his eyes, we are but more outsiders, come to plague his native land."

"He took our coin readily enough," said Roland.

Declan arched an eyebrow.

"He may love our money, but not us I'm thinkin'."

They had chosen to sail with Master O'Bryne when they learned he was bound first for Carrickfergus in the north of

Ireland. Before they departed Shipbrook, they'd considered the safest route to reach Declan's home in Tyrone. The two nearest ports on the eastern coast of the island were Dublin in the centre and Carrickfergus in the north.

"A landing in Dublin means a three days' ride through the de Lacy lands in Meath to reach the border of Tyrone," said Sir Roger.

"And the Dub Gaill still call Dublin their home port," added Roland. "They'll not have forgot the beating they took from the Invalid Company at Deganwy. Haakon the Black might be dead, but if any of that lot recognize me, we'd not make it out of the city without a fight."

"You can reach Tyrone from Carrickfergus in only a day and a half," said Sir Roger, "though I don't like ye passing through John de Courcy's domain. In truth, I don't trust de Lacy or de Courcy. Either man might look with suspicion on two knights crossing over into Tyrone—particularly if one of those knights is Irish."

Declan nodded. He'd listened carefully to the arguments for both routes. This was his journey and he knew it was his decision to make.

"We'll take our chances with Carrickfergus," he'd said with finality.

Now, their course set, they leaned on the rail of the *Trosc* and watched the shoreline fall away as they reached the protected estuary of the Dee and sailed toward the Irish sea proper. An hour before, the cog had sailed past the last ford on the river. Shipbrook was little more than a mile away from that ford, but not visible from the river. To port, they had seen the top of the cross that marked the final resting place of Sir Alwyn Madawc. Shipbrook's old Master of the Sword now stood constant watch over this ancient crossing point between Wales and England.

As the *Trosc* entered deeper water there was a brisk wind, but fortunately no large swells. As the land receded, Roland leaned in close to his friend and laid a hand on Declan's shoulder.

"How does it feel sailing for Ireland, Dec? I know ye've been of two minds on returning there."

"Ye know I've oft thought about taking this journey, Roland, but one thing or another has inclined me to put it off."

"Your father?"

"That—and a crusade and a civil war."

Roland smiled.

"Aye, you've had a busy ten years."

For a while they stood together silently watching Cheshire recede behind them.

"Tell me about Fagan," Roland said. "You've not had much time to grieve."

"Ahh, Fagan. As a boy, I confess I near hated him. He was six years my senior and regularly beat me when no one was watching. When I look back now, I think I understand. Ye know my mother died givin' birth to me and I think he blamed me for it."

"Hardly fair," said Roland, "but it's what a boy might dwell upon."

"Aye, but I feared him and we do come to hate what we fear."

"What of Keiran?"

"Keiran…Keiran was a gentler soul than Fagan, though on occasion he joined in the beatings. I always thought he was bullied into it by Fagan. He would come around later and say he was sorry and bring me a sweet cake or some other peace offering. Finbar says he should recover if the wound does not fester, but he is not dealing well with the loss of his hand."

"Would you?"

"Probably not, to be sure. But after seeing what the Invalids can do in a fight, I'd be ashamed to complain about such a loss."

"Have you thought about meeting your father?"

"I honestly don't know what I'll say to him."

"I'd give anything if I could see my father one more time," said Roland solemnly.

Declan looked over at his friend.

"Your father didn't give you away."

Declan O'Duinne

By midday they were out of sight of land and, as the sun set over the port rail, the wind held steady, driving the *Trosc* to the northwest. As night fell, the moonless sky grew crowded with stars. With the sun's departure, Brother Cyril had fallen promptly to sleep curled up in his warm robes, while Finbar kept to his perch on the bale of wool and tilted his head back to gaze at the heavens. Roland and Declan lay on their backs looking up at the display as well.

"What do ye reckon they are?" asked Declan. "My father told me as a child they were precious stones that belonged to the old gods, the gods of the Druids. He said they were fleeing the wrath of the Christian's one God and spilled them across the sky in their haste."

Roland smiled. He liked that story. It reminded him of one his grandfather had told him when he was very young.

"My grandsire claimed they were the hearth fires of Asgard where Odin and the gods of the Danes dwelled," Roland offered, "but my father wasn't so sure. He thought the gods of the Danes had long ago been overthrown by the God of the Christians and if those lights were fires, then it would for angels standing guard to keep the old Norse gods at bay. My mother claimed it was all nonsense and that any thinking person knew the stars were seeds dropped by the sun in its passage."

There was a long silence, before Declan spoke again.

"That actually makes sense."

Roland laughed.

"Maybe..."

"I think the stars are other worlds, some like this one, some very different." It was Finbar. He had dozed off and on and hardly spoken since they took ship in Chester, but it seemed the old man had been listening all the while. Roland and Declan sat up.

"You've learned some English these past ten years," Declan said admiringly. It seemed age had not slowed Finbar's curious mind.

"Aye, some," Finbar said. "To know your enemy, it helps to understand their speech."

"Fair point," said Declan, "but these other worlds you think are up there, do they have people and horses and such like?"

"I don't see why not," said Finbar. "If God made this world, why should he not make others?"

"Better ones perhaps?" suggested Roland.

"God works to perfect this world." Now it was Brother Cyril who weighed in. Having been roused from his own slumber by the discussion of the heavens, he sat up and yawned.

"Perhaps he does," said Finbar, "but I fail to see his progress."

"You must have faith, my friend."

Finbar shook his head.

"Faith we have aplenty in Ireland, even if the Pope and the English church think otherwise. It is not faith we lack, but strength, strength enough to throw all the English back into this sea," he said gesturing to the waves sweeping by the bow of the *Trosc*. "*That's* what I pray for."

"Perhaps the Irish should invest in good mail and heavy cavalry rather than prayer," countered Declan. "God did not throw the Normans into the English Channel despite all the prayers of the Saxons and I doubt he will smite the English on behalf of the Irish now."

Declan looked at his old family counsellor and expected the man to take some umbrage at his harsh words, but Finbar just nodded eagerly.

"It is as you say! If we are to remain free, we must learn how to beat these English with their enormous horses and their armoured men," he said fiercely. "We have neither the horses nor the armour, but there are surely other ways."

Declan stared at the old man for a moment. Finbar had spoken little since arriving, exhausted, at Shipbrook—beyond the news of the recent Irish defeat and his clan's grievous losses—but Declan could see that he was recovering some of his strength and all of his conviction. This was the Finbar he remembered from his boyhood.

"Finbar, I know you see and hear everything that passes through my father's house and much else besides. We are less than a day's sail from Carrickfergus now and we need to know what you know. What will we be ridin' into?"

The old man did not reply at once, but sat there stroking his long grey beard.

"Lord, in truth, we'll be ridin' into the eye of a storm. In three days' time, the Mac Lochlainns and the O'Neills will meet at Armagh to choose a king. If yer sire lives and can ride, he will be there. I know not if Keiran will make the effort."

"Will it come to a fight?" asked Declan.

"Well, there hasn't been an O'Neill take the kingship in a hundred years," said Finbar, "but Hugh O'Neill believes it is time that changed."

"And the Mac Lochlainns?"

"Believe otherwise, of course," said Finbar. "So, yes, it might well come to a fight, but it does not need to be your fight, lord. If yer sire is not at Armagh, we will ride on to our rath by the Blackwater. There we will visit his bedside or, God forbid, his grave. In any case, I'd advise we not tarry in Armagh."

Declan nodded.

"On that we agree. I'm not coming to Tyrone looking for a fight."

"Then I will pray one doesn't find you, my lord," Finbar said and climbed back atop his bale of wool.

"Thank you, Finbar. You still see further than most men."

Finbar yawned sleepily and pulled his robe close around him against the sea breeze.

"It is my job, lord," he said. "It's all I'm good at."

***

Dawn broke clear with the wind still steady from the southeast. At first light, a sail was sighted to the north and the crew of the *Trosc* brought pikes and axes onto the deck should the unknown ship have hostile intent. After a few tense moments, the sail disappeared over the horizon and was seen no more. The crew returned the weapons to the hold and the *Trosc* continued to run with the wind.

True to Master O'Byrne's prediction, land was sighted at mid-morning. Roland and Declan stood by the port rail and watched it emerge out of the morning mists. The coast was low-lying with a few green rolling hills, dotted with cattle.

"Lovely land," said Roland.

Declan sighed.

"I'd almost forgot how green it all is."

Finbar joined them at the rail.

"I heard one of the crew say we will make port within the hour," he said.

Roland and Declan looked at each other. The two had stayed awake well into the night worrying over what they would find at Carrickfergus. Finbar had passed through the port in route to Chester but a week ago. He'd told them there were armed men patrolling the docks, but that none had questioned him.

But Finbar was an old man, leaving the country. Two armed men entering de Courcy's domain might generate more interest. One thing was certain, they could not admit they were bound for Tyrone without arousing suspicion.

As the night wore on, they'd tried to concoct a credible lie as to the purpose of their visit, but a convincing story proved elusive. In the end, they'd given up and drifted off to sleep on the deck.

Declan turned to Roland and asked again the question they'd struggled with through the night.

"What if we're questioned by de Courcy's men?"

Roland shook his head.

"We must hope the guards at the docks are not that curious," he said at last.

Finbar snorted beside him.

"Hope in one hand and spit in the other," he said, acidly, "then see which one fills up first."

Carrickfergus

*T*he castle stood on a rocky crag that rose on the north shore of a wide bay. Like the Tower in London, its square stone keep loomed unnaturally over the surrounding land. But unlike the gleaming white of London's Tower, the dull grey stone of Carrickfergus seemed to draw in and deaden the light of the sun rather than reflect it. It proclaimed, with no room for argument, that John de Courcy ruled this land.

As the ship drew near the dock, O'Byrne proved his skill with the steering oar, bringing the *Trosc* in to touch the side of the pier as gently as a head striking a pillow. Two of his crew leapt over the rail with lines in hand and lashed the cog to the dock. Other crewmen drew forth heavy timbers that served as ramps to bring up the horses from below.

Roland took the reins of The Grey and led gelding up onto the deck. Crewmen had removed a section of railing and the horse stepped from deck to dock without hesitation. It was The Grey's first voyage and the big horse had handled the journey with its usual steadiness.

Declan's chestnut mare was skittish, but the Irishman had a natural gift for handling horses and calmed the animal with a few strokes of his hand on its neck and a few whispered words. Reaching the dock, he handed the reins to Roland and went below to fetch the palfrey Sir Roger had given to Finbar. The old Irishman stepped gingerly onto the dock as his mount came up from below. Brother Cyril had chosen to bring his own tall, gangly mare. The horse shied away from the ramp at first, but after a stern scolding from the monk, followed its master docilely up and onto the dock.

All members of the traveling party safely ashore, Declan turned and waved to the master of the *Trosc*.

"Well done, Master O'Byrne!" he shouted.

Domnall O'Byrne stared at Declan for a long moment then turned and spat into Carrickfergus Bay.

***

They had barely got clear of the dock and onto dry land when two guards posted at the waterfront saw them. One pointed and the other marched down to meet them.

They were not going to pass through Carrickfergus unnoticed.

"You there! Who are ye and what's yer business in Antrim?"

Roland glanced at Declan, who was looking back at him expectantly. Roland cleared his throat.

"Well, we…," he began hesitantly, but was cut short by Brother Cyril who stepped in front of the guard.

"We travel to Down," the monk said with authority. "I've come at the behest of the Bishop of Chester to pay homage at the tomb of the blessed Patrick and to confer with the fathers there. These two," he said, motioning absently toward Roland and Declan, "are for my protection. It seemed hardly necessary, as God watches over me, but the Bishop insisted."

The guard stared at the monk, then at the two armed men flanking him for a long moment.

"What about him?" he asked pointing at Finbar.

"My clerk. I will be expected to give the Bishop a written report of my pilgrimage, but alas, my writing seems to be hard on the man's eyes, so this old scribbler has been sent along to chronical everything."

By now, the second guard had joined the first.

"What's this lot about?" he asked as he studied the new arrivals.

"Traveling to Down on church business, they say."

The second man looked them over.

"Church business or no, we have our orders. Any man who carries a weapon is to be taken up to the keep fer questionin', so these two," he said pointing to Roland and Declan, "have to go. Might as well take the others. Ye know how his lordship loves to talk to churchmen."

The first guard, finding no fault with that assessment, nodded.

"All of ye. Leave yer mounts here and follow me," he ordered and turned toward a path that led from dockside up a narrow ravine. The second guard hailed a boy who'd been hovering nearby and ordered him to take charge of the four horses.

"Give them water and hay and there'll be a coin in it for you," Declan called to the boy as they were led away up the path.

As they walked, Declan sidled up to the monk.

"Down?" he asked in a whisper.

Cyril had a pained look.

"You kept me awake half the night, my lord—the two of you worrying about what story to tell when we landed," he whispered back. "I finally drifted off without knowin' if you came up with a good lie."

"We didn't."

"So it appeared to me," said Cyril. "But while I laid awake I thought of one myself. Hope you didn't mind."

Declan threw an arm over the monk's shoulders as they walked.

"I knew ye'd prove useful!" he said.

The path ran a short way up the ravine toward an earthen ramp that led up into the town. As they walked, Declan's eyes were drawn to the right where the grey walls of the keep loomed a good eighty feet over his head. The square tower covered one corner of the rocky crag that thrust out into the bay and a stone curtain wall, twenty feet tall, encircled the rest. The ravine where they were being led was ten feet deep and twice as broad. It was partly a natural cleft in the rock and partly excavated, cutting across a narrow neck of land to serve as a kind of dry moat on the landward side of the fortress.

Formidable, he thought.

The opposite side of the ravine was topped by a wooden palisade that protected the small trading village that served the port and the castle. The guard led them up the broad earthen ramp and through a wide gate set in the timber wall. Inside were the usual storehouses, stables and markets of a port town as well as the houses of merchants, traders, laborers and soldiers who made their homes there. By the look of several of the larger houses, the place was prospering. It was certainly busy. The narrow streets were fairly clogged with men, though only a few looked to be conducting the business of the port.

Declan nudged Roland in the ribs and inclined his head toward the knots of armed men loitering everywhere among the buildings. A half dozen of these, unmistakably soldiers, lounged near the gate while another group sat on benches outside a shed where a smithy was hammering away at a glowing length of steel. The men contented themselves throwing dice to pass the time as they waited on repairs to weapons or mail.

"Heavily armed for a trading town," Roland whispered.

Declan nodded. The business of every port city he'd ever seen was business, but this looked like more of an armed camp than a trading centre. It would appear that the primary business of Carrickfergus was not wool or cattle or slate.

It was war.

***

Their escort led them through the crowded streets to a wooden drawbridge that spanned the ravine. Passing back over the dry moat they turned left along a path that clung to a narrow strip of land between the stone curtain wall and the natural escarpment of the rock crag that dropped into the sea. Sixty yards on, they finally reached the gate of the castle.

Declan took careful note of the layers of defence that protected de Courcy's stronghold. To enter the castle at Carrickfergus one had to pass through the walled and garrisoned town, then cross the wooden drawbridge that spanned the dry moat. If the drawbridge was up, the castle was protected on three sides by water and the fourth by the deep ravine. And even if the bridge was down, it did not lead directly to the castle gate. To reach that, one had to cover another sixty yards along the base of the looming curtain wall to find the one arched entrance to the inner ward. Any attacker would face a rain of death from the defenders on the wall simply to reach the only gate and once there would find there was no room to employ a ram.

Whoever built this knew his business, Declan thought.

As they approached the gate, a troop of ravens perched above the arched opening took noisy flight, drawing Declan's attention. Their departure revealed a sight that made him stop in his tracks and grasp Roland by the arm. Above the gate, maintaining a sightless vigil over all who entered or left the castle, was the severed head of man. The thing was mounted on a spike, its eye sockets empty and its mouth agape as though in a final agony. It wasn't the first time Declan had seen such a thing, but it served as a sobering reminder that they were not in a peaceful realm.

Two guards stood watch at the gate, but recognizing their escort, waved them by without ceremony. Passing through the arched opening in the curtain wall they entered a small square, surrounded on all sides by fine buildings, some of stone and some half-timbered. On the right, the largest of these looked to be a great hall of some sort, perhaps for conducting the routine business of John de Courcy's domain. To the left was a small chapel and along the west wall were various storehouses and workshops. Looming over all and taking up the northwest corner of the enclosed space was the massive keep.

Their guard guided them across the square to a set of narrow stone steps that led up to the only door in the structure, set fifteen feet above ground. They were met there by another guard.

"New arrivals fer questionin'," their man explained. "Two armed, one churchman and a clerk." The guard at the top of the stairs eyed them for a moment, then waved them through the entrance and into a small antechamber.

"Drop yer weapons here," the man ordered.

Roland and Declan exchanged glances, but complied without complaint, unbuckling their sword belts. It seemed reasonable that armed strangers would not be allowed into the keep.

"Wait here," ordered the first guard who disappeared through a narrow door. They could hear footsteps ascending a stairway on the other side. The man left to keep watch on them looked bored, but attentive to his duties.

"Nice keep," Declan said cheerily.

The guard stared at him, but made no reply. Declan shrugged.

"Quiet, too."

Any further attempt at conversation was interrupted by the return of the first guard.

"This way," he ordered, and disappeared back through the narrow door.

***

They followed the guard up a narrow spiral stairway to the second level, where they were ushered into a large chamber with a high ceiling and windows set high up on each wall. There were two men in the chamber. One was a priest in fine black robes and the other was, unmistakably, the Prince of Ulster. John de Courcy was as Sir Roger had described him— tall, well over six feet in height, with broad shoulders and long, muscular limbs. His hair was cropped short and flecked with bits of grey, framing an angular, clean-shaven face burnt brown by the sun. He looked every bit the warlord that he was. Hearing them enter, he cut short an animated conversation he was having with the priest and crossed the chamber to greet them.

"An emissary from the Bishop of Chester, I'm told, and a pilgrim to the shrine of the good saint Patrick!" he said with a booming voice.

"I am Brother Cyril, at your service, my lord," the little monk managed as de Courcy gripped his slim hand in a meaty fist.

"We don't get many such visitors, Brother Cyril. May I inquire as to the health of his excellency, the Bishop?"

"Oh, very fine, my lord. Very fine indeed! He sends his blessings to all who sustain and advance the study of the works of the venerable Patrick."

De Courcy started to speak, but the black-robed priest tugged at his sleeve and whispered in his ear. The Prince gave him a sour look, but nodded.

"My friend, Father Tibold," he said, nodding toward the priest at his side, "had the pleasure of spending a day with your Bishop last summer while passing through Chester. He was wondering if His Excellency still keeps that tavern girl...," de Courcy turned back to the priest, who whispered once more into his ear, "...the tavern girl, Tessa, in his chambers?" Roland glanced at Declan. This could only be a test of Brother Cyril's bona fides.

Cyril did not flinch.

"I know naught of this Tessa you speak of, my lord."

De Courcy arched an eyebrow.

"Perhaps she was the Bishop's ward before Hilde." Cyril continued. "Hilde was a most comely young maiden whom the Bishop took under his wing last winter. Though last I heard, he had discovered the girl lacked sufficient *piety* and sent her away. He's recently adopted Sybilla, a more God-fearing maid."

De Courcy glanced over at the hovering priest who raised both eyebrows and shrugged. The Lord of Carrickfergus turned back to Cyril with a small smile.

"Well, Brother Cyril, it seems your news on that front may be fresher than ours," he said with a wink. "It's hard to keep current with the good work your Bishop is doing on behalf of the young women of Chester! But I am glad he has sent you. There is much the English church can learn from the works of Patrick! He was an Englishman, you know."

Cyril nodded eagerly.

"Aye, lord, I know Patrick's story well! I have long been fascinated by the works of the saint and, for me, this pilgrimage is very personal."

"Personal?"

"Aye, my lord. Like Patrick, I too was taken as a slave from my home in England and carried off to a foreign land. And like Patrick, I escaped and took priestly vows on my return. His story has inspired my own journey of faith!"

"Splendid!" said de Courcy and slapped Cyril on his bony shoulder. "I've taken Patrick as my guide as well. He lifted the pagans of this island up from darkness and into the divine light of Christ, though many have fallen back into apostasy. In the lands we English have yet to control, the most loathsome and barbaric practices are performed with the sanction of the Irish church. By God, I fear many souls are being lost to this blasphemy! It must end, and by all that is holy, I will end it!"

De Courcy's face slowly became flushed as he spoke, his eyes burning with intensity. Declan had seen this before—in the eyes of the holy warriors who fought for Saladin and in those of the Knights Templars at Acre. They were the eyes of men burning with a passion for a world beyond this one. They were the eyes of a fanatic.

"God's will be done," Cyril replied calmly.

"I will see to that!" de Courcy said with finality. "Now who are these others? Guards and a clerk, I'm told."

"Aye, my lord, these are dangerous times and the Bishop insisted that I take precautions," he said gesturing toward Roland and Declan. "I've hired these knights for escort. They tell me they fought with King Richard in the Holy Land. The Bishop also insists that I chronicle all that I see and hear at the shrine, my lord. It pains me to say that the clerk is along because my writing is hurtful to the eyes of His Excellency."

De Courcy nodded sympathetically.

"We can't all be scribblers, father. I, myself, can neither read nor write. As for your guards, you will have no need of them, I assure you. All the land between here and Down lies within my domain, and I do not tolerate brigands."

De Courcy motioned toward an alcove in one corner of the vast room and a monk, dressed in the black robes of the Benedictines scurried over.

"Prepare a letter of introduction for Brother Cyril to Abbot Layton at Down and also grant him safe passage through my lands."

"Aye, your grace," said the monk, bowing quickly and hurrying back to his alcove.

As the clerk disappeared, de Courcy beckoned Cyril to come closer and draped a huge arm across the monk's shoulders. He leaned in close and whispered.

"While you are in Down, father, you must have the Abbot show you the bell."

"Bell, my lord?"

"Aye, the very bell used by Patrick himself to call the faithful to worship. It is encased in a shrine of bronze and gold and is the most sacred relic in all Ireland. I took it from the heretics of Tyrone a fortnight ago and with it came a great blessing.

"What sort of blessing, my lord?" asked Cyril.

"Visions, Brother Cyril. I've had visions in the presence of the shrine. Patrick himself...he speaks to me. He has blessed all my works!"

He drew back and smiled again.

"So, you may be off with my blessing. I ask only that you pass this way on your journey home. I would hear of your commune with Patrick."

"Of course, my lord," Cyril said hastily. "We've already taken up far too much of your time. I will remember you in my prayers at Down."

Cyril brought his hands together prayerfully and made a small bow. The clerk came running over, blowing on a small sheet of parchment to dry the ink. He handed the safe passage document to Cyril who shoved it into his robe. He bowed again and turned to go, but de Courcy reached out and grasped him by the arm. His grip was like a vise.

"One more thing, father," he said. "As you have no real need for guards, I will keep one of yours here, as my *guest* until your return."

Cyril started to protest, then bit back his words. The keeping of hostages was a common enough practice when nobility wished to bind someone to their word. To refuse was out of the question. To balk at this would only draw suspicion from a man who was suspicious by nature. He could see in de Courcy's face that there would be no appeal to this order.

"Very well, my lord. I will leave Sir Roland Inness here in your keeping," he said, gesturing Roland forward. "My other man speaks a few words in Gaelic and may be of more use to me."

The Prince released his iron grip on the monk's arm as Roland stepped forward and gave a small bow.

"Inness...that name sounds familiar to me. Have we met, Sir Roland?"

"Nay, my lord. Not to my knowledge."

De Courcy studied him closely.

"From where do you hail, Inness?"

"Derbyshire, my lord," he answered honestly, "the high country."

De Courcy rubbed his chin.

"That's de Ferrers land, is it not?"

"Aye, lord, though Earl William is presently in exile."

"As well he should be! He should have had his head removed along with the King's brother—traitors both! I don't know if Richard really understood how close he came to losing his throne. But tell me, while you were in Chester, did you see any preparations being made? "

"What sort of preparations, my lord?"

"Invasion preparations, Inness. Troops being mustered, ships being outfitted, that sort of thing. Surely you know Earl Ranulf is planning to find his own piece of Ireland to conquer—all the Marcher Lords are."

Roland knew that some of what de Courcy claimed was quite true. Since Strongbow's invasion thirty years ago, most of the Marcher Lords had financed expeditions to carve out new lands across the Irish Sea. But the Earl of Chester stood as a singular exception. Ranulf, he knew, was content with controlling Cheshire and keeping the border with Wales secure. The Earl had no designs on Ireland.

"I saw none of that, my lord. I'm told the Earl is now in France with the King."

De Courcy scowled.

"No doubt making plans," he said sourly. "The Earl stood with Richard against John. He'll be looking for reward and where better than here in the north of Ireland? He has the money and the men to do it. I'm told Ranulf has a troop of Crusader veterans who fought for him at Towcester, maimed and wounded men I've heard. They say they are the King's best troops, yet they sit there in Cheshire under Ranulf's control instead of in France. Why is that, Sir Roland?"

"I couldn't say, my lord."

Now de Courcy was beginning to pace back and forth as he spoke.

"I too stood with the King against John when some barons here did not!" he said, his voice rising. "But what thanks do I get for that? None! Mark my words, Inness, Ranulf will land troops here within the year, but he will find no welcome from me. I have sworn to almighty God to finish the sacred task I took up twenty years ago. It's His will that I rule all of Ulster. Ranulf of Chester had best look elsewhere for land!"

Roland stayed silent and tried not to show his astonishment at the man's raving. After a moment, de Courcy stopped pacing and placed a gentle hand on Roland's shoulder.

"So tell me, Sir Roland, what action did you see in the Holy Land? I will someday take the Cross myself, as Jerusalem remains in the hands of the Saracens."

"I fought at the siege of Acre, my lord."

"A great victory there," De Courcy said, "and did you serve the King in the recent civil war against his brother?"

"Aye, lord. I fought at Towcester under Earl William Marshall," he answered, which was close enough to the truth.

De Courcy frowned.

"Marshall, now there's a Marcher Lord with one foot already in Ireland. He married Strongbow's daughter and now has claim to Leinster—without raising a finger to earn it! What I rule here in Ulster, I claimed with my sword. Still, Marshall did good service at Towcester. I would have liked to have been there to see it. Quite a number of the Irish who fought on the other side that day—those that survived—made haste to come home after that whipping. Some are even now in my employ. John's mercenary cavalry was the best money could buy and I would be keen to know how you beat them."

"With longbows and good ground, your grace."

"Truly?" the tall Norman lord asked with an arched eyebrow. "That simply? Perhaps I should count myself fortunate that the Irish have no longbows and are content to fight on ground I choose. Sir Roland, I shall want a full account of the battle while you are my guest."

"With pleasure, my lord," said Roland.

De Courcy took a step back and looked slowly from Roland to Declan.

"Were you at Towcester as well?"

"Aye, lord," said Declan.

"Good! I am in need of men like you two. I can offer silver or land or both to those that prove themselves. There will be profitable work here in Ulster in the coming weeks."

"We are not averse to profit, my lord," said Declan.

"Nor fighting," Roland added.

"Splendid, splendid! I'd not deprive the Bishop's emissary here of his traveling companions until his work is done, but once the good father is aboard ship for Chester, I invite you two men to stay. For now, Sir Roland, you will be my guest. We'll find you a place here where you will be comfortable."

He turned back toward Brother Cyril and laid a hand on the monk's skinny shoulder.

"You should not tarry, Brother Cyril. If you leave now, you can reach the inn at the ford of the River Lagan by nightfall. It's the only lodging you'll find twixt here and Down."

Cyril bowed and turned toward the door to the chamber where the guard who had escorted them from the docks was waiting. As they filed out past Roland, Declan whispered.

"Back in a fortnight. Don't do anything stupid."

Roland nodded.

"The same to you."

The Road Home

*O*nce the three travellers passed through the castle gate, their guard lost all interest in them. Alone, they made their way back through the town and down toward the docks. As he walked, Declan edged close to Cyril.

"That was well done, friar," he said quietly to the monk. "We'd all likely be confined to the dungeon right now had ye not invoked the name of Patrick, but was there no other way than giving him Roland as a hostage?"

Cyril shot him an acid look.

"You were there, lord. Who would you have suggested I name—you? Master Finbar? Myself?"

Declan knew it was an unfair question. Of course there had been no other choice, but it still rankled.

"John de Courcy is a frightening man," he said finally.

"That's plain enough," Cyril agreed. "Did you see his eyes? There is madness there! My knees were shaking all the while, my lord. De Courcy is what I call a righteous sinner. Many men find it convenient to invoke God to justify their actions, but a man like de Courcy actually believes that his basest desires are God's will. Such men will commit every sort of horror in the name of the Lord—without mercy or remorse. I can better understand Sir Roger's refusal to serve such a man."

As they reached the ramp that led down from the walled town toward the dock, Finbar touched Cyril's sleeve.

"How did you know about your Bishop's...ward?"

"I didn't," said Cyril, "I hardly know the man, but it is a common rumour in Chester that the Bishop has this...*weakness* for young women. No doubt Father Tibold knew of this and sought to use that knowledge to test me."

"But what of this Tessa the priest spoke of?"

Cyril shook his head ruefully.

"I spoke the truth when I said I did not know of her, but I doubt there was ever one named Tessa. I believe the priest was laying a clever little trap for me. If there was no Tessa and I claimed to know of her, I would have been revealed for certain as a liar. I depended on the simple fact that I, having just arrived from Chester, would have more current news of the Bishop's indiscretions."

"And the names you gave?" Finbar asked, genuinely curious.

"Made up," said Brother Cyril with a smile. How would the clever Father Tibold know if there was now a Hilde or Sybilla?"

"Clever," said Finbar.

"Thank you."

***

When they reached the landing beside the dock, Declan saw that the *Trosc* had already unloaded its cargo and was sailing south across the bay. With relief, they found their horses tethered to stakes in the ground and happily munching on fresh hay. The boy left in charge stepped out between the animals and presented an upturned palm.

Declan had taken little note of the lad as they were being led away to meet de Courcy, but now saw that the boy looked to be around ten years of age and was as ragged and dirty as a street beggar. He was gaunt and his clothes were threadbare, but his carriage was not that of a beggar. Declan flipped a small silver coin his way and the boy snatched it out of the air with alacrity. After a brief examination of his prize he slipped it into a small leather pouch at his waist.

"Thank ye, m'lord," he said solemnly.

Declan dipped his fingers into his own coin purse and drew forth a larger silver piece, holding it up for the boy to see.

"Now, lad, we'll be takin' but three of these beasts with us. The last, that big grey fella yonder, belongs to our friend, Sir Roland Inness. You recall the tall man with dark hair that was with us?"

The boy nodded eagerly, not taking his eyes off the coin.

"Aye, he's a soldier, like you, m'lord."

"Aye, he's a soldier alright. He'll be staying behind here at Carrickfergus. It's his horse and I want it stabled and cared for until we return or he comes to fetch it. This is enough silver to pay for its fodder and stabling for a fortnight and a daily walk as well," he said, still holding the coin up before the boy. "If it's longer that, there will be more. Understood?"

"Aye, lord, but your friend, Inness, where is he? How will he know where to find me if he wants to fetch the horse?"

Declan couldn't help but glance up at the brooding square tower looming over the landing.

"He's in the keep, I expect—a guest of Lord de Courcy."

"A hostage then," the boy said, flatly.

Declan raised an eyebrow.

"What's yer name, lad?"

"Finn Mac Clure, m'lord."

Declan looked at the boy carefully and wondered if he could be trusted. Once they were out of sight, he might run right to the castle and tell all to de Courcy's men, but he thought not. The lad looked half-starved and barely clothed. The coin in Declan's hand was enough to handsomely cure those ills, which was more it appeared than anyone at Carrickfergus had ever done for this lad. Declan leaned in close and placed the coin in the boy's dirty palm.

Finn did not immediately drop it into his purse.

"His lordship keeps a fair close watch over his guests," he said. "He'll not be at liberty to fetch the horse."

"Perhaps not, but one never knows. The situation could change. You look like a clever lad. Inness is clever too. He may grow tired of the Lord's hospitality and find himself in urgent need of his horse. Can you get word to him where he might find you and his horse—should the need arise?"

The boy gave a sly smile.

"I expect I could, m'lord, but I'll need two of these for the trouble," he said, pointing to the single coin in his hand.

Declan looked hard at the boy, as though truly seeing him for the first time.

"You're a thief!" he said.

The boy returned the gaze without flinching.

"I've been called worse," he said, "but if I'm to risk my neck consortin' with one of the Lord's hostages, I'll be paid for it!"

"Well paid," Declan said sourly, but he fished his hand in his pouch once more and produced another coin. He placed it in the boy's hand.

"Do we have an agreement?"

Finn spit in his right palm and held out his hand. Declan took it.

"Deal," the boy said solemnly and dropped the coins in his purse.

"Now, Master Finn," Declan said, "when you speak to Sir Roland, tell him we will do as we promised the Prince and return with a report from Down in a fortnight. Tell him he is to enjoy de Courcy's hospitality in the meantime and wait for our return. He's not to do anything stupid. Can you tell him that exactly?"

"Aye, lord," said the boy.

"Keep your part of our bargain and I will have another coin for you. Break it and you have my word I will not be forgiving. Understood?"

"Aye, m'lord."

Declan looked up to see that Brother Cyril and Finbar had already mounted. He pulled up the stake securing his chestnut mare, stepped into his stirrup and swung himself into the saddle. He turned away from the boy and eased his horse up beside Finbar.

"Which way?"

Finbar gave a little nod toward a road that ran between the timbered walls of the town and the bay. Declan turned to Cyril.

"Let's be on to Down," he said, loud enough so that anyone nearby would hear. "We've a saint to consult."

***

The road that led away from Carrickfergus skirted the northern shore of the bay for ten miles traversing a rocky shoreline and mucky bogs along the way. Declan led the way at a good clip until they were well out of sight of the castle. Then he reined in and turned to look back in the direction they'd come.

"So what is to be done now?" he asked, as much to himself as to his companions. "We've told a bold lie to get past John de Courcy and now we are entangled in it. How far to Armagh, Finbar?"

"A good two day ride, lord."

"And to Down?"

"One long day and a bit of another."

"We cannot return to Carrickfergus without visiting the shrine of Patrick first. That much is for certain. De Courcy knows the place and those who tend it too well. He'd know a lie before we finished tellin' it. We must go to Down."

"Aye," said Finbar, reluctantly, "but first Armagh and yer sire, lord. We have a fortnight to return to de Courcy before suspicions are aroused. See your father, then attend to getting your friend free of de Courcy."

Declan sat his horse and stared back toward Carrickfergus for a long time before speaking.

"Very well. We go to Armagh first. I'll see to my father, whether alive or dead. He and I will say our piece, if he is still above ground, but I will not tarry there long while Roland is under that madman's control. De Courcy may fancy himself Prince of Ulster, but it will be a short reign if any harm comes to Roland. That I swear."

"He is a dangerous man," Finbar agreed, "but has a reputation for keeping his word. I believe your friend Inness will be safe enough, as long as we do nothing to arouse de Courcy's suspicions. If Brother Cyril can convince the priests at Down of his bona fides and return with a report to de Courcy as promised, I believe Sir Roland will survive being in Sir John's custody. In fact, he can enjoy a fortnight of snug lodging and good food while he awaits our return!"

Declan rubbed his chin, still staring back toward Carrickfergus, then shook his head.

"Most men would do exactly that, but ye don't know Roland Inness, Finbar. I do. I fear he won't sit idly waiting for us to return."

Finbar looked confused.

"He will…attempt an escape?"

"If the opportunity presents itself, he well might."

Finbar snorted.

"Why would he risk such a thing?"

Declan turned and gave the old counsellor a hard look.

"It's an uncertain world, Finbar. He knows we might not return as promised. We might catch the pox or drown crossing a river or be killed by brigands. He knows that nothing short of death would keep me from returning for him, but he also knows death is easy to come by in these parts. For that reason, I doubt he will just wile away the time waiting for us to return. He won't like having his life in the hands of a man like John de Courcy. He'll take his leave of Carrickfergus if he has a chance and I would do the same!"

"But ye've seen the place, both the town and the castle. There is no escaping Carrickfergus!" Finbar protested

Declan furrowed his brow.

"Aye, it's a formidable place, but you underestimate my friend, Finbar. He once escaped from Saladin's dungeons in Jerusalem. I doubt Carrickfergus will hold him if he's a mind to leave."

"But he doesn't know this country! Where would he go if he frees himself?"

Declan frowned.

"Now that, I cannot tell you."

***

It was twilight when the three mud-spattered riders neared the ford of the Lagan and saw the small inn. Declan looked at his companions. Cyril seemed none the worse for the journey, but there was exhaustion written on Finbar's aged face. He reined in his horse beside the inn.

"We can pass the night here," he said and started to dismount.

"No," said Finbar, "these inns do not suit me—too many eyes—and I would not want to tarry so near now to home. Only God knows if yer sire still lives or if the hour of his passing is near and I've not made this journey only to have you arrive late!

I know I must rest, but let us press on, at least for a few hours more."

Declan did not object and turned his horse's head to the south. The inn had been built on the last stretch of high ground before the road descended into salt marshes that lined both sides of the river. The ford was near where the Lagan spilled into the bay. There the tides had deposited a bar of hard packed sand that horses could manage at low tide.

The sun was setting as the three riders splashed across the ford and climbed to higher ground south of the river. A mile further on, the road split with one track continuing south and a smaller track branching off to the southwest.

"Down lies to the South," said Finbar, pointing along the main track. He turned and pointed to the smaller path. "That way lies the River Bann and Armagh. The clan chiefs will already be gathering there. The Council is to begin in three days. If yer father lives and has any of his strength back, he will be there."

For two more hours they rode southwest in the fading twilight until it became dangerous for the horses to continue. Declan led them off the trail and over a rise to a secluded patch of woods near a meadow. He built a small fire as a soft rain began to fall. As the three men gathered around the flickering light, Declan tilted his head back and let the fine drops fall on his face.

"Ireland," he sighed, "so green, so wet." He lowered his head and turned to Finbar.

"This council at Armagh. You've said that Hugh O'Neill intends to challenge Mac Lochlainn for the kingship. What lies behind his challenge—other than the old bad blood between the clans?"

Finbar looked across the fire at the young knight.

"As you've already surmised, if bad blood was all that was needed to start a civil war between the O'Neill's and Mac Lochlainns there would never be peace! So, yes, there is more to it than that."

The old man took a sharp stick and began to scratch in the dirt next to the fire. He made a ragged line and near the centre drew an equally ragged circle. He turned to Declan and gestured to the young monk by his side.

"You will know much of what I say now, my lord, but yer Brother Cyril here needs to understand the situation. It may help him survive."

Cyril nodded vigorously and leaned in to watch as the old Irishman stabbed the point of his stick into the centre of the circle. He was not fluent in Gaelic, but the Abbot who had instructed him as a novitiate in Northumbria had been Irish and he had learned enough to follow conversations.

"Here is Lough Neagh," Finbar said, "the biggest lake in all Ireland and this," he said, pointing to the lines on either side of the lough, "is the River Bann that feeds the lough in the south and carries its waters off to the sea in the north. It is the traditional boundary between Tir Eoghain to the west and Down and Antrim in the east. De Courcy now rules Down and Antrim and most assuredly has designs on Tir Eoghain."

"He is planning something for certain," Cyril observed. "All those men we saw in the village of Carrickfergus—they were not merchants or tradesmen."

"Aye," said Finbar, "de Courcy has grown bolder these past few years in his sallies across the Bann. A year ago he struck in the north, crossing the Lower Bann and pillaging as far as Derry. Last month he led the force up from Down in the south and struck at Armagh."

"Where my brother died," said Declan.

"Aye, along with many another man of the Cenél Eoghain," Finbar said gravely.

For a long moment, the old Irishman fell silent as though in reverence for the many fallen. Then he spoke with a touch of bitterness in his voice.

"Our dead King, Muirchertach Mac Lochlainn, insisted on that battle, though he has lost every time he's ever fought against these English. What's more, he ordered the most sacred relic of our faith, the bell of Saint Patrick, to march in the vanguard. He was hoping, I suppose, that divine intervention could make up for poor generalship. The bell was lost along with the King's life."

Finbar stopped and seemed to be gathering his thoughts as the rain fell harder, the drops hissing as they struck the coals of the fire.

"John de Courcy may be mad, but he is a brilliant general," he said, squatting close to the flames now and holding out his thin, wrinkled hands to warm them. "I know not whether he will strike next in the north toward Derry or the south toward Armagh, but strike he will."

He twisted about as he sat on his haunches and looked at Declan. There was fear in his eyes.

"From Armagh it is but a half day's ride to the Blackwater and our rath, lord."

"And while the Cenél Eoghain bicker, de Courcy gathers men," said Declan.

"Hugh O'Neill could stop him!" Finbar declared with certainty. "Hugh is a fighter and no fool. He says he can keep these English bastards out of Tir Eoghain—if he is king."

"And the Mac Lochlainns?"

Finbar snorted.

"Think otherwise."

Declan did not reply. He stirred the fire with a stick and lifted his face once more to the soft rain.

Ireland, he thought. *So green, so wet,...so cursed.*

***

They arose while stars were still visible in the sky and were riding west at first light through low rolling hills. The three riders passed few on the road at this hour, only a herdsmen or two driving cattle toward their rath for morning milking. As they neared a second ford over the winding Lagan River, they saw a new motte being raised south of the road.

Declan reined in his mount. He pointed to the naked mound of earth rising off to the left of the road. There, trees had been felled and draft horses could be seen hauling carts filled with local clay up a switchback ramp to be deposited on the top.

"More of de Courcy's work?" asked Brother Cyril.

"Aye, it's grown since I passed this way ten days ago," said Finbar.

Declan stared at the mound. In another month, this heap of earth would be topped with a log palisade and would command this road and the ford over the Lagan. De Courcy was leaving nothing to chance. Near the base of the mound, he saw three men watching them. One gestured in their direction and all three began to move toward their horses tethered nearby.

"How far to the ford, Finbar? " Declan asked as he watched the men untie their mounts. "I'm not in the mood for a fight before supper."

"Not far, lord."

"Very well. I think it best we not dawdle on this side of the river," he said and spurred his chestnut mare into a trot.

***

The sun had set when they reached the River Bann. At the ford, the river was no more than thirty yards wide, but this was late spring and the current was strong in the shallows. Had they been mounted on the small Irish ponies, they'd have been soaked to the thighs making the crossing, but aboard their taller English horses they scarcely splashed their boots. As his mount scrambled up the western bank of the river, Declan looked around him. While this land was in the province of Armagh, the men of Tir Eoghain had ruled it for generations.

Tir Eoghain.

He felt a lump in his throat as he reined in on the high ground above the river. It had been ten years since he'd set foot on his native soil. The land looked unchanged, but he could not say the same for himself. He looked across a flat boggy expanse to green hills two miles distant and thought of the day he'd left this land. It had been a bitter one. The memory of it had gnawed at him for ten years.

Given away.

He shook his head. They would reach Armagh by the next afternoon and find his father alive or dead. What would he say to the man? What would Cathal O'Duinne say to him? He guided the chestnut mare off the road and found a hidden glade to spend the night. He lay awake long after the others had fallen into sleep—wondering what the new day would bring.

***

60

Declan O'Duinne

It was a little past noon when the spire of Saint Patrick's church at Armagh came into view. The road they'd travelled since crossing the Bann approached Armagh from the northeast and was often used by pilgrims from Antrim coming to worship at this church founded by Saint Patrick. The O'Duinne rath lay to the west of Armagh just beyond the Blackwater River and as a boy Declan had come many times to the abbey town with his father and brothers on feast days. But he had never approached the town from this direction and the view of the church, sitting atop the steep northern slope of Armagh's hill, was breathtaking. Cyril and Finbar hastened to keep up as Declan dug his heels into the flanks of his horse and urged the animal into a trot.

The road did not run directly into the abbey grounds, but turned sharply to the right and curved around the steep hill, passing over a low shoulder and turning south. The land in that direction was mostly level and had been cleared for crops and pasturage. Cows and sheep browsed spring grass and Declan could see some of the abbey brethren at labour in the fields. A quarter mile on, they reached another road that ran from the central square of the abbey toward the O'Neill stronghold of Dungannon, fifteen miles to the west.

As they reached the western road Declan reined in for a moment and looked off in that direction. This dirt track ran for six miles to a ford over the Blackwater River. A mile beyond the ford lay the O'Duinne rath where he'd been born. Turning back to his left, he saw that the abbey grounds looked much the same as they had when he'd last seen them as a boy.

He nudged his chestnut mare into a walk and followed the road up a gentle grade as it passed between a monk's dormitory on the left and a large stable on the right. The road ended at a cobbled square that sloped gently up to the north and ended at the entrance to Saint Patrick's church, which sat on the crest of the hill. On the eastern side of the square was another dormitory and the abbey's chapter house and library

When they reached the centre of the square, Declan saw a banner raised in front of the chapter house. A steady breeze snapped the flag out stiffly. He'd been gone ten years, but he could hardly fail to recognize the bloody red hand on the white field. It was the symbol of the O'Neills—the Red Hand of Ulster. He dismounted and led his mare toward the banner. If Cathal O'Duinne was in Armagh he would be somewhere nearby.

Groups of well-armed men were gathered in front of the squat abbey buildings and he could see tents set up in the open spaces between the structures. Finbar veered off to the right and began making inquiries among some of the clansmen idling in the square. Declan turned abruptly to his left to head toward the row of tents between the chapter house and the monk's dormitory. He expected that the small O'Duinne sept might not rate lodging in in either building.

Brother Cyril, following obediently behind, noted the sudden change of course and realized too late that the Irish knight had not seen a young woman striding across the square, directly into his path. The monk called out a warning just as Declan ploughed into the girl and sent her sprawling.

For a long awkward moment there was stunned silence on all sides, then Declan began to sputter an apology and knelt at the girl's side to help her to her feet. She slapped away his proffered hand and scrambled up on her own, her cheeks flushed red and her eyes blazing.

"Miss, please forgive me, I did not…"

"Ye did not look where ye were goin'!" the girl cut him off as she brushed some dust from her dress. "Are ye blind?"

"No! No, my lady, just clumsy and in too great a hurry."

Declan watched as the girl patted down her hair and continued to inspect her clothes for dirt. He could not help but notice that she was quite beautiful. Her hair, though a bit mussed, was as black as a raven's wing and her eyes were pale blue. With a start, he realized that he had stopped halfway through his apology and was simply staring at the poor girl. She, in turn, was looking him up and down with a frown.

"I beg yer forgiveness, my lady," he began again. "It was all my fault." He gave the girl a small bow and a smile.

It was not returned.

"Aye, it was that," she said with a sniff. "Yer with the O'Neills?"

"Not exactly, miss. I'm a visitor."

"Then stay out of my way, visitor," she said and stalked off.

"You seem to have made your first new friend here, my lord," Cyril said cheerily.

Declan shook his head as he watched the girl walk away toward the opposite side of the square. The dormitory on the eastern side of the square had its own banner hoisted. It was also one he recognized—the three crescent moons of the Mac Lochlainn clan.

"I would not like to be that one's enemy," he said as she disappeared into a crowd.

Just then he was hailed by Finbar who had missed the incident in the square entirely. The old counsellor beckoned him with an excited grin and pointed down a row of tents. At first Declan could not see what the man was pointing to—then he did and it made the breath catch in his throat. There, sitting on a short stool sharpening his long-handled axe, sat a very pale, but very much alive, Cathal O'Duinne.

Though the brown hair and beard were shot through with grey, there was no mistaking his father. Declan was frozen to the spot, but Finbar did not wait. He brushed past the young knight and hurried to greet his master. Cathal O'Duinne looked up as his old friend's shadow fell across his work. For a moment he did not seem to recognize Finbar, then his eyes grew wide. He tried to leap to his feet, but only rose to a crouch before sitting back down heavily, a hand clutching at his wounded side.

"Help me up, damn it all," he growled and extended his hand.

Finbar grasped him by the wrist and managed to haul the bigger man upright. Once standing, Cathal wrapped his arms around the thin old man and pulled him close. After a long embrace, he stepped back, his hands still gripping Finbar's shoulders.

"I thought you dead," he said, his eyes shining. "They told me I'd sent you off on some fool's errand whilst I had the fever.

I swear I have no recollection of it! When I came back to my senses, I sent riders out to find you and bring you back, but by then you had vanished. I paid a priest at Dungannon to say prayers for your safe return!"

"The prayers worked, my lord, for here I am," Finbar said simply.

"Your good wife told me that you had set out to fetch my youngest son back from England," he said, draping an arm around the man's thin shoulders and shaking his head. "It's been ten years since I let that boy go, Finbar, and what's done is done. I live with that loss, but these are bad times for the O'Duinnes. I've lost Fagan and Keiran is now a shadow of himself. I could not stand to lose you as well, old friend. Gone to England? Good God, Finbar, did you even make it beyond the Bann? Did ye get as far as Dublin? Where have you been wandering all this time?"

Finbar had waited patiently for his master to have his say. Now the old man broke into a wide smile.

"Why I crossed the Bann and the Irish Sea as well, my lord, and I wandered all the way to England."

Finbar paused.

"And I've brought ye back a keepsake."

"Keepsake?"

"Aye, lord," said Finbar and stepped back, pointing to Declan who stood, still as a statue, at the end of the row of tents. For a moment Cathal O'Duinne said nothing, then his chin began to tremble and he clutched at Finbar's arm to steady himself.

"My God," he gasped, releasing his hold on Finbar and lurching forward.

Declan saw the recognition in his father's eyes and came to meet him. He tried to speak but did not know what words to say. The two men embraced in the crowded alleyway as Finbar looked on, a satisfied smile on his face.

"Father..." Declan croaked, his throat tight.

Cathal O'Duinne sobbed, his shoulders heaving as he held his lost son in an iron grip.

"Blessed Jesus," he finally managed, "ye've come home."

Declan O'Duinne

Reunion

The two men stood embracing in the alleyway for a long time, then Declan finally drew back. Both men's eyes were red.

"Yer wound…" Declan began.

"I've had worse," Cathal said, brushing aside his injury with a wave of his hand.

"Finbar thought ye might die, so I came."

Cathal shook his head.

"He tells me I sent for ye, lad, but I have no recollection of that. By the time my fever broke, Finbar was gone. I never thought he'd come back alive, much less with you, but I thank God he did." The older man took a step back to get a better look at the young man standing before him.

"You look as though England has agreed with you, son," he said.

Declan shrugged.

"I've no complaints," he began, then stopped. He looked at his father, then blurted out the question that had gnawed at him for ten years.

"Why did you do it?"

His son's words struck Cathal O'Duinne almost like a physical blow. He staggered a half step back and looked shaken. Finbar grasped the man's arm to steady him and glared at Declan.

"Shame!" he shouted, waving a finger at Declan. "I've not brought ye back here to speak so to yer sire!"

But the burly clan chief pulled his arm away and held up a hand to silence his old counsellor.

"It's a fair question," he growled at Finbar, "and who has a better right to ask it?" He turned his gaze back to Declan, his cheeks now wet with tears.

"Not a day has passed in ten years that I did not see you, perched up behind that big Norman on his enormous horse, riding away. It broke my heart, Declan. Every day since, I've wondered how you fared—whether you were alive or dead."

O'Duinne stopped, searching for the words to explain what had happened so many years ago. Declan broke the silence.

"When I was younger," he said, his voice husky as he fought back tears of his own, "I invented a grand story and told it to any who wondered how an Irish boy came to be squire to a Norman knight. In my story, the Norman knight bested you in battle, then spared your life. That much I know to be true. The rest I had to invent. In my telling you commended me into Sir Roger's service because you saw in him a man of gallantry and honour. Though Sir Roger de Laval is those things and much more, I never really believed that part of the story. Now, Father, I would have the truth. Why did you do it?"

Cathal O'Duinne took a deep breath.

"Very well then, the truth," he said, "or at least the truth as best I can recall it. The story ye told was not a lie, son, but it was not the whole truth. Yer Sir Roger did best me that day. I swear, I've never seen a more deadly man in a fight than that Norman! The blow he laid on my helmet came out of nowhere and, next I knew, I was looking up at the man, my head in his lap. Instead of finishing me, as any man might, he gave me water and checked the lump on my head. Very odd behaviour from an enemy, especially a Norman! Then you arrived with Finbar and yer brothers. My head was swimming, but I saw that it was you who came at the man with murder in your eye and an axe in your hands. The damned axe was nigh as big as you were. I saw the Norman back away, but knew he might have to kill you to save himself."

"So ye ordered me to put down my axe."

"Aye, I did."

"For that I thank you, but why save me, only to bind me over to the man's service?"

Cathal did not answer for a moment and seemed to sway on his feet. Finbar started forward again, but O'Duinne waved him off.

"Ye know I lost yer mother the day you were born, son," he began. "She was…everything to me and I never wed another. I miss her still. And you…you were so much like her! Not in appearance so much, but in spirit. Slow to anger, quick with a smile—and you had her laugh. When you were a boy, I would hear it across the rath and, for a moment, she would be back with me."

"Then why send me away?" Declan asked, his voice cracking.

Cathal shook his head.

"That day…it was not the first time I'd faced the Normans and lost. I had been fighting them since I was a boy. I marched with our clan to face them at Down when you were but a babe. In that great battle, we outnumbered the Normans three to one and yet, we were routed. They seemed to be…unbeatable and I saw nothing but war and defeat ahead for the Cenél Eoghain. Perhaps it was the blow to my head, but when I saw you come at that big Norman with your axe, all my despair and all my fears for the future seemed to be coming true. You were only twelve years old, Declan. I did not want you ground up in this losing fight against the English and it struck me you might be better off serving the victors and not dying with the Irish. It was selfish of me to make such a decision for ye. I realized that almost as soon as ye'd gone, but it was too late then. I'm sorry, son, truly I am."

Cathal finished his answer and looked up at his son, hoping for understanding if not forgiveness. Declan looked at his father swaying in the alleyway and could see the pain in the man's eyes. It had not occurred to him until this moment that their separation had been more wrenching for the older man than for himself. He reached out a hand and laid it on Cathal's shoulder to steady him.

"Thank you," he said softly. "For ten years I wondered what was in yer heart that day and now I know. Had I stayed, yer fears might have proven true. Perhaps I'd have been long dead now instead of here before you. You judged Sir Roger de Laval more rightly than ye knew—no fiercer or more honourable man walks the earth. Sending me away with him was a gift, though I did not think it so at the time."

Cathal O'Duinne tried to hold back a sob, but could not. Declan draped an arm over his father's shoulders as he wept out his relief. Finbar watched for a moment, then turned away, allowing the two men their reunion. He'd done his job.

***

The afternoon passed quickly as the two sat before Cathal's tent and revelled in each other's company. Declan listened with interest to his father's account of the years he'd been absent, tales of the home rath and his brothers. Woven throughout the telling were accounts of the never-ending struggles of the Irish against the English and amongst themselves.

"I am sorry for Fagan, Father, and for Keiran's wounding," Declan said when Cathal related the latest bloody encounter with the English east of Armagh.

Cathal sighed.

"Aye, I saw Fagan fall early in the battle, but there was naught I could do for him in the heat of the fight. I did not know until I'd recovered a bit from my own wounds that he'd died and that Keiran had lost his hand."

The clan chief paused and looked off into the distance.

"Fagan was a good fighter and brave as any of the Cenél Eoghain, though he was quick to anger and headstrong. He was eldest, but I had my doubts he was suited to lead the clan upon my death. I never told him that, but he knew it and thought ill of me for it. I've wondered if the lad took risks in that fight to prove me wrong."

Declan laid a hand on his father's shoulder.

"In these times, men live by the sword and die by it—if fate or chance decrees. In battle, a half inch and a half second separate the living from the dead. Fagan died a man's death, fighting for his clan and his country. In this world," he said waving a stick at the alley choked with tents, "that may be the best any of us can hope for."

"But tell me of Keiran," he said.

69

Cathal gave a little smile and shook his head.

"Yer middle brother is more level-headed than Fagan and less truculent by nature. A bit like me I'm told," he said with a little chuckle. "Keiran was quick with a blade, and clever as well, but that did not protect him against the English. One of their knights took off his sword hand at the wrist and he near bled to death. One of my men closed the wound with a hot blade and that saved him, but the loss of his hand seems to have unmanned him."

Declan nodded.

"I've seen it happen. Some men cannot abide the loss of a limb, but others can and do. I've seen men with worse injuries than a lost hand outfight men whole in body. I've led such men. When you have done with this council, we must go to the rath. I will speak to Keiran."

"He will be shocked to see you, no doubt. Perhaps it will rouse him from the ill humours that seem to have possessed his mind. He will not listen to me."

As they sat and talked through the afternoon, Cathal was eager to hear Declan's tales of the crusade and the civil wars that had wracked both England and Wales in recent years, as well as his description of his life at Shipbrook.

"You've grown into a fine-lookin' man, Declan," he said, with pride in his voice. "And it sounds like yer Sir Roger has done right by ye. Have ye wife, or child?"

"No, no," Declan answered, with a sheepish grin. "Out on the Welsh border, there aren't many young women to court."

Cathal laughed at that.

"There are always young women to court, lad, if you look about ye. At yer age, I was more interested in hunting and fighting than in courting—until the first time I saw yer mother. She was sloppin' hogs I believe. Up till then, I'd paid little attention to the girls. Afterwards, I paid all my attention to her, until she agreed to marry. I think she did it to get some relief from my constant courting," he said with a wry smile. "I wish ye'd known her, lad. She was a beauty and as kind a woman as God ever made. If ye find one like that, son...," he said, his voice trailing off.

"I'll court her till she's sick of me!" Declan said with a grin.

For a while the two sat silently, happy to be in each other's company, then Declan spoke up.

"The battle at Tandragee—Finbar spoke a little of it. What happened there?"

Cathal O'Duinne sighed and rubbed his chin.

"It was a disaster, lad. We had greater numbers than they, but when we met on the road, the English drew back to high ground. O'Neill counselled against attacking them there, but the King would not listen. So in we went. We were on the right and pushed the English and their Irish levies back, but each time we'd break their lines, their armoured knights would seal the gap. You've fought with them, son, and must know how hard they are to kill."

"Aye, mail makes a man very hard to bring down with a blade, but there are ways."

"Then, the Mac Lochlainn's on the valley floor were broken by the English cavalry and it became a rout. Thanks to Hugh O'Neill, we were able to withdraw in some order, though our losses were heavy. The slaughter among the Mac Lochlainn clans was worse."

"So now the Cenél Eoghain must decide what is to come next," Declan said. "Tell me, what is to happen at this council?"

Cathal shrugged.

"I'm sure Finbar has told ye the gist. The Mac Lochlainn's wish to retain the kingship of Tir Eoghain, despite the disasters they have led us into. Hugh O'Neill served the old king reluctantly, but faithfully. He gathered his clans when Muirchertach Mac Lochlainn summoned them to battle. He will not do so for the new claimant."

"But won't the clans fight if de Courcy makes a new incursion?"

"If Hugh O'Neill is king, they will!" Cathal said fiercely.

"When I passed through Carrickfergus, I saw what was being gathered there and it is a formidable force."

Cathal's head came up at the mention of the great fortress on the bay.

"You passed through that place?" he asked.

"Aye, we made port there and the place looked more like a military camp than a trading town. We were hauled before de Courcy himself for questioning before being sent on our way."

"You spoke with John de Courcy?"

"Aye, and I can tell you he is gathering an army and means to use it."

Cathal O'Duinne rose to his feet, still stiff from his wound.

"Come with me," he ordered. "You need to meet Hugh O'Neill."

Hugh O'Neill

*T*he dormitory that had until recently housed Augustinian monks was now crowded with armed men. Some tossed dice on a rough wooden table near the entrance, others gathered in quiet corners to tell tales and drink ale. As he trailed Cathal through the press of men Declan noted the sights, sounds and smells of the place. What had been a quiet dwelling for pious monks was now like barracks the world over. A place to eat, rest and wait—until time to do violence once more. It felt like home to him.

Unlike the dormitory for lay monks on the west side of the square, this building was home to the monastic brethren who rated better quarters. After passing through a number of outer rooms and down a corridor, Cathal led his son to a door that opened onto a small cloister. This peaceful refuge at the heart of the dormitory had a stone fountain at its centre surrounded by a garden rampant with spring flowers.

The open space was less crowded than the interior of the building, but there were knots of men about. These clansmen looked oddly out of place among the delicate flowers in bloom. Yarrow, woodbine, poppy and fairy thimble in their spring finery combined to make even the most elegantly dressed chieftain look dull and drab by comparison. Near the centre of the cloister, on a stone bench, sat Hugh O'Neill.

Cathal did not point O'Neill out, but he did not need to. The number of men gathered around the figure on the bench was identification enough, though the clan chief looked nothing like Declan expected. Having served Richard the Lionheart, Prince Llewelyn and William Marshall he'd come to expect war leaders to look as imposing as their reputations, but Hugh

O'Neill did not. He was of average height, with dull brown hair and a round belly that could only be called corpulent. Cathal turned and saw the look on his son's face as they neared the leader. He leaned in close as they walked.

"They call him Hugh the Stout behind his back," he whispered, "but don't let that fool ye. He's a fighter!"

Declan surveyed the group gathered around O'Neill. There was no question these men were warriors. They looked to be men ready to do violence when called upon, but they all showed deference to the portly man sitting on the bench. Despite the crowd around O'Neill, the clan chief noticed their approach and hailed Cathal.

"O'Duinne! Yer looking fitter today. How fares the wound?"

Cathal bobbed his head, the only formality seemingly required when addressing the chieftain, and gave a small laugh.

"It heals up slower than it did ten years ago, Hugh, but it hasn't festered so I expect to live."

O'Neill slapped his knee at that and hopped to his feet.

"Let me see!" he said with genuine interest.

Cathal did not hesitate, but pulled up his tunic to show the angry red scar along his ribs. Hugh O'Neill bent down and carefully examined the wound.

"Nasty cut there, Cathal, but it looks clean. How is yer lad, Keiran? I hear he is recovering, but takes his wound badly."

"Aye, he'll live, but I'm not sure he wants to. His body will heal in due time, but I worry for the lad's spirit."

O'Neill nodded gravely.

"I can't say how I would cope with the loss of a limb myself, Cathal. Probably just as badly. I'll say a prayer for the lad."

"That would be most kind, sir."

"Not at all!" O'Neill said, turning his gaze toward Declan. "But tell me, who is this sturdy young man ye bring with ye?"

Cathal cleared his throat.

"Ye recall ten years ago, the fight down near the Bann over the herd of cattle?"

For a moment Hugh O'Neill furrowed his brow trying to recall the incident, fights over herds of cattle in Ulster being as commonplace as thunderstorms in the summer. Then his eyes brightened.

"Ah, yes. I recall it. You took a blow to the head and were tended to by the man who laid on that blow. We all thought it most unusual behaviour for a Norman!"

He started to continue then stopped and looked hard at Declan.

"Then…bless me, this must be the boy—the one you sent off with the Norman."

Declan glanced at his father who had a pained look on his face. He'd wondered what story Cathal O'Duinne might have told about that day. It appeared the man had told the truth.

Declan gave Hugh O'Neill a small bow.

"My lord, Declan O'Duinne, at yer service."

O'Neill looked him over, then turned back to Cathal.

"He has yer colouring, Cathal, but for certain he's his mother's son with those eyes."

Cathal nodded.

"I always thought so. And he's done well, Hugh. He fought with the English on crusade and was knighted by King Richard himself at the battle of Acre."

A faint look of distaste showed on O'Neill's face.

"So I see you became a Norman yourself…*Sir* Declan."

Declan bristled.

"Not a Norman, my lord, though I make no apologies for serving one. The man I've given my oath to is as good a man as any in England—or Ireland, I expect."

O'Neill bristled back.

"Normans are a plague," he stated flatly.

Cathal laid a restraining hand on Declan's elbow, but to no avail.

"Normans outfight the Irish," he replied, an edge in his voice. "Whose fault is that? Are they more a plague than the men of Connacht or Tir Connell who ravage Tir Eoghain every generation or so? You can curse the Normans or you can learn how to beat them, my lord. You had best do the latter, for you will face them again and soon, I expect."

"What do you mean, sir?" the clan chief demanded.

"I mean that Carrickfergus is bursting with armed men and Sir John de Courcy is preparing to go to war."

"And how do you know the mind of that bastard?"

"I landed at Carrickfergus two days ago and was dragged before de Courcy himself. He questions all armed men who pass through his port."

"You spoke with de Courcy?" O'Neill interrupted him.

"Aye, lord. The monk who came with us on this journey did most of the talking, but I was present."

"And what did you learn from this 'Prince of Ulster'?"

"I learned he's a madman, my lord, who thinks dead saints speak to him. Apparently they tell him to conquer all of Ulster."

Hugh O'Neill shook his head.

"I've heard of his obsession with Patrick, but sadly, he is more than a madman. He hasn't ruled a third of Ulster for twenty years without being clever and a capable war chief." O'Neill looked over his shoulder at the cluster of men waiting for him by the bench, then turned back to the O'Duinnes, father and son.

"I have unfinished business to attend to, Cathal, but I would pursue this further. Come to me an hour after dark—and bring him with you," he said, pointing at Declan.

***

In the spring, in the north of Ireland, sunset is long in coming. With Finbar dispatched to the O'Duinne rath to look in on Keiran and Brother Cyril allowed to venture down the hill to seek out his fellow monks, Declan and his father spent the time speaking of their ten years apart.

"Even here, in far off Tir Eoghain, we heard tales of the English king they call the Lionheart and of his exploits in the Holy Land," Cathal said as he added wood to the campfire outside his tent. "More recently, word reached us that men loyal to King Richard had beaten Prince John's mercenaries at a place called Towcester."

"I fought there," said Declan.

"As did more than a few men from Tir Eoghain," Cathal observed.

Declan gave a small laugh.

"I hope they hold no grudges."

"Why should they? They were paid to fight. Had Richard offered them more they would have been on your side."

Declan looked up at the western sky, which was turning shades of orange as the sun dipped low on the horizon.

"What will Hugh O'Neill want of me tonight?"

Cathal shrugged.

"He'll likely want to know everything you can tell him about de Courcy and the force he's gathering at his accursed fort at Carrickfergus. Beyond that, I cannot say."

"That I'll do willingly, Father, but you must understand I came here to see you, not to join in a war. I've given my oath to Sir Roger de Laval and will honour that as long as he wishes to have me. He will choose what wars I fight, not I."

Cathal O'Duinne did not reply at once. He sat silently for a while, watching as the sun disappeared completely behind the dormitory that housed the Mac Lochlainn clans. Then he turned back to Declan.

"Son, I know what I did all those years ago can never be undone, though I have wished a thousand times I had not done it. And to see you now, come home to Tir Eoghain, a man in full. It made me wish—made me hope—that you would stay."

"Father, I…"

Cathal raised a hand to silence his son.

"I can see now that, with the help of God and your Sir Roger, you have built a good life for yerself in spite of my own foolishness. It seems a life worth holdin' on to, son. I hear your king fights the French these days, but there is peace in England, so you should get yerself back there before war finds ye here—as it surely must if ye stay. I've had enough of dead and wounded sons to last a lifetime."

Declan felt a lump in his throat. When he'd last known his father, he'd been twelve and the man had loomed over everything in his life like a giant. Now, with his hair going to grey and his face etched with lines, the clan chief looked merely human. Declan crossed to where Cathal sat and dropped down beside him.

"Father, I will stay for this council and give Hugh O'Neill what information I can. Before I leave, I'll visit my brother as well, but I cannot tarry more than a few days. Then I must go on to Down and then back to Carrickfergus."

Cathal looked at him quizzically.

"Why back through Carrickfergus? Ride down to Dublin and take ship there. It's the sensible thing to do."

"Not in this case, Father. We had another member of our party when we arrived on these shores, a fellow knight who is more brother to me than Fagan or Keiran. De Courcy forced us to leave him hostage at Carrickfergus until our return. Whatever Hugh O'Neill may want of me, I will not leave Roland Inness in that man's hands longer than needed, nor will I risk his life. I told him I would return in a fortnight to fetch him."

"But why Down? It's hardly on the way to Carrickfergus."

"Aye, but we had to have a story that would not arouse de Courcy's suspicions. We've told him that Brother Cyril was traveling from Chester to confer with the monks at Down and he expects us to give him an account of our visit when we pass back through his port."

"So you would ride back into the lion's den for this man, Inness?"

Declan did not hesitate.

"I've given my word. And Roland Inness would do it for me."

***

With the coming of darkness, clouds blew in from the west hiding the moon and stars and leaving only guttering torches to light the cobbled square at Armagh. Declan and Cathal made their way back to the main entrance of the monk's dormitory and were directed to a corner room where Hugh O'Neill sat on a wooden chest holding court. When the clan chieftain saw the two men enter, he politely asked the four men with him to leave.

"Come in, come in, have some ale," he said, gesturing toward cups and a pitcher on a small table by the lone window of the room. Declan glanced around as Cathal poured two cups of the amber liquid. It was truly a monk's lodging with nothing more than a wooden crucifix on the wall for ornamentation and a straw mattress beside the chest where Hugh O'Neill was perched. A half dozen stools had been dragged in from elsewhere in the building to accommodate the many clansmen who had business with the leader of the O'Neills.

Cathal handed a cup to Declan and the two men settled onto stools. O'Neill took a deep draught from his own cup and rose, looking out the tiny window into the black of the night.

"After the last battle, all the clans limped back to Armagh or further into Tir Eoghain to bind their wounds and mourn their many dead," he began. "All thought…all hoped, that there would be no more campaigning after such a battle. For, while the Cenél Eoghain suffered terrible losses, the English were bloodied as well. Then, a fortnight ago, we heard reports from Carrickfergus that de Courcy was gathering new forces to continue his campaign against us. That is the last information we have received. Our man who watched the comings and goings at the port and castle has gone silent." He stopped and turned toward Declan.

"I asked you here, in part, to find out what you saw there."

Declan grimaced.

"Lord, there was a head on a spike over the castle gate. That might explain the silence of your spy."

O'Neill frowned.

"I expected as much. Fergus was a brave man and deserved a better fate, but his loss has left us blind. So tell me, what did you see or hear as you passed through that damned place."

"I did not count heads, my lord, but in the town itself I saw at least a hundred fighting men lounging in the streets. Some looked to be Irish, but others had the look of Englishmen. I saw two men with longbows—likely Welsh archers. If I saw that many fighting men on the street, I'd guess as least three times that number were in the taverns and barracks."

"And the garrison?

"No more than eighty men."

O'Neill took another drink from his cup of ale.

"Your interview with de Courcy—tell me about that."

"Most of the conversation centred on Brother Cyril's story that he was a pilgrim sent by the Bishop of Chester to confer with the Abbot at Down regarding the saint, Patrick. De Courcy heartily approved of such a pilgrimage and gave us a letter of safe passage and introduction for the Abbot at Down. He strongly urged us to view for ourselves the bell of Saint Patrick, which I gather he placed in the abbey after the battle."

This caused Hugh O'Neill's face to redden.

"We played right into de Courcy's hands by parading the saint's bell before our army that day. I saw him take the bell from the dead hands of Eamon Maelchallain after they broke our lines. It was a grievous loss, Sir Declan. Saint Malachy himself entrusted that bell to the Cenél Eoghain and the Maelchallain clan. Now it's in the hands of our enemy. It's loss has caused many to lose heart, but not the O'Neills!" The clan chieftain slammed a fist down on the table causing a cup of ale to spill and drain out on the floor.

"This de Courcy is a clever man. In many ways, he understands the Irish better than any of the English barons. He has used our divisions to defeat us in battle and has venerated our saints to ease the burden of his rule. De Courcy has elevated St. Patrick to a more exalted position than even the church of Rome has. He seeks to sway the Irish to his side by his reverence for our greatest saint, but I for one see through him. He may pay his respects to our saints but he has no respect for the Irish themselves. He has banished the Irish priests at Down who had maintained the church there since Patrick founded it seven hundred years ago and brought in droves of English monks to replace them. Still, I'm not sure his veneration of Patrick is just an act."

"My lord, the man believes Patrick speaks to him," said Declan, "and it is no act."

O'Neill shook his head.

"I had not heard that he was in direct contact with the dead saint, but I'm not surprised. De Courcy is half mad. Did he have anything else to say?"

Declan thought for a moment.

"He seemed most interested in the fact that my comrade and I fought under Earl William Marshall at Towcester. He wanted to hear a detailed account of how we beat Prince John's mercenaries. Sadly, he kept my friend, Sir Roland Inness, as a hostage until our return from Down. I expect it will fall to Roland to explain how we bested John's army."

"Towcester—that ended John's rebellion against his brother, or so we heard."

"Aye, it was John's last throw of the dice and he had the stronger force that day, but we had the better strategy."

O'Neill arched an eyebrow.

"Then perhaps I should ask the same question that de Courcy asked—how *did* you beat John's army?"

For the next hour, Declan related the details of the battle at Towcester that secured Richard's throne. Throughout his telling, Hugh O'Neill peppered him with questions on terrain, tactics, and weaponry.

"Longbows?" he asked, after Declan recalled the death rained down on the mercenaries by Earl Ranulf's Danish archers. "I thought only the Welsh used that weapon. De Courcy hires as many of them as he can find."

"Aye, I think if the English themselves ever come to fully appreciate the power of the longbow, they might conquer the whole world. But they are as stubborn as the Irish. They have been taught from boyhood that it is the armoured knight and the motte that wins wars. They find it hard to change."

"So how are we to win, without archers?"

Declan ran a hand through his hair. The longbowmen had played a crucial role in the battle. The ability to strike at the enemy foot as they advanced up the long slope and again at the armoured knights when they came within close range had been decisive. But the bow was not a weapon much favoured by the Irish. He thought back on what he knew of Irish war tactics and brightened.

"Do you still employ hobelars, my lord?"

O'Neill nodded. Since earliest times, Irish clans had used the nimble little ponies bred on the island in the incessant wars between petty kings. Men who trained as hobelars would dart in close to enemy lines mounted on the swift little beasts, hurl light spears at their enemies, then turn and gallop away before the infantry could close on them.

"We have made use of them on raids and ambushes. But in a pitched battle, they would be cut to pieces by the English cavalry."

Declan shook his head.

"Not if you pick the right ground, my lord."

Hostage

"Psst...Master Inness!"

Roland's head snapped up at the hissed greeting. He was passing by the arched opening in the eastern wall that served as the entrance to Carrickfergus Castle. He'd spent his first night as the guest of Sir John de Courcy in a room attached to the barracks in the inner ward. It was small and spare with a straw mattress on the floor and a stool, but wasn't a gaol as there was no lock on the door. The guard who had escorted him there explained that guests of Sir John had the run of the inner bailey so long as they made no move to exit the castle gate and returned to their rooms at sundown.

He'd passed the morning wandering between the buildings that crowded the space within the castle walls and walking the perimeter of the curtain wall assessing the strengths and weaknesses of the fortifications. He'd found few weaknesses. Now he'd been hailed, but no one was in sight.

He glanced through the passageway at the two men-at-arms stationed at the gate itself. They were talking to a woman who held a basket of washing under her arm and were paying no heed to him. He swivelled his head around. There were only a few tradesmen and men-at-arms going about their business in the bailey and none seemed interested in him. But someone had called his name. He hadn't imagined it.

"Up here!" came the voice again from directly above him. He looked up and found himself gazing at the round face of a boy, peering down from the wall walk above the gate. The boy motioned urgently for Roland to join him, then drew back out of sight.

Roland glanced at the gate guards. They were still engaged with the washerwoman. He moved casually to the stone steps that led up to the wall walk. At the top of the stairs he stopped and lifted his eyes to the towering keep. There was a lookout on duty on the roof, but the man was looking off to the west. Lowering his gaze, he searched for the boy, but saw no one.

"Psst, in here," came the voice again.

The sound came from a small wooden structure that overhung the gate. The place was used to drop stones or boiling water on attackers attempting to breach the gate and could be accessed from the wall walk by a narrow door. Glancing around once more, Roland slipped through the door into the cramped compartment. It took a moment for his eyes to adjust to the dim light. He heard the boy before he could plainly see him.

"Yer Inness, are ye not?" the boy asked quietly.

"Aye, lad. I'm Inness."

"Then I have yer horse and yer kit too. The horse, he's a good 'un!"

Roland smiled. His eyes had adjusted to the light and he saw it was the boy who been left in charge of the horses on their arrival.

"Aye, he is, lad. I call him The Grey and he's the best horse I've ever had."

"Ye must be rich to own such a one as that," the boy said, with just a touch of wistfulness in his voice. "I'll need silver to keep him in hay and water."

Roland looked hard at the boy. This was no doubt a lie. If Declan had left The Grey in this lad's care, he would have paid. But the hollow cheeks and thin frame were no lie. This boy was fighting his own battle to survive in Carrickfergus. He took a coin from his purse and handed it over.

"What's your name, lad?"

"I'm called Finn, m'lord. I work down at the stables in town. Yer friend, the one with red hair, he gave me a message for ye."

"What was the message, Finn?"

"He says they will be back in a fortnight to fetch ye. Yer to stay put and enjoy the food and lodging here until they return. Yer not to do anything stupid."

Roland stifled a laugh. It was sound advice, but Declan knew he might well ignore it. When he'd been imprisoned in Jerusalem's dungeons by the great Saladin, there'd been other Christian prisoners there and all were waiting for King Richard to take the city and release them. But he'd seen Jerusalem's walls and knew what a daunting task that would be. He chose not to wait and had found a way out. The men who had stayed behind were all dead now. It was a lesson he hadn't forgot.

"You speak good English, Finn."

The boy frowned.

"I speak it. I have to or I'd starve. I've more use for English than Irish in my work."

"But you are not English."

"No," the boy said and spit in disgust. Then he realized who he was speaking to. "No offense, Master Inness."

"None taken, but you said you might starve. Have you no family?"

The boy shook his head.

"None hereabouts." My people are from Ulaid—what the English call Antrim. It was once ruled over by my grandsire as vassal to de Courcy."

"Once?"

"Aye, once, my lord. Three years ago, my grandsire rose against Sir John, but was brought to heel. He swore to remain loyal to the Prince, but he went back on his word and rebelled once more. This time de Courcy was not so gentle. He crushed the rising and left my grandsire dead upon the field, I'm told."

"What of your father and mother? How did you come to be here in Carrickfergus?"

"They are both dead. My mother died of a fever two springs ago and my father was killed."

"Killed? In battle?"

"No," said Finn and paused for a long moment before continuing.

"When first my grandsire rose against de Courcy and lost, he was forced to provide a hostage to ensure his future loyalty."

"Your father was the hostage."

"Aye, he was like you," the boy said. "He was a *guest* of Sir John."

"But your grandsire rose again."

"Aye lord, and the Prince had my father's throat cut."

Silence fell in the dim interior of the alcove.

"I'm sorry, Finn."

Finn shrugged his skinny shoulders.

"My grandsire was a fool to break his word and de Courcy...he's a bad man, Master Inness, a dangerous man."

"Aye, lad. That's plain enough and I thank you for the warning." Roland took another coin from his purse and held it up.

"You seem a clever lad and it seems you can come and go as you please around here. How would you get out of Carrickfergus if you were me?"

The boy gave a small smile. He reached out and took the coin.

"Let me think on that, Sir Roland."

The Council

*T*he dawn broke with no sun to be seen, only dark clouds rolling in from the west and a fine drizzle soaking the abbey, the town and all in it. In late morning, a horn sounded from the top of the hill near the church announcing an hour until the beginning of the council of the Cenél Eoghain. Near noon, the sun managed to show through a break in the overcast as Hugh O'Neill strode out of his quarters in the monk's dormitory followed by thirteen men. A dozen of these were the heads of the major O'Neill septs. One was not.

Declan stood nervously with the sept chieftains, the only man among them who was not a known leader within the O'Neill clan. A messenger had appeared at Cathal's tent a little after dawn with the unexpected request that he attend the council. He'd pulled a clean tunic from his kit and brushed the mud from his boots and now stood with men who looked at him curiously.

Some of the older chiefs he recognized from his childhood, but he was struck by the number of younger men among this gathering, no doubt the legacy of the slaughter inflicted on the clans not ten miles from where they now stood. That defeat had thinned the ranks of veteran sept leaders, men of his father's generation. Now their sons had taken on the burdens of leadership.

As they waited for Hugh to lead the way up to the church the older men yawned and scratched themselves while the younger men tried not to look nervous. Hugh turned to look at his followers.

"Weapons?" he demanded.

All raised open palms and shook their heads. No man was to bring a weapon to the council, which was being convened in the church. The meeting would be overseen by the Archbishop of Armagh as further hinderance to any bloodshed between the parties. But Hugh knew these men and knew the violent history between his own clan and their cousins, the Mac Lochlainns. He intended to take no chances.

"Any man among ye that raises a hand to a Mac Lochlainn, lest it be in his own defence, will answer to me," he announced. "The Archbishop has my word on this and any of ye that makes a liar of me will regret it." He paused and looked at each man in turn.

"Are we clear on that?" he asked finally.

A chorus of ayes came back and he nodded.

"Right then," O'Neill said, airily. "Let's go see what the new Mac Lochlainn chief has to say for himself."

He turned on his heel and started across the rain-slicked square toward the stone church that crowned the highest point in the town. It appeared that the entire populace of Armagh had gathered at the edges of the square to look on. Monks, novitiates, tradesmen, warriors, fat merchants and skinny boys shirking their chores all watched as the O'Neills assembled. This gaggle buzzed with excitement as Hugh led his men toward the church.

On the opposite side of the square, another group was forming. Declan looked over his shoulder and could see a youngish man addressing the Mac Lochlainn clan leaders, but could not make out what was being said. The appearance of the Mac Lochlainns caused a new round of excitement among the onlookers. All knew that the men gathering in the church would soon decide who would rule Tir Eoghain and its people.

As O'Neill and his followers neared the church, they saw a figure standing in the entrance. It was Tomas O'Connor, the Archbishop. Tall and thin, the prelate was an imposing figure, clad in a spotless white linen cassock accented by a silk tunic of green and gold. A peaked mitre sat atop his head and in his left hand was a long staff of oak, topped with a cross of gold, a symbol of his spiritual authority.

Declan O'Duinne

Tomas O'Connor was of the royal line of Connacht—grandson to one Connacht king and nephew to two others. He had taken holy vows as a boy and was reputed to be devoted in his faith, but he was no simple, humble priest. He was a prince of the church and he held himself like one.

"O'Connor was Muirchertach Mac Lochlainn's choice for the Archbishopric, but he's purported to be his own man," Cathal whispered to Declan as O'Neill halted his party in front of the church. "He has met more than once with de Courcy, but no one doubts his loyalty to the Irish church or the Cenél Eoghain. His opinion will carry weight here."

A moment later, the Mac Lochlainn chieftains arrived, led by Conor Mac Lochlainn. Declan had seen kings and princes at close hand. He'd fought under Richard the Lionheart and helped Llywelyn ap Iowerth win his throne. He knew the look of royalty and this young Mac Lochlainn had that look. He was tall and slender and wore an embroidered linen shirt over tight-fitting breeches. A dark blue cape was thrown over one shoulder and a silver crucifix hung from his neck.

Declan glanced at the portly Hugh O'Neill and sighed. If the choice of king was to be decided on looks alone, the O'Neill cause was lost. As he looked at the two contenders, he was reminded of King Guy of Jerusalem and that gave him some comfort. King Guy had looked every inch a king—tall and handsome and elegant, but the man had led his small kingdom into ruin. Regal looks alone did not make a king.

As Conor's followers gathered around, Declan saw that, like the O'Neill chiefs, they were a mix of young and veteran clan leaders, their own ranks painfully thinned at the battle at Tandragee the month before. He was about to turn his attention back to the Archbishop when he was shocked to see a woman among the rough clan chiefs—the very woman he had knocked off her feet in the square the day before.

Declan elbowed his father.

"The woman..."

Cathal O'Duinne leaned in close, a small smile on his lips.

"She's a Maelchallain and a fetching lass she is," he whispered. "The Maelchallains are the hereditary Keepers of

Saint Patrick's bell. Her father fell in the battle and her younger brother is but thirteen years old. He will not be of age until the end of summer. She leads her sept until then."

"Her name?"

"Margaret, though many call her Meg. I've heard she may marry Conor Mac Lochlainn."

To his surprise, Declan felt a small twinge of jealousy.

"Pretty girl," he said, wistfully.

Cathal snickered.

"Prickly, I'm told."

***

The benches in the nave had been rearranged so that they faced the aisle. As Archbishop O'Connor led the clan chiefs in, the Mac Lochlainn adherents found places on the left side of the nave and the O'Neills occupied the benches on the right. Once all had found a place, the Archbishop began a prayer of benediction.

Declan found his eyes straying to the Maelchallain woman, but jerked his head away when her eyes unexpectedly met his. He felt his face flush, embarrassed that he had been caught staring and was thankful when the Archbishop finished his prayer and began the proceedings.

"Welcome all to the house that Saint Patrick built. May his spirit speak to each of you as you determine what course the Cenél Eoghain must follow. The chief of the Mac Lochlainns called for this Council of the clans to assemble and, by rights, should speak first."

Conor Mac Lochlainn, son of the dead King, rose to speak.

"Archbishop O'Connor, I thank you for your good offices in arranging this gathering," he began. We value your wise counsel as we consider what is to be done."

The Archbishop gave the speaker a small nod to acknowledge his role in bringing the clans together. Mac Lochlainn then turned to face the O'Neill chiefs directly.

"Men of the O'Neills," he began, "our two clans have ruled the Cenél Eoghain since the days of Niall of the Nine Hostages. For three hundred years we have kept Tir Eoghain free of foreign invaders, be they the Northmen or the ambitious kings of Connacht and Meath."

Mac Lochlainn stopped his speech suddenly, his face reddening. He turned to the Archbishop, whose grandfather and uncles he had just labelled as foreign invaders.

"Your excellency, I…"

O'Connor waved a hand in front of his face as though brushing away any offense.

"You will hear no disagreement from me that my kinsmen from Connacht have, more than once, cast covetous eyes on this land," he said affably. "So do not fret, my lord. Your speech is well begun. Please continue."

Conor Mac Lochlainn cleared his throat and began again.

"Men of the Cenél Eoghain, we have never failed to turn back invaders in the past. By the blood of our fathers and the favour of God, we have kept this land free. Would that it should remain so for a thousand years more."

The young leader paused and looked keenly at Hugh O'Neill.

"But, my lord, you know what the English are doing east of the Bann. New mottes go up every month topped with timber walls. We have no engines to breach those walls, so if we strike into Down or Antrim, we must bypass them, only to have the English sally forth and attack us in the rear. Because of these forts, we cannot risk taking the fight to them."

There were murmurs of agreement from the Mac Lochlainn chiefs at this.

"But they can and do bring the fight to us! We have been losing battles to the English for twenty years now, even when our numbers are greater. Their archers and their armoured horsemen—we have nothing to counter them," he said and there was genuine anguish in his voice.

"The Mac Lochlainns lost four sept chiefs and our King at the Tandragee. Our holy relic, the bell of Saint Patrick, was taken. I cannot but see it as a sign of God's displeasure. He has withdrawn his favour from us and all we have left is our blood—and the English are happy to take that."

Hugh O'Neill leapt to his feet, shock written on his face.

"Where are you heading with this, Mac Lochlainn?" he demanded. "Are you suggesting surrender, sir?"

The O'Neill chiefs started to rise behind their leader, but he whirled around and glared at them.

"Sit down!" he bellowed.

They sat.

Declan, who had not risen with the others, watched O'Neill bring his chieftains to heel. It was an impressive display. These were all men used to giving orders, not taking them, but they'd instantly obeyed this command. And their obedience was not out of fear. He'd seen what that sort of obedience looked like. No, they'd obeyed Hugh O'Neill out of respect. The man might be short and thick in the middle, but his complete command over these rough warriors erased any doubts in Declan's mind about O'Neill's qualities as a leader.

Having brought his own men under control, O'Neill now turned back to Conor Mac Lochlainn.

"I asked you a question, sir! Are you suggesting surrender?"

Mac Lochlainn turned a baleful eye on his own men. Most had leapt to their feet at O'Neill's accusation of surrender, but a few, including the woman, had not. Declan stole a glance at Margaret Maelchallain. She was sitting stiff and upright on a back bench with a stricken look on her face.

Conor waited until all were back in their places, then turned back to O'Neill.

"Not surrender, my lord, peace. I have been approached by an intermediary with a message from John de Courcy. He offers us a treaty of peace and the return of our sacred relic. He offers us continued possession of our lands and property and governance of our own affairs. He will acknowledge our Archbishop, Tomas O'Connor, and confirm him in his position at Armagh. All this he offers."

"In exchange for what?" O'Neill demanded. "What is de Courcy's price for this 'peace'?"

Mac Lochlainn spread his hands.

"The price is less than I feared, my lord. We—all of us here—must swear fealty to de Courcy as our overlord. He will then grant us back our lands to rule as we see fit."

This was met with an angry rumble from the O'Neill men, silenced by a dark look from their leader.

"What else?" O'Neill asked.

Mac Lochlainn shrugged.

"Not so very much. We are to come at his summons should any invade his lands east of the Bann and he, in turn, pledges to come to our aid against any attack from outside Tir Eoghain."

"That's all?"

"No. We…we are to allow de Courcy to construct a fort west of the River Bann and another at the ford on the Blackwater—to be garrisoned by his men."

Hugh O'Neill stood there, his jaw muscles working and his fists clenched, fighting to contain his anger. It took him a long moment to gain control of his fury, then he spoke.

"My lord, Mac Lochlainn. We have lost a king and you have lost a father. We have had our most precious relic taken from us. These are bad times for the Cenél Eoghain, but this…this is a peace for slaves! I'll not deny that your father and I rarely agreed on matters, but I swear by all that is holy, we would have agreed on this. The Cenél Eoghain will not sell our freedom so cheaply!"

"And I shall not see my people slaughtered for the pride of the O'Neills!" the young Mac Lochlainn shot back. "The kingdoms of Ireland have fallen to these English bastards one after another. The High King has submitted to the English King. Why should we be different? Why should we fight a war we cannot win?"

"Let the other kings do what they will," O'Neill countered. "We are the Cenél Eoghain and we can beat the English!"

"So says you!" Mac Lochlainn shouted, pointing a finger at the O'Neill chief.

Hugh raised a hand to cut off any uproar from his own men before it began, then turned away from Conor Mac Lochlainn spoke directly to the Mac Lochlainn clan chiefs.

"There is a man in my company who knows the English way of war. He fought with Richard of England on Crusade and with William Marshall, Lord of Leinster, at the Battle of

Towcester. On that field, Prince John's army—an army very much like that led by John de Courcy—was routed."

Now there was low murmuring on both sides of the nave. Every man there had heard of this battle. That day had put an end to Prince John's hopes of wresting the English throne from his brother and had sent many an Irish mercenary—those that survived the carnage—back home. Most gathered in Saint Patrick's church knew at least one Irishman who had fought there, though few of the returning warriors spoke of that day of slaughter.

Declan had been curious as to why O'Neill had invited him to this council. Now, with a sinking feeling, he knew.

"This man you speak of, where was he a month ago when de Courcy put our army to rout?" Conor asked with a sneer. "We could have used his *wisdom* there! And where is he now, my lord? We would all like to hear what magic must be conjured up to defeat warbows and heavy cavalry!"

There were jeers and hoots from the Mac Lochlainns as their leader finished. Hugh O'Neill turned to Declan, motioning for him to stand.

"Here is the man, Conor—Sir Declan O'Duinne. He knows how to beat the English."

"By God, he is English himself!" shouted Mac Lochlainn, pointing an accusing finger at Declan. "You say he fought for Richard of England and for William Marshall. If not in breeding, then in body and soul he is English."

O'Neill raised a hand to object.

"He is an O'Duinne, sir. The blood of the Cenél Eoghain runs in his veins! And who better than one who has fought with the English to teach us how to beat them?" O'Neill asked calmly. "He is the oath man of an English knight, but why should that cause *you* concern, my lord? A moment ago you were suggesting we should *all* give our oath to an Englishman. Let the man speak."

Mac Lochlainn sputtered a protest, but he'd been undone by his own words and knew it. He turned and raised his hands to his own followers then turned back to face the O'Neills. He stared at Declan, then nodded.

"Say your piece then," he said and sat down heavily on the wooden bench.

Declan looked across the aisle at the Mac Lochlainn chieftains who now sat with arms crossed and sour looks, save for the one woman, Margaret Maelchallain. There was still a pained look on her face, but she was leaning forward, waiting to hear what he had to say. Declan cleared his throat and began.

"As Hugh O'Neill said, I have given my oath to an Englishman and I make no apologies for that. There is no better man on either of these islands than the man I serve. He, like most who rule in England, is of Norman stock—a warrior race to be sure, but no more so than those they have conquered and no more so than the men here today. It is not Norman valour that has given them rule over half of Europe, it is the Norman way of war. The way they wage war has beaten down the Saxons and the French and the Sicilians and it is now grinding down the Irish."

"They fight like cowards, covered all over with mail!" a Mac Lochlainn chief shouted. "Even their horses are armoured!"

"And our forefathers went into battle naked, I'm told," Declan shot back. "Does that make you a coward for wearing clothes now or carrying a shield?"

"Where then are we to get mail?" another man asked. "Our smiths do not know the craft of making such things."

"And what about the horses?" yet another man added. "Our Irish ponies can't match those beasts!"

Declan shook his head.

"The Ostmen smiths in Dublin know the craft of making mail. You could go there and offer a man enough gold to come north and teach your smiths the secrets. You could send merchants to England to buy horses. You could hire Flemish mercenaries who know the craft of building siege engines that can knock down the walls the English build. All these things you could do, but you do nothing but fight in the same way as your fathers fought. That is what lost half of Ireland to the English and will lose the other half in due time.

"So you would make us Normans?"

This question came, surprisingly, from the Maelchallain woman.

"Nay, my lady. I do not say you must become Normans to beat them."

"How then?" she asked, with genuine curiosity in her voice. "To do the things you say will take months if not years. De Courcy won't wait for us to ship over horses from England."

Declan drew a breath. How to explain this? He found himself wishing that Roland Inness, with his clever mind for tactics, was here to lay out a plan, but his friend was still a hostage. It was up to him to convince his own people they could win a war against the English.

"First, you must not allow any of their mottes to be built on your land," he began and saw Conor Mac Lochlainn scowl at that. "The English plant these wooden forts at choke points—fords and passes through the hills. As my lord Mac Lochlainn noted, once a motte is in your rear, your lines of supply or retreat are at risk. It only takes a small garrison of mounted troops, secure on top of their hill, to threaten any force that passes by and once the wooden fort is built, a stone one will soon follow. Unless you are prepared to pay a very high price in blood, you must not allow them to build these things."

"We had no mottes in our rear a month ago and still we lost," Margaret Maelchallain noted.

"Aye, my lady, but had the English built a motte here in Armagh they could have blocked your retreat and you would likely not be sitting in this church today as free men and women. I was not there, but I've been told what happened that day. If I've heard aright, you were bound to lose that fight."

This brought a renewed outcry from the Mac Lochlainns. A few brandished their bandages and scars received on that day. More than a few insulted the O'Duinne family name. Conor Mac Lochlainn let the uproar go unchecked for a bit then stood and raised his hand to quiet his men.

"Let him finish so we can be done with this...lecture," he said, disdain clear in his voice. "Tell us, Sir Declan, why we were bound to lose that day."

Declan did not hesitate.

"On better ground, you might have won, my lord, but you fought the English on ground of their choosing. It was ground favourable for their heavy cavalry. On that sort of ground, no men on foot can stand against them."

Declan paused and looked at the men across the aisle. Some seemed to be listening. He could not read the look on the face of their leader or that of the Maelchallain woman. It mattered not at this point.

"I'm told the centre of your line was on the valley floor, on level ground, with nothing but flesh and blood to stop their charge. As I said, my lords, you were bound to lose."

With that, Declan sat down. Archbishop O'Connor, who had been watching the rancorous debate from a bench set in the middle of the aisle, rose quickly to his feet.

"My lords, we have heard much today and have much left to decide. I think it best to take our leave to consider all that we've heard here. Tomorrow is the sabbath. Let us take that day to lift up prayers and beg God for wisdom in these matters, and come back together the day after."

* * *

Declan felt numb as he joined the O'Neill chiefs filing out into the square. The Mac Lochlainns held back, wisely avoiding the chance that a harsh word might incite a brawl inside the holy confines of the church. Declan glanced over his shoulder and saw that the Mac Lochlainn chiefs had clustered around their young leader, leaving Margaret Maelchallain alone on the bench. She had asked the sort of questions he might have expected from the clan chief, but Conor Mac Lochlainn had shown little interest in what he had to say. As for the Maelchallain girl, her curiosity did not seem to be welcome among her fellow chiefs.

For his part, he had known Hugh O'Neill was prepared to make a case for fighting the English, but he had not expected to be called upon to personally sway the Cenél Eoghain towards war. Hugh O'Neill had used him for his own purposes and without apology, but such was the habit of great men. He'd been used by Richard of England when he and Roland had been sent off to scout Saladin's army and by Earl Ranulf when he needed to retake his city of Chester from William de Ferrers.

This day he'd been used once more, but not ill-used. His brief meeting with the Prince of Ulster had told him all he needed to know about John de Courcy. Submitting to him would be the end of the Cenél Eoghain. If his words had swayed those who thought to surrender to de Courcy, then he had no regrets. Besides, every word he'd spoken was the truth.

Allies

*I*t was well past dark when a man appeared at Cathal O'Duinne's tent in the alleyway. They were being summoned once more to attend the O'Neill clan chieftain. The messenger led the two men around to the entrance of the dormitory and back to the corner room that served as O'Neill's reception hall. Hugh was perched once more on the big chest, but he was not alone.

Two finely-carved chairs had been brought in for these new guests. Declan was surprised to see them occupied by Archbishop O'Connor and Margaret Maelchallain, both known to be supporters of the old Mac Lochlainn king. O'Neill slid off the chest as the newcomers arrived and made the introductions.

"Your Excellency and Miss Maelchallain, I believe you both know Cathal O'Duinne," he began and both nodded at the leader of the O'Duinne sept. "This is his youngest son, Sir Declan," he added. "Sir Declan has travelled from Cheshire to see his family."

"And to trample local girls," Margaret Maelchallain added acidly. Declan reddened as the three other men in the room looked at him curiously.

"I did, indeed, manage to trample Miss Maelchallain in the square yesterday, for which I am heartily sorry. I was relieved to see her at the council this morning, looking uninjured from the experience and full of questions."

He gave the girl a small bow.

"If I might be of some service to you...to make amends."

Margaret Maelchallain shrugged at that.

"If I should think of something, Sir Declan, I will let you know," she said with a smug look. "In the meantime, all I ask is that you look where you're going!"

Before Declan could reply, the Archbishop rose from his seat and strode over to Cathal, placing a hand on the man's shoulder.

"I heard of your loss, Cathal. I know my prayers will be of little solace to you, but I will say them nevertheless. Surely your son is with our Lord in heaven even now and for all eternity."

Cathal kept his head high.

"I thank you for yer prayers, your excellency. My boy died bravely and I must hope, not in vain."

The churchman stiffened.

"As long as the Cenél Eoghain remain free, he will not have died in vain," he said grimly.

Declan noticed the change in the man's tone. It was curious. At the council, the Archbishop had spoken softly amidst the angry voices on both sides. He had tried to calm the passions that threatened to tear apart the Cenél Eoghain. Now, as the churchman spoke of his countrymen's struggle for freedom, he had fire in his voice. Even more curious was the simple fact of the man's presence here with Hugh O'Neill.

Cathal had told him that O'Connor's candidacy to fill the role of Archbishop of Armagh had been supported by King Muirchertach Mac Lochlainn. The Archbishopric of Armagh, centred as it was on the mother church of Ireland, was the highest office in the Irish church and gave its holder spiritual authority over all of Ireland's Christians. The Pope had confirmed the appointment and O'Connor had been loyal to the Mac Lochlainns ever since. Yet here he stood before the chief of the O'Neills. Declan wondered if Conor Mac Lochlainn knew of this meeting, and suspected he did not.

Margaret Maelchallain's presence was also surprising. It had been a Mac Lochlainn king who had named the Maelchallains as protectors of Saint Patrick's bell, the clan's greatest honour. The clan, in turn, had given their complete loyalty to the Mac Lochlainns for generations. Yet here she was.

Hugh O'Neill had not failed to note the churchman's tone when he spoke of freedom for the Cenél Eoghain and knew when to press home a point.

"You spoke of freedom, your excellency," he began. "We are of like mind there it seems. Conor Mac Lochlainn wants to avoid bloodshed, I know, but at what price? If we agree to de Courcy's offer we will surely lose our freedom *and* our blood. Most of the men we fought at Tandragee were the men of Antrim and Down. Does anyone think the Cenél Eoghain won't be used in the same way when de Courcy takes up arms against the men of Connacht or Donegal? We will shed our blood, not for ourselves, but for our new master's ambitions."

He paused for a moment to gauge O'Connor's reaction, but the churchman simply stood there, his face revealing nothing. O'Neill changed tacks.

"Your excellency, I am aware that, with de Courcy holding the east and de Lacy the south, you are confined here in the northwest, cut off from your flock outside of Tir Eoghain. I know de Courcy's offer to preserve you in your position as Archbishop and prelate over the holy church in Ireland would free you to be a shepherd to all Irish Christians. It must be tempting."

Now the Archbishop's face betrayed him. He scowled.

"Is that what you think of me, O'Neill?"

The chieftain's face reddened and he started to reply, but Tomas O'Connor cut him off with a raised hand.

"De Courcy is a clever man," the churchman said, his voice full of scorn. "He thinks to buy me, but knows not how. I need no Englishman to grant me powers already granted by the holy father in Rome!"

Once more O'Neill made as though to speak, but the prelate raised his hand again and he fell silent.

"You are also a clever man, Hugh O'Neill, and ambitious. You want my help, but I trust you are not foolish enough to bribe me with power or position."

"You have me there, your excellency, on both counts. I am ambitious and I do need you. But if not power or position, what then is the price of your support?"

101

O'Connor's eyes gleamed like an old testament prophet as he leaned in toward the O'Neill chief.

"You must fight!" he snarled. "You must never surrender."

For a moment, O'Neill just stood there. Declan knew the man had misjudged the Archbishop and insulted him in the bargain, but instead of a rebuke, O'Connor had revealed where his heart lay to the O'Neill chief. And O'Neill sensed that much depended on his response at this moment.

"Your excellency, while I have breath in my body, I will not bend the knee to the English—not to de Courcy or de Lacy or any of that ilk. The O'Neills will fight, whether the Mac Lochlainns join us or not. This I swear on my soul."

"Then you should be our king," the churchman said simply and sat back down on his chair.

"You will support me?" O'Neill asked eagerly.

"I will not oppose you," the prelate said.

"A weak endorsement for the man you think should be your king, don't you think?"

The Archbishop sniffed.

"I loved Muirchertach Mac Lochlainn, with all his many faults. Out of respect for him, I will not openly oppose his son's bid for the throne. Nor will I oppose yours, Hugh. If you are as clever as I think you are, then that will be all you need. If you can persuade enough of the Mac Lochlainn septs to support your claim to the throne, then you will be king. Some, I believe prefer to continue the fight," he said, glancing over at the Maelchallain girl, "so there is opportunity there."

All eyes turned toward Margaret Maelchallain. Hers was not the largest sept in the extended Mac Lochlainn clan, but as Keepers of Saint Patrick's bell it was one of the most prestigious. Her presence here suggested the Maelchallains were not ready to make peace. The young woman had sat quietly while O'Neill and O'Connor had sparred with each other, but Declan could see she was not at all cowed by either man.

"There are those among our septs who do not agree with Conor Mac Lochlainn," she said flatly, "though they are loathe to speak against him. Conor is a good man and wants to do what is right, but I fear that with the loss of his father and so many of our clansmen, he has lost heart for this fight. Our sept's loyalty to the Mac Lochlainns runs deep, but Conor is not the man who can preserve the freedom of the Cenél Eoghain," she said, looking hard at Hugh O'Neill. "I am here tonight to judge for myself if you are."

"I know what you risk by coming here," O'Neill said softly. "The kingship is rarely decided without blood being spilt and it may well come to that, though I pray it does not. I expect there are those in your camp who would not hesitate to kill a clan chief they thought disloyal, no matter the sex."

The girl shrugged.

"There are those in my camp who despise me simply because I am a woman who speaks my mind and others who dislike that I speak against this base surrender that de Courcy offers. If they knew I was here, they would not hesitate to kill me. But there are others who feel as I do."

"Yet you are here and not they," said O'Neill.

"They all deferred to a lady to speak for them," she said with a wry smile.

Hugh O'Neill returned her smile.

"So tell me, what must I do or say to convince you that I am the man to be king of Tir Eoghain?"

For the first time since Declan and Cathal had entered the room, Margaret Maelchallain stood up.

"You've given me part of what I came to hear. You will not accept the peace offered by the English and will fight them to the end. That is a sentiment I share, but it is not enough. If we follow you into war and lose, then Conor Mac Lochlainn will have been right—needless blood spilt for the same outcome. So what I need to know, sir, is, can you win? This is why I asked that you have your Sir Declan join us tonight. I have other questions for him."

"Fair enough. Ask him what you will."

Declan rose to his feet. He had not expected to once more be questioned.

"What is it you want to know, my lady?"

"I want to know who you are and if you truly know whereof you speak, sir. O'Neill says you are a knight, Sir Declan. That title carries little weight among the Irish, but I would know who made you so and for what. He speaks of far off battles you've fought and I would know more of those. Your words were persuasive this morning," she said tartly, "but anyone can spew words."

Declan clenched his teeth. The woman's questions might be reasonable, but her tone was insulting.

"Say please," he said, simply.

The girl looked at him incredulously.

"What?"

"You must ask me nicely, if you wish me to answer, my lady."

"Declan!" Cathal laid a hand on his son's arm, but Declan pulled it away.

"Father, I came to Ireland because I was told you were dying. I did not come here to be used by Hugh O'Neill in his campaign to be king or to be insulted by this young lady," he said nodding toward Margaret. "She will say please, or I will say no more." He turned to Hugh O'Neill. "And you as well, my lord."

An embarrassed silence fell over the room. For a long moment, no one spoke. Then the Archbishop gently poked Margaret Maelchallain's arm with his staff. She turned and glared at him, but he just inclined his head toward Declan. Slowly she turned back.

"Very well," she said through gritted teeth. "Please continue, Sir Declan."

"Yes, please do, Sir Declan," added Hugh O'Neill with an amused smile.

Declan nodded and turned to look directly at the girl.

"As for who I am, miss—I am an O'Duinne, a clan as old as yours though not as famed. I was knighted by Richard the Lionheart at the siege of Acre. I and eighty other fools were the first wave up the breach in the wall. Only forty came back down. It was at Acre that I understood that flesh and blood alone cannot take a fortress. You must have siege engines to breach the walls—or you must starve out the garrison. The Irish have not the skill to build these engines nor the men to sustain long sieges. This is why I said you must not let the English build fortresses on your land. On that same campaign I rode with King Richard's heavy cavalry when we smashed through the lines of the Saracens at Arsuf. When on favourable ground, no men on foot can stand against Norman cavalry. Doing so got your King killed a month ago."

"I was also at Towcester the day we broke Prince John's cavalry. That day we fought on ground of our choosing. The Prince had summoned his army to London and we placed our smaller force athwart the only decent road leading there, which compelled them to attack us where we stood. Earl Marshall set our men at the top of a long, muddy slope with deep forest on each flank to anchor our lines. We buried sharpened stakes into the ground to our front and set our spearmen in the front rank to blunt the shock of the heavy cavalry."

"Just as de Courcy did against the Cenél Eoghain, the enemy sent their foot in first to weaken our lines, but we held. Then the heavy cavalry was ordered forward to break through and begin the slaughter, but their great warhorses found little purchase in the mud of that slope. When they reached our lines, there was no momentum in their charge. An armoured knight on a warhorse at full gallop is almost impossible to stop or to kill, but the same man, on a horse brought to a standstill by mud, or spikes or spears, can be taken down. This we did at Towcester. We butchered their cavalry on that muddy slope."

"In the war you face here, de Courcy's cavalry are the key. Give them the right ground and they will ride you down. Choose more wisely and they can be broken. That is what I've learned from serving a Norman for ten years."

Declan stopped. It was the longest speech he'd ever made.

"Did I answer your questions, my lady?" he asked at last.

Margaret Maelchallain did not speak as silence descended on the room. Then she hiked up the hem of her dress and walked past Declan to the door. She took hold of the handle and looked back at him standing there.

"Yes," she said softly. "Yes, you did."

The Broken Brother

*D*eclan awoke to the sound of the abbey bells calling the monks of Armagh to Matins. Near him in the dark he could hear his father snoring contentedly, his sleep untroubled by the bells. Silently he rose and slipped out of the tent. It was still dark, with barely a hint of dawn to the east and there was a slight chill in the air, but the sky was clear and it promised to be a fine Sunday. He stretched and walked out onto the abbey square. No one else was about yet.

As he watched the sky begin to lighten with the approaching dawn, he saw a man stroll out from the dormitory across the way where the Mac Lochlainn clans had found quarters. He raised a hand to acknowledge the newcomer's presence, but the man just stared at him and did not return the gesture. Declan sighed.

As gratifying as his reunion with his father had been, being drawn into the bloody politics of Ulster was another matter. The relentless aggression of the English and the endless bloody infighting among the Irish had changed not at all since he'd left ten years before. It left a sour taste in his mouth.

The man who had joined him on the square returned to the dormitory where the crescent moon banner of the Mac Lochlainn's hung limply in the still morning air. He wondered if his words the day before had reached the Mac Lochlainn chiefs. By all accounts their young leader, Conor Mac Lochlainn, was no coward. He'd heard that the man fought bravely at Tandragee and barely escaped with his life. But he knew that such a crushing defeat could weaken a man's resolve, even if it did not make him a coward.

In the end, perhaps Mac Lochlainn was right to seek the best terms he could get to have peace with the English. With de Courcy to the east and Walter de Lacy to the south there were threats enough to consider such a course, particularly if there was no unity within the Cenél Eoghain. With the O'Neills and Mac Lochlainns contending for leadership, the unity needed to face the English seemed unlikely. But he knew now that Hugh O'Neill would never accept such a peace. The man had sworn to the Archbishop to die first and he meant it. If Conor Mac Lochlainn hoped to avoid more blood, he was going to be sorely disappointed.

Down the hill to his left, he saw a line of monks making their way up toward the church, answering the call of the bells. Evicted from their dormitories by the arrival of the Cenél Eoghain chiefs, they had spent the night in whatever accommodations they could find in the small village at the bottom of the hill.

Near the end of the line, Declan saw Brother Cyril, trudging uphill with the others. Cyril had spent the night with his brother monks and gave Declan a cheery wave as he passed by. The Irish knight had admired the courage of the skinny little monk when first they'd met in Wales and had further warmed to the churchman during this journey. Seeing him grinning as he followed his Augustinian brethren up the hill for Matins services lifted his spirits.

As the monks filed into the church, the bells fell silent. For a moment the calling of birds was the only sound filling the square, then a soft chanting rose from the church as the monks began their devotionals. Declan turned and walked back toward his father's tent and saw Cathal O'Duinne step out of the opening.

The man still moved a bit stiffly, favouring his left side where the English broadsword had left its mark, but he looked fitter than the day before. Clearly he was recovering his health and vigour. Seeing his son, Cathal beamed and came to meet him. He took Declan by the shoulders, holding him at arm's length as though admiring some fine object.

"I still can't believe yer here lad, but it's grand to have ye, if only for a while," he said, then pulled his son close and wrapped an arm around his shoulders. "Come, have some breakfast. One of my boys will be here soon with the horses. It will take half the morning to reach the Blackwater from here."

Declan pulled up a stool by the fire that Cathal was busily stoking. When the blaze was sufficient, the older man ducked back inside the tent and reappeared with a pan, a half-pound of cured pork and a loaf of brown bread. He settled the pan in the coals and dropped in the pork. It had begun to sizzle when Hugh O'Neill came around the corner and headed their way.

"Sleep well?" he asked Declan as he squatted by the fire and warmed his hands.

"Aye, lord, right well, and you?"

O'Neill shook his head.

"Nay, I was up till an hour before those damned Matins bells. After ye left last evening, I sat with each of my clan chiefs, one at a time. I had to be sure they were with me in this. You know it will be bloody before we're done."

"Aye, lord. I've no doubt of that."

O'Neill turned back toward the elder O'Duinne who had been tending to the pork sizzling in the pan.

"Smells good," he said.

"Yer welcome to have some, Hugh. Give it another minute."

O'Neill looked up at the sky, which had gone from near black to pale blue as dawn arrived.

"I'm obliged, Cathal. All of this politics makes a man hungry!"

Cathal speared the pork and flipped it to brown on the other side for a bit then cut it into three pieces. He gave his chief and his son each a slab of dark bread and a hot, greasy hunk of meat.

For a while they squatted quietly by the fire, enjoying a fine breakfast on the Sabbath. Then O'Neill broke the silence.

"Cathal, I've been thinking on yer son, Keiran. I lost my herald at Tandragee—a good man and dependable. I need another. I would be pleased to have yer boy take his place if he is up to it. It might give the lad something to occupy his mind other than the hand he lost."

Declan watched tears well up in his father's eyes, but the man fought gamely to hold them back.

"It's a kind offer, Hugh, and I am obliged to ye for it," he said, his voice husky, "but I fear he may refuse. The heart seems to have gone out of him."

O'Neill frowned.

"Then make it an order—from me," he said.

The O'Duinne chief started to protest, but O'Neill held up a hand to silence him.

"Listen to me Cathal. This isn't pity. I know yer boy. He reminds me of you. There is a war coming and I will need men such as he if we are to win it. If he can walk and sit a horse, I will expect you both to be back here before the council reconvenes on the morrow. I'd like you there as well, Sir Declan."

The clan chieftain paused and laid a hand on Cathal's shoulder.

"Thank you for breakfast, old friend, now go see to yer son," he said and headed back up the alley without another word.

Declan watched him go and shook his head. Hugh O'Neill was a man standing at a crossroads for his country. His people, the Cenél Eoghain, were divided and a relentless enemy was on their doorstep. The council that had been called to heal the divisions and meet the threat had, thus far, come to nothing. The weight of it all had to be on the man's shoulders, yet Hugh O'Neill had heard the pain in Cathal O'Duinne's voice and had come to offer what help he could to an old friend.

There walks a king, Declan thought as the man disappeared around the corner

The sound of hooves on cobbles announced the arrival of the boy with their horses. The two led their mounts across the square and, skirting the crowded alleyways around the Mac Lochlainn quarters, made their way to Dungannon Road. It was a fine morning for a ride and Declan let his father set the pace on his smaller mount.

As he gazed around at the countryside, memories came flooding back to him. He'd often ridden with his father and brothers to Armagh to trade cattle and horses with the monks there and the land had changed little in ten years. For the first few miles, the country was open pasturage and mostly flat, with hedges and stone walls separating neighbour's fields. At this time of year, the green of the land was almost luminous.

Passing out of the open grazing land, the road snaked through low, wooded hills. As a boy, he'd sometimes set snares and hunted red squirrels with a sling in this forest. Another two miles brought them to the broad valley of the Blackwater river. Here the road descended gradually toward the river and the trees gave way to pastures and peat bogs. He saw two cows sunk up to their hocks in the spongy soil beside the road contentedly chewing their cud. There was a boy with a long switch trying to drive them to higher ground. The boy was half covered in the black mud of the bog and the cows eyed him with docile indifference. The scene transported him back to his boyhood.

Ten years ago, that would have been him.

Well before noon they splashed across the ford and rode for one more mile to the O'Duinne rath. Declan felt a tightness in his chest as the familiar timber enclosure set on a small rise came into view. He'd ridden out of this place in haste ten years ago, not knowing he'd not return. Looking at it now, it seemed that time had frozen in place. Cattle browsed in the lush spring grass of the surrounding pastures, women tended the large vegetable garden that was snugged up to the south side of the palisade and a shepherd, no more than eight or nine years old, was driving a flock of sheep down toward a small pond for a morning drink.

A man standing near the timber gate saw the riders approach and, recognizing Cathal, gave out a loud hallo. This brought a few of the household folk scurrying to the gate and others soon joined them. Finbar had returned to the little fortified village in the valley of the Blackwater the day before with news of Declan's return and it seemed the entire population of the clan chief's rath had turned out to greet the long lost O'Duinne son.

As the riders reached the gate, there was a excited buzz in the gathered crowd. Cathal reined in his pony and dismounted. Declan did the same. They handed their reins to eager boys who had appeared from every direction to see what the excitement was about.

Cathal raised a hand and the crowd quieted.

"For ten long years, our rath has had an empty seat at the feast table, a missing laugh in the courtyard, a missing voice, when voices were raised in song. Now, my son…my dear son Declan has come home!"

A cheer went up as men and women, some Declan recognized and some who were strangers to him, crowded around, shaking his hand and slapping him on the back. Amidst the welcoming crowd, Declan saw his father craning his neck to look up toward his own house. Given the uproar in the courtyard, he would have expected his brother to emerge from the arched door of the clan chief's house to greet them but there was no sign of Keiran. Cathal had told him his brother was not bedridden when he'd departed just three days ago, but a chill thought struck him. Had the wound festered in the few days since?

As they broke free of the crowd and hurried across the courtyard, Finbar suddenly stalked out of the house, a frown on his face. The counsellor hurried forward to greet them.

"Welcome home, lord," he said with a slight bow toward Cathal, "and to you, lord," he added, nodding toward Declan.

Cathal brushed aside the niceties.

"Where is Keiran?" he demanded.

Finbar shook his head sadly.

"He's inside, lord. I told him of your arrival, but he refuses to step outside, even to greet you and his brother."

"His arm?"

"Is healing well, lord. There is no putrefaction there that I can see."

Cathal sighed and turned to Declan.

"This wound…it has affected the lad's mind."

Declan nodded.

"I've seen such as this before and it's as bad as the rot." He looked at Finbar.

"Take us to him."

Finbar led them into the main room of the house and pointed toward a door on the left. Cathal pushed it open and stepped into the dimly-lit room with Declan close behind. Keiran was lying on his cot with his eyes open, but he did not rise.

"Ahh," he said dully, "my long lost brother. Come home at last."

Declan walked past the cot and pulled the shutters open on the lone window, letting light pour into the room. Keiran groaned and shaded his eyes with his one good hand.

"And it's good to see you too, brother," Declan said briskly. "How's the hand?"

Keiran sat up, a crooked smile on his face.

"Why it's gone, little brother," he said, brandishing the stump at Declan. "Misplaced it somewhere. Have ye seen it?"

Quick as a snake, Declan reached out and grabbed his brother's wounded arm above the elbow and jerked the man to his feet.

Keiran howled but dared not pull away as Declan stuck his nose down and sniffed at the stump where the man's right hand had once been.

"Smells as clean as fresh mown hay," he observed, then drew back and sniffed again, wrinkling his nose, "which is more than I can say for the rest of ye."

"Declan!" Cathal shouted and laid a hand on his son's shoulder as though to restrain him. "Is this how ye greet yer brother?"

Declan did not answer. He pulled away from his father's touch and released his grip on Keiran's arm. His brother snatched it back, glaring at him.

"Why have ye come back here?' he snarled. "We did well enough without ye!"

"And I did well enough without you, but I came to see our father—and to see my brother as well."

"Well now ye've seen me," Keiran said, bitterly, "so get out and leave me be."

Declan shook his head.

"Oh, I've seen *you*," he said with disdain, "but *not* my brother Keiran. I've been gone for ten years, but I remember *him* well. Fagan bullied me. Keiran never did. It was him I looked to when I was in trouble. It was him who took my side, even when I'd been up to mischief. I loved my brother Keiran, but I do not see him here."

Silence fell over the small room as the two brothers glared at each other. Keiran seemed to sway a little and reached out with his good hand to steady himself against the wall.

"I...," he began, but the words caught in his throat. "I...," he tried once more, but the words would not come. His shoulders began to heave and he slowly slid down the wall to the floor, an anguished sob escaping his lips.

Declan squatted on the floor beside his weeping brother.

"Keiran," he said, "let me tell you of the men of the Invalid Company."

***

Cathal and Finbar slipped quietly from the bedchamber, leaving the two brothers alone. Declan told Keiran of his first encounter with the Invalids. They had been mustered outside the walls of Oxford with orders to ride into Wales to find Ranulf of Chester. Half had been drunk and the rest ill from the effects of drink.

"Three men puked from horseback that morning and half a dozen were dead asleep in the saddle before we got them moving. These were men who'd stormed the city of Messina, fought their way into Acre and charged with King Richard against Saladin's cavalry at Arsuf. They'd been hurt, many more grievously than you, Keiran, and sent home. Out of gratitude, the King offered them pay and quarters in London, but gave them no duties. After months living on the King's coin they turned to drink, lechery and banditry. In time, the good folk of London insisted they depart. That's when they were put into our care."

As Declan talked of the Invalids, Keiran remained sitting on the floor with his back to the wall and his arms circling his bent knees. His eyes were cast down, his chin resting on his chest.

Declan wasn't sure if his brother was listening, but continued to talk.

"Thomas Marston, who the men call Patch, is the senior sergeant of the company. He lost an eye at Arsuf. Sergeant William Butler, lost a leg at Acre. Sir John Blackthorne lost an arm above the elbow at Sheffield. Sir Edgar Langton has a crippled leg. There are one hundred twenty men in the Company and each of them has suffered grave injury."

There was no reaction from Keiran.

"These men were castoffs. For a long time they behaved as you do now, as though they were of no worth to themselves or to others, but an odd thing happened. They were given a job to do, a job they did not want and that none who knew them thought they could do. I was there when they went into battle against long odds, against hard men, mercenaries who had not known defeat. I saw them slaughter those men. The Invalids are feared now, and justly so. They helped save the very crown of England for their King. And all it took to claim back their pride was being given a job to do."

Declan paused and looked at Keiran who had still not moved.

"If they can, my brother, so can you."

Declan stopped and let silence fall over the room. For a long time, Keiran didn't move, but at last he raised his head and met Declan's eyes, his own red-rimmed. But he said nothing and Declan could not read what was behind his brother's eyes.

"Hugh O'Neill has asked for you to be his herald, Keiran. In truth he has ordered you to come take up that duty at Armagh tomorrow. You are being given a job, brother."

Keiran shook his head slowly.

"Out of pity," he said.

"Perhaps, though he said he knew you and needed men such as you. It matters not what Hugh O'Neill thinks. There is a war coming and soon. If you lie here and let other men fight in yer place, you are as good as dead."

Declan rose to leave. Keiran stayed on the floor. He looked up at his brother, but did not speak. Declan turned as he reached the door.

"You are more than a sword hand, brother," he said.

***

A short walk from the O'Duinne rath was a small hillock that looked down on the valley of the Blackwater River. Save for a few trees, the hill was covered with grass and at its summit lay the graves of generations of the O'Duinne clan. After the initial round of welcomes had been completed, Cathal had led Declan up the hill. The newly turned earth marked where Fagan had been laid to rest, next to his mother, Maeve.

Declan had come here often as a boy. It was a good spot to hide from Fagan or from Cathal if he wanted to avoid some chore. But he would also pass the time having conversations with his dead mother, a woman he'd never known. But today was not the day to commune with the dead. The demands of the living were too urgent. Together they stood silently over the graves for a while, then said a quiet prayer and turned to go.

They both stopped as they saw Keiran climbing the hill towards them. When he arrived at the top, a little breathless, he nodded to his father then turned to Declan.

"I can barely scratch my arse with my left hand, brother," he said.

"Then ye should master that trick before picking up a sword," Declan said with a grin.

It was a start.

***

The three men were up and on the road to Armagh by dawn, riding down to the ford through mists rising up from the Blackwater. The council was to reconvene at noon and it would not do to be late. They spoke little as they rode, but Declan stole glances at his older brother. That morning in the stable, Keiran had struggled to put the bridle on his pony with one hand, but had managed it. As he rode, he looked pale and uncertain, but the air of bitter despair that had marked him was not there.

The day before, Cathal had left them alone among the graves on the hill and they had talked until the sun was well down in the west. They spoke not of battles they'd fought, but of their lives since the day they were parted ten years before. They might have talked on for hours more but for a passing rain squall that sent them hurrying back to find shelter inside the rath.

Now as they rode out in the dawn, Declan felt a sense of peace. He'd sailed for Ireland to find his father, whether alive or dead, and had found much more. He'd brought old wounds with him and the scars were still there, but the gnawing pain in his heart was fading. As with Keiran, it was a start.

Margaret Maelchallain

*T*he abbey bells were announcing Sext when the O'Duinnes rode into the square fronting Saint Patrick's Church. Cathal led Keiran off to present him to Hugh O'Neill and Declan took their horses down the hill to the stables. As he walked back up the slope, he saw Margaret Maelchallain coming his way, leading a pony by the reins. The girl ventured a little smile as he approached.

"My lady," he said and made a small bow.

"We don't much use that form of address here in Tir Eoghain," she said, her voice playful, "but I rather like the sound of it."

"Then I shall not fail to use it as much as possible, my lady," he replied with a grin.

"Walk with me down to the stables," she said.

"With pleasure."

As they walked, Declan could not resist stealing glances at the girl. On a bright afternoon in early May, she looked especially striking. Her dark hair fell in cascades over her shoulders and her blue eyes were almost a perfect match for the clear sky overhead. And unlike their earlier meetings, her mood seemed lighter, less guarded.

"I wish to apologize for insulting you at our last meeting," she said, turning serious. "You appeared here at Armagh as if you dropped from the sky and I was suspicious, but I had no cause to be rude."

"Perhaps I took offense too easily, my lady. But tell me, do you still find me suspicious?"

She stopped and looked him directly in the eyes, as though trying to divine what lay behind them. Then she arched an eyebrow.

"No more so than any of Hugh O'Neill's adherents!"

There was a bit of mischief in the girl's eyes when she spoke, but Declan recognized her words were only part in jest. He might have been gone ten years, but to her, he was an O'Duinne and the O'Duinnes were loyal to O'Neill.

"My lady, I am an adherent of no man," he said, earnestly, "save the one I've given my oath to."

Margaret looked at him now with genuine curiosity.

"This English lord you are pledged to—he must be an unusual man to inspire such loyalty."

"Sir Roger de Laval is most unusual, my lady. Should you ever meet him, you would know it."

"I expect I would. I've always liked unusual men."

There was a teasing note in her voice, but then she turned serious once more.

"You will be returning to England—to your Sir Roger?"

"Aye. I've given my word."

"But are you not tempted to stay here, with your own people? You said yourself that John de Courcy intends to invade, and soon. If he does, the Cenél Eoghain will need men such as you—men who understand the English."

Listening to Margaret Maelchallain and looking into her sky blue eyes might be enough to tempt any man, but he recognized flattery when he heard it.

"Of course I am tempted, my lady, but Sir Roger raised me—every bit as much as my own father did and I've come to find a home there in Cheshire. If you could see Shipbrook, sitting there looking down on the River Dee, you would understand better why I am drawn to return."

"It sounds like a lovely place, Sir Declan, but I would have thought it took more than a scenic spot by a river to make you leave Ireland behind. Do you not have a wife or a sweetheart back there in your Shipbrook?"

"Why no...no, my lady, I do not," he answered honestly.

"Pity," the girl said, though she did not seem at all sorry for his single state.

"My lady,...," he began, a little flustered by this unexpected turn in the conversation.

Now Margaret waved a hand to stop him.

"Oh please," she pleaded. "I find I've already grown weary of all this 'my lady' business. Call me Meg."

Declan smiled, grateful to be done with this questioning of his plans and his status.

"Fair enough, Meg, but you must call me Declan."

"I will," she said gaily. "'Sir Declan' sounds so very formal. So, tell me...Declan, if the girls of Cheshire do not interest you, how did you find the Saracen women on Crusade? Were they as beautiful as the stories make them out?"

Declan wrinkled his brow.

"My lad...eh, Meg, the few women I saw there were either poor farm wives or prisoners in Acre. The former generally fled as we came near and the latter were more woebegone than beautiful. Life is not easy there for women."

"Life is not easy anywhere for women," the girl said, turning suddenly serious.

"I expect that is especially so for one who must lead a clan in times such as these."

She gave a little shrug.

"It is only until the end of summer when my brother will be of age."

"And when summer is over, what will you do? I'm told yer betrothed to Conor Mac Lochlainn."

She shot him a hard look, searching to see if there was some censure in his words. Seeing none, she shrugged again.

"That was my father's doing—an agreement he struck with the old King. Both are dead now."

"And where does Conor Mac Lochlainn stand on the issue?"

She let a small smile come back to her lips.

"You'll have to ask him, Declan, but I suspect I am out of favour just now."

They reached the stables and Margaret turned her pony over to a boy to be fed and watered.

As they turned to retrace their steps up the hill, she reached out to touch his arm.

"When will you leave?" she asked.

"In three days. Brother Cyril and I must pay a visit to Down, then return to Carrickfergus before taking ship for home."

"Why would you risk passing back through that place—and why Down first?"

He quickly related the circumstances of their arrival at Carrickfergus and the necessity of returning there.

Meg nodded.

"I see," she said. "De Courcy is more than a little mad. I hope your friend is delivered back safe into your hands."

As they reached the square at the top of the hill, Margaret turned back to him and gave a little curtsy.

"Is this how they do it in England?" she asked sweetly, her blue eyes wide and questioning.

For a moment he felt a wild urge to tell her to renounce her betrothal to Conor Mac Lochlainn and come back to England with him, but knew such a demand could only be met with shock and disdain.

"I've never seen it done more beautifully," he said—and meant it.

***

Long into the night and through the next day, the factions of the Cenél Eoghain met in the nave of the church without result. Cathal attended as chief of clan O'Duinne and Keiran sat near Hugh O'Neill, should he have any messages to dispatch. Margaret Maelchallain took her position with the Mac Lochlainn chiefs, but said little as the two sides argued and cast dispersions on each other.

On the second day, Brother Cyril took leave of his monastic activities to pay Declan a visit. He had spoken little to Cyril since they'd arrived and the skinny monk had much to report.

"The brethren here at the abbey are Augustinians!" he said with obvious pleasure. "Much less rigid than those Benedictines in Chester."

"Aye, or that Father Tibold that attends Lord de Courcy," Declan added. "His robes marked him as one of the Black Monks."

Cyril gave a little shiver.

"Aye, that man looked to have no bend in him."

"The abbey at Down is Benedictine I heard," Declan pointed out.

"It is," said Cyril with a sigh. "The brethren here at Armagh say that de Courcy ousted the Augustinians from the abbey there and installed the Black Monks. There is bad blood between Armagh and Down over the matter."

"Wonderful," said Declan, sourly. "All we need is a religious feud to smooth our way!"

Cyril shrugged off the concern.

"God will protect us, lord—even from Benedictines. And if we leave on the morrow we will arrive on the Feast of Ascension."

Declan furrowed his brow.

"There will be crowds at the abbey on a feast day," he noted, a touch of concern in his voice.

"It will distract the Abbot and the brethren," Cyril said airily. "They will likely bring out their relics for a processional, which will make them less likely to concentrate on us."

Declan did not argue. He had a hostage to collect and had no wish to tarry at Down Abbey.

"I'll want to leave at dawn," he said.

"I'll be ready, lord."

***

Late on the afternoon of the second day, Finbar rode into the square at Armagh and sought Declan out. He'd come to say his farewell, but not only that. He did not mince words.

"Ye should stay here," he declared. "Whatever yer ties to England, yer needed here with yer own blood! Yer father needs ye and so does yer clan, my lord."

Declan sighed. He knew his father had held out hope that he would stay and that had tugged at his heart. But in the end, Cathal O'Duinne had accepted his decision to go with grace. Finbar, however, was not a graceful man.

"You yerself saw what de Courcy is gathering at Carrickfergus. He'll not have those men sit around eating his food and drinking his ale all summer. No! He'll march on Tir Eoghain before the harvest is in. But I guess that's all our misfortune and none of your own," he said bitterly.

"We do not know what is in the mind of John de Courcy," Declan said gently. "He may come next week or not at all. When he does come here, one more sword will not sway the balance, Finbar. The Cenél Eoghain have survived ten years without me. I think they can manage."

Finbar scowled at him.

"As you said to yer brother, lord—yer more than a sword hand!"

Declan laid a hand on the old man's shoulder.

"Finbar, you've given yer oath to my father, have ye not?"

Finbar looked at him and squinted.

"Aye, of course I have. All know it."

"Have you ever thought to break that oath?"

Finbar started to answer, but stopped.

"Ah, yer a clever lad," he said, shaking his head. "Of course I've never broken my oath and here I am asking ye to break yer own."

Finbar's shoulders slumped. He knew when he was beaten.

"Well then go," he said at last, his voice resigned, "and I'll not wish ye ill, lad. You were a good boy and have growed to be a fine man. Losin' ye near broke Cathal's heart all those years ago. Findin' ye again mended it. I must be content with that."

Declan wrapped the old man in an embrace, his eyes stinging.

"You did a fine thing coming to find me, Finbar. I did not know I needed to come home until you brought me here. Thank you."

The old man nodded.

"I did it for yer father," he said simply.

Declan walked with him back to where he had tethered his pony and watched his father's counsellor ride back down the hill and set out to the west—to the Blackwater River and home.

The encounter had left him feeling glum. He would be departing in the morning for Down and might never see Finbar or his kin again. To shake the melancholy that clung to him, he walked down to the stables to check on the chestnut mare. He was examining the horse's hooves when his father found him.

"Making ready to leave for Down on the morrow, son?" he asked.

"Aye, that's the plan, father. How goes the council?"

Cathal frowned.

"I think more of Mac Lochlainn's chiefs are leaning toward O'Neill's position, but none have spoken up. I fear they value loyalty above good sense."

Declan smiled at that.

"I'd reckon they'd say the same of you and the other O'Neill men. Are you not loyal to your chief?"

Cathal looked uneasy at that.

"Aye, I am and that is why I've come to find you. There has been a request—from Hugh O'Neill himself. He asks a personal favour of you."

"What sort of favour?" Declan asked, uneasily.

"He asks that you take Margaret Maelchallain with you to Down."

"What?"

Declan wasn't sure he had heard his father correctly.

"Margaret Maelchallain is the Keeper of the bell," Cathal replied by way of explanation.

"I know who the woman is and what she does, but why, in God's name, would she be going to Down?"

"It seems she wishes to see the bell of Saint Patrick for a last time—or so Hugh told me."

"This makes no sense, father. We are going there only to make a show and will leave as quickly as we can—in and out! Then it's on to Carrickfergus to retrieve my friend. We do not need this woman along to complicate things."

"I told Hugh ye wouldn't like it," Cathal said, apologetically, "but he asked me—as a personal favour."

"Gad! Yer high chiefs here are no different than the great lords in England," Declan said, his voice rising. "They know damned well a favour requested is as good as an order."

"Perhaps you should speak to him," Cathal suggested.

"No!" he said, turning on his heel. "It's Margaret Maelchallain I'll speak with!"

***

He'd sent a boy with an urgent message for her and she met him by the stables as the abbey bells finished tolling the mid-afternoon call to prayer. Margaret had been light-hearted and playful two days before. Now the girl once more appeared guarded and serious.

"You are angry with me," she said before he could speak.

"What did you expect?" Declan answered, trying to keep his temper in check. "Or do you not understand that going to Down will be dangerous, not only for me and Brother Cyril, but for my friend who is in John de Courcy's hands?"

"I do, Declan, honestly I do, but please understand. My family are the Keepers. My father died trying to protect the bell. Its loss is a stain upon the Maelchallain name. I'm told you have a letter from de Courcy that will grant you access to the brethren who now hold the bell. I wish only to look upon it for one last time—to see that it is being properly venerated by these English monks. I will not make trouble."

"I am sorry for the loss, my lady, truly I am, but seeing the bell won't bring it—or yer father—back to ye."

The girl's eyes began to well and a tear trickled down her cheek. Declan waved a finger at her.

"Oh for God's sake, Margaret—tears? You don't need tears to get yer way. You've already run to Hugh O'Neill behind my back. He needs yer support to be king and what's my life or the lives of my friends next to the support of the Maelchallain clan for his ambitions? For my father's sake, I cannot refuse this request, but there are conditions."

Margaret's eyes quickly dried.

"What are your conditions?" she asked.

Declan held up a single finger.

"I will take you only as far as Down, but not back to Armagh. I've a promise to keep to my friend who is hostage at Carrickfergus and I've lingered too long here as it is."

"Fine," she said quietly. "I will bring one of my men along to ride with me back to Armagh, so you may be on your way with all due haste."

"That will do," he said and held up a second finger.

"Until we part company, you will follow my orders, in every particular, or I swear I will send you and your man packing, back to Armagh."

The girl briskly wiped away the last of the tears that had fallen on her cheek with a dainty finger.

"Agreed," she said. "When do we ride?"

***

In the grey light before dawn, Declan stood beside his father and brother as the three men gathered by the fire to say their farewells. Further down the alleyway, Brother Cyril was already mounted on his bay mare and Margaret Maelchallain stood beside her pony talking softly to the young warrior who had been assigned to escort her to and from Armagh.

Much had passed between the three O'Duinne men in only a week's time and Declan struggled with what to say in parting. In the end it was Cathal who broke the awkward silence.

"Stay safe, son," he said as he draped an arm over Declan's shoulders. "And if life in England ever grows old, you will always have a home here in Tir Eoghain."

"If fortune allows, I will come this way again, Father," Declan said and turned to Keiran, extending his left hand. His older brother took it.

"It's been good to see you again, little brother. Perhaps if peace ever settles in these parts I'll come to visit you over there in England. I'd like to meet these Invalids you speak of."

Declan smiled.

"You would be at home among them, Keiran."

Looking down the alley, he saw Margaret mount her pony and heard his own chestnut mare nicker. It was time. He mounted, raised a hand in farewell and rode out of Armagh to the east.

Declan O'Duinne

Leap of Faith

By his seventh day as a guest of John de Courcy, Roland had poked his nose into every part of the inner ward, making mental notes of everything he saw. He found no weakness he could use to aid in an escape and though Finn had appeared twice inside the walls, the boy had exchanged nothing with him beyond a quick glance. With nothing new to explore and no duties to attend to on a grey and drizzly afternoon, Roland made his way to the shed where the castle smith forged nails, weapons, pots and hinges for the lord of the castle and the tradesmen in the town. His offer to work the bellows was gratefully accepted and helped lift his boredom.

Roland had worked up a good sweat when a shout from the lookout atop the keep drew his attention. The man was pointing across the inner ward toward the bay and the open sea. The lookout called down to the man standing guard at the entrance to the keep. Over the pounding of the smith's hammer, Roland could not make out the message, but the guard disappeared inside. Curious, Roland excused himself from bellows duty and climbed to the south wall of Carrickfergus. He looked out to sea and saw a grand sight.

Five sailing cogs had entered the mouth of the bay and were ploughing through the swells straight toward the protected harbour of the castle. An onshore wind had their square sails taut and he could see crewmen scurrying about working the lines. Such ships were common trading vessels in these waters, but the cargo of this small fleet was not wool or slate—it was men.

Even at this distance there was no mistaking the men crowding the deck of each ship. Sunlight glinted off spear tips and steel helmets. There were at least forty men on each of the cogs. Roland could not guess where they had come from, but there was no doubt as to their purpose.

As the five boats passed south of the castle, they fell into single file and began making graceful turns to starboard to enter the break in the jetty that formed the anchorage of Carrickfergus. Roland followed their progress and moved along the wall walk until he reached a point that overlooked the harbour. He watched as each boat edged up to one of the two long piers and secured their lines.

"Beautiful sight, is it not?"

Roland jerked around to see John de Courcy coming toward him. He'd been so engrossed in watching the troop ships he'd not heard the big man's approach.

"Aye, my lord, as long as you were expecting company."

De Courcy laughed at that.

"Oh, aye. This isn't some invading force from Chester, Sir Roland. These men come from all over England and they are the best money can buy. With them and my local troops, I have what I need to finish these stiff-necked Irish here in the north," de Courcy said, a gleam in his eye. "Look off west, Sir Roland. The land beyond the horizon is there for our taking! In Tyrone, the fields stay green all winter long. There are cattle and sheep in their thousands."

"And stiff-necked Irish in their thousands as well."

De Courcy shot him a dark look, but then chuckled.

"Yes, that is a complication, but one I will soon overcome and if you've grown tired of being a hostage, sir, my offer still stands. If you join me, there will be silver and land. It will take three days to muster my Irish levies. Once they join me, we march. Fight for me and carve out a new destiny for yourself!"

"Your offer tempts me, my lord. I will think on it."

De Courcy slapped him on the back with his massive hand.

"You do that, Inness. It will pay better than the wages yer getting from that little churchman."

The lord of Carrickfergus started to turn away, then stopped.

"My guards tell me that you've been busy, inspecting every inch of my castle. I hope you aren't finding your stay here too confining."

"Not at all, my lord," Roland said with a smile. "I do love to roam about, but having a few weeks of decent food and a roof overhead is nothing to complain about."

"Good! Good!" de Courcy said. "But tell me, when you roamed about on my battlements, did you find any weaknesses in the defences of Carrickfergus?"

Roland shook his head.

"None, my lord," he answered honestly. "You've built well."

***

Roland passed what was left of the afternoon back at the smith's shed working the bellows and keeping a watch on the castle gate. He doubted any of the newly-arrived English mercenaries would know him, but he wanted no surprises. With the arrival of these hired swords and the news that de Courcy would march on Tyrone in three days, the need to escape from Carrickfergus had become urgent. Somehow he had to get free of the Prince's hospitality and get a warning to Declan before his friend got swept up in a war. Lost in thought as he pumped the bellows, he almost missed the arrival of the English.

Two men, dressed in good mail and sporting expensive cloaks, presented themselves to the guards at the gate and were ushered into the keep. Roland was relieved that neither man looked familiar. In less than an hour the two reappeared on the steps of the keep and were escorted back through the gate. Roland guessed the new arrivals would be quartered in the town. John de Courcy might be a bold man, but he was no fool. He would not invite two hundred heavily armed mercenaries to enjoy the run of his fortress. Such men might come to covet the place.

The sun was hovering just above the western wall of Carrickfergus, when he saw Finn scurry through the gate and look around. Roland stepped out of the smith's shed and caught the boy's eye. Finn made no acknowledgement of the glance, but turned and hurried up the stone steps to the wall walk above the gate. Roland made his apologies to the smith and wandered slowly across the cobbled courtyard. There were more than the usual number of people about, hurrying to complete their business before nightfall, but none paid him any mind. He climbed the steps and ducked into the cramped wooden structure where he had first met the boy.

Finn was waiting for him.

"The situation has changed, Master Finn," he began. "I need to take my leave of Carrickfergus—tonight if possible. You said you would think on a way that I might get free of this place unnoticed."

The boy screwed up his face and shook his head.

"Oh, that's why I come t' see ye, lord. I had a plan and a good one, but it can't be done as quick as all that. Once a week, I come with a cart to the inner ward and muck out the stables there. Ye see, Lord de Courcy pays for the stablemaster's services in part with horse shit and the stablemaster sells it to the farmers to spread on their fields. It's a profitable trade."

"I see," said Roland. "You would have me buried beneath the horse turds."

"Exactly, my lord! I have never had a guard take a second look at that dung cart as I've passed through the gate. I'd have trotted ye right over to the stables, put ye on that big grey horse and off you'd go."

"It's an excellent plan," Roland agreed, "but...."

Finn spread his hands and shrugged.

"But I may only come on the assigned day and that is four days hence."

Roland sighed. De Courcy and his army would be a full day's march ahead of him by then. He needed to be gone well ahead of them if he was to get a warning to Declan.

"Is there no other way out of here, Master Finn?" he asked quietly. "I believe I may need to leave this very evening."

Finn's shoulders slumped and he did not speak for a long time, then his head came up.

"There is a way, my lord, but I doubt ye'll like it any more than the horse turds."

"Tell me, lad."

"Well sir, the gate is closed tight at full dark and well-guarded. There'll be no escape through there," the boy said. "So, if you are to escape Carrickfergus tonight, you'll have to go over the wall."

Roland frowned at that.

"It's a good twenty-foot drop to the path that runs from the gate to the drawbridge, boy. It could be done, but not without being seen by guards on the wall, even in the dark. Once they raise the alarm, I'd not get far."

Finn shook his head vigorously.

"No, not that wall! Even if the guards did not see ye, there are two more men on duty at the drawbridge over the dry moat, and it will be raised after dark."

"Then where?" Roland asked, beginning to get exasperated.

"The west wall, sir."

Roland stared at Finn in the dim light. Perhaps he'd misheard the boy. He'd seen the west wall that overlooked the harbour when they'd docked days ago and had studied it carefully since in his inspection of the castle grounds. There was nothing but jagged rock extending out from the bottom of that wall for ten feet. Beyond that was the water of the harbour.

"The west wall, you say? Do you think I have wings?"

"Wings, sir? Why would you need wings?" the boy asked, genuinely curious. Then before Roland could answer, Finn brightened.

"Oh! I suppose ye've only seen the bottom of that wall at low tide, sir. Hereabouts, the water rises over ten feet at high tide and covers most of the rocks. The next one will be when ye hear the bells ring for Compline tonight. If ye take a good long jump, ye clear the rocks and land safe in the water." The boy paused, then added, "Can ye swim?"

Roland reassessed his judgement of the boy. This plan was less revolting than hiding under horse manure, but considerably more dangerous. Still, it might work, and he'd take his chances with the rocks and water rather than trust to John de Courcy.

"Aye, Finn, enough to paddle to shore. If I go tonight, can you have my horse saddled near the harbour and ready to ride?'

Finn rubbed his chin.

"Aye, I could sir, but…"

Roland smiled. Finn gave up nothing without payment.

"What is your price?" he asked.

The boy fixed him with a pleading look.

"Take me with ye when ye go, Master Inness."

Roland had been reaching for his coin purse and had not expected this answer.

"No," he said firmly.

"Then ye can find yer own horse," the boy replied softly.

"Finn, if we're caught, de Courcy will take no account of your youth. You'll be killed."

Finn snorted.

"If I deliver your horse to you from the town stables, how long will it be before they know it? If I help ye, I've a better chance to stay alive going than staying."

Roland looked at the boy in the dim light. He was coiled up in the corner of the tiny room, his eyes full of fear and defiance, like some small animal brought to bay. Roland sighed. This boy, he knew, had an instinct for survival and had weighed the risks with a clear eye. They would, in time, learn that he had abetted the escape. Besides, he'd taken a liking to the lad—and he had to have his horse.

He held out his hand.

"Agreed," he said.

Finn spit in his hand and reached out to grip Roland's, sealing the bargain.

***

As the sun dipped below the western wall of the fortress, Roland dutifully headed for his room in the barracks. He looked up at the sky and saw a line of grey clouds moving in from the west. It would likely be a moonless night, which was both good and bad. The deep darkness would make it easier for him to gain the west wall unseen by the night watch, but the thought of leaping blindly into the darkness was daunting. It meant putting all his faith in Finn's assurance that the evening high tide would be sufficient to keep him from being smashed on the rocks beneath the wall.

Finn was to wait near the harbour with The Grey and a mount of his own until midnight. Beyond that time, the ebbing tide would make a plunge off the wall suicidal. For his part, Roland would wait until he heard the chapel bells ring the call for evening Compline prayers, then slip out of the barracks and make his way to the west wall.

He reached his small room and sat down on the straw mattress to wait. There was a small window set high on the wall that let in whatever lingering light there might be and he watched as the view through the opening slowly darkened. The chapel bells rang out the call for Vespers, marking several more hours until the call to Compline. He'd just stretched out on the straw mat to rest, knowing he would likely get no sleep this night, when there was a rap on his door. Startled, he leapt to his feet and opened the door to find a page standing there. The boy bowed, then issued an invitation.

"His grace, the Prince, wishes you to join him for the evening meal, Sir Roland. He says he wishes to hear more of the Battle of Towcester. You are to follow me."

Roland's stomach clenched. Now, of all nights, to get such an invitation! He thought to grab the boy, haul him into the room and knock him cold, but one of de Courcy's men-at-arms was lounging in the corridor leaving him no opportunity. The page had already turned back the way he had come and Roland hurried to follow, cursing under his breath. He now had to hope that the evening meal would conclude before midnight or there would be no escape this night.

The page hardly looked back as he hurried across the bailey and up the stone steps of the keep. Once inside, he led Roland up the narrow spiral stairs, to the second floor. The great hall that had been largely empty the week before during de Courcy's rambling interrogation was now filled with tables and benches and a few high-backed chairs.

Most of the lower tables were already occupied by Sir John's retainers and what appeared to be prosperous local tradesmen from the town. Most paid no attention to his arrival, occupied as they were with each other and the pitchers of wine on the table. There was no sign of the lord of Carrickfergus or any of the newly-arrived English mercenaries.

"The Prince will be here shortly," the page announced as he guided Roland through the throng to the high table at the south end of the hall. "You will sit at his table."

Roland noted that his place was near the end of the high table, next to a fat and florid man who was dressed like a merchant and barely looked up as he took his seat. At the opposite end of the table sat the dour priest, Father Tibold, who, between gulps of wine, darted glances in his direction. Roland inclined his head toward the churchman in greeting, but Tibold chose to look away rather than return the gesture.

From his seat, he scanned the hall. Directly opposite him was the large arch of the main entrance. Through that door was the spiral stairs that led to the first floor and the only way into or out of the keep. He twisted around and noted two smaller archways behind the high table on either side of the hall. Where they led, he could not tell. When he turned back he saw three men enter the hall, flanked by a page. Roland had seen two of the men earlier when they had come to pay their respects at the keep. The third man had not been with them, but he was clearly their leader. The man was tall and lean and though his carriage was relaxed, there was a hint of coiled energy in his bearing. Roland did not recognize him, but he knew that look. It was the look of a man accustomed to violence and to command.

As the new arrivals made their way across the hall, Roland casually slid a carving knife off the table and tucked it into his boot. Thankfully, the fat man to his right was already in his cups and did not notice. As he watched the three men make their way through the hall, he saw little likelihood of trouble, but that was exactly when trouble tended to occur. The page directed two of the Englishmen to lower tables. Their leader he guided through the crowd toward the Prince's table.

As the mercenary captain approached, Roland watched the man's eyes casually scan those already seated. When his gaze landed on Roland, it lingered for a moment, then moved on. The page led the man to his place at the right hand of de Courcy's throne-like seat, marking him as the guest of honour.

The mercenary's face showed little more than boredom as Father Tibold tried to engage him in conversation. The fat drunkard seated next to Roland belched loudly, just as a page rose to announce the arrival of their host.

"His grace, the Prince of Ulster!" the man intoned solemnly above the buzz of the dinner guests.

The room fell silent as all present rose and bowed as their host entered the feasting hall through the small arched door farthest from Roland. Sir John de Courcy looked resplendent in white robes set off with three crimson eagles embroidered on his left sleeve. He beckoned everyone to sit and after much scraping of chairs and benches, the dinner guests settled back into their places. The lord of Carrickfergus greeted his mercenary commander warmly before taking his own seat and soon the two men were deep in conversation.

Roland did not object when the fat merchant draped a meaty arm over his shoulders and poured wine into his empty cup while mumbling drunkenly in his ear. He preferred ale, but took a long swallow of the red liquid. It looked to be a long night.

As soon as de Courcy was seated, the kitchen staff began bringing in large trays laden with food. It seemed the Prince of Ulster did not spare expenses when entertaining guests. There were platters piled high with roast grouse and partridge and trays groaning with choice cuts of beef. Baskets full of fresh brown bread were placed on every table along with delicacies such as boiled crab and steamed oysters.

For a time, the buzz of conversation quieted as men tucked into this feast. Roland's table companion had been regaling him with rambling details on the leather trade in Ulster, but turned his attention to the delights of the meal as soon as the food reached the table. Roland had little appetite, but stabbed a roast quail with a fork and forced himself to eat. If he made it out of the castle this night he would be on the run and one never knew when or where another meal might be taken.

He cast a quick glance at the centre of the table. De Courcy had taken even less food than Roland had—a few oysters and a chunk of brown bread, which he picked at as he listened to something his guest of honour was saying. He had seen nobles give lavish feasts before and the host usually led the revelry at such events, but de Courcy seemed disinterested in the food and drink.

A strange man, Roland thought.

***

An hour into the meal, trays and platters were still arriving from the kitchen and the merchant was snoring beside him. Through the thick stone walls of the keep and above the drone of the diners he heard the faint sounds of bells. It was the hour of Compline, leaving little more than two hours until midnight. He had a growing fear that the feast would drag on past that critical hour and his chance to escape would be lost for this night. Then there was a tap on his shoulder and he looked up to see the page bending over him.

"Lord de Courcy requests your company, Sir Roland—if you please."

Roland nodded and rose from his chair to follow the page. As he approached de Courcy, the Prince was still in animated conversation with the mercenary captain, but looked up as Roland neared and beamed.

"Sir Roland, good of you to come!" he said above the buzz of conversation in the hall. "May I present Captain Charles Oliver, commander of my English mercenaries. Captain Oliver, this is Sir Roland Inness. He's come from Chester and is my guest for a fortnight or so. As it turns out, he was at Towcester, same as you—but fighting on the winning side!"

Oliver gave Roland an odd look, but laughed at de Courcy's jibe.

"I trust I've chosen my sides more carefully for this campaign, my lord!" he shot back.

"No doubt you have, sir," de Courcy replied then turned back to Roland. "I thought it would be fascinating to hear how your accounts of that day might compare."

As de Courcy spoke, Roland looked at Charles Oliver. The man was staring at him now.

Trouble.

As de Courcy finished his introductions, Oliver spoke up.

"My lord, I did not realize you had Sir Roland Inness as your guest!" he boomed and stuck out a hand to Roland. Roland took it with a sinking feeling in his gut. The mercenary turned back to de Courcy.

"Has Sir Roland brought his Invalid Company with him? By God it would be a relief to be on the same side for once! I rode with Prince John's heavy cavalry at Towcester. We struck the centre of Marshall's line that day, but it would not budge. I learned later it was held by Earl Ranulf's Invalids, commanded by Sir Roland here," he said shaking his head and turning back to Roland. "It's a pleasure to meet you, sir. Your boys can fight. If they be cripples, I saw no sign of it that day!"

As the man spoke, the smile on de Courcy's face faded and his face grew flushed. Captain Oliver seemed prepared to continue, but de Courcy raised a hand to silence him rising to his feet and pointing an accusing finger at Roland.

"You have played me false, Inness! Bodyguard for a priest? Bah! I should have seen from the start that this *pilgrimage* was a farce. You, sir, are a spy for Earl Ranulf!"

"I am not, sir!" Roland shot back.

De Courcy turned to Oliver, who stood there, looking shocked at this sudden turn.

"Imagine that, Captain! Sir Roland proclaims his innocence, yet he has flown a false flag while enjoying my hospitality. We shall see! I have men who can put him to the test. It's a painful process, but always brings forth the truth in the end."

Roland began to back slowly away. De Courcy drew a dagger from his belt and handed it to Oliver. The mercenary, like all of de Courcy's guests, had been disarmed before entering the hall.

"Seize him, Captain!" de Courcy ordered.

By now the mercenary had recovered from this surprising turn of events and he did not hesitate. He stepped around de Courcy and moved toward Roland, his knife held low.

"This is out of my hands, Inness," he said quietly. "Don't make it hard."

Roland reached down and drew the carving knife from his boot.

"Hard for you or hard for me, Captain?"

Oliver just shrugged and kept coming, though a bit more cautiously. Roland took a quick glance at the far end of the hall. The two men-at-arms stationed at the main entrance had seen the sudden commotion at the high table and were forcing their way between the dinner guests who, oblivious to the drama playing out, clogged the aisles between the tables. Roland backed slowly toward his only clear path to an exit, the small arched door in the corner of the hall behind him.

"Take him!" de Courcy roared, goading the mercenary into action.

Oliver feinted low with his blade, then thrust at Roland's chest. It was a move Roland had learned to counter long ago after hours of practice under the watchful eye of Sir Alwyn Madawc. As the mercenary chief changed the angle of his thrust from low to high, Roland followed, bringing his knife hand under Oliver's and forcing the man's arm upwards. In the same motion, he stepped forward and brought his boot down on the man's knee, forcing it back at an unnatural angle. The mercenary screamed in pain and collapsed to the floor.

Roland did not waste the opportunity. He turned and bolted for the door. Behind him, Sir John de Courcy, his face a mask of rage, picked up his own carving knife and gave chase. As Roland passed the merchant, still snoring in his seat, he grabbed the top of the man's chair and tipped it backwards. The fat man landed with a crash, then struggled noisily to his feet, momentarily blocking de Courcy's path. In the next instant, Roland was through the door.

He found himself on a small landing. To his right, spiral stairs twisted up to the third floor of the keep and then on to the roof. There would be no escape in that direction. To the left more stairs wound down to the first floor and the exit from the keep. He started in that direction, but could hear shouts and laughter rising up from below. The first floor held the guardroom of the keep. There would be upwards of a dozen men at the bottom of the stairs.

From behind, he heard de Courcy screaming at the fat merchant to get out of his way and ordering his men-at-arms to make haste. He took a step toward the stairs that led down to the guardroom. There was little hope he could fight his way to the keep's exit, but he resolved to try. He would not be taken alive to be tortured by John de Courcy. A sound from behind made him whirl around. A man stepped out of a narrow passage he had not seen in the dim light. He was hitching up his pants and looked up in time to be clubbed unconscious.

Roland stepped over him and stuck his head in the narrow opening. It smelled foul and he realized that it must be the keep's privy. He grabbed the unconscious man by the wrists and dragged him into the small alcove. Looking up, he saw a few steps leading up to a stone bench with a hole carved in the seat. Behind him he heard men burst through the door from the hall and onto the landing. He turned and made ready to kill whoever came through the small opening.

On the landing, he heard de Courcy order one guard up the stairs to the right and the other down the stairs to the guardroom. From the sound of the footsteps on the stairs, the Prince had followed the man he'd sent up towards the third floor. As the clamour faded, Roland leaned against the stone wall and tried to think. The chase had passed him by for the moment, but it wouldn't be long before a thorough search of the keep was launched and this privy would not be overlooked.

There were hours yet until midnight and if he could reach the west wall, there would still be time to jump. But reaching that wall seemed impossible. There was no access to it directly from the keep and the only way out of the keep was on the first floor.

"I will not die in a privy," he said grimly and stood up. He resolved once more to go down the stairs and hope for the best. Perhaps he would surprise whoever was in the guardroom long enough to make it to the door.

Unlikely, he thought, but steeled himself for the attempt.

Then he heard a sound, one he had not noticed before. It was a soft roar, followed by a quieter hiss. It was the sound of waves striking rocks. It was the sound of the sea. He turned and looked down through the hole in the privy bench and saw nothing but yawning blackness, but there was a light breeze rising up through the hole into the small alcove. The breeze carried the expected unpleasant odours expected from a privy, but there was also the smell of salt and seaweed.

From above he heard steps on the stairs, returning from the third floor. There was no more time for thought, no time to weigh risks. He set aside his carving knife and crawled back onto the stone bench, dropping his legs through the hole. Leaning forward, he supported his weight on his elbows and slid his rear off the stone bench and into the void below. He bent his knees, planting his feet against the stone of the keep wall and lowered himself slowly, until only his head and arms remained above the hole. He could hear urgent voices on the landing.

Roland took a deep breath, gripped the smooth edge of the privy seat with both hands and squeezed his shoulders through the opening. It was a tight fit and he had to dip one shoulder then the other to finally slide through. For a moment, he hung there in space, his feet having slipped from the stone wall of the keep to dangle beneath him. The drop from here was twice that from the west wall, but it no longer mattered. He gritted his teeth and edged his hands back along either side of the privy hole until he could once more touch the outer wall of the keep with his feet. He bent his knees, took a deep breath and lunged out into the blackness.

The fall seemed to last an eternity as he plunged through the dark, expecting at any moment to smash into the rocks below. Then he struck the water hard and plummeted straight to the bottom. The tide had done its work and instead of slamming into rock, his feet sank, ankle deep, into the muck of the harbour bottom. Though the fall had not killed him, the impact with the water left him stunned and disoriented.

But the muck at his feet told him which way was down and which way up. He bent his knees and lunged upwards. For a moment the bottom sucked at his feet but they slipped free and he burst to the surface, sucking in huge lungfuls of air. He was no great swimmer, but the shore was only twenty feet away and he managed to splash his way over to the narrow fringe of rock at the base of the great keep that still stood above the tide.

He looked up at the dark mass of stone rising above him and had the strange urge to laugh. But there was no time to enjoy his own relief. Carrickfergus would soon be like a disturbed ant bed and no place for him to linger. He rose, a little unsteadily, and picked his way along the narrow ledge of rock until he reached the arc of sand and mud that formed the landward side of the small harbour. Two wooden piers stretched out into the water and three of the sailing cogs that had delivered the mercenaries were still tied up there.

As he stepped onto the sand, he prayed that Finn had kept his part of the bargain and was somewhere waiting in the dark with The Grey. If the boy failed him, he planned to strike out on foot for the range of mountains he'd seen to the north in hopes of eluding capture. He was not familiar with the land hereabouts, but liked his chance better in high country where mounted pursuit would be limited. He guessed it would take him half a day to reach the hills, staying clear of any roads.

Roland moved quickly until he reached the ravine that cut across the neck of land occupied by the castle. He saw no one and the only sounds he heard were shouts coming from within the inner ward of the castle—no doubt the guard being turned out. Staying low, he ran in a crouch across the mouth of the ravine, then stopped once more to listen. Still nothing. Then he heard a familiar whinny.

It was The Grey.

In the dim light, he saw Finn creeping carefully along the base of the wooden palisade that enclosed the town, leading the big gelding and a small Irish pony. Roland was relieved to see his longbow, quiver and kit all lashed to his saddle. The boy was stopping every few yards to look about and listen. Roland stood up.

"Finn," he hissed. The boy jumped as Roland stepped out of the shadows.

"Bless me," he managed, trying to catch his breath, "ye gave me a fright!"

Roland could not help himself. He grabbed the Irish boy and hugged him.

"You are a fine sight, Master Finn, a very fine sight."

Finn pulled away, wrinkling his nose.
"Why do you smell like a privy?" he asked.

Pursuit

John de Courcy was first to find the unconscious man in the privy and the abandoned carving knife on the bench. It took him a moment more to comprehend that the spy he'd unmasked had used the castle's garderobe to make an escape.

"Damn!" he said in amazement, peering down through the hole in the bench. Below, he saw nothing but darkness. The fall was forty feet or more, so most likely this Sir Roland was lying bloody and broken on the rocks at the base of the keep, but the tide was in and if the man had somehow cleared the rocks... He would not leave such a thing to chance.

Within minutes, the glow of torches lit up the inner ward of Carrickfergus Castle as the guard was turned out. The light quickly spread to the port town as de Courcy led a score of his men over the drawbridge and down toward the harbour. For long minutes, men clambered along the narrow fringe of rock that stood along the base of the keep looking for a body, but found none.

A boat put out into the harbour to look for the fugitive and the three cogs were searched from deck to keel, all to no avail. Then a sharp-eyed local discovered hoof prints in the fringe of hard-packed sand that rimmed the harbour. The prints might be innocent, left by a townsman or one of the newly-arrived English mercenaries, but de Courcy thought not. The Prince turned the search of the local area over to the Captain of his guard and hurried to the stables in the town with ten of his men.

The spy's body might lay at the bottom of the harbour and not float up to the surface for a day or two, but John de Courcy's instinct told him Inness was not dead. He'd somehow survived the fall and managed to steal a horse. But there had been two sets of tracks in the sand. Had this spy had an accomplice?

As de Courcy's men hurriedly saddled the best mounts in the stable, the Prince considered where the fugitive might head. With nothing but water to the south and east Inness had to have gone north or west. To the north there were few roads or places of refuge. A man on foot might choose that direction, but not a man with a horse. Surely Inness had gone west. There was a decent road that ran along the bay in that direction and the man's fellow spies had ridden out that way a week ago. He spurred his horse up to the westward road with ten men in his wake.

The road that ran along the shore of the bay was good by Irish standards, but rough—even in broad daylight. In the pitch dark of a moonless night, it was treacherous. With de Courcy himself in the lead, the riders moved cautiously but relentlessly through the dark. The going was painfully slow, but it would be the same for the man they pursued. Their quarry was a good hour ahead of them, but his men were mounted on the best horses in Ireland. If Ranulf's spy was on this road, they would catch him. When they did, he would see that the head of Roland Inness joined that of Hugh O'Neill's spy on a spike above his castle gate!

***

In the pitch blackness, Roland placed his trust in his big, sure-footed gelding and The Grey did not let him down, picking its way carefully along the rutted and rocky road that ran beside the bay. Where the track looked to be most dangerous, he dismounted and led the horse on foot with Finn following behind. The boy's native Irish pony seemed untroubled by the uneven ground or the dark.

As they moved through the night, Roland tried to consider what to do. The simple fact was he did not know where to find Declan. He knew Down lay somewhere south of the bay and Tyrone was further west. God willing, this road would lead them to one or the other and, hopefully, to his friend—if they could stay ahead of the pursuit. Each time he'd dismounted, he

145

let the horses settle and listened for any sounds on his backtrail. If de Courcy discovered he'd survived the plunge from the privy, the Norman would surely guess that they had fled down the westward road.

He figured they had perhaps an hour's start on the Prince and his men, but his lack of familiarity with this road was a hinderance. Twice they had strayed off the main track in the dark only to find the path they'd taken petering out in jumbles of gorse or turning off towards the mountains north of the bay. They'd had to retrace their steps in the gloom, losing valuable time with each misstep.

Near dawn, he heard a horse whinny in the distance behind them. For the sound to reach them, the pursuers had to be close. In the half-light he clucked to The Grey and the horse picked up the pace. Roland looked behind him and saw that Finn was gamely trying to keep up on his pony, but while these small horses could trot all day, they were no match for the speed of the long-legged English horses. He eased in on his reins to let the boy catch up.

By sunup they had reached the head of the bay. Topping a small rise, Roland saw the land sloping down to the southwest following the shoreline. Such bays usually were fed by rivers. He turned to Finn who had just ridden up behind him.

"Is there a river yonder?"

Finn raised himself up and looked down toward the head of the bay.

"Aye, sir. There is a river there. It's called the Lagan. My home was upstream on the far side, a half day's ride from here I'd reckon."

"Then we will follow it to your home and return you to your people."

"No!" the boy blurted out with a mixture of fear and anger. "I'll not go there! They left my father to die and gave not a thought to me. They are still under de Courcy's rule and would turn me over to him."

"Then where are you to go?" Roland asked, exasperated.

"With you! We had an agreement." the boy said indignantly.

"I agreed to take you away from Carrickfergus, lad, not to adopt you! What am I to do with you?"

"That is for you to decide, lord. But we have an agreement. I go with you."

Roland shook his head. There was no time to haggle with this boy with riders not far behind. He pointed down toward the river.

"Is there a ford?"

"Oh, aye, sir, down near the river's mouth," Finn said, brightening. "There's a big sandbar there that's firm enough to cross when the water's low."

Roland cast an eye toward the shoreline and saw a wide strip of mud exposed along the edge of the bay. He had made the leap into the harbour at Carrickfergus before midnight when the tide was nearing its highest. Judging by the mud, it was now near low tide, but it would take another hour to reach the river. It wouldn't be high tide, but the water would be rising.

Regardless, they would have to cross. He looked back to the east as the disc of the sun broke above the bay. Back along the road, he saw a flash of sunlight reflect off burnished metal

They're getting close, he thought.

***

John de Courcy reined in his black palfrey on the small rise and looked toward the head of the bay as the sun rose behind him. The clouds that had made the night so dark had blown away in the dawn leaving a clear blue sky. A mile to his front, he saw two riders heading west. The sight gave him grim satisfaction.

When no body had been found on the rocks below the keep, he'd sensed that Inness had somehow survived the drop from the privy. And when his men found fresh hoofprints from two horses in the sand, that had settled the issue with him. An accomplice must have been waiting outside the castle with horses when Ranulf's spy made his escape. And for men on horseback, only one direction might lead to safety—west.

All through the long night, he had relied on that logic and his own instincts to push his men westward along this road. Now his quarry was in sight.

But who was the second rider? he wondered.

Perhaps it was the other man who had been in the traveling party with the priest—or perhaps Inness was not the only man Ranulf had sent to spy on him! The thought troubled him, but no matter. He knew he had the better horses and would ride these two down in time. And when he did, they would tell him if there were other traitors in his midst. He turned to his men.

"There they are, lads," he said with a wolfish grin. "A gold coin for the man who takes Inness alive. A silver if you have to kill him."

He jerked his reins around and spurred his palfrey into a trot.

***

Roland had not told Finn that he'd seen de Courcy's men on their trail, but as they neared the ford on the Lagan, the boy looked back over his shoulders and cried out in alarm. Even at a quarter mile away, the tall figure leading the chase could not be mistaken.

"Sir Roland!" Finn shouted, pointing back toward the riders. "It's the Prince!"

Roland had been holding The Grey in check on the level ground to allow Finn's pony to keep pace, but now he reined in. As Finn pulled up beside him, Roland offered the boy his hand.

"They'll not catch us on The Grey," he said.

Finn took another look at the approaching riders and grabbed Roland's hand in a death grip. Roland pulled the Irish boy up behind him on the big gelding and gave the horse the spurs.

The Grey leapt forward, churning up sand as he galloped. The horse slowed his gait only a bit as it plunged into the water. With the incoming tide fighting the outflow of the river, treacherous currents swirled around The Grey's chest, but the horse never lost headway and scrambled up on the opposite bar. A dozen long strides more and it reached the river bank.

Roland reined in and slid out of the saddle.

***

De Courcy saw the rider pull what appeared to be a young boy up behind him and splash into the ford. They had steadily gained on the pair since sunrise and now the chase was nearing an end. His riders knew it too. Three of his younger men, their blood up, spurred their mounts into a gallop as they reached the sand bar. De Courcy let them go. It was good to encourage such eagerness.

He lifted his gaze to the opposite bank and was surprised to see the big grey horse standing there, unmoving, with naught but the boy on his back. As he watched, the man he sought stepped out from behind the horse. Even at this distance he recognized Inness. The sight stirred him into action. He touched his spurs to the palfrey's flanks and set out after the riders ahead of him.

But then he saw the longbow and knew why the rider had stopped on the far bank. He reined in sharply and watched as Inness drew, aimed and released his arrow in a low arc toward his men in the river. The third man into the ford was whipping his horse to catch the other two when he pitched backwards into the water. He floundered in the swirling current for a moment, clutching at the shaft in his chest than sank beneath the brown water. The two riders in the lead did not see the man fall and did not seem to realize their danger.

De Courcy started to shout out a warning to the them, but knew they would not hear. Then one of the two took an arrow in his eye and was dead before he hit the water. The lone rider in the river saw his comrade go down and reined in sharply, sliding out of his saddle and shielding himself behind his horse. De Courcy watched it all with a mixture of shock and anger. As the remainder of his men gathered around him, he waited for the surviving rider to stumble back out of the river. On the far bank, Inness stood there watching them.

De Courcy had hired many a Welsh archer over the years and knew well the power of their longbows. To try to cross the river without shields would be suicide. He gritted his teeth in frustration and had to stifle an oath that would have been blasphemous. He'd never seen an Englishman use a long bow. It was the second time this man Inness had surprised him. He vowed it would not happen a third time. Without a word, he signalled for his men to turn back toward Carrickfergus and home.

***

On the opposite side of the river, Roland watched de Courcy and his men ride away and climbed back on The Grey. He clucked to the horse and the big gelding trotted effortlessly down the road to the south, its long strides eating up the ground. The boy had watched the skirmish at the ford with wide-eyes. He leaned forward and shouted above the wind and the pounding of hooves.

"I've not seen the like of yer bow, lord."

Roland just nodded.

"Teach me to use it!"

Roland did not answer. He let The Grey run and tried to think.

What was he to do with this boy?

Down

*T*he road south from the ford over the River Lagan was poor. Unlike in Britain, Roman legions, and the long, straight roads they built, had never reached as far as Ireland. This road wound around hillocks, ploughed into bogs and was little more than a trail when it passed through forested land. Roland let The Grey pick its own way along the rutted path. The horse hardly made a false step, but the going was slow.

As he rode, he tried to reason out what to do next. Everything depended on finding Declan, but he was uncertain where his friend would now be. As they rounded yet another bend in the road, they came upon a smaller trail that led off toward the west. Roland reined in The Grey and twisted around in the saddle.

"How well do you know the country to the west?" he asked Finn. "Do you know the way to Tyrone?"

Finn studied the new trail off to his right and furrowed his brow.

"I know it's west from here, lord, but not much else. I've heard it's beyond a river called the Bann, but I've not seen that river. My people call it Tir Eoghain and say it is a big place full of bad people."

Roland grimaced. He'd managed to get free of John de Courcy, but now found himself in a land he knew little of. He cursed his own lack of preparation for this journey. Declan and Finbar knew the route from Carrickfergus to the O'Duinne rath on the Blackwater River, but they were not here and he had not bothered to ask them the way. It was a careless mistake.

He knew Finn was right when he said Tyrone was a big place and while the people there might not be bad, they would not likely welcome strangers wandering aimlessly through their land. He had learned a good bit of Gaelic from Declan over the years, but not enough to pass as a local, even with the boy Finn in tow.

Then, there was the matter of time. Declan had pledged to return to fetch him in a fortnight and one week had already passed. He was certain that his Irish friend would have travelled first to Tyrone to see to his father. He also knew they would not risk returning to face John de Courcy without having paid their respects at Down Abbey. Brother Cyril would want to prepare a convincing report for the Prince and to do so would require a visit with the Abbot there.

He looked off to the west then back to the south. Declan and Cyril might even now be at Down or even on their way back north to retrieve him. He turned back to Finn and pointed south.

"Will this road take us all the way to Down, boy?"

Finn poked his head around Roland's chest and looked ahead.

"I believe it will, sir. There's only one road I know of that runs south from the ford on the Lagan and that goes to the Abbey at Down."

Roland nodded.

Down it would be.

***

As the sun dropped low in the west, Roland guided the big gelding off the road and into a thick copse of trees nestled in a little ravine. A little ways on they found a small pool where rainwater still stood and a few patches of spring grass, enough for The Grey's supper.

Roland sent Finn to gather wood. Wary of pursuit, he had watched his backtrail all afternoon, but had seen no sign of de Courcy or his men. He'd dropped two men at the river and wasn't surprised that the Prince had abandoned the chase. However mad the man might be, he was no fool when it came to assessing his chances in a fight. It should be safe enough for a fire.

Shadows were long as he nursed a small flame into life and laid out his bedroll. Finn unsaddled The Grey and came to squat by the fire. He'd been looking keenly at the longbow ever since they had settled into camp and now with arrangements made, he pressed Roland to have a closer look.

Roland handed the rough yew staff to the boy who ran his hands along its length. The thing was a foot longer than the boy was tall.

"It's not a pretty weapon," Roland said, "not like a sword."

"I never saw a sword kill a man at two hundred paces, lord, but this thing did!" he said in admiration as he held the unstrung bow in his left hand and pretended to draw it. "I've seen Welshmen with bows like this, but never saw them used."

Roland walked over and took it from the boy.

"First rule is, don't string it unless you expect to use it. Strings are near as hard to make as the bow and will lose strength if left taut for too long."

"Show me," Finn asked.

Roland pulled the loose string away from the wood.

"You step through with your right foot and use the left to anchor the bottom, like this," he instructed. "Then grasp it as near the top as ye can, and lean yer hip into it."

Finn nodded his understanding.

"Once you have it flexed, you slide the loop up over the notch, like this and it's strung." He completed the steps with a long-practiced motion and handed the strung bow to Finn.

"This is a warbow, Finn, and it's been fashioned for a full grown man—one practiced in its use. You are neither, so you cannot expect to draw it, or even string it."

Finn raised the bow and pulled gamely back on the taut string. It moved but a few inches as the skinny Irish boy grunted with the effort. He finally gave up and handed it back to Roland with a sheepish grin.

Roland couldn't help but grin back.

"What is your clan name, lad?

"Mac Clure, lord."

"If you will not go back to the Mac Clures, what am I to do with you, Finn?"

A sly smile played over the boy's face.

"Yer a knight are ye not?"

"Aye, though a poor one."

"Poor or not, a knight should have a squire."

Roland sighed and raised his eyes to heaven.

***

Declan was first up on the morning of the Feast of the Ascension. They'd spent their second night on the road in this small patch of woods, near enough to Down Abbey to hear the bells calling the monks to prayer. The day dawned chilly and grey with the promise of rain later and he added fresh wood to the fire they'd built the night before, kneeling to blow on the white coals. They glowed red beneath the ash and flames flared back into life.

The movement woke Margaret Maelchallain, who threw off her cloak and rose, her dress wrinkled and her hair in tangles. The girl looked at the sky and frowned, then, taking a bundle under her arm, she slipped off to see to her morning toilet in the bushes. Brother Cyril rose next and trudged over to warm himself by the growing fire.

Only the three had made camp here. The young warrior from the Maelchallain clan assigned to escort Margaret back to Armagh had been left to wait for them in a thick stand of oaks five miles back up the road. As Cyril watched the girl disappear into the bushes, he hoisted the back of his robes to let some of the heat rising from the growing flames warm his backside.

"I must remind myself to occasionally thank God that he made me male," the monk said, nodding toward where Margaret had disappeared from sight. "It makes the morning routine much simpler."

He rose and went off to relieve himself behind a tree. A minute later, he was back.

"And, of course, there is child birth," he said, adding to his list of the advantages of manhood.

"Amen to that," agreed Declan.

He rose from tending the fire and took down a bag he'd secured to a low limb. He withdrew a small loaf of barley bread and a hunk of hard cheese. Walking back to the fire, he saw Margaret Maelchallain emerge from the bushes, transformed.

The girl was now clad in a long dun-coloured dress of undyed wool, with a brown scapula draped in front and back. Her raven hair was completely hidden beneath a tight-fitting white coif that framed her face. From her neck hung a simple chain with a wooden crucifix. She looked at the two men standing by the fire and smiled nervously.

"The Archbishop gave me these. He thought I would attract less attention as a nun," she said, turning to the skinny monk.

"Do I look right, Brother Cyril?"

Cyril nodded eagerly.

"You look every bit the daughter of the church, Sister Margaret!"

His answer made her giggle. The laugh caught Declan by surprise and reminded him of the day they had walked back from the stables. He crossed his arms and refused to smile. She swung around to face him and did a slow turn.

"Will I pass, Sir Declan?" she asked sweetly.

He studied her for a moment and rubbed his chin.

No harm in being civil, he thought.

"The Benedictine sisters in Chester dress in black habits," he said, which turned the girl's smile to a frown. "But I'm certain Tomas O'Connor knows best," he added, "and ye do look every inch a nun." The smile returned to her lips.

"Thank you, Sir Declan!" she said brightly.

"Though there *is* the question of your comportment."

Margaret furrowed her brow.

"Comportment?"

"Aye, my lady. While ye look the part, I wonder if ye can act it. The holy sisters I've known have all been women of a quiet and pious manner. Do you think you could affect such a pose for an entire day?"

For a moment she stared at him, her face reddening, then she heard Cyril cackle and broke into a laugh of her own. She brought her hands together in mock prayer.

"I shall ask the Lord's help to bank my fires for at least one day, Sir Declan," she said as she stepped near the fire.

"Divine help may be yer best hope," Declan said, as he took out the knife he kept in a sheath on his belt and cut a slab of bread and one of cheese and handed it to her.

"Best fortify yerself for the effort with some breakfast."

"Thank you," she said softly.

He cut chunks of bread and cheese for himself and Cyril. Together they stood over the fire and broke their fast. The laughter had done them all good, but there was no escaping the fact that they were soon to be riding into peril and they ate their food in silence. Declan looked at the little monk who was wolfing down his bread and cheese. Much would depend on the quick mind of Brother Cyril. He'd fooled John de Courcy, but would he fool the Abbot at Down?

It was essential that he did. Declan had no doubt de Courcy would question them closely about their visit to Down on their return to Carrickfergus. For their own sake and for Roland's they could not be caught in a lie, so a visit with the Abbot and to the gravesite of Saint Patrick was necessary. But best to keep both short, then get out.

Keep it simple, he thought.

There would be crowds at the abbey for the Feast of the Ascension. Cyril had said that was a good thing as it would preoccupy the Abbot and the monks. In that throng they would just be a few more pilgrims, though with the extra status afforded by de Courcy's letter of introduction. That letter should get them an audience with Abbot Layton, even on a feast day. A quick interview with the Abbot, a visitation at the grave of the saint, then off.

That should be simple enough.

***

Three roads converged at the hill of Down where John de Courcy had endowed his abbey to honour Saint Patrick. One came up from the south, up from Dublin, through the port of Dundalk and on to Down. Another ran down from the north, crossing the River Quoile at a ford, then swinging west past the Mound of Down. There, men in the pay of John de Courcy manned a log palisade that sat atop the natural motte, providing security for the abbey and its village. The last road came from

Armagh, passing over a ford on the River Bann, then running due east across flat and open pastureland to reach the abbey. It was on this road that Declan, Cyril and Margaret Maelchallain now rode toward the abbey amidst growing crowds of pilgrims.

The feast day had dawned grey and dreary, but the threat of rain was banished as the sun burned away the morning mists and breezes blew away all but a few white clouds. Declan looked up at the blue dome of the sky and thought it a good day for a parade and a celebration. The first sign that they were nearing the abbey was the top of a slender stone tower visible above the trees.

As they came around a bend in the road they saw a prominent hill nearly encircled by marshes to the west and a broad river to the north. The stone tower was fully visible now and beside it a large church stood, nearly finished, but with scaffolding on one side for stone masons to complete their work. All around the base of the hill was a low, earthen berm meant to define the grounds of the abbey and village more than for defence. Friar Tuck had once explained to him that these low ridges marked the boundary between the church's domain and the King's.

"Separating the sacred from the profane," the monk had observed.

Inside the enclosure were huts and buildings of various sizes comprising the village that existed to support and profit from the abbey. The road they were on swung just south of the marshland and entered the abbey grounds from the southwest. As they approached the entrance, Declan could see entire families of local Irish trooping in from every direction, come to celebrate Christ's ascension into heaven.

"A good turnout," observed Brother Cyril admiringly.

Declan grinned at that and glanced over at Margaret who was paying no attention to the gathering crowds. She had her eyes fixed on the church at the top of the hill, the church where the bell of Saint Patrick—her bell—was said to be kept in a vault. Declan marvelled again at the power that these sacred relics held for those who venerated them.

He himself believed in the one God with utter conviction, but wondered if the shinbones of saints and the like really held miraculous powers. When King Guy of Jerusalem marched out against Saladin on the field of Hattin, his priests had carried the One True Cross ahead of his army. Years later, on a moonlit night, he and Roland had ridden over the bones of the Christian soldiers who'd been slaughtered on that field.

He glanced once more at Margaret and saw how her eyes shone as she looked longingly up at the church. Perhaps a shinbone was nothing but a shinbone and a bell nothing more than a bell, but men—and women it seemed—believed they could produce miracles. True or not, that gave these relics great power.

Declan reined in his chestnut mare and dismounted outside the earthen berm that encircled the hill. There were two armed sentries on either side of the gap in the berm that served as the entrance to the abbey grounds, but they looked bored and disinterested in the crowds that were streaming past them and up the hill. Sitting atop the berm was a small group of boys entertaining themselves by watching the crowd pass by. He motioned to the biggest among them. With a coin for a deposit and another promised upon return, he arranged for the safekeeping of their mounts.

Together, the knight, the monk and the false nun joined the crowd marching up the hill toward the church.

***

Roland was up at first light and shook Finn awake. Thin tendrils of fog swirled among the trees as they broke camp. Hours before dawn, he had heard the faint sounds of church bells to the south. He'd grown familiar with the schedule of the bells during the siege of Chester when, despite the bombardment of the town, the monks of Saint Werburg's Abbey had not once failed to mark their calls to prayer.

In late spring, they rang the bells for Matins hours before dawn. As he saddled The Grey, he reckoned that if the bells were from Down Abbey, they were only an hour or so from the place. He swung into the saddle and hoisted Finn up behind.

"I heard bells in the night, my lord."

Roland smiled. Finn looked to be a light sleeper, a useful habit for an orphan trying to survive in a hard world.

"Aye, lad. I expect they're the Abbey bells at Down. We should reach there by mid-morning and I hope to find my friends there, the ones who paid you to mind our horses. They will be traveling to Down, if not this day then soon."

"The Irishman and the monk?" Finn asked.

"Aye, the very same. I need to find them."

"How'll ye do that, my lord? Will ye ask the Abbot if they've seen 'em?"

Roland shook his head.

"I don't think that would be wise. My friends have a letter of introduction for the Abbot from the Prince, but I do not. To question him about my friends might be viewed with suspicion."

"I could see it might, sir. I've heard these English monks at Down are entirely de Courcy's creatures. I wouldn't trust 'em."

Roland shrugged.

"I don't."

"Then how will ye find yer friends, lord? I've heard there are soldiers at Down as well as monks and they'll want to know yer business if yer just pokin' about the place."

Roland frowned. The Irish boy had a point. He reined in The Grey and twisted around in the saddle to look at the boy.

"Alright, Finn, out with it," he ordered.

"Lord?"

"You've told me how I shouldn't go about this. Now tell me how I should."

The boy looked abashed, but did not hesitate to speak up.

"I meant no offense, my lord, but *you* can't do it," he said flatly. "Ye've said ye can't ask the Abbot or the monks directly about yer friends and don't think de Courcy's soldiers won't notice ye ridin' in on this fine English horse. Ye'll get us both caught fer sure, my lord."

"Then how?" Roland demanded.

"I'll do it m'self, lord," the boy said earnestly. "No one notices a boy like me. I can stroll around the abbey grounds and spy out the place. I recall yer friends well enough to know 'em on sight and if I don't see 'em, I won't ask the monks. I'll ask the locals. They won't care what my business is, if there's a coin or two in it for them."

Roland stared at the boy for a moment then shook his head. He pulled out his coin purse and fished out two small silver pieces and handed them to Finn. The boy slipped them into his purse, where they made a clinking sound as they joined a growing hoard in the little leather pouch.

"You'll have more silver than I before we're done, Master Finn."

The boy just smiled as he tucked the purse into his belt.

***

Declan cleared a path through the crowd gathered outside the church of Saint Patrick and made his way to the arched entrance of the nave. Two monks flanked the opening, one of middle years and plump, the other hardly beyond boyhood and gangly. They were gently but firmly turning away worshipers clamouring to enter the church. Locals were advised that the nave was being used to prepare the holy relics for the processional that would begin in half an hour. In the meantime, they were to wait outside.

As Declan approached, the two men eyed him. His dress separated him from the local peasantry, but the two were unmoved by appearances and disinclined to make an exception for him. But before they could issue a rebuff, Brother Cyril, with Margaret Maelchallain in tow, stepped to the front and greeted his fellow monks heartily.

"Brothers, this is truly a day the Lord has made," he proclaimed, speaking to them in English, "and we have ridden far to share in your celebration of His ascension into the heavens."

The two monks smiled sympathetically, but shook their heads sadly.

"You are most welcome here, Brother," the older of the two said sadly, "but the nave is in use just now."

Cyril frowned and drew forth a roll of parchment from his robes.

"I had not thought this necessary," he said with a sniff, "but Lord de Courcy was good enough to provide me with a letter of introduction to the Abbot—when last we spoke."

He handed the parchment to the monk who had addressed him. The man unrolled it and squinted at the words. Declan saw the monk's demeanour change as he reached the bottom of the document where de Courcy's own seal was affixed.

"You are Brother Cyril?" he asked meekly.

"I am. I come at the behest of the Bishop of Chester to pay respects at the tomb of Patrick and commune with my brother monks here at Down."

"Oh, good Brother Cyril!" he exclaimed, plastering a hasty smile on his face, "forgive our lack of hospitality. It's the feast day, you see and the locals...they are like unruly children and require a firm hand. But come, no need to wait in this crowd. It is quieter inside." He gave a short bow and motioned for them follow him into the nave.

Cyril beamed back at the man.

"Thank you, Brother...?"

"I am Anselm, Brother Cyril, at your service, and this," he said pointing to his companion, "is Brother Martin. He'll keep watch on the door and I'll take you to the Abbot. He is always most anxious to welcome visitors sent our way by the Prince. Did you know that it was Lord de Courcy who provided the funds to build our abbey here. He is a most devout man and a great benefactor. Together we are leading these Irish out of sin and into the light!"

Cyril smiled benignly.

"The Prince informed us of the good work you do here, Brother Anselm."

Anselm sighed loudly.

"We try, Brother, honestly we do! But the Irish here cling to many of the old ways, no matter how blasphemous. You know that as a novitiate, I spent a year at Norton Priory in Runcorn. Now there was a holy place!"

A sly smile flickered across Cyril's face.

"So you were once an Augustinian like myself, Brother Anselm?"

Anselm looked a little sheepish.

"Aye, I was, Brother, but I found I was ill-suited for a life tending the sick and the poor. I do admire those like yourself who go out among the people, but I shudder to think what that would be like among these stiff-necked Irish! For me the more contemplative life of a Benedictine has great appeal." This he said as he turned his attention to Margaret and contemplated her. Cyril saw the shift in the monk's interest and made the introduction.

"Brother Anselm, may I present, Sister Margaret. She is Irish herself, but for several years now has resided with the sisters at Chester Priory. It was there she began her study of the life of your great Saint Patrick and looks forward to learning more."

Anselm stared at Margaret with more than an ecclesiastical interest, unconcerned that he had just insulted her countrymen and the Irish church. He reached out pudgy hands and clasped hers.

"Sister, I am perhaps the most knowledgeable in the teachings of Patrick amongst our brethren here and would be *most* pleased to instruct you."

Margaret blushed prettily at the man.

"You are most kind, Brother Anselm. I have many questions and much to learn from one as wise as you."

"Yes, yes," he said, absently licking his lips, "but come, I must conduct you to the Abbot!"

He reluctantly released Margaret's hands and turned back to Cyril.

"Please follow me," he said.

As he started into the dim interior he hesitated.

"He is with you?" he asked, nodding toward Declan.

"Aye, brother, my bodyguard, Sir Declan. The Bishop insisted."

Anselm nodded.

"A wise precaution in this country. I rarely venture off the abbey grounds myself. In truth, I do not look forward to these holy days. Who knows what sort of brigands might conceal themselves among the crowds. We have de Courcy's garrison nearby, but they are far more interested in protecting their little fort atop the mound than we poor monks here at the abbey!"

Cyril patted the fat monk's arm and winked over his shoulder at Declan.

"Well, you can rest easy today, brother," he reassured the man. "No villain will come near you with Sir Declan at hand. He was knighted by King Richard himself!"

Anselm glanced once more at Declan and, for the first time, really looked at him. The monk had seen much over the years, including his share of fighting men.

"He looks very capable, Brother Cyril," he said, "but time is short and the Abbot must be informed that we have guests!" He stepped into the nave and motioned for them to follow.

The inside of the church was illuminated by a few large candles near the altar and by faint sunlight that found its way in through small windows set high up along both walls of the nave. To the right of the altar was a heavy oak door with elaborately forged iron hinges and polished carvings on its outer face. The door was half open with two men-at-arms keeping watch over a cluster of black-robed monks bustling in and out of the hidden chamber.

"That is the sacristy," Brother Anselm said in a low voice as they drew near. He laid a hand on Margaret's shoulder and whispered to her. "Here we keep our holy relics. There is a lock of Saint Ita's hair in a silver locket, a knuckle bone from Saint Brendan and our most prized possession…,"

"The bell of Saint Patrick," Margaret said finishing the sentence. "I'd heard it was here," she added breathlessly.

"And you shall see it!" the monk assured her as they neared the front of the nave.

Overseeing the buzz of activity at the front of the nave was a remarkable looking man. William Layton, the Abbot of Down, was dressed all in black and towered over the monks scurrying around the sacristy. Declan guessed the man was a half head taller than himself, with steel grey hair and dark eyes set deep beneath brows that sprouted tangles of hair like briar patches. The Abbot was barking orders in a clipped voice as they approached.

"Drape this white silk over the arms of the crucifix," he said handing a bolt of shimmering cloth to one of the brethren. He stood back and watched the man hang the cloth on the ornate rood. A frown creased his face as he saw the result.

"No, no, no! Drape it evenly," he said, his voice rising in exasperation as he shooed away the monk and fiddled with the silken cloth, "like so!" He stood back and admired his handywork. As he did so, Brother Anselm caught his attention.

"Father Abbot, we have distinguished guests," he announced and handed the parchment to the man. He took the roll with a trace of annoyance, but brightened upon seeing the seal at the bottom.

"Brother Cyril! You've come on an auspicious day for our abbey. You and your party are most welcome here."

Cyril bowed to the man.

"I can see you are in the midst of preparations for the processional observing our Lord's ascension, Father Abbot, and I fear we will be in the way."

"Nonsense! All are welcome in the sight of the Lord and most particularly those who come from Chester. I studied there at the abbey as a young monk myself and have fond memories of my time at Saint Werburg's." He gazed off in the distance as though calling those memories to mind, then turned back to the newcomers.

"Chester is a much more civilized place than this rude abbey," he said wistfully, "but with the support of our most gracious Prince, we will make it into something grand someday. As for now, I insist you join us as we make our processional! Tomorrow, when things are calmer, we can visit Patrick's grave and speak of his ministry here."

"You are most kind, Father Abbot," Cyril said. "It will be our honour."

Pleasantries exchanged, Abbot Layton turned his attention to retrieving the relics from the sacristy and arranging the order of march for his monks. Two of the sturdier looking brethren were assigned to carry the crucifix that would lead the processional while two of the frailer brothers were given the task of parading with the knuckle bone of Saint Brendan and the locket of hair from Saint Ita. Finally, the Abbot motioned Brother Anselm into the sacristy. The burly monk emerged a moment later holding up the Abbey's prized new possession—the shrine and the bell of Saint Patrick.

Declan drew in a breath. Margaret had told him that the saint's bell was iron and of the simplest construction, but the shrine that had been crafted to contain it was a true work of art. She had not exaggerated. The bell shrine was exquisite in its intricacy and beauty. The body of the shrine was composed of four bronze plates trimmed in silver and covered in gold filigree shaped into complex swirls and symbols. Eight precious stones were set into the front face. Even in the dim light of the nave, the thing seemed to glow.

Abbot Layton pointed to the monk holding the silver locket on a small embroidered pillow.

"You will follow your brother with Saint Ita's hair, Brother Anselm" he directed. "Hold the shrine high for all to see and for all to understand that we are the true heirs of Patrick, come to bring them into the light!"

He turned back to Cyril.

"You and your companions may follow Brother Anselm."

With that, he strode through the nave to the door of the church. Black-clad Benedictines now lined the first forty feet of the road that led down from the top of the hill to the entrance to the abbey grounds. They had moved back the crowd to make way for the processional and now, with a small a gesture from the Abbot, the brethren began to chant, softly at first but with their voices slowly rising.

At the doorway, a monk stepped to the front with a smoking censer and walked out between the ranks of his brothers. The Abbot waved forward the men bearing the Crucifix and fell in behind them as they exited the church. The bearers of the holy relics came next. As the nave emptied, the three newcomers looked at each other. Declan shrugged.

"I love a parade," he said as he fell in behind Anselm.

***

A mile and a half from the church on the hill, The Grey scrambled up the muddy bank of the ford on the River Quoile.

Roland looked off to the west where the land was low and the river had spread out into a broad tidal marsh full of reeds and flocks of water fowl. The road clung to a forested fringe of higher ground and swung southwest. He clucked to the horse and The Grey needed no prompting from the reins to know where to go.

In less than a mile, the woods dwindled to a few patches and the country opened up to the south with fields and pastureland replacing the trees. A few rough huts appeared among the fields, but there was no sign of the inhabitants. North of the road, the broad marshland continued as far as the eye could see, the view interrupted only by a cone-shaped hill that rose from the reeds and was topped with a wooden palisade. This would be John de Courcy's garrison, keeping watch over the ford and the abbey. Further west, he saw the top of a slim tower above the horizon.

Down Abbey.

As The Grey passed de Courcy's motte, Roland waved to three sentries who stood watch on the causeway that led across the marsh to the foot of the fortified hill. They did not return his wave. He counted another half dozen men-at-arms on the timber walls that circled the hilltop.

Ahead, the hill of Down came into view with a large stone church at its crest. An earthen berm, about the height of a man ran along the base of the hill in both directions as the road curved off to the south again. To his front, he now saw a few people on foot hurrying up the road, some dragging small children along in their haste. A few of the more nimble had climbed over the berm and were cutting across the grassy hillside, taking a shortcut toward the church.

Roland looked over his shoulder and spoke to Finn.

"What do you suppose the rush is?"

Finn screwed up his face in thought, then brightened.

"Feast of Ascension, I believe, lord. They was planning a processional for it at Carrickfergus 'for we left. It was set for today, I believe."

Roland reined in The Grey and considered what to do next. The feast day would mean crowds at the abbey. Crowds could affect the plan—for good or ill.

"Are you still game to spy out the place, lad?"

Finn nodded vigorously.

"Aye, lord, it'll be easy with all these folk about. I'll fit right in!"

Roland smiled at the boy's bravado, but worried for his safety.

"Take no chances, Finn," he warned as he watched the people hurrying south along the road. The main entrance to the abbey grounds would no doubt lay in that direction, away from the river and the threat of flooding. "I'll hide myself in the nearest patch of woods south of the abbey. If any of the monks or guards take an interest in you, you must get yourself out of there and find me. Do you understand?"

"Right, lord. I'm to run fer it if they're on to me," he said.

A little ahead of them, two boys broke away from their family and clambered over the berm, racing each other up the hill toward the church. Finn slid off the back of The Grey and patting the big gelding on the haunch, set off at a sprint to follow them. Roland watched the boy go, his skinny legs pumping as he chased the two local boys up the long slope. He watched until Finn disappeared over the crest and tried to shake off a nagging sense of dread.

Over the years, he'd grown used to sending men into peril, but those were men who'd freely chosen the life of a soldier. Nothing about young Finn Mac Clure's life had been freely chosen. Orphaned and abandoned, the boy had simply done what he must to survive. Now the lad was going into harm's way, more from necessity than choice. Sending Finn into the abbey might be the best way to find his friends, but if anything happened to this boy, Roland knew he would have much to answer for, if only to God and himself.

But like an arrow once loosed, there was no retrieving the boy now. He clucked to The Grey and rode south. Somewhere ahead he heard the faint sound of voices raised in song.

***

The processional moved slowly down the south slope of the hill from the church to the entrance of the abbey grounds. The Benedictine monks kept up their rhythmic song, punctuated by occasional pronouncements in Latin by Abbot Layton. As the Crucifix passed by, the faithful fell to their knees, bowed their heads and crossed themselves.

But moments later, their heads came up and a buzz ran through their ranks. They'd all seen the knuckle bone of Brendan and the hair of Ita on past holy days, but this was their first view of the holiest relic in Ireland, the bell of Saint Patrick. A woman broke from the crowd and went down on her knees before Brother Anselm, weeping and praying loudly to the dead Saint.

Anselm never broke stride as he stepped around the woman and continued down the hill. Margaret stopped and knelt beside the weeping woman, laying a comforting arm across her shoulders. The poor woman whispered something, then kissed Margaret's hand before crawling back into the crowd.

"She was begging Patrick to give her a child. Hers died in the winter."

When the head of the processional reached the break in the berm at the bottom of the hill, the lead monk turned and followed the barrier to the west. The crowd followed along, some racing ahead and some falling in behind. When they reached the northern extent of the abbey grounds, they turned up hill and headed for the tall stone tower that rose high above the church.

As he marched up the hill, Declan considered how to complete their visitation at the abbey. The Abbot had offered to grant them time the next day to consult with him and the monks, but he had no intention of staying any longer than needed. He felt certain that, by the time these services were done, Cyril would have enough information on the abbey and its residents to construct a convincing report. The skinny Augustinian had a sharp eye for detail and could transform a half day's visit into a week-long sojourn for the Prince's report.

At the top of the hill, the Abbot halted beside a newly-erected high cross. At the base of the cross was a mound of carefully chosen stones marking a gravesite. Carved in the centre of the stone cross was the name "Padraig". Declan had been ten years in England with occasional forays to the Holy Land and into Wales, but his heart remained Irish. He felt a lump in his throat as he looked upon the final resting place of Patrick.

Abbot Layton stood beside the grave in silence for a long time waiting on the gathering flock still trudging up the hill. The abbey monks fell silent. When the crowd settled, the tall churchman raised his hands to heaven.

"Today, we celebrate the Ascension of our Lord into Heaven!" he exclaimed in English. The crowd remained silent. The Abbot gestured for Anselm to come forward and he took the bell shrine from the monk. He raised the ornate shrine over his head.

"And we celebrate," he continued, his voice rising to a triumphant shout—"Naomh Padraig!"

Saint Patrick's Bell

Finn Mac Clure watched as Abbot Layton raised the shrine and shouted Saint Patrick's name to the masses in poorly accented Gaelic. He had caught up with the processional as it reached the northern end of the abbey grounds and followed the monks up the hill, forcing his way through the crowd to get a better look at the ceremony. He squeezed through to the front rank of onlookers just as the Abbot made his dramatic presentation to the gathered faithful.

All around him people turned their gaze up to look upon the holy relic and murmured prayers. Finn kept his eyes to the front scanning the crowd anxiously. Then he saw him! At the top of the hill, among a cluster of monks was the red-haired knight who'd given him silver back in Carrickfergus.

In his excitement, Finn was tempted to break away from the crowd and run to take this news to Sir Roland, but he hesitated. No doubt word that his friends had been located would be well received, but why not wait for the end of the ceremony and simply take the Irish knight to where Sir Roland was waiting? Surely it was the sort of thing a good squire might do for his master. He decided to wait.

Satisfied with the effect Patrick's bell shrine had had upon the locals, Abbot Layton rushed through a final benediction and ended the service. He and his gaggle of monks turned away from the crowd and made their way across the top of the hill to a side entrance to the church. Finn watched them file inside with Sir Declan, the skinny monk he'd seen in Carrickfergus and a nun trailing behind them. He found a nice spot beneath a sapling and sat down to wait and watch.

170

Declan O'Duinne

***

It took a moment for Declan's eyes to adjust from the bright sunlight on the hilltop to the interior of the church as they passed through the narrow side door. Most of the monks had dispersed to other duties without entering the church, but the relic bearers gathered at the door to the sacristy to put away their treasures until the next holy day.

Abbot Layton, pleased with the ceremony, had a rare smile on his stern features.

"Did you see how they wept at the sight of this?" he asked, rubbing his hands together in satisfaction. "Our benefactor, Prince de Courcy, knew what a prize he had when he took it from a dead heretic on the field of battle and placed it with us. The bell is proof that God guides our hands and that we are the true heirs to Saint Patrick!" he exclaimed.

Declan stole a look at Margaret. The dead heretic had been her father. The girl's face was turning a bright shade of crimson and her jaw muscles worked as she fought to contain her fury. No one seemed to notice, as all eyes were on the bell shrine. He laid a gentle hand on her arm, but she jerked it away.

He'd feared that bringing her here was a mistake. He knew now that it was. She'd come for a last look at the bell that meant so much to her family, but seeing it in these men's hands must have felt like a sacrilege. Seeing it thus would give her no peace. He felt sorry for the girl, but there was nothing to be done.

The Abbot handed the shrine back to Brother Anselm, and turned to Cyril.

"These public ceremonies are a drain," he said, wearily, "but I will be refreshed on the morrow and will look forward to consulting with you, Brother Cyril."

"I'm honoured, Father Abbot," Cyril replied.

Declan felt his tension ease a bit as this engagement with the Abbot was ending. By morning, he planned to be well on his way back to Carrickfergus, leaving the Abbot to wonder what had become of his visitors from Chester. Then he saw Margaret lay a dainty hand on Brother Anselm's arm as the man was turning to enter the sacristy and his tension flooded back.

"Brother Anselm, could I possibly hold it?" she asked the monk sweetly. "Just for a moment—it's so beautiful!"

Cyril cast a worried glance at Declan. This was not part of the plan. Declan scowled and tried to catch the girl's eye, but she ignored him. Brother Anselm looked to the Abbot for guidance. For a moment the tall cleric stood stone-faced, then gave a reluctant nod. Anselm turned back to the girl.

"Why, yes, Sister, but please do be careful. The gold scrollwork is very delicate."

He placed the shrine gently in Margaret's hands and beamed down at her. Margaret Maelchallain hardly looked at the shrine. Instead, she kicked the monk in the crotch. Anselm howled and bent double, then crumpled to the floor, writhing in agony. Abbot Layton looked on, his mouth agape, but recovered quickly. With a snarl, he lunged at Margaret, his hands reaching for the bell. Declan moved to shield her, but Brother Cyril was quicker. He stepped between the Abbot and the girl and punched the startled churchman in the nose. A bright spatter of blood fell on the man's immaculate black robes as he reeled backwards.

"Oh good God!" Declan blurted and whirled around to see who might have witnessed this sudden assault. There was a monk and one of de Courcy's men-at-arms standing in the main doorway of the nave. They had been engaged in conversation, but turned together to see what had caused the sudden uproar inside. The monk's eyes grew large when he saw one of his brethren writhing on the floor and the Abbot leaning on a bench for support, holding a hand over his broken nose. The guard was not so slow to react.

"You there!" he ordered. "Don't move!"

Declan moved.

He grabbed Margaret by her wrist and bolted toward the side entrance of the church with Cyril following close on his heels. Behind him he heard the guard raise a hue and cry. There had been a dozen or more armed men from de Courcy's garrison assigned to keep watch over the feast day activities at the Abbey and they would now be alerted to trouble.

The three fugitives burst out into the daylight at the side of the church and stopped. A boy sitting under a sapling sprang to his feet and stared at them. The crowd of worshipers had mostly dispersed, but a little ways down the hill a few of the laggards caught sight of them. One gaped at Margaret and pointed at the object she held tightly to her chest.

"An clog!" he shouted in awe and crossed himself.

"Damn!" Declan cursed. Saint Patrick's bell and Margaret Maelchallain were about to get them all killed! His first thought was to flee north. That side of the hill was empty all the way to the berm at its base, but the land beyond was hemmed in by the river and marshes and their horses were in the opposite direction. Without mounts they would not get far, but to get to them they would have to pass through the heart of the abbey. Now that an alarm had been raised, de Courcy's guards would surely be gathering there. Still, without the horses they were doomed. South it must be.

He turned to his left and, keeping close to the west wall of the church, headed south. He still held Margaret's wrist and she did not try to resist as he pulled her along behind. Cyril brought up the rear, casting anxious eyes back toward the side entrance of the church should pursuit come from that direction.

When they reached the front of the church Declan stopped and looked down the long sweep of the hill. Near the first line of buildings, ten men-at-arms were forming a loose line and moving uphill toward them. A hard looking man, no doubt a sergeant, saw the three at the top of the hill and barked out an order. His men spread out further, intending to come at their quarry from front and sides.

Declan released Margaret and drew his broadsword.

***

Forty paces behind the three fugitives, Finn Mac Clure stood frozen to the spot, watching in horror as the Irish knight drew his sword. He couldn't believe his ill luck. He'd found the folk Sir Roland had asked him to find and now they were all about to be killed! This would be a black mark against him for certain and that was something he couldn't abide. He set off down the western slope of the hill until he was out of sight of the approaching soldiers. Once there he broke into a sprint. No one paid any attention to the skinny boy running like the Devil was on his heels toward the south entrance of the abbey.

***

For an hour, Roland had kept watch from a small patch of woods a quarter mile south of Down Abbey. He'd seen the processional reach the south entrance to the abbey and turn west. There had been a cluster of black-clad monks trailing behind a raised Crucifix and a large crowd of locals swirling around the edges, but that was all he could make out. If Declan or Cyril or Finn was there, he could not see them.

He watched the crowd disappear around the hill and could do nothing but wait. Finally, people appeared, coming over the crest of the hill in ones and twos at first, then in larger groups. A half dozen boys chased each other down the slope and out the south entrance to the abbey grounds. Crowds of locals followed them and begin to stream out of the abbey grounds, marking the end of the feast day services. All seemed as it should be as he waited anxiously for Finn's return.

Then an uproar broke out near the top of the hill.

Something he could not see had caused an alarm to be raised and soldiers who had been lounging around the abbey grounds were suddenly running towards the church. He could hear shouted orders and saw the men-at-arms forming up just below the crest of the hill.

Something had gone terribly wrong.

He swung up on The Grey's back and dug his heels in the gelding's flanks. The horse broke out of the trees and bounded across the open field that lay between the woods and the abbey. As he rode, Roland scanned the hill to his front. The soldiers had shaken out into a line and were moving cautiously up the hill. He could not yet see what their target was.

Could it be Finn?

He doubted an unarmed boy of ten would call for such an extreme response from de Courcy's garrison troops, but something was amiss and Finn had not returned. He gave The Grey a slap on the haunches and the horse broke into a gallop, eating up the ground even faster. A half minute later, he reined in near the cut in the berm. A big farm boy was sitting on the berm eyeing him leerily. Near the boy were three horses staked to the ground. The little Irish pony meant nothing to him, but the chestnut mare he knew well. It belonged to Declan O'Duinne and the long-legged bay was Brother Cyril's mount.

He swung down off The Grey, strung his longbow and draped his quiver over his shoulder. The farm boy did not wait around for his promised coin. He scrambled down off the berm and ran. Roland climbed to where he'd been sitting and drew an arrow from his quiver. A hundred paces to his front, he saw a familiar figure.

Finn Mac Clure was running down the hill toward him, his skinny legs churning.

***

Declan stood at the top of the hill and watched the soldiers closing in. A few of those on the flanks looked to be local boys, recruited to help man the garrison, but a half dozen in the centre he marked as trained men. He could tell by the way they moved and the way they held their weapons. The sight made him wish he hadn't left his mail hauberk rolled up and lashed to his saddle.

He looked over his shoulder to see Cyril and Margaret huddled a few yards behind him, the girl still clutching Saint Patrick's bell to her breast. He wondered what they would do to her if she were taken. It would not be pretty. Abbot Layton would see to that.

"If I can cut a hole in their line, we run for the horses," he called back to them. "If they cut a hole in me, fend for yerselves."

"God will not fail us!" Margaret assured him.

"We'll see," Declan muttered to himself and began to move down the hill toward the advancing soldiers. It was always best to take a little of the initiative away from men coming to kill you.

***

A young soldier on the left end of the line was unsettled by the sight of the man striding down the hill toward them. A moment before, he'd been thrilled at the prospect of killing or capturing these folk who had committed some transgression on the abbey grounds. The son of a pig farmer, he'd joined the garrison at Down to escape the filth and boredom of his life and to impress a local girl, but a year of guard duty at the motte had proven to be more boring than slopping hogs. It had left him longing for something to relieve the tedium. When the sergeant sounded the alarm and ordered him into ranks beside nine of his comrades he'd felt no fear—only excitement.

But now the man was only thirty paces away and the wicked steel blade he swung looked deadly. The boy felt his gut twist and his legs start to go wobbly. In a panic, he cocked his arm and launched his spear at the man's chest. It never reached its mark as it was slapped aside with the flat of the man's sword as though it were an annoying fly. The sergeant screamed a curse at the boy, who turned and fled down the hill.

***

Declan watched the lad break and run. The local boys who remained all looked nervous, but the half dozen men at the centre of the line did not waver. They were veterans and would know how to use their spears. He broke into a trot straight at them then cut to his right. The man to his front lunged forward with a hasty underhand thrust of his spear. Declan brought his blade down in a quick chopping motion, slicing cleanly through the spear's wooden shaft, its iron point falling harmlessly into the grass. He shifted his weight and launched a vicious backhand slash that caught the man on the side of his helmet, dropping him in a heap.

From the left, another spearpoint came at him in a blur. He jerked backwards from the waist, but the blade ripped the front of his tunic, cutting a furrow across his chest. He grabbed the shaft and yanked its owner toward him. This soldier was no green pig farmer and neither was he a fool. He let go and scrambled backwards. Two more spears were thrust at him, narrowly missing and forcing him to move back uphill.

"Throw down yer sword and ye'll live," the sergeant called to him while motioning for his men to circle around on either side.

"I doubt that," he replied, nodding toward a tall, black-clad figure hurrying up behind the line of soldiers. It was Abbot Layton, his face a mask of fury and still smeared with his own blood. "I believe we've upset the Abbot."

The sergeant shrugged.

"That's between you and the Abbot," he said.

"Kill him," the Abbot screamed at the sergeant. "He has defiled the church of Saint Patrick!"

The sergeant shrugged again.

"I take me orders from Sir Randolph Quincy at the fort and he takes his orders from the Prince. If this lot will come peaceable, we'll put 'em under lock and key and ye can take it up with them."

Abbot Layton sputtered and issued threats, but the sergeant stolidly stuck to his duty as he saw it.

Declan smiled at the man as he edged backwards.

"You're a good man, sergeant, but I doubt we would fare any better with de Courcy than with the Abbot, so I'll have to refuse your invitation to lay down my sword."

The sergeant shrugged and signalled to his men to close in. He'd taken two steps forward when a scream escaped his lips. He dropped his spear and staggered, then went down on all fours, an arrow protruding from his hindquarters. As the sergeant groaned and fell on his side, Declan looked down the hill and wanted to weep. Roland Inness was standing on the berm there and his bow was drawn.

Seeing their sergeant take an arrow, the veteran soldiers on the hill instantly recognized their danger. They wore no mail and had no shields. They threw themselves to the ground and made themselves as small a target as possible for the archer down the hill. The new men, seeing the veterans rooted to the ground, tried to burrow into the hillside as well. Abbot Layton's face turned ashen and he began backing away toward the church. Declan turned to Cyril and Margaret and motioned them forward.

"You were right, Margaret," he said as she reached him. "God did not fail us. He sent us Roland Inness."

***

Roland saw the men-at-arms drop to the ground and lowered his longbow. He watched Brother Cyril and what looked to be a nun stepping gingerly between the soldiers hugging the grassy hillside. None rose to stop them as they joined Declan. Together, the three ran down the long slope to the berm where their horses were tethered. When they reached the bottom of the hill, Declan, grabbed Roland in a bear hug.

"God knows how ye got here, Roland, but yer a damned welcome sight!"

"He dropped from a privy!" Finn put in cheerily.

Declan arched an eyebrow.

"Now there's a tale I'll want to hear," he said, releasing his friend and looking back up the hill where the garrison troops were beginning to rise from the ground. "But no time now. The Prince's men will be along 'for long and they'll bring shields I'd wager."

Roland looked past his friend and saw two soldiers being dispatched on the run to carry the alarm to the garrison a mile down the road.

"You're more right than you know, Dec, the Prince's men are coming and not just the men from the motte east of here. Five shiploads of English mercenaries landed at Carrickfergus just two days ago. De Courcy has summoned Irish troops from Antrim and when they arrive he said he would march against Tyrone. He wanted me to join him!"

Declan grimaced.

"So soon? I'd hoped to get clear of here before the next war began."

"Might be sooner, once this news reaches him," Roland said, standing back and looking at Declan's bloody shirt. "We need to see to your wound."

Declan waved him off.

"Later. It's not deep and we've no time now."

Roland saw the two runners sent to alert the fort scramble over the berm and pelt down the road to the east. Declan's injury would have to wait, but another pressing question came to mind.

"Your father?" he asked gently.

"He lives!" Declan answered brightly, "It was a worse wound by far than this one," he said looking down at his torn shirt, "but he is a tough old man. You'll like him."

Roland smiled.

"I've no doubt of that, but tell me," he asked inclining his head toward the beautiful young woman climbing onto the bare back of an Irish pony, still clutching the bell shrine to her chest. "Who is the nun and is that the bell de Courcy spoke of?"

Before Declan could answer, the girl pulled the tight-fitting white coif from her head and shook loose a cascade of raven hair.

Declan shook his head.

"Aye, that's the bell of Saint Patrick, but the girl is no nun!"

***

Declan winced as Margaret dabbed blood from the wound on his chest with a piece of damp cloth she'd ripped from the sleeve of her nun's habit.

"Hold still," she said softly. "I'm almost done."

They'd ridden hard for an hour through open country to put Down and its garrison behind them when they came to a stretch of woods. Roland had demanded they get off the Armagh road and see how bad the wound was under his friend's blood-soaked shirt.

The girl finished cleaning the jagged cut and bound it with a another piece of cloth she'd torn from her discarded scapula.

"There," she said, standing back and inspecting her work. "That should heal with nothing more than a bit of a scar."

"Not my first," Declan said sourly.

"I can see that," Margaret said, glancing over the half dozen marks left by old wounds on the young Irish knight's arms and torso. "You seem to collect them."

Declan stood up and frowned at her.

"You should see the men who gave them to me," he said as he gingerly pulled his one spare shirt on over his head, "but you'd have to dig them out of the ground."

This made the girl laugh.

"Yer a bold man, Sir Declan," she said. "I didn't think I'd like you when first we met, but you do grow on a girl."

Declan ignored the olive branch.

"You almost got us all killed back there, my lady."

Margaret stiffened.

"I did not intend to," she replied, tartly.

Declan gave her a hard look.

"Did you intend to steal the bell all along?"

Margaret dropped her eyes. Then looked over at the sacred object sitting near her. Even in the shade of the old trees, the shrine shone brightly.

"I must confess, the thought did enter my mind, but Hugh O'Neill knows me too well. He warned me not to do it and I promised to follow his advice."

"But you didn't."

"I couldn't. You heard what the Abbot said. That sack of horse turds called my father a heretic! What would *you* have done?"

Declan started to reply, but then looked over at Cyril and Roland. The two had been hovering nearby watching Margaret minister to him.

"What say you two?" he asked.

Brother Cyril rubbed his chin for a moment.

"Well, theft is a sin, sure enough," he opined solemnly, "but I'm not sure if this could properly be ruled a theft, since the lady was simply retrieving what was her family's to begin with."

Declan scoffed.

"A fine legal point, Brother Cyril, but this," he said, sweeping his arm in an arc to take in the thick woods, "is not the Hundreds Court!"

He looked at Roland.

"What say you?"

Roland shrugged.

"I know little of this bell, save that John de Courcy puts great stock in it. I'm not surprised those he took it from feel the same."

He walked over to where Margaret had gently laid down the precious relic and picked it up, giving it a gentle shake. A dull clank could be heard, but nothing that sounded like the ringing of a bell. The girl leapt to her feet, her fists clenched.

"Be at ease, miss, I'll not harm it," Roland assured her as he examined the object. "This jewelled case—the bell is inside it?"

Margaret stepped forward with her hands out.

"I'll show you."

Roland handed the ornate shrine to the girl, who flipped it over and fiddled with a hidden latch. A moment later, she slid the bottom bronze panel out to the side. With great care she reached in and drew forth the bell of St. Patrick. The girl's eyes were shining as she held it up for all to see.

For a long moment there was silence as everyone in the little clearing stared at this object held in such reverence by the Irish.

"It looks like a cowbell," Finn said, disappointed.

Margaret shot him a dark look.

"We were almost killed over a cowbell," Declan said sourly.

Margaret's eyes welled with tears and she thrust the dull iron bell back into its bronze shrine.

"My father *was* killed over this," she said, her voice a mix of pain and defiance. "I suppose a man like you who fights for Normans couldn't understand such a thing!"

Now it was Declan who bristled, but before he could speak, Roland laid a hand on his arm.

"What would you have done in her place, Dec? If they'd killed your father for this thing?"

Declan jerked his arm away, but the question seemed to cool his fury. He turned to look at the girl who was glaring at him, tears streaming down her face. It was to her he spoke.

"My pardon, Margaret. It is a fine bell—just the sort a saint would have." He shot a look at Finn, who needed no coaxing.

"It's a very nice bell, my lady," he said sheepishly. "I'm sorry I called it a cowbell."

Margaret seemed to soften a bit at Finn's sorrowful apology. She turned back to Declan, not yet ready to forgive.

"What would you have done in my place?"

"In your place," he said, "I'd 'ave taken the bell, killed the Abbot and not lost a moment's sleep over it."

***

With Declan's wound dressed and the bell returned to its shrine, the riders mounted and rode through the afternoon. They picked up Margaret's escort on the fly and, as darkness fell found a sheltered ravine to pass the night and made camp, only a half day's ride from Armagh. Finn went instantly to sleep after eating a cold supper and Margaret Maelchallain did the same, exhausted, but still clutching the bell of Saint Patrick to her chest. Roland and Declan left Cyril tending a small fire and walked out to the edge of the ravine as the stars started to show in the sky.

"I see young Finn has attached himself to you," Declan said as he found a seat on the thick trunk of a deadfall tree.

"Aye, he has. I'd have never got free of de Courcy without him. He has ambitions to be my squire, but I'm not sure I can afford him. His services don't come cheap!"

Declan laughed at that.

"Oh, I can vouch for that. I'd like to see what's in that boy's coin purse. I'll wager its heavier than yours or mine!"

"I'd not take that bet, but you can't blame the lad. An orphan boy has to shift for himself."

"And Irish lads do make the best squires," Declan said with a grin.

Roland sat down next to him on the tree trunk. It had been a long time since the two friends had shared a campsite and they sat for a while in silence, just enjoying the company. Somewhere in the distance an owl hooted, calling to its mate.

"What will you do now?" Roland asked quietly.

Declan shrugged.

"I did not come to Ireland looking for a fight. When we left Carrickfergus, I'd hoped to simply see to my father and brother, put in an appearance at Down and get back to de Courcy with a story that would satisfy him and get you out of there," he said gazing up at the lights in the sky. "Didn't know ye'd already managed the trick."

"Or that Lady Margaret had plans of her own," said Roland.

Declan gave a little hoot at that.

"Aye, she did and we're lucky it didn't end badly. Had we been taken with you still in de Courcy's hands, we all would have lost our heads I expect."

"That's why you're so angry at the girl?" Roland said.

"I think I've a right!" he said. "That bell means more to her than flesh and blood and it was very nearly our flesh and blood today—and could have been yours as well. She knew you were a hostage, but gave no thought to what de Courcy would do to you if she stole his bell."

Roland shrugged at that.

"People put great store in such things, Dec. How many men died trying to take back Jerusalem from Saladin? It wasn't the city they wanted—England did not need another city—it was what the city stood for."

"That's true enough," Declan admitted. "But the damned girl still almost got us killed."

"She's pretty though, isn't she," Roland said.

Declan nodded, his anger spent.

"Very. And she has courage. She had to kick a fat monk in the balls to steal the thing, which I rather enjoyed!"

Roland laughed at that.

"I'd have liked to seen that, but Dec, you haven't answered my question. I know you didn't come looking for a fight, but it seems one has found you."

Declan rose to his feet, agitated.

"What we should do is deliver Mistress Maelchallain to Armagh, say our farewells and head south to take ship in Dublin," he said wistfully. "We could be back home in a week."

"And leave Tyrone, your clan and Mistress Maelchallain to their fate?"

Declan groaned.

"Sir Roger did not send me off to fight a war in Ulster, Roland, and I am his man."

Roland stood and looked Declan in the eye.

"Roger de Laval would be the last man on earth to ask you to abandon your people when they are in peril," he said flatly.

"The Irish are always in peril," Declan said glumly, "but very much so at the moment. My heart tells me I must stay and help them...."

Roland laid a hand on Declan's shoulder.

"Then we'll stay and see this through."

"No!" Declan said fiercely, pulling away from Roland's touch. "Not you! This is not your fight. You must return to Shipbrook and tell Sir Roger that I'll be back when the danger here is past."

At this Roland burst into laughter.

"You want me to stand before Sir Roger de Laval and, God forbid, Millicent Inness, and tell them I left you behind in Ireland? Are you daft?"

Declan managed a sheepish grin at that, but would not concede his point.

"These are my people, Roland, not yours," he said.

"Ah, but you're wrong there, Declan. Have you forgot the night in Towcester on our way to Richard's coronation? That night I confessed to you that I had killed three of the Earl of Derby's men. I stood there, an admitted criminal, and you did not haul me off to face justice. Instead, you took me into your clan. I still have the scar here on my hand where we shared our blood. From that day, I've considered myself an O'Duinne—if not by birth, then by blood. Would you expel me from the family now?"

Declan knew when he was beaten. He plopped back down on the log.

"Stay then and tell me what ye know of de Courcy's plans. We'll reach Armagh in the morning. The Cenél Eoghain chiefs are gathered there. They'll need to know of the trouble heading their way."

"The Prince didn't confide much to me, Dec. I gather he's been waiting for his English mercenaries to arrive. On the day they disembarked, he said it would take three days to muster his Irish levies and then he would march."

"Which would be..." Declan said, mentally counting the days.

"Tomorrow," Roland said.

184

Declan cursed softly.

"That would put him at the fords over the Bann three days from now!"

"If he comes this way," Roland cautioned. "He did not tell me where, exactly, he planned to strike."

"When news reaches him of the theft of the bell, I think there is little doubt he'll march to Armagh," Declan said flatly. "Beyond the mercenaries, what do ye reckon his strength to be?"

"I spent some time watching the town from the curtain wall of the castle and counted heads as best I could. I'd guess he has four hundred men quartered there, mostly English and some Irish. Finn tells me upwards of eighty English-bred war horses are stabled in the town, so there will be that many heavy cavalry. And now he has two hundred English mercenaries—well-armed veterans.

"And probably five hundred Irishmen from Antrim he can call upon," Declan added. "Let's call it twelve hundred or more—a formidable host."

"Tell me what your Irish can muster to oppose him," Roland said.

Declan sighed, glad that his friend could not see the pained look on his face.

"It's hard to say," he began. "If all the factions of the Cenél Eoghain unite, they can field perhaps seven hundred foot, some light horsemen and no heavy cavalry."

Roland grunted. It was far from favourable odds.

"And will they unite?"

Declan shrugged in the dark.

"I've met the man who could bring the clans together. Hugh O'Neill is not much to look at, but he is clever and has no surrender in him. Sadly, the old King's son believes he should succeed his father. They were still arguing over it when we left Armagh. It's the bane of the Irish to fight amongst themselves, even with foreign invaders at the door."

He looked up at Roland.

"I'm sorry I've dragged ye into all this."

Roland sat down beside his friend and draped an arm over Declan's shoulders.

"We've been dragged into every war we've ever fought, Dec. I don't recall you or I ever starting a single one."

War Clouds

Five miles west of the River Bann, six riders were up and in the saddle before first light. By midmorning, the spire of Saint Patrick's church was in sight atop the hill of Armagh. A sentry posted down by the road saw them coming and hurriedly mounted, galloping his horse up the long slope to the abbey with news of their approach. By the time they reached the square that fronted the church, men were beginning to gather.

Declan reined in his chestnut mare and signalled for Roland and Brother Cyril to hang back. Margaret Maelchallain needed no word from him to know that this moment was hers. The girl guided her Irish pony to the centre of the square, as curious clansmen converged on her. Still dressed in her nun's habit, she reached into the woollen bag at her side and without a word drew forth the shrine of Saint Patrick's bell, hoisting it triumphantly over her head.

The men in the square all stood frozen as though thunderstruck. Then, amid cries of shock and joy they fell to their knees. Disturbed by the sudden clamour in the square, Hugh O'Neill came rushing out of his quarters and saw the girl with the shrine held high. He went down on one knee, crossing himself, then rose and hurried to Margaret's side, helping her slide down off the horse.

"My God, Meg, what have ye managed?" he asked, his voice choked with emotion as men all around rose to their feet and crowded in around the girl and her sacred treasure.

Aroused from prayer, Archbishop O'Connor appeared at the door of the church. He looked across the square at the growing crowd and at its centre he saw it, still held high over the girl's head.

The bell!

He leaned against the door frame for support as his knees went weak. He raised his eyes to heaven.

"Thank ye, Lord," he whispered and rushed to join the crowd celebrating the return of the relic.

Roland dismounted and Finn slipped off the back of The Grey as the uproar in the square brought more men streaming in from all sides, among them Cathal and Keiran O'Duinne. Declan saw his father and brother forcing their way through the crowd toward him and hopped off his mare to greet them. Cathal grasped his son in a bear hug.

"I'd not thought I'd see ye again, son," he whispered.

When Cathal released his embrace, Declan took Roland by the arm and pulled him forward.

"This is de Courcy's hostage, father, and my good friend, Sir Roland Inness."

Cathal's eyes darted between Roland and the girl in the centre of the square holding up Saint Patrick's bell and shook his head.

"I don't know how ye managed to collect the bell and yer friend and get back here alive, but it will be a story worth hearing," he shouted above the noise.

For a while, the men stood off to the side and watched the outpouring of joy in the abbey square. Roland leaned over and whispered to Declan.

"I can see now why she stole the thing."

Amidst the tumult in the square, Hugh O'Neill edged his way out of the crowd and managed to reach Declan and his companions.

"I'd not thought to see ye back here, O'Duinne," he said.

"I'd not thought I'd be back, my lord, but Margaret Maelchallain had other ideas."

O'Neill winced.

"I told the lass not to cause trouble," he said and sighed. "but following sound advice is not her nature. Still, she's done a grand thing here. Her name will be venerated by the Cenél Eoghain."

"Aye, she's a brave woman," Declan said. "They'll likely write songs about her, but taking the bell will prove easier than keeping it."

O'Neill stared at him.

"What do you mean?"

"My lord, John de Courcy has gathered a thousand men or more at Carrickfergus and may already be on the march. He intends to strike at Tir Eoghain and could reach the Bann in three days."

O'Neill's eyes grew wide.

"How do you know this? We've heard nothing."

Declan turned to Roland and motioned him forward.

"This is Sir Roland Inness, my lord, the fellow knight I spoke of and my closest comrade. De Courcy held him hostage as surety for my return. He escaped three days ago. While he was hostage, Sir John spoke freely to him of his plans to march against Tyrone once he received additional troops. Two hundred English mercenaries disembarked at Carrickfergus three days ago."

O'Neill looked hard at Roland.

"You saw these men?"

"I did, lord. I watched five cogs tie up in the harbour and I counted heads as the men came ashore."

"English mercenaries, you say."

"Aye, they wore mail after the English fashion and I was introduced to their captain at de Courcy's keep. They are English and veteran men, lord."

"And you saw others?"

"Aye, lord. Before the mercenaries arrived, I counted four hundred men already quartered in the town, some Irish and some English—and there are eighty English-bred warhorses in the stables there. I understand that de Courcy can also muster Irish levies."

O'Neill's shoulders sagged a little at this news.

"Aye. If he really intends to strike at Tir Eoghain, he'll have that many or more Irish from Antrim and Down to call upon, but tell me, Sir Roland, why would de Courcy confide his plans to you?"

"He invited me to join him, my lord," Roland said. "Three days ago, we stood on the curtain wall at Carrickfergus and watched the English mercenaries disembark in the harbour. He said there was land and gold to be had in Tyrone for men like me—once he'd chastised you stiff-necked Irish."

O'Neill bristled at the insult for just an instant, then he chuckled.

"Perhaps ye should have taken the man's offer, Sir Roland. If he crosses the Bann with a thousand men, it might be the better choice!"

Roland shook his head.

"My lord, I've kept company with a stiff-necked Irishman for five years. They make for better companions than de Courcy."

O'Neill smiled at that, but turned quickly back to business.

"I'm not surprised that de Courcy plans to strike against us, but I'd hoped to have more time."

"My lord, he now has six hundred men quartered at Carrickfergus. No baron, not even the King of England, would keep that many men fed and paid for long without finding a use for them," Roland said. "Three days ago he said they would march within the week. I believe him."

O'Neill nodded.

"And if I know John de Courcy, the loss of the bell will goad him."

"What will you do, lord?" Declan asked.

"I'll fight, by God!" he snapped. "I'll have scouts out at the fords over the Bann by day's end and I'll summon my men to Armagh."

"You believe he will strike here then?" Declan asked.

"Until now, I had not thought so. A year ago he struck north of Lough Neagh and last month he marched west from Down and reached as far as Tandragee. I had expected him to strike north toward Derry again, but the theft of the bell changes all that. De Courcy will take the loss as a personal affront. The Maelchallain rath is but three miles south of here and while they are Keepers of the bell, they hold it for the Archbishop of Armagh. De Courcy knows this. He *will* come for the bell, Sir Declan. Whatever his plans were, he will change them. He's coming to Armagh. I'd wager my best bull on it."

"You'll fight him here?" Declan asked.

O'Neil's face grew hard.

"I fear I must! This is sacred ground. I can hardly leave it to de Courcy without a fight," he growled, pounding a clenched fist into his palm. Declan and Roland glanced at each other.

Jerusalem.

" But I fear it won't be enough," O'Neill added with a frown and pointed across the square.

The sight made Declan's heart sink.

The half-moon banner of the Mac Lochlainns was nowhere to be seen.

"Gone?" Declan asked, shocked.

Seamus O'Cahan, Hugh O'Neill's most powerful clan chief, had torn himself away from the crowd still gathered around Margaret to join his chieftain. He heard the question and did not wait for Hugh to reply.

"Bastards slunk out 'for dawn this morn—too ashamed to do it in daylight!" he muttered.

"I can see they're gone, lord, but why?" Declan asked.

O'Cahan scowled.

"Conor Mac Lochlainn's position was weak and he knew it! Our people back Hugh, to the last man. His people waver. He knew if he pressed for the kingship now, he would fail. So he's left, and I say good riddance to him and to them all!"

Declan shook his head.

"You'll wish them back, lord."

Before O'Cahan could protest, Hugh laid a hand on the man's arm.

"Seamus, de Courcy is on the march with a thousand men. He may reach Armagh in four days, maybe less."

O'Cahan's face turned pale.

"Are ye sure of this, Hugh?"

"Aye, Seamus. I just bet my best bull on it."

***

Fifty miles to the northeast, a lone rider reined in his mount as he neared the fortified port of Carrickfergus. He'd ruined two horses in his haste to reach Lord de Courcy with Abbot Layton's message and now the Prince's castle was in sight, perched on the shore of the bay. He had been forced to slow the horse to avoid trampling any of the hundreds of men who were congregating around the coast road. The men were moving between scores of tents pitched along both side of the track. Some were cooking a noon meal, some sharpening weapons and some casting lots—all signs of an army waiting to march.

When he reached the shingle by the harbour he leapt from his saddle and hurried up the ramp and into the town. Guards tried to bar his way, but he waved a scroll with the seal of the Abbot of Down affixed to it and bullied his way to the very entrance of the keep. There the guards were less impressed.

"The Prince is done with audiences for the day," one guard said flatly. "Come back tomorrow."

The man stuck the parchment under the guard's nose.

"If I come back tomorrow it will be so I can see the birds peckin' at yer stinkin' head stuck up above the gate there," he screamed hoarsely, pointing at the entrance to the inner ward.

That gave the man pause and he snatched the scroll from the courier. He unrolled it and made a show of scanning the words, though he could not read a single one. He did, however, recognize the blob of red wax with the seal of the cross. That seal belonged to the tall, frightening Abbot of Down. He'd seen enough.

"Very well," he said officiously. "I will inform the Prince that he has a message from the Abbot."

***

Orders had been given for the army to march at dawn the next day, but an hour after the message from Down reached Carrickfergus, new orders were issued. Sir John de Courcy sat atop his magnificent white warhorse and watched as tents were struck, packs shouldered and men shouted into ranks by their sergeants. He knew they would not get far before darkness forced a halt, but he'd be damned if he'd sit idle after the report arrived from Down.

They had stolen his bell!

He'd immediately dispatched couriers to Down with orders relieving Sir Randolph Quincy of command of the garrison there and sacking Abbot Layton. He had entrusted his most precious possession to these two men and they had failed him miserably! But he reserved part of his rage for himself. The Abbot had reported the thieves had a letter of introduction—a letter that bore his own seal!

The moment his scribe read those words, he'd known. His suspicions about the Earl of Chester were no imaginings! This man Inness had already been exposed as Ranulf's man and his companions had used his letter of introduction to get near the bell. He couldn't fathom the Earl's purpose in these strange events. Perhaps he simply wished to stir the Irish up against him, but that hardly mattered now. The thieves had fled to Tyrone with the bell and he would have it back!

With the sun already low in the sky, the army of the Prince of Ulster lurched into motion, trudging west along the bay. As he rode, de Courcy was flanked by Sir Charles Oliver, captain of his English mercenaries and by the senior chieftain commanding his Irish troops. He slowed his horse to a walk and addressed them.

"I had thought to march north of Lough Neagh then swing south to strike at the O'Neill stronghold at Dungannon, but there is a new plan. We will march on Armagh. They have taken something of great value to me, and I expect I will find it there. If the Irish do not come out to meet us we will sack the town and destroy the church and the abbey there. I'll not want one stone sitting atop another when we are finished! If they do defend the place, we will crush them and then destroy the church and abbey. In either event, we *will* recover the bell of Saint Patrick. Patrick himself has assured me of this!"

The two men shot quick glances at each other, but rode on in silence.

***

Hugh O'Neill did not dally. Within the hour, a dozen men were dispatched to watch the fords over the Bann and four of his best riders were ordered to range further east and north to find John de Courcy and his army. More riders were sent west to summon the fighting men of the Cenél Eoghain clans to Armagh. With his scouts and messengers dispatched, he called a hasty meeting of his clan chiefs in the nave of Saint Patrick's church.

O'Neill asked Declan to collect Margaret from the crowd and bring her to the council of war. By now the crush around the girl had thinned a bit and he could see that the triumphant light in her eyes was fading into weariness. She looked wrung out, but the girl managed a small smile as he reached her side.

"O'Neill has called his chiefs together and asks you to attend," he said.

She gave him a sceptical look.

"I am no O'Neill chief," she said dully. "I must see to my own."

She doesn't know, he thought.

"Meg," he said gently, "Conor and the Mac Lochlainn chiefs have gone."

Margaret blinked in disbelief.

"Gone? Why would they go?" she demanded.

Declan spread his hands, a pained look on his face.

"The O'Neill men give dark reasons, Meg, but I don't know."

"Nor do the O'Neill chiefs!" she snapped. "They do not know Conor Mac Lochlainn."

"But do you really know him, Meg?" Declan asked, touching her arm. "I mean truly?"

The girls shoulders slumped.

"I wondered why I did not see him in this crowd. I had not thought he would go." she admitted sorrowfully.

"Nor did O'Neill," Declan said.

Margaret looked up at him.

"What will we do, Declan? De Courcy will come for the bell!"

"O'Neill knows that and I believe he'll fight him here at Armagh."

"Without Conor's men, he will lose," she said and stuffed the bell shrine back into her bag. She seemed at a loss of what to do next.

"Come, walk with me," Declan said and offered his hand.

She looked past him and saw the O'Neill chiefs hurrying toward the church

"The council...," she said, her voice weary.

"They can wait a bit for the Keeper of the bell," he said.

She nodded and let him take her hand. Together they walked across to the monk's quarters on the western side of the square, abandoned now by Conor Mac Lochlainn and his followers. As Margaret approached the empty building, she looked shaken.

"Tempers run high when thrones are at stake," Declan said gently as he led her to a wooden bench that sat against the wall of the dormitory. "Perhaps he felt he had no choice."

Margaret slumped down on the bench. She hung her head and twisted her fingers into knots, then looked up at Declan, her eyes red-rimmed.

"I don't think a man like you can understand Conor Mac Lochlainn. You never seem in doubt, even when you're wrong, but Conor...Conor has the weight of six generations of kings on his shoulders. It makes him doubt everything, including himself. He is a decent man, but proud. He knows in his heart that O'Neill would make the better king, but his pride will not let him accept that—will not let him be the first Mac Lochlainn in a hundred years to not be king of Tir Eoghain."

Declan looked down at the girl. He had not thought a woman with her spirit could ever be an object of pity, but at this moment she seemed genuinely pitiful. He laid a hand on hers to still their nervous movement and she did not pull away.

"Meg, I do not know what's in Conor Mac Lochlainn's mind, nor will I judge him. I may have been born into the Cenél Eoghain, but I've been gone ten years. I'm little more than a stranger here now, but this much I know. War is coming and if the men of Tir Eoghain do not unite, neither Mac Lochlainn nor O'Neill will rule here. De Courcy will."

Margaret gave him a dark look.

"We were united at Tandragee and still we lost."

Declan stood up.

"I've fought in three wars, Meg, and nothing is certain once swords are crossed. The English can be beaten, but not by the O'Neills alone."

"Then make my apologies to Hugh O'Neill and his chiefs," she said rising quickly to her feet.

"What will you do?" Declan asked.

"I will go to my chief. I will make him see. Conor Mac Lochlainn may not want O'Neill for his king, but he'll have John de Courcy if he will not listen."

***

He found Margaret a fresh pony and sent word to her young clansman that she would be in need of him once more as she went in search of her missing chief. The girl stood there, still half covered in mud, her face grey with fatigue, as they waited for her escort to arrive. She wearily wrapped a slender hand through her pony's mane to haul herself up, then stopped. She turned back to Declan.

"I've been a lot of trouble," she said. "I'm sorry."

Declan looked at her. There was a small clot of dried mud on one cheek and he gently brushed it away with his hand.

"Meg, you've been a great deal of trouble," he said, "and I'm not sorry for any of it."

For a moment the fatigue vanished from her face. She leaned in quickly and kissed him gently on the lips, then drew back.

"You're a good man, Declan O'Duinne," she said. "You should stay here."

Before he could reply, she turned and hauled herself up on her horse.

"I see my escort has arrived," she said, looking over Declan's head. He turned and saw the young warrior who had ridden with them to Down trotting up from the stables. He turned back to the girl, searching for the proper words.

"Meg...,"

She laughed at him.

"I didn't mean to cause more trouble," she said, but the look in her eyes said the opposite. She made a little clicking sound and the pony pricked up its ears and started forward. He watched her ride off to the west on the Dungannon Road until she was out of sight.

***

In the nave of the church there were heated discussions underway when Declan entered. His father was seated on one of the benches that had been pulled into a half circle facing Hugh O'Neill. He motioned for Declan to join him.

O'Neill had not missed his entrance and abruptly halted the debate, intercepting Declan near the door.

"Margaret?" he asked tersely.

"Gone, my lord. Gone to find her chief."

"The bell?"

"Gone with its Keeper."

O'Neill sighed.

"Meg's a hard-headed lass. I hope she knows what she's doing."

"She headstrong to be sure, lord," Declan said, "but she sees thing clear enough."

"Then let us hope she can lift the scales from Mac Lochlainn's eyes."

***

Through the long afternoon debate raged over how best to meet the new threat from John de Courcy. Most argued for defending Armagh to the death, relying on the high ground the church and abbey occupied and the presence of Saint Patrick's bell to make up for their lack of numbers. Hugh O'Neill chose not to tell them that the bell was no longer in the abbey town.

Others argued that defending the town without the Mac Lochlainn men was suicide.

"We should fall back and harass de Courcy wherever he may march!" Seamus O'Cahan demanded.

"And abandon Armagh?" Archbishop O'Connor asked sharply.

Before O'Cahan could reply, a man shouted from the benches.

"And how far shall we fall back, O'Cahan? To the Sperrin Mountains? To the western sea?"

"We've used the Sperrins as a refuge in times past," O'Cahan retorted, "and could again. I'll avoid the western sea as I cannot swim!"

That brought a chorus of laughter and not a few derisive hoots from the gathered chiefs.

Aidan Mac Gorley stood and pointed a finger at O'Cahan.

"Our raths are east of here, Seamus, and yours are out near the Sperrins. A retreat there would be convenient for you but disaster for us!" he shouted.

Hugh O'Neill rose quickly and raised a hand for silence. If the debate grew much more heated, weapons might be drawn. It was time to end the discussion.

"We will do what we must to defend Armagh," he said with finality. "If John de Courcy gains this place, we'll never get it back and it won't end here. Dungannon will fall and Omagh and Derry. De Courcy means to have all of Ulster, so we must stop him here. We have three days to prepare."

With that he adjourned the meeting. As the clan chiefs filed out of the church, Hugh beckoned Declan and Cathal to his side.

"Sir Declan, you did not speak," he observed. "Did you have nothing to say?"

"I didn't think it wise, lord. Would yer clan chiefs have listened to an outsider on a matter of this weight?"

This brought a small smile to O'Neill's lips.

"So you *do* have an opinion?"

"Oh, aye, lord. Only two choices were offered—starve in the Sperrins or be slaughtered here in Armagh. Neither looks good to me."

O'Neill frowned.

"You have a better plan?"

Declan shook his head.

"Not yet," he said truthfully.

O'Neill's frown deepened.

"Then ye'd best work on one," he said.

Conor Mac Lochlainn

*C*onor Mac Lochlainn called a halt at mid-afternoon by a clear stream with good grass for the horses. He and his clan chiefs had ridden fifteen miles up the rough road that ran northwest from Armagh toward Derry and would spend two more days in the saddle to reach the Mac Lochlainn stronghold there. The young chieftain wandered down by the stream as his men made camp. He had a need to be alone after a week filled with conflict and disappointment.

After the defeat at Tandragee, some of his chiefs had advised him to wait before making his bid for the kingship of the Cenél Eoghain, but he had insisted on quickly calling the council at Armagh. He knew that Hugh O'Neill would challenge him, but thought that, in the end, the clans would turn once more to the Mac Lochlainns for leadership. He'd been bitterly disappointed when they hadn't.

What made matters worse were reports that some of his own adherents had favoured O'Neill, among them Margaret Maelchallain. Her reported defection had been a particularly painful blow. As Keeper of the bell of Saint Patrick, the chief of the Maelchallains carried far more influence than the sept's small size would warrant. But the pain was more than political—it was personal.

He was in love with Meg Maelchallain—had been for years. He'd known her since he was a boy and even then he'd been drawn to her wit, her daring and, yes, to her beauty. Unlike most, she seemed entirely unimpressed that he was the King's son and that had made her friendship all the more precious to him. When his father had arranged his betrothal to Eamon

Maelchallain's oldest daughter, he'd been secretly overjoyed. Yet he'd never told her that.

Now she had turned to Hugh O'Neill to lead their people, or so the whispers suggested. And there were other reports that tore at him. Meg had been seen having genial conversations with this outsider, Sir Declan O'Duinne. This he'd dismissed as an innocent encounter until she had insisted on riding off with this stranger to Down. He could not help but feel a sharp pang of jealousy at the thought of it.

It had all been too much. He'd ordered his clans to pack up and head home. He sat down and leaned against a sapling, closing his eyes and listening to the gurgle of the stream. It had been an exhausting week.

***

"Conor!"

Mac Lochlainn jerked awake. For a moment he was unsure of where he was, then realized he had fallen asleep down by the stream. Standing over him was Trian Mac Shane.

"You have a visitor, Conor," Mac Shane said.

Conor scrambled to his feet, brushing leaf litter from his breeches.

"Who is it?"

"It's Meg."

Conor stopped brushing himself off.

"Thank you, Trian. Would you see her to my tent? I'll be along in a moment."

"Aye, Conor. I'll tell her that."

The young chief of the Mac Lochlainn clans watched Mac Shane head back to the campsite and took a deep breath.

It was time to see for himself where Meg Maelchallain stood.

***

She was standing outside the tent when he got there, looking more weary than he'd ever seen her.

"Meg, I'm pleased to see you safe back from Down. Please come inside," he said, holding the tent flap back. She nodded and stepped through the opening. He followed her through and helped her off with her cloak.

200

"I had not expected to see you here," he said. "Why have you come?"

"I had not expected to find you gone when I returned from Down," she replied, turning to face him. "Why did you leave Armagh?"

"Answer my question first," he said. "Why have you come here?"

"You are my clan chief," she said simply.

"Am I still, Meg? There are reports you have found a new chief to follow."

Margaret's face flushed at that.

"Have you set spies on me, Conor?"

Mac Lochlainn shook his head.

"I've not, Meg, but people see things. They hear things. They tell me you prefer Hugh O'Neill to be king. Is that so?"

Margaret stood very still in the centre of the tent as his question hung in the air.

"I do, Conor. I'm sorry, but I do," she said finally.

"You would have me submit to O'Neill then? Support him as our king?"

"Yes! I know you have a claim, Conor, perhaps the stronger claim to the title, but the O'Neill line is as royal as your own."

Conor Mac Lochlainn stared at her, his face pained.

"I had expected loyalty from my chiefs, Meg, especially from the Maelchallains. Especially from you…"

Margaret shook her head.

"Our clan has been faithful to your line for longer than we've guarded the saint's bell, but I will not see the Cenél Eoghain made slaves for the sake of the Mac Lochlainns. Your father was a good man, but no leader, Conor. You are a good man too, but you are not the man the Cenél Eoghain need at this moment."

"And Hugh O'Neill is," the young chieftain said bitterly.

"I believe he is," Margaret replied without hesitation. "He understands that we can have peace with de Courcy, but only at the price of our freedom. You think that price is bearable. He does not, nor do I."

"So you turn against me?"

"Not you, Conor, not you."

He turned on her, his face cold.

"I have tried to chart a course that might save our people from destruction. I am sorry that in so doing, I've lost your regard, Meg. You are leader of your clan and must do as you think best for your people. I will release you from our betrothal," he said. "It seems your heart lies elsewhere these days—with O'Neill and perhaps with this new man, come from England."

"Conor Mac Lochlainn!" she lashed out. "You may do as you wish with the marriage agreement our fathers made. I've never once heard from your own lips that you approved of the match in any case! As for Declan O'Duinne, he is a good man, but ill-disposed to be my suitor after what I did at Down."

"Did he make advances?" Conor asked, suddenly concerned.

She couldn't suppress a laugh at the notion.

"Sir Declan? No! He was at all times proper with me, even when I angered him."

"How did you anger him?"

"I stole back our bell," she said simply, reaching into her bag to draw it forth and handing the bell shrine to the shocked clan chief. Mac Lochlainn's eyes grew wide

"My God, how…"

Margaret shook her head.

"I did not intend to do it, but the damned English abbot maligned my father's good name and I lost control of my senses for a moment. After that, of course, it was too late."

"I can see why this Sir Declan was upset with you," the young man said, the anger drained from his voice. "It was a foolish thing to do, Meg. You might have been killed—or worse."

Conor handed the bell shrine back to her.

"But it's a miracle," he said in a hushed voice.

"And we are now in need of another," she said.

"What do you mean?"

"Conor, John de Courcy is marching on Armagh with a thousand men. He could be at the Bann in three days and Armagh in four. I believe O'Neill will defend the place."

"He'll lose," Mac Lochlainn snapped.

"Perhaps," she said, "but at least he will fight and the Maelchallains will be with him. Will you, Conor?"

The Gathering Storm

A score of warriors from the O'Duinne clan, bristling with axes, spears and shields, were the first to answer Hugh O'Neill's summons, their lands being only six miles away along the Blackwater River. Finbar Mac Cormaic, perched atop a shaggy pony, followed them into the square at Armagh. Cathal O'Duinne and his sons were there to greet them as they marched in.

Next to arrive were fifty warriors of the O'Hagan clan. They had been sighted on the Dungannon Road at noon and trooped into the square an hour later after a long march from their raths near Tullyhogue.

Roland stood next to Declan as they filed into the square.

"How many more do you think?" he asked.

"The O'Neill men should be here from Dungannon by tomorrow. Hugh says he expects two hundred warriors from his own clan. But he worries about the O'Cahans. They have over a hundred men, but their raths are out near the Sperrin Mountains. Seamus O'Cahan sent his best rider on his fastest horse with the summons, but it could take three days or more for them to reach us. My father says the other septs might bring another hundred all together.

"So, half the strength de Courcy has—if the O'Cahans arrive in time."

"It's good Lady Catherine taught you sums," Declan said grimly, "though yer answer provides little comfort."

"Aye, no comfort at all. How many will this Mac Lochlainn bring if he returns?

Declan rubbed his chin.

"They took heavy losses at Tandragee. I'd guess he has no more than three hundred men fit to fight."

"Can eight hundred defend this town?"

"Well, I'd not count on those three hundred from Mac Lochlainn, but let's have a look at the ground," he said and headed up the hill toward the church.

Roland followed him through the graveyard on the east side of the church and out to the crest of the hill. From this vantage point, a grassy slope fell away steeply to the north.

"Good high ground here, Dec," he said.

"Aye, but that road troubles me," Declan said, pointing to the dirt track that came in from the northeast, then turned west and ran along the base of the hill. "That's the road we travelled to get here from Carrickfergus and if de Courcy marches on Armagh, he'll likely so the same."

Roland looked at the road snaking over rolling green fields to the northeast. He walked along the crest of the hill toward the west following the road's course as it curved along the base of the slope before passing over a low rise and turning south. A quarter mile on, it intersected with another road running off to the west.

Where the roads met just west of the abbey, there was nothing but gently rolling fields and pastureland that came right up to the edge of the abbey grounds. He shook his head. From that quarter, Armagh would be very difficult to defend. Declan joined him.

"See the problem?" he asked.

"Aye. If we can't block that road, de Courcy will just follow it around and attack from the west. We'll be hard pressed to hold the place if he does."

Declan looked back to the northeast. He could see for miles in that direction and it was a beautiful sight—green rolling hills to the horizon. But beyond that horizon, he knew John de Courcy could already be on the march with twice the strength O'Neill could muster—and he'd bring with him veteran mercenaries and heavy cavalry. On proper ground, O'Neill's outnumbered clansmen might hope to make a stand against a force such as that, but while the hill he stood atop was good ground to defend, the road was a fatal weakness. Flesh and blood, no matter how courageous could not stop heavy cavalry down on level ground like that.

"I doubt the road can be held against de Courcy's cavalry, even if Mac Lochlainn brings in his men," he said. "I'll have to tell O'Neill."

Roland laid a hand on his shoulder.

"Better you than me."

***

"You would have us abandon Armagh without a fight?"

Hugh O'Neill rose from his seat at the suggestion, his face turning crimson.

"Do you not understand what this hill and this church means, O'Duinne? Your own brother died at Tandragee to keep it out of English hands as did many another good man. Now you would have me tell my clan chiefs we can't hold the place? That they must abandon their raths and flee into the Sperrins to live like wild animals?"

Declan did not flinch from O'Neill's anger. He had expected it.

"My lord, I do understand what Armagh means to the Cenél Eoghain, but that does not change the fact that the road de Courcy is likely to come down runs right around the high ground to open fields and pastures!"

"We'll block the road." O'Neill insisted.

Declan shook his head.

"Ye've seen what English cavalry can do to foot on open ground like that, my lord. They'll punch right through whoever you put there to block the road and be in your rear in short order."

O'Neill brushed aside his words as though shooing away annoying flies.

"If Mac Lochlainn rejoins us, we can make a fight of it! Or would you have us turn tail and flee?"

"No lord. I would not have you flee and certainly not to the Sperrins. If de Courcy drives the Cenél Eoghain into those mountains, I doubt you'll ever recover your land. The English can be beaten, but not if they can ride into Armagh from the west on level ground. We must find another way."

"Another way? If yer friend here is right," he said, pointing at Roland, "de Courcy could be crossing the Bann in two days!"

***

It was growing dark when Ronan Mac Ada guided his horse off the road and into a strip of trees that grew along the banks of the River Lagan. He had ridden hard since before dawn, covering twenty miles of bad road from the River Bann to reach this place. A half mile to the north was a ford over the Lagan. He planned to cross it at first light, but first he had come here.

On the far side of the river he knew there was a neck of land protected on three sides by a bend in the river. And on that neck of land a motte had been rising since early in the spring. It would be completed by winter, but it was not the fortress that interested him. This protected neck of land would be an easily defended place for an army to pass a night.

He slid off his pony and tied the reins to a branch well back from the river. He crawled on his belly through the underbrush until he reached the riverbank. From there he had a good view of the far shore, but in the dim light of dusk he could see nothing but trees lining the northern bank of the river and the top of the earthen mound set back from the water. He settled in to wait.

Soon he began to hear faint sounds—a horse whinny, the clatter of metal on metal and muted voices. Perhaps it was just a labour detail wrapping up their work on the mound, but then he saw a score of men troop down to the river to fill wooden buckets with water. This was more than a work detail.

He lay there for another half hour as the darkness grew, then he saw a light flare among the trees opposite him, a campfire being stoked. Then he saw another and another. By the time it was full dark he counted almost a hundred fires. He turned and crawled back through the brush to his horse and mounted. He'd found what Hugh O'Neill had sent him to find.

Now, darkness be damned, he had to get back to Armagh.

***

Dawn brought clouds and thick fog that clung to the low places beneath the hill of Armagh. The stone church atop the hill seemed to float above the surrounding countryside. Three men and a boy sat around Cathal O'Duinne's cookfire waiting for a small cauldron of porridge to come to a boil. Finn, who'd claimed a preference for sleeping in the stables, had joined them as soon as it was light and stood eagerly over the pot with an empty bowl.

"Yer new squire looks hungry," Declan said.

Roland sniffed.

"I can't afford a squire."

"Neither could Sir Roger when he took on a second one, as I recall."

Roland gave him a sour look and changed the subject.

"Now you've slept on the problem, have you a plan to beat de Courcy? Your man O'Neill seems averse to fleeing to the Sperrins. He sees only one course, defend Armagh to the death."

Before Declan could answer, Cathal O'Duinne spoke up.

"Fagan and I spent a summer and fall in the Sperrins two years ago when de Courcy threatened Derry. Those mountains can barely sustain a few hundred fighting men in any season. The clans cannot shelter their women and children there. They'd all starve! If we let de Courcy drive us into those mountains, the Cenél Eoghain are finished. Better to die here on the hill of Armagh."

Those gloomy words cast a pall over their gathering, save for Finn.

"Porridge is ready!" he announced eagerly, stirring the thickening mixture with a wooden spoon.

Declan looked across the fire at Roland.

"No great plan came to me in my dreams, Roland. I'm good with this," he said holding up his sword, "but yer the planner—what say you?"

Roland frowned.

"We know more about what de Courcy brings to the fight than what the Irish will bring, what with the Mac Lochlainns in doubt and the O'Cahans fifty miles away. Hard to make a plan around that."

Declan sat silent for a while, poking at the fire with a long stick.

"What we need is time," he said, "time for the O'Cahans to reach us and time, I pray, for Mac Lochlainn to have a change of heart."

"If it's more time you need, I doubt John de Courcy will oblige," said Roland.

Declan stood up and dropped his stick into the flames.

"Then we mustn't leave it up to him. He has to cross the Bann to get here. Perhaps we can slow him there."

Roland stood up.

"Then let's ride out that way and have a look."

Seeing the two knights stand, Finn hastily shovelled porridge in his mouth and held up a finger.

"I'll fetch the horses, my lords," he managed as he gulped down two more spoonfuls of breakfast.

***

The road that ran northeast from Armagh was better than most. It was a pilgrimage route for the faithful from Antrim, who from time to time made the trek south to worship at Saint Patrick's church and to see the Saint's bell on feast days. Thus Tomas O'Connor, Archbishop of Armagh, set aside funds to have brush cleared away and logs set in the low places to smooth their path. Pilgrims brought offerings to Armagh, so it was only good business.

Three riders followed the road as it ran through gently rolling hills for seven miles. Two miles from the River Bann, the hills gave way to land as flat as a tabletop and nearly treeless. The riders reined in atop the last of the high ground as a weak sun broke through the clouds. Patches of fog still clung to low land beyond the hills, but the riders could make out a dark line in the distance—a fringe of trees marking the river's course.

They covered the last two miles at a canter and drew up at the ford. Here the banks of the river were low and the Bann was only sixty feet wide. Roland clucked to The Grey and guided the horse out to mid-stream. There was a stiff current, but the water only rose to the horse's belly.

"Not much of a barrier for a warhorse," he said.

"It's dropped a bit since we crossed a week ago," said Declan, edging his mare up beside the big grey gelding.

As they headed back to the western bank, they saw Finn craning his neck and looking past them to the other side of the river. They turned to see a rider approaching the ford from the east. The man was in a hurry, but reined in sharply when he saw horsemen on the opposite bank. He hailed them.

"Hello at the ford!" he called out in Gaelic.

Declan stood up in his stirrups and leaned forward.

"Hello to you!" he called back. "Are ye O'Neill's scout? I'm O'Duinne."

The man had been sitting tensely atop his pony, ready to turn and flee if need be. Now he leaned forward and stared back for a long moment. Then he relaxed and guided his horse into the stream.

"I'm Ronan Mac Ada," the man said as he drew near. "I recognized yer English horse. Yer that Irish knight that took Meg Maelchallain to Down."

Declan could not help but smile at that.

"Aye, and I barely survived the journey!"

The man urged his dripping pony up on to the western bank. The tired animal struggled to make it out of the water.

"Best ye not stay around here overlong," he said as he reined in beside them. "I sighted the English army camped eighteen miles to the east last night. They could reach the river by sunset."

"I'm obliged for the information," said Declan.

Roland turned to Finn.

"Give this man yer horse, lad. His looks all used up."

Finn didn't argue, nor did the scout. They switched mounts hurriedly.

"I'll be on to Armagh then," Mac Ada said.

"After ye tell O'Neill about the English, give him a message from me," Declan said. "Tell him if he'll give me forty men with shovels, I can give him another day before de Courcy reaches Armagh."

The man looked puzzled for a moment, but then gave a curt nod of his head.

"Aye, I'll tell him, just what ye said."

"And tell him they'll need ponies as well."

"Aye, shovels and ponies," he said, turning his new mount's head to the west. Then he stopped and looked at Finn.

"Obliged to you fer the fresh horse," he said, then headed off to the west at a fast canter.

"Forty men with ponies and shovels?" Roland asked. "It sounds like you have a plan."

Declan shrugged.

"Not to beat de Courcy, just to slow him down."

"That's a start," Roland replied, "but tell me how you'll slow down a thousand men with forty?"

Declan turned back to the river.

"We begin by ruining this excellent ford," he said and climbed down from the chestnut mare. "As it is, a sow with shoats could cross the river here in less than a minute."

Roland hopped off The Grey and joined him where the road emerged from the river onto the gentle slope of the west bank.

"Aye, this is no good," he said.

"No good at all," Declan agreed. "So this is where we dig a trench." He scrambled off the road and walked downstream along the bank. For fifty feet the bank was clear, but beyond that oak and beech and willow grew right up to the river's edge. Declan stopped there.

"We dig to here," he said.

"And to the trees there," Roland added pointing upstream. "If we dig it wide enough and mound the earth, even The Grey would balk at making the jump!"

"Aye," said Declan. "They'll have to send infantry across to drive us off, then fill in the ditch before the horses can cross,"

"With forty men defending the ditch, that will take time, but we can't hold forever," Roland said with a frown. "Once de Courcy takes the ditch and brings over his cavalry, it will go poorly for our lads. Ponies won't outrun English-bred horses on this open ground."

"That's where yer wrong," said Declan with a grin.

He walked back up to the road and motioned for Roland to join him. He followed the road for a hundred paces and stopped. A stone's throw from where they stood a half dozen of the shaggy Irish cattle browsed lazily on spring weeds. Roland looked across the open grassland and shook his head.

"This looks no better than the fields near Armagh," he said. "Good ground for cavalry."

"Looks can be deceivin'," Declan said with a small smile. "This isn't a pasture, Roland. It's a lovely peat bog!"

He motioned for Finn to come up. Finn nudged his pony in the flanks with his heels and trotted up beside them.

"Finn, lad, be so kind as to drive those cows up here on the road," he ordered.

The boy gave a little whoop, and guided the pony down off the road and into the bog. Despite its fatigue, the sturdy little horse splashed through the shallow pools and the muck with ease and the boy soon had the cows on the move. For a second time in days, Declan had the strange sensation of seeing his younger self, but now the sight of the boy did not bring melancholy, it brought hope.

He edged his own mount off the road and guided the chestnut mare in amongst the tussocks of moss and grass. A few yards in, the mare began to struggle, its hooves sinking deep into the black peat. The horse balked at going further. Declan swung around in his saddle and looked up at Roland on the road above him.

"Now *this* is lovely ground for heavy cavalry," he said.

"Point taken," said Roland.

***

It was late afternoon when they saw riders coming up the Armagh road. They counted only thirty men, but they all carried shovels, spears and axes. Cathal O'Duinne rode at the head of the column and Declan recognized most of the men behind him as warriors from his own sept. Bringing up the rear on his long-legged mare was Brother Cyril.

212

"Hugh would have sent more," Cathal explained, "but there were only thirty shovels to be had at Armagh. It's only thanks to Brother Cyril we found that many. He begged his Augustinian brethren for help and they emptied their tool shed. Felt they owed him for retrieving their bell."

Declan nodded.

"Thirty will have to do then."

Fight at the Ford

Men dug as though their lives depended on it. All through the late afternoon and into twilight they dug. Riders appeared on the far bank of the Bann and watched them, then turned and spurred off to the east. Night fell and still they dug, piling the black earth of the river bank behind the growing ditch. It was past midnight when Declan called a halt to their labours. The trench was six feet wide and four feet deep with another four feet of packed earth on the far side. It was a hundred feet long and slashed across the road just feet from the river's edge.

Their work done, men set aside their shovels and lay down behind the ditch to await the dawn, their weapons close at hand. Roland sent Finn to watch the horses and with strict instructions to ride away if it looked like their ditch was being breached. The boy started to argue, but Roland cut him off.

"Squires never dispute their master's orders," he said.

"So I am to be yer squire, lord?" the boy asked eagerly.

"Not if you argue with me, now see to the horses, lad."

Finn ran off to the tree line where the ponies were tethered. Roland saw Brother Cyril sitting on the newly-built berm and sat down beside him. Both men had taken their turns with the digging and both were covered in black mud.

"I had not thought to see you here," Roland said. "Did the labours of your Augustinian brethren grow wearisome?"

Cyril laughed at that.

"Not so much wearisome as boring, lord! For a few days, I found the simple routine of the abbey to be a tonic, but by the third day.... I mean really, day after day, work, pray, pray some

214

more, then work and finally bed, only to be roused to pray in the middle of the night? No, lord, monastic life is not for me. I think I found my calling as chaplain to the Invalids!"

"And they are lucky to have you, Cyril."

"Thank you, sir."

Roland slapped the monk on the shoulder.

"Best get some rest. There'll be hot work come morning."

Cyril yawned and slid down behind the earthen berm where he curled up in his mud-covered robes. In the darkness, he was nearly invisible against the black earth.

***

The men dozing fitfully along the ditch heard the enemy before they could see them. Across the narrow river a horse nickered and a man coughed. Soon, whispered voices could be heard, carried across the water in the dark stillness. Men reached for their spears and axes and peered over the earthwork toward the eastern bank. Slowly the darkness gave way to a ghostly predawn light and the grey shapes of trees on the far bank emerged like phantoms. A thin layer of fog hung over the water itself as men gripped their weapons and waited.

Then it came—a dozen arrows buzzed by overhead and others buried themselves in the black dirt of the berm. There was a grunt of pain from a lone man who had ill-advisedly taken that moment to stand and relieve himself. The arrow struck him in the back of the neck and he never finished his morning toilet.

"Damn! They have archers," Declan hissed.

"Longbowmen, I'd guess, given the range," Roland said, keeping his head down. "Probably Welsh."

Men flattened themselves against the reverse slope of the berm and waited for another volley, but none came. Instead a new sound reached them, the sound of pounding hooves. Declan raised his head in time to see a score of men on mail-clad warhorses pounding down the road and plunging into the river.

"Here they come," he said quietly.

Roland peeked over the berm and drew an arrow from his quiver.

215

"It appears the Prince does not wish to be detained," he said as he nocked the arrow.

"Aye," Declan replied, "he thinks to punch right through with this lot and scatter us."

"And they will if those horses get over the ditch," Roland said as he stood quickly and loosed a shaft at the lead rider. It struck the man full in the chest, toppling him over the haunches of his charger and into the river. He sank out of sight, but managed to gain his footing and stand up, waist deep in the river. He looked dazed, an arrow protruding from his hauberk.

"Good quality mail," Declan observed.

There was no time to reply as the charge of the heavy cavalry reached midstream. Roland rose again and loosed a second arrow, striking a rider in the helmet. It knocked the man senseless. He toppled into the river and did not rise.

Before he could loose another shaft, an arrow struck him a glancing blow on the thigh, tumbling him backwards, but not penetrating his mail. He scrambled to his feet and drew his short sword. Declan had his broadsword ready as the wall of men and horses splashed out of the water.

Three riders in the lead whipped their mounts forward. The warhorses gathered themselves on their massive haunches and attempted to leap the ditch and berm. Only one cleared the barrier and gained any purchase on the mud of the berm. The others fell short and slid back down into the muddy trench and became hopelessly tangled with each other.

One rider was crushed beneath them as they thrashed about trying to escape. The other managed to crawl out of the ditch and stagger back toward the river. An O'Duinne clansmen leapt the trench and ran him down when he was knee deep in the river, dropping him with one vicious swing from his axe. The clansman was cut down before he could scramble back to safety.

The lone rider who gained the top of the berm was instantly attacked from both sides as O'Duinne men rose up and pulled him from his saddle. His riderless warhorse bolted off down the road toward Armagh. Seeing the chaos at the trench, the other riders drew back. A zealous few dismounted and tried to cross the ditch and scale the dirt berm on foot. They did not survive the effort, being met at the top by a wall of spears and battleaxes. Even good mail could not save the men from this onslaught. Their bodies slid back down to be trampled by the frantic horses still struggling to escape the ditch.

With six men dead, the rest turned and rode for the eastern bank of the Bann. A few of the O'Duinne men stood atop the berm to jeer at them as they retreated across the ford, but scrambled back behind their hasty earthwork as more arrows whistled past them. The warhorses floundering in the trench finally managed to haul themselves out. With their riders dead, the two horses stood about nervously at the river's edge for a moment, then plunged back into the stream to follow the retreating riders who were nearing the opposite bank.

It had all taken less time than it took to savour a cup of good ale.

"What's next," Declan asked as he rested his back against the mud of the berm, "infantry?"

"I'd imagine," Roland said and drew another arrow from his quiver.

***

"How many men hold this damned ditch?" de Courcy demanded of his cavalry commander. The man would not meet his gaze.

"I'd guess sixty or seventy, my lord."

De Courcy mentally halved that number. Beaten commanders always exaggerated the enemy strength.

"Do you know what it costs me to keep you men in good horses, sir? Do you?"

"No, my lord," the man croaked.

"For that expense, I expect my cavalry to produce better results, but we will do a proper accounting of your worth another time. For now, you will stand aside and let my foot shoo away these O'Neill men. Scouts say the ground west of the river looks to be pastureland. Once we are over their ditch they will scatter like so many grouse. Those my infantry don't kill, I expect you to! Is that understood?"

"Perfectly, my lord!"

***

It was midmorning when the Irish levies made their charge. They entered the river at the run, their column six men wide and twenty deep. The front ranks carried shields and those that followed crouched as they came on.

"They must've heard there was a longbowman over here," Declan said as he watched the men splash into the Bann.

Roland didn't answer. This was a greater threat then the cavalry had been. He nocked his first arrow and loosed it into the middle of the column. One of de Courcy's Irishmen took it in his neck and pitched forward adding a ribbon of red to the green-brown water of the Bann. Men around him crouched lower, but kept moving. At midstream, the water came to a man's chest, and the headlong rush slowed. Three more of Roland's arrows found their mark, but now de Courcy's foot began to reach shallower water. A low growl came from their ranks as their charge regained speed.

Then they struck the ditch.

The front rank dropped into the trench, turned on their backs and braced their oaken shields above them. Men in the ranks behind used the shields as stepping stones over the ditch and onto the mound behind. In seconds, a dozen men had gained the berm and were scrambling up it. The men of clan O'Duinne rose to meet them. This was war as the Irish knew it. Sword and spear, axe and dagger, with nothing between a man's heart and his enemies' blade but cloth and skin.

Declan and Roland vaulted to the top of the berm as de Courcy's infantry clambered up the muddy sides. Declan did not bother thrusting. There were too many targets as men came swarming across the shields bridging the ditch. He drove them back with long sweeping slashes of his broadsword. None could find a way to get inside the killing arc of that blade and survive.

"Come on!" Declan taunted them in Gaelic, his blood up. "Come see what the Cenél Eoghain have for ye!"

One eager young warrior heard the challenge a he splashed out of the river. He looked up at the swordsman on the berm. The men ahead of him had seen their comrades fall to the red-haired warrior at the centre of the line and were edging to the left and right to avoid the man's deadly broadsword. Declan saw the man staring at him and knew the look. This man would not shy away from his blade. Whether the lad wanted reputation or thought he could not die, he came straight in, raising his long-handled axe as he ran toward the berm. Declan watched him come and saw him plant his foot on a shield in the ditch. The edge tilted and the young man lurched off balance to the right. A moment later, he slid down into the ditch with neither life nor reputation left to him.

To his right, Declan heard Roland screaming English oaths at the Irish. None could understand the words, but none would mistake their meaning as Roland's blade grew stained with blood. To his left, Declan saw his father hacking at men with his long-handled axe as though clearing a field of saplings. He dodged to his left as a man with a long spear jabbed at him. Below him, the trench was filling with the enemy dead and wounded, but he knew the O'Duinne men were taking losses of their own. As with all battles, the issue here would be decided by who broke first.

There was a final surge from the men from Antrim and Down that was met at the top of the berm and turned back. Finally, the carnage at the ditch was too much. Somewhere an order rang out and was repeated down the line. Men drew back from the berm and the trench, dragging wounded comrades with them back across the ford.

Declan breathed a sigh of relief and slid back down behind the mound of dirt, breathing hard. It had been a close run thing. He looked down his own lines and saw six of the O'Duinne men sprawled lifeless behind the berm and others binding up wounds. They could not sustain another attack. He rolled over and looked at Roland.

"When next they come…"

He didn't need to finish his thought. They both knew it would be time to run.

***

Hugh O'Neill arrived at noon along with a half dozen of his own O'Neill warriors, men who formed his personal guard.

With him was his herald, Keiran O'Duinne. Cathal and Declan saw the riders coming and went to meet them a hundred yards up the road from the berm.

"Best dismount here and walk, Hugh," Cathal advised. "There are archers on the far bank."

O'Neill glanced off toward the river and hopped off his pony. As they moved toward the berm at a crouch, he turned to Declan.

"Ponies and shovels," he said shaking his head. "If it wasn't for yer sire, I might've ignored that request, lad, but he's convinced ye do know how to beat these English. For my part, I thought I'd find ye all dead or halfway back to Armagh by now. Didn't see how ye could slow down an army with but thirty men, but damned if you haven't!"

They reached the berm and O'Neill crawled to the top to look over. A score of bodies or more lay piled in the ditch on the other side. More men lay on the river bank and a few, partly submerged in the stream, jerked as though still alive as the current tugged at them. O'Neill slid back down behind the muddy mound and shook his head.

"Ponies and shovels," he muttered to himself.

***

A hundred yards from the ford, John de Courcy paced back and forth across the road and stared at the far side of the river. He turned to the man standing beside him.

"Captain Oliver, we've wasted most of a day trying to cross this river. I want you to take your men across and fill in that damned ditch. It's time you started earning your pay."

The last comment was clearly a taunt, a fact not lost on Charles Oliver. Since the day Sir Roland Inness made him look the fool in front of the Prince, de Courcy had used that humiliation to goad him. It rankled, but in his business there was no profit in challenging your paymaster, so he had swallowed the insults.

The blow he'd taken to his knee as Inness escaped had left him with no permanent injury—except to his reputation and in his work, reputation was everything. When some of his own men proved bold enough to make jests at his expense, he'd knocked heads together to put an end to that. Still, the injury to his pride stung. He looked across the river and wondered if the man who'd done him that injury might be over there with the Irish. De Courcy suspected Inness had fled to Tyrone. Though Oliver had come to doubt much of John de Courcy's wild speculations, in this, he hoped the man was right. Killing Inness would do much to restore his standing with his men and with future employers.

Oliver looked across the river at the trench and the berm and the bodies. He'd seen worse. His men would make short work of this primitive little earthwork and its Irish defenders.

"Consider it done, my lord," he said.

It was late in the afternoon when Oliver led his English mercenaries into the River Bann. Two hundred strong they came, draped in good mail and carrying shields. They did not hurry as had the Irish, for to lose footing on the mucky river bottom might doom a man so heavily armoured. But they came on steadily.

De Courcy mounted his magnificent white stallion and rode back to where his column of heavy cavalry was assembled on the road, waiting patiently for the Englishmen to clear the ditch. Once done, these horsemen would have their chance to avenge their losses from the morning. But he would not leave the outcome to chance. When the cavalry went in, the Prince of Ulster would lead them.

He drew his longsword, rested it across his saddle and waited.

***

Roland sent a half dozen clothyard shafts at the men crossing the river, but they were aware of the threat from the archer on the far bank and kept their shields high. Declan tapped his shoulder.

"Time to go," he said.

Roland loosed one more arrow and stepped away from the berm. Together they ran for the trees where their horses were tethered. Hugh O'Neill, his guard, and the O'Duinne warriors were all mounted on their ponies.

Finn was waiting for them and handed Declan the reins of the chestnut mare and Roland the reins of The Grey. Brother Cyril was already mounted on his lanky bay mare.

"You understand the three of us will be on the road, lad," Roland said to Finn as he climbed up on The Grey. "These big brutes will sink in the bog and so will those horses coming across the river. You stay on your pony and stay with the O'Duinne men—all the way back to Armagh! Understood?"

"Aye, lord. Ye already told me that," the boy replied tartly. He grabbed his pony's mane and dragged himself up. "Don't let the Prince catch you!" he added and dug his heels into the small horse's flanks. The other riders were already fanning out into the bog and the boy easily caught up to them.

"I like the lad's advice," Declan said as the first English mercenary managed to hoist himself up to the top of the mud berm. "He'll make a good squire."

Roland shook his head, then guided The Grey up onto the Armagh road. Declan and Cyril joined him and all reined in fifty yards from the berm. Mercenaries were clambering up and over the mound and some were starting to loosen the packed mud with their swords, pushing it down into the ditch. None made any effort to advance toward the riders sitting and watching them. That would be the cavalry's job.

***

De Courcy saw Captain Oliver's signal and led his mounted men across the Bann. The ditch had been filled in across the width of the road and the horses bounded up and out of the ford without hesitation. As he reached level ground, de Courcy saw three riders mounted on English-bred palfreys watching them from up the road and wondered who they were. In these parts few would have such mounts. He knew his slower warhorses could not hope to ride them down and so he paid them no further mind.

North of the road he saw more horsemen mounted on Irish ponies moving slowly to the west across the open grassland. Their lack of haste puzzled him, for on open ground like this, he knew his heavy cavalry could catch the smaller Irish ponies. He turned to one of his lieutenants and ordered him to take forty men and chase down the riders north of the road. The rest he would lead on toward Armagh.

The man saluted and barked orders to the riders behind him. He spurred his horse in the flanks and the big animal plunged off the road. Three riders followed close behind. Within yards, all were flailing in the sucking mud and hopelessly mired. Seeing the danger, de Courcy whirled around and screamed at the next rider to halt. The man managed to back his horse out before it became entrapped in the bog. De Courcy leaned forward and stared at the ground beside the road.

A peat bog!

He knew of no bogs like this in Antrim or Down, but he had seen one, years ago on a campaign north of Lough Neagh and should have recognized the signs! He cursed under his breath, then quickly sent up a prayer of contrition. This had been his own fault. He'd already lost most of a day to this unexpected rebuff at the ford and it had galled him. He'd been too hasty, too careless, too certain.

God punishes the prideful!

He looked across the flat expanse of the bog at the horsemen lurking there. Most had halted and were looking back at him, but some were beginning to edge back toward the road. Their ponies splashed through the standing water and managed to keep their footing in the spongy peat. They did not charge. They simply picked their way across the firmest ground they could find until they were close enough. Then their riders began to hurl their throwing spears at the men jammed together on the road.

A prickle of apprehension ran through him. He'd faced light cavalry like this before—hobelars the Irish called them. They had always been easily driven off by his own heavier mounted troops, but now, protected by this damned bog…

Perhaps it would be best to move on to Armagh.

He turned and ordered the column forward. The word was passed to the rear and the infantry began crossing the ford. North of the road, the men on ponies waited to greet them.

***

223

For two hours they harassed the advancing English host tramping along the road, darting in on their ponies to strike at them with throwing spears. A squad of Welsh longbowmen tried to protect the column, but they could not be everywhere. The men on the road shouted curses at these nettlesome riders and vowed vengeance, but could do little else. To leave the road would have been death.

When the English column finally reached firmer ground, the riders melted away and found smaller paths that joined the Armagh road miles ahead. Declan, Roland and Cyril were waiting at the rendezvous as the riders straggled in. Men and horses were caked with mud, but the three on the road were relieved to see Cathal, Keiran and Finn among them. When the last man closed up on the road, Hugh O'Neill counted heads. No one was missing.

O'Neill rode up beside Declan and looked up at the young knight aboard his much taller mount.

"Ye've given me an extra day, Sir Declan and I'm in yer debt. Now let's be on to Armagh and see what use I can make of yer gift."

The Eve of Battle

*T*wilight had settled over Armagh when a sentry on the road saw them coming and galloped up to the church to pass the word. Clansmen hurried into the square to greet the mud-spattered riders. Many had expected the next riders to appear from the northeast to be de Courcy's men and cheered at the sight of their chieftain as he led his exhausted men into the abbey town. Archbishop O'Connor hurried down from the church to meet him.

"You look like hell, O'Neill," he said with real concern.

"And I feel the same, excellency, but we bought ourselves another day."

"Then it was time well spent. You'll be pleased to know that the last of your own clansmen arrived in the early afternoon and the O'Cahans are just two hours away. When they arrive, you'll have over four hundred men!"

Hugh O'Neill gave the churchman a weary smile.

"That is good news, Tomas. Now do ye suppose ye could ask some of your monks to bring up buckets of water? My lads did themselves proud, but it was filthy work."

The monks from the abbey were immediately put to work hauling oaken buckets up from the abbey well to the square where men lined up to scrub off the dried mud from their clothes and faces. Declan had just turned a bucket of cold well water over his head when he saw Margaret Maelchallain coming toward him across the square. He squeezed the water from his hair and went to meet her.

"You're back," he said simply.

"Aye, and yer alive," she said with visible relief. "I arrived this morning to find you had gone off to the Bann to fight de Courcy with thirty men. It did not sound promising."

"I told ye I knew how to beat the English," he said with a grin.

"Aye, ye did, but ye didn't say ye'd survive the effort."

"I never expect to die, Meg."

Margaret laughed at that.

"Then one day yer in for a big surprise, Declan O'Duinne! But tell me, are the English beaten?"

"No, not yet. But we bought time and now O'Neill has most of his men here."

"Plus forty from the Maelchallains," she added. "My clan will stand with the O'Neills to defend Armagh."

"And Conor Mac Lochlainn?"

The girl's face fell.

"I think not. I begged him, but he is too proud."

"Too proud to listen to his betrothed?"

The girl started to answer, but seemed to notice for the first time the crowd of men standing nearby.

"Come and walk with me," she said.

He followed her as she walked up toward the church. It was fully dark now and as they walked, she looked up at the night sky. There were portents of rain, with low clouds blotting out the moon and stars. She sniffed the air.

"Storm coming," she said.

Declan nodded. He felt it too.

When they reached the edge of the slope that fell away to the north she froze. A half mile from where they stood, scores of campfires blazed in the night casting a ghastly yellow glow on the low-hanging clouds.

John de Courcy had come to Armagh.

"So close!" she gasped.

"Aye, I expect they'll come at first light."

"Do we have a chance?"

Declan wanted to reassure the girl, but this was no time for lies.

"Not much. Not without Mac Lochlainn's men."

Margaret's shoulders slumped.

"I thought I knew him," she said sorrowfully, "I truly did."

"You did what ye could, Meg. It's all any of us can do."

The girl did not speak for a while as she stood and looked at the evil glow in the northern sky.

"After this is all done," she said, "if you live, what will you do?"

"Go home, I think, back to England...back to Shipbrook. And what of you, Meg?"

She gave a short bitter laugh.

"Well, there is to be no marriage to Conor Mac Lochlainn. That's for certain! And in another three months, my brother will take the leadership of the clan. There won't be much expected of a clan chief's spinster sister I presume. Perhaps I'll put back on the nun's habit and take vows."

Declan reached over and took her hand.

"That would be a terrible shame," he said and drew her to him. She did not protest, and in the glow of the enemy campfires, he kissed her and she kissed him back. When at last they drew back she wrinkled her nose and giggled.

"You smell like a peat bog," she said.

"My apologies," he said with a grin.

She raised a hand to touch her lips, her eyes shining.

"That was my very first proper kiss, Sir Declan," she said and stepped back into his arms.

"But not yer last," he said and kissed her again.

***

The Compline bells had rung when Declan saw Margaret back to her quarters. Returning to his father's tent, he found Roland sitting with Cathal and Keiran around the cookfire. He beckoned to his friend and together they walked out into the square. It was practically empty as men made preparations for the next day or tried to get some rest.

"Tomorrow will be bad, I think," he said as they walked.

"It doesn't look promising," Roland agreed.

"It's not too late for you and Cyril and Finn to ride south to Dublin."

Roland shook his head.

"I've spoken with Cyril. He won't leave. The boy was sleeping last time I checked. I'll let him rest, then order him to get clear before things begin."

Declan nodded. They had walked across the square and out to the Dungannon Road that passed through a gap between the monk's dormitory and the stables on the western edge of the abbey. Here were the open fields where de Courcy would no doubt array his heavy cavalry on the morrow. Roland kept walking and Declan followed until they came to the place where the road from the northeast met the westward road that ran from Armagh to Dungannon. Roland stopped and turned around, looking back up the road toward the abbey. He stared at the scene for a long time, then muttered something to himself.

"Gad, Roland, speak up!" Declan implored. "Have ye thought of something?"

Roland shrugged.

"Nothing brilliant, but your trench down at the ford put me in mind of something. This road passes between the dormitory and the stables," he said. "The walls of both buildings are near as high as the walls of Shipbrook."

Declan looked at the layout of the buildings and understood instantly what Roland was thinking.

"If we can block up this one road and barricade the gaps south of the stable…," he said in an excited voice.

"It might not stop them," Roland said, "but they will pay hell getting into the abbey."

"I knew you had a plan in you!" Declan said and slapped Roland on the shoulder. "Let's go find O'Neill."

***

The last of the O'Neill clans rode into Armagh on their shaggy Irish ponies as the monks filed down through the square at the end of Compline prayers. The O'Cahans, one hundred twenty strong, had covered the fifty miles from their raths near the Sperrins in two days.

An hour later, Hugh O'Neill called his chiefs together on the hill behind the church. Margaret Maelchallain was there as chief of her clan as was Cathal O'Duinne who brought Declan with him. They stood beside Seamus O'Cahan, Turlough

O'Hagan and a half dozen chiefs from smaller septs as Keiran O'Duinne lit a torch and O'Neill issued his orders for the defence of Armagh. The clan chieftain used a sword to draw an oval in the dirt.

"Here is the hill and here is the church," he said, marking a cross on one end of the oval. "De Courcy is here," he said, pointing his sword tip just north of the oval. "We will form lines twenty paces below the crest of the hill here to block his way directly into the town. If we are pushed back to the hilltop, I will give the signal to fall back to the church to form a new line."

Declan nodded. O'Neill was showing a clever grasp of terrain and tactics. He would use the steep slope to maximum advantage, but if his men were forced back to level ground, that advantage would be lost. Retreating the hundred yards to the church would allow him to reform his men into shorter lines between the church and the abbey buildings.

O'Neill took the point of his sword and scraped out a furrow that ran toward the oval on the ground, then curved around the hill.

"This is the road Sir Declan says we cannot hold. I've looked at the ground there and, sadly, I must agree with him. We all were at Tandragee and saw what de Courcy's heavy cavalry did there. I won't make the mistake Mac Lochlainn made."

There was a low buzz of agreement at that.

"But that leaves the western approach to the town open."

The buzz of agreement turned to worried muttering.

"So we are going to barricade every road, alleyway and garden path on the west side of the abbey that opens onto the square. If we can keep their heavy cavalry out of the town, we have a chance. I've spoken to the Archbishop and even now his monks are blocking every way into town from that quarter. I want the O'Duinne and O'Hagans to man those ramparts. My O'Neill men, the O'Cahans and the Maelchallains will hold the line here on the north slope."

No one spoke. O'Neill glanced over at Declan who gave him the slightest of nods. It was a simple plan, but with barely five hundred men to defend the abbey town against twice that number, it had merit. It did not ensure victory, but did guarantee that the English would endure a bloodbath to take the place. Having nothing better to offer, Declan held his peace.

"Are there any questions?" O'Neill asked. No one spoke.

"Then see to your preparations. Assemble your men when you hear the bells toll the hour of Prime and may God and Saint Patrick be with you and the Cenél Eoghain on the morrow."

The gathering broke up as a stiff wind picked up from the west. Off in the distance, there was a rumble of thunder and a flash of lightning. Declan felt a first fat drop of rain slap against his arm as the storm approached

O'Neill gestured for Margaret to stay behind.

"Meg, I am indebted to you—for all ye've done. You are the Keeper of the bell and leader of yer clan—and no man could have done better. But none here expect ye to stand in ranks with yer men when the fighting begins. Be here on the morrow and show the men that Saint Patrick is with them, The Archbishop will bless the men, then both of you must shelter in the church once we are engaged."

Declan stole a glance at the girl and saw her bristle.

"As you say, O'Neill, I am the Keeper and the leader of my clan. I would just be in the way in the shield wall, but I will not cower inside the church. The Maelchallains need to see their leader is with them and all the Cenél Eoghain need to know the bell and the spirit of Saint Patrick has not fled at the sight of the enemy. I will stand with my men!"

O'Neill sighed.

"Yer a headstrong woman, Meg. Do what ye will."

***

The fat drops of rain turned into a downpour as Declan and Margaret sought shelter in the entrance to Saint Patrick's church.

"This plan of O'Neill's," she said over the pounding of the rain, "will it work?"

"It's as good a plan as any, given the men we have," Declan said, trying to sound more confident than he was.

230

The girl stood quietly for a long time watching the rain beat down on the cobblestones of the abbey square.

"I've...I've not been in a battle before, Declan. I'm afraid."

"So am I," Declan answered honestly. "A battle is a dreadful thing."

"But I'm leader of my clan. I'm the Keeper. I must be there...," she said, her voice trailing off. She lay her head against his chest, shivering in her soaked clothes. He wrapped her in his arms and stroked her hair.

"Duty is a hard master," he whispered to her.

***

While he waited for Declan and his father to return from O'Neill's war council, Roland shared Cathal's cookfire with Finbar. Raindrops hissed and sizzled on the hot coals as the storm blew in. The old counsellor looked across the fire at him and shook his head.

"Cathal has ordered me out of Armagh by morning," Finbar said, his voice resigned. "He's knows I'm of no use as a warrior, so I'm to mind the rath till he returns. But what of you, Sir Roland? Why are you staying here. If I was an Englishman about to be caught up in this fight, I'd think about saddling my horse and riding for Dublin—tonight."

Roland shrugged.

"I sometimes feel only barely English, but for this fight, I will be Cenél Eoghain. Did Declan not tell you? I'm an adopted O'Duinne."

Finbar snorted at that.

"Oh, I did hear something about that—boys swearing blood brotherhood! Very touching, but this is no boy's game, Inness. There's a good chance we all die tomorrow. You should go."

"With respect, Master Mac Cormaic, boys or not, Declan was my family when I needed one. I've come to Ireland to watch his back, and that's what I will do."

"Then God help ye, lad," Finbar said and shuffled into the tent to pack his kit.

Finbar's words made Roland think of another boy. He left the fire behind and headed down the hill as the rain began to fall in sheets. He found Finn in the stable, curled up on a stack of hay near The Grey's stall. He shook the weary boy awake.

"My…my lord," Finn stuttered.

"Sorry to wake you lad, but we must talk."

Finn rubbed his eyes and sat up. Roland sat down beside him.

"The English will attack tomorrow," he said.

"Aye, lord. We all know that."

"I want you gone from Armagh when they do."

Finn frowned.

"Do not squires stand with their masters in battle, lord?"

"You are not my squire, Finn. You can sleep until you hear the bells toll the hour of Prime. Then you will saddle The Grey and ride south. The first good patch of trees you find that way, hide yourself there. If I don't come for you in a day, do not come back here. Find your way to Dublin. Take ship for Chester in England. When you reach there, you will go to a place north of the city called Danesford. Folk in Chester will know of it. Tell them at Danesford that I've sent you. You'll be welcome there. Do you understand?"

"Aye, lord," the boy said quietly, "Dublin, then Chester, then Danesford."

"Good lad! I know you have money, Finn, a good deal of it from Sir Declan and me, but not enough to buy your passage to Chester. Sell The Grey in Dublin if you must to pay your way. You'll get a good price."

He reached in his belt and drew out a dagger. A bright red stone was set in the handle. He passed it to the boy hilt-first.

"Take this with you. It is for my son. He will be at Danesford."

Finn took the dagger. It was a blade that had once belonged to the assassin Ivo Brun. He looked up at Roland.

"I'd a been a good squire," he said, his eyes welling. Then he turned away, but Roland had already seen the tears he wished to hide.

Onslaught

Sir John de Courcy, Prince of Ulster, looked up through the driving rain at the thin line of Irish troops arrayed near the top of the slope. Their line curled around the crest of the hill with the spire of Saint Patrick's church visible behind them. De Courcy frowned. It was good ground to defend, particularly with the storm turning the grassy hillside slick.

He looked off to the west and squinted through the downpour. His scouts had reported that the road curving around the hill to the west was clear, but he could hardly believe it. He had expected the Irish to block that road and defend it to the death. For if the steep slope on the north side of Armagh's hill was good ground to defend, the western approach to the abbey town was anything but. There was nothing west of the abbey but open ground and the gentlest of slopes.

He shook his head. These Irish might fight like devils, but they were children when it came to planning a real battle. Now he would make them pay for their failure to block the westward road. He'd decided that he would not destroy Saint Patrick's church, but where the abbey now stood he would raise a motte. Then any who made the pilgrimage to Armagh would do so only on his sufferance.

He wiped the rain from his eyes and peered once more up the hill at the centre of the Irish line. Standing in front of the line was a man de Courcy knew all too well. Archbishop Tomas O'Connor, prelate of the Irish church, stood with his arms outstretched exhorting the defenders, his fine linen robes hanging sodden on his thin frame. De Courcy uttered a soft curse. He'd offered O'Connor his full support as head of the

Irish church. In return, he'd only asked the man to stay neutral in this fight. He now had O'Connor's answer, but no matter. Irish priests had roused their countrymen against him on other battlefields and had died for their trouble.

Of more interest was the woman who stood beside the Archbishop. She held an object aloft and even at this distance, there was no mistaking the shrine of Saint Patrick's bell. He felt his face grow hot, even in the chill rain. He had counted on his victory at Tandragee and his seizure of the bell to leave the men of Tyrone disheartened and in disarray. Now they had the bell back and had gathered once more to fight him.

He wondered if the woman parading the shrine before the Irish host was the one who had stolen it from Down, but that was of little consequence. De Courcy leaned forward in the saddle, as though he might simply reach out and pluck the treasured artefact from the woman's hands. Then he rocked back and stared up the hill grimly. He had taken the bell once from the dead hands of a clan chief and it mattered not to him if he took it now from the dead hands of a woman.

Patrick had promised it to him!

As he looked up the hill, he saw a single banner snapping in the blustery wind. Emblazoned on it was the familiar blood-red hand of the O'Neills. That was no surprise. He'd known he'd never seduce the O'Neill chief. He was pleased to note the absence of the crescent moon banner of the Mac Lochlainns. De Courcy had thought the young Mac Lochlainn heir could be bought, but he'd not received an answer to his offer of peace. Perhaps the boy was straddling the fence, awaiting the outcome of this campaign before picking sides.

Foolish lad, he thought. *My price for peace will be higher, once O'Neill is off the board.*

De Courcy counted no more than three hundred men at the top of the hill, further evidence that not all of the Cenél Eoghain had rallied to the call. He had five hundred Irish foot at his command, men from Antrim and Down, ordered to be here by their chiefs who now answered only to him as Prince of Ulster. It was more than enough men to send against the thin Irish line atop the hill.

He called forward the commander of his Irish levies. When the man reached him, he pointed to the top of the hill.

"Drive those men off that hill and hunt them down," he yelled above the roar of the storm. "I do not wish to see them again a month from now on some other field. I want them dead! Is that understood?"

"Aye, yer grace," the man shouted back.

"And you see the woman there, the one with upraised arms?"

"Aye, lord."

"If you or your men take her, the thing she holds in her hands is mine! Any man who thinks to keep it for himself will wish he had not. Is that clear?"

"Aye, yer grace. None of my men will touch the thing."

"Good man! Now wait for my word to advance."

The Irish commander hurried back to his men and began barking out orders in Gaelic.

De Courcy twisted around in his saddle and looked down the column formed up on the road behind him. Waiting patiently in the rain were four score men mounted on English-bred war horses. These were the men who had broken the Irish line at Tandragee a mere month ago. On that field, his horsemen had slaughtered hundreds of these stubborn Irish.

Standing in ranks behind his heavy cavalry were his mail-clad English mercenaries, veterans all. He sent word for his cavalry commander and Captain Oliver to come forward. When they arrived, he pointed up the Irish line.

"My Irish infantry will occupy those men on the hill," he shouted. "Once they are engaged, we will follow this road and attack the abbey from the west. The ground is good there. If the Irish on the hill haven't broken by the time we enter the abbey, we will take them in the rear.

He pointed toward the woman on the hill, still holding Saint Patrick's bell high overhead.

"I know not who that woman is, but she has my bell and I will have it back! If they run, we will follow them, come what may. If I am wounded, or my horse stumbles and falls, you are not to turn aside. Is that clear?"

"Aye, your grace," both men shouted back.

"Return to your men and wait for my command," he ordered.

The cavalry commander wheeled his warhorse around and trotted back to join the rest of the horsemen on the road. Captain Oliver trudged back through the mud of the road to where his men stood in ranks.

De Courcy now motioned to a lieutenant to send the archers forward. A few shouted commands were issued and the Welsh longbowmen, all business, tramped forward through the pelting rain and planted their spare arrows into the ground at their feet. They drew waxed bowstrings from their tunics where they had secured them against the rain and strung their bows. He'd only been able to hire a score of the Welshmen, but that should be sufficient to further thin the ragged line on the hill before he sent in his infantry.

As the Welsh archers prepared for their first volley, de Courcy looked back up the hill at the sodden ranks of Irishmen and shook his head.

They never learn, he thought.

***

The movement of the archers had not gone unnoticed up the hill. A sharp command from Hugh O'Neill brought the Archbishop and Margaret Maelchallain hurrying back to the rear of the Irish lines. Both were drenched

"Best get back to the church," said O'Neill brandishing his shield as they passed. "Those robes won't stop an arrow."

The Archbishop nodded to the burly chieftain.

"God be with you, Hugh, and all here this day," he said as he passed.

"And with you," Hugh said absently, as he watched the movements on the road at the base of the hill.

Roland Inness stood a few feet away from Hugh O'Neill. He had chosen to begin his day atop the hill where he could more readily use the range of his longbow. He watched the Archbishop retire to the church and looked at the girl who was trailing behind him, trying to shield the ornate bell shrine with the sleeves of her robe. Her black hair clung wetly to her cheeks and her dress was soaked, but her eyes were shining and her jaw was set in grim determination. To his surprise, she stopped and picked up a shield. Roland turned to O'Neill.

"My lord...the Lady Maelchallain ..."

Hugh O'Neill frowned and shook his head wearily.

"You try talking to the lass, Inness. She'll not listen to me. Says the men will lose heart if she runs to the rear with the bell."

Roland watched as Margaret raised her shield and crouched behind it, ready to receive whatever the English sent her way. Below, he heard a barked command in Welsh. It was one he'd heard before and he raised his shield.

Below, twenty longbows were drawn in unison. The distinct snap of twenty bowstrings sounded and a score of arrows arced through the rain, falling among the Irish on top of the hill. Most struck nothing but mud at the feet of the defenders or were impaled on linden wood shields, but two men, less careful than the rest were struck and went down. An angry growl rose up from the packed ranks of the Irish. Men began to bang swords and axes on their shields and shout insults at the Welsh archers gathered at the bottom of the hill.

"Steady, lads," O'Neill called, as the next flight of arrows dropped from the stormy sky. Roland caught a shaft on his shield then set it aside to quickly draw a waxed string from his leather jerkin and string his longbow. He nocked an arrow and turned to O'Neill.

"With your permission, my lord."

"By all means, Sir Roland."

Roland looked over the heads of the Irish warriors closely packed to his front. He could see the archers below reaching for their next arrow. He elevated his bow, drew the string back to his ear and loosed an arrow into the storm. A moment later the first Welsh archer lurched backwards into a pool of muddy water, a clothyard shaft in his chest. Roland had come to know many Welsh bowmen during his time fighting with Llywelyn and hoped that none of those men were down below.

More's the pity if they are, he thought.

He nocked another arrow and drew his longbow.

***

237

John de Courcy watched as four of his twenty Welsh archers died one after another. He hastily ordered men forward with shields to protect the remainder. A moment later, men in the massed ranks of his infantry began to fall. He had counted the shafts and the time between shots and knew it was but a single man—but a man with damned good aim. He unhooked the shield strapped to his saddle and raised it to his chest. His exquisite mail shirt would protect him from edged weapons, but not an arrow with a bodkin head.

He knew not where the Irish had found a longbowman, but was thankful they had not found more. One archer, no matter how good his aim, could not stop what he was preparing to send up the hill at O'Neill's men. He sent word back for the Irish foot to advance.

A dull drum beat began as the men of Antrim and Down shook out into a line three-deep for the attack. More commands rang out and men began moving forward up the grassy slope, their leaders screaming at them to stay together and keep the line solid.

De Courcy watched them go. This was the only moment in a battle that left him anxious. Once the lines met and men began to hack and stab at each other, the worry departed, replaced by a wild quickening of the blood. He was a man born to war and knew it. Some might say his lust for battle was a sin, but he knew better. His love of battle was all part of God's plan. The Almighty had been vexed by the Irish for too long and had sent John de Courcy to chastise them.

***

On the hill, Roland watched as the line of Irish warriors moved up the slope. He sent arrow after arrow into their ranks as their leaders screamed at the men to move faster and stay together. On top of the hill men hurled insults down at the approaching attackers. Somewhere a chant rose up and spread down the entire length of the Cenél Eoghain line.

"O'Neill, O'Neill, O'Neill!" they roared.

Hugh O'Neill raised his hand high overhead as the enemy line drew within twenty yards of his men. When he dropped it, a hail of spears came whistling out from the rear ranks of defenders. The spears tore ragged gaps in the enemy line, but these were quickly closed. Roland loosed his final arrow, laid his bow down and drew his short sword. It would be close work now.

On both sides, men sent up fervent prayers, gripped their weapons tighter and girded themselves for the carnage about to descend on the hillside. Some screamed defiance, some cursed the enemy and some pissed themselves in terror, but none turned aside, their fear of dishonour stronger than their fear of death. The shouted orders of their leaders meant nothing now as the two lines met with a sound akin to the rumble of thunder.

Shield met shield, axes arced overhead, swords and spears hacked and thrust, seeking exposed flesh. Men began to fall onto the wet grass of the hillside, some dead, some wounded and some simply losing their footing and being trampled in the melee. Once down, few rose again.

Roland looked over at Hugh O'Neill. The man had dismounted and, taking his battleaxe in hand, moved along the centre of his line, letting himself be seen by his men. The clan chief was short and squat, but on this day he carried himself like a warlord. Roland had but a moment to admire the O'Neill's mettle, before a huge man with a two-handed sword managed to burst through the line to his right.

The man turned to strike at a defender from behind, raising his long blade overhead for a killing stroke. Too late, he saw a blur of motion as Roland's short blade drove in under his armpit. The sword slid in and out in the blink of an eye. The man screamed, staggering backwards and sat down hard on the grass. Blood foamed at his mouth as he slowly toppled over, a surprised look still on his face.

The gap in the line sealed, Roland looked to his left and saw Margaret Maelchallain , still clutching her shield and holding the bell of Saint Patrick to her breast with a free hand. There was a look of horror on the young woman's face. Courage she had aplenty, but butchery such as this she had never witnessed. He hurried to her side.

"My lady," he shouted. "You've done your duty here."

He pointed to the bloodbath a few yards to her front.

"We cannot afford to lose the bell or its Keeper just yet. Please get to the rear."

The girl didn't seem to hear him, her gaze fixed on the chaos before her. She turned to Roland and tried to say something but no words would come. To her front a man staggered backwards and fell at her feet, a spear in his chest.

"Go!" Roland screamed and shoved her toward the rear. She dropped her shield and ran for the church as Roland turned back to the fighting.

Here and there along the line, de Courcy's men were breaking through, but each breach was quickly closed. Off to his left, Roland saw Hugh O'Neill twice use his battleaxe to strike down men who had managed to hack their way through the ranks of defenders and into the rear. Near the clan chief, he watched Keiran O'Duinne kill one of the Irish levies with a vicious one-handed slash of his sword.

At the foot of the hill, he saw that de Courcy had waited for the assault to begin before sending his heavy cavalry up the road to the west. He caught sight of the last few riders disappearing around the hill. The English mercenaries followed them at a steady trot up the muddy road. Soon they would be striking the defenders at the western barricades.

From where he stood, Roland could see that the O'Neill line, was bending, but not yet breaking, though the sheer weight of numbers was pushing the defenders back. The rear rank was already standing on the level ground of the hilltop.

Time to fall back, he thought.

***

Down the hill and to the west, men stood anxiously behind hastily built barricades of overturned water troughs, farm carts, barrels of ale, benches from the nave of the church and any other solid objects the monks could find to block the spaces between the buildings. An hour before, they'd all knelt beside these barriers as Margaret Maelchallain paraded Saint Patrick's bell before them and Archbishop O'Connor called upon almighty God to give them strength.

Now, from up the hill and beyond the church, they heard the chants for O'Neill and the sound stiffened their resolve. Then the chanting on the hill ceased, replaced by a sound like a thousand swords being forged on a thousand anvils, a chaotic wall of noise that heralded a battle being joined.

The fight for Armagh had begun.

Along the barricades, men stood to their posts, gripping their spears and axes and waiting for the assault they knew would come. Declan stood next to his father atop an overturned bench. Forty men stood with them to guard the longest of the barriers, thrown up between the lay monk's dormitory and the stable. It was here that the Dungannon Road entered the abbey grounds and ran right up to the square. Smaller barricades blocked alleyways and farm paths that ran between the buildings south of the stable.

To his front were green pastures and a few patches of rye and oats, no doubt to brew the abbey's ale, but his attention was fixed on the road coming in from the northeast. It was from that quarter that trouble would come. He did not have long to wait as a tall man on a white charger came over the low rise where the road swung around the hill of Armagh. Behind him came a column of heavy cavalry. The men were spattered and smeared with the mud of the road, but they were still a splendid sight, clad in mail and mounted on the finest English-bred horses in the north of Ireland.

They followed the road south as it ran along the western edge of the abbey, passing in front of the O'Duinne and O'Hagan clansmen as though on parade. When the lead rider reached the Dungannon Road he held up his arm and the column halted. At another signal, the riders wheeled their horses to the left to face the abbey. The man on the white horse edged his mount forward, studying the barricades that had been thrown up between the buildings.

Declan watched him turn in his saddle and look to the north where over the rise came a thick column of foot soldiers marching up the muddy road. These were the English mercenaries Roland had seen at Carrickfergus, the same men who'd taken his trench at the ford on the River Bann. He doubted a few carts and barrels would stop them, but it was better than nothing. He drew his broadsword as the English infantry formed up in front of the horsemen.

***

Brother Cyril rooted through his few belongings in the dim interior of the wattle and daub hut he shared with eight other Augustinian monks until he found what he was looking for. It was a short sword he'd carried with him all the way from Chester—a gift from the men of the Invalid Company. Until this moment he had not felt a need to take it from its leather wrapping, but he had just seen the English mercenaries forming on the Dungannon Road and thought it was time.

He was a man of peace and would not go out of his way to kill another man, but neither would he stand about like some sacrificial lamb to be slaughtered. Sir John Blackthorne, the finest swordsman in the Invalid Company had given him some rudimentary lessons in blade work and he had once been forced to defend himself during a bloody melee on the banks of the River Conway. Since then, there'd been many prayers of penance for the man he'd killed there, but he made no apologies to God for having survived the encounter himself.

He popped out of the opening to the hut and was met by one of his new friends among the monks of Armagh. The man looked askance at the blade in Cyril's hand.

"No need for that, brother," Brother Cormac said. "Stay with us. We will hide you."

Cyril was touched by the man's offer, but knew that to accept it would only get them both killed. De Courcy would suspect that the monk who had lied to him and engineered the theft of Saint Patrick's bell would be somewhere here in Armagh and would leave no stone unturned to find him. Better to die a swift and honourable death than to fall into that man's hands!

"No, brother," he said, giving the blade a few tentative swipes. "It's an Englishman who's about to sack your abbey. It's my duty as an Englishman to stop him!"

***

The downpour had eased to a light rain as Captain Charles Oliver halted his column in front of de Courcy's cavalry and looked at the flotsam stacked between the buildings. He was not impressed. He trudged through the ankle deep mud to de Courcy's side to await the man's orders. The Prince pointed to the barricades.

"Captain, it seems our Irish friends insist on putting impediments in my way. I would like your men to clear a path through that rubbish. You can manage that—can't you?"

Oliver gritted his teeth and bit back the angry retort he wanted to deliver. He looked up at De Courcy.

"We'll clear the way for you, my lord," he said grimly.

For an moment, John de Courcy wondered if this was what he had looked like twenty years ago when he had led a handful of his fellow knights into the north to find his destiny. He expected it was and the thought did not displease him. He beckoned the man closer and leaned down to issue his orders.

"Once you clear a path for my cavalry, Captain, you are to move with your men up toward the church. If the O'Neill men on top of the hill have not yet broken, you will take them in the rear. I will lead my cavalry into the square behind you and that will be the end of Hugh O'Neill!"

Oliver looked up at the man and had to suppress a shiver. There was a gleam of madness in de Courcy's eyes that unsettled him.

"And, Captain," the Prince continued, "as I told my Irish troops, I want no prisoners. After this day, I want the power of the Cenél Eoghain broken forever!"

"No prisoners, my lord?"

"You heard me, Captain. Together we will kill them all. Is that clear?"

Oliver drew his sword and looked at the thin line of clansmen peering over the top of the barricades.

"Aye, lord, kill them all," he agreed. "And the church? Its treasures are ours?"

De Courcy nodded.

"But only at the end of the day, Captain, only after all the Irish are hunted down. Then you may take what you will, though any holy relics are mine."

The Englishman nodded. This would be a fine bonus for a day's work. Perhaps enough to make him forget the bloody work he'd been ordered to perform and the insults he'd had to swallow.

He turned and called his sergeants to him. These were men who'd stormed castle walls. He was certain these pitiful barricades would not stand long before them. He divided his force into two, the smaller group to test the barricades south of the stable. He would command the bulk of his men assaulting the barricade on the Dungannon Road. Before he released the sergeants he beckoned them in close.

"No prisoners," he said.

Abbey Square

Declan glanced down the line of men mustered at the barricade across the Dungannon Road. The gap between the monk's dormitory and the stables where the road entered the abbey spanned a good thirty yards, but only forty men manned the makeshift barrier there. With smaller barricades to defend south of the stables, it was all that could be spared to block this main entry into the abbey grounds.

He had picked his way carefully up the jumbled pile of benches and barrels and found a spot with good footing and a clear line of sight. The view was not encouraging. To his front, he watched a tall man striding in front of the assembled English mercenaries and barking out orders. A small group peeled off from the formation and moved to the south—no doubt to assault the barricades there, but the main body—well over a hundred strong—stayed formed-up on the Dungannon Road.

Up the hill behind him, the roar of battle waxed and waned, but he paid little mind to what was happening elsewhere. He had trouble enough to his front, where out on the road the leader of the English mercenaries was pointing a sword directly at him and screaming a battle cry. With a roar, the mercenaries charged the barricade.

Declan shoved his steel helmet down snuggly on his head. It looked to be a hard morning ahead.

***

Archbishop O'Connor stood in the doorway of the church and saw Margaret Maelchallain come running around the corner of the building. He anxiously beckoned for her to join him and shelter inside. She saw the churchman and started to run to the doorway, but stopped. She looked down at the shrine she still held in her hands then back at the Archbishop. He was waving frantically at her to hurry, but she did not move.

Behind her she could still hear the sounds of the bloody mayhem at the crest of the hill. Across the abbey square, a new roar rose up as the English began their assault on the barricades there. She knew Declan was down that way and felt a wave of concern and a pang of guilt. If not for her theft of the bell, the young Irish knight and his companions would likely be on a boat bound for England now instead of facing death in a fight not of their own making.

O'Connor was shouting something at her, but she could not hear his words. She felt frozen with indecision. It would be very easy to run to the church, to hand the thing to the Archbishop and seek sanctuary there, but she knew in her bones that would be futile. A man like de Courcy would respect no sanctuary that stood between him and what he wanted.

She looked again at the bell and found herself wishing Saint Patrick had lost the damned thing in a bog. She wished she had not stolen it, wished she had not brought it here to Armagh along with the carnage that followed in its wake. The bell and its shrine only weighed a few pounds, but at this moment it felt like she was carrying an anvil.

Still, that morning she'd watched as men prayed and wept at the sight of it. Burden or not, it could still inspire men to fight and she would not be the one to hide it away in some sacristy when it was needed most. She turned away from the church door and walked to the centre of the square. There was a high cross there, tall and weathered and older than any in Armagh could recall. Margaret climbed up on its pedestal and stood there, the bell cradled in her arms.

Come what may, she was the Keeper.

***

North of the church, the steady pressure from below had finally forced O'Neill's line back to the hilltop. Roland waited to hear the signal to fall back, but none came. He looked off to his left and saw no sign of Hugh O'Neill. For a dreadful instant, he thought the clan chief had fallen, then he saw that the man had forced his way into the front rank of defenders, wielding his axe with a savage fury.

He'd seen this before—leaders getting caught up in the battle fury and losing themselves in the fight. Richard of England was famous for leading from the front rank in battle and men loved him for it, but there was a time and place for personal valour and this was not one of them. The O'Neill men needed a commander, not another axe man.

He ran down the line toward the clan chief but saw O'Neill was too entangled in the fighting to be distracted. He caught sight of Keiran O'Duinne who had fallen in behind his chief, protecting the man's flanks in the melee. Roland grasped the herald by the arm and pulled him to the rear.

"Give the signal!" he screamed over the din.

Keiran hesitated. He looked back at O'Neill, desperately hoping for some sign from the clan chief. Roland grasped his tunic.

"Blow the damn thing or we're all dead men!" he shouted.

Keiran O'Duinne had been at Tandragee. He'd seen what happened when a line was broken and men put to panicked flight. He drove his short sword into the ground at his feet, raised the horn to his lips and blew three long wailing notes.

All along the crest of the hill men had waited for the sound of the horn. When it came, scores of O'Neill men in the rear rank pulled their last throwing spears from the ground and hurled them at the attackers. This sudden rain of missiles felled dozens of de Courcy's men and caused others to draw back. As the enemy recoiled, the men at the top of the hill began a slow withdrawal toward the church and the abbey grounds.

Hugh O'Neill heard the horn as well and the sound seemed to break the spell of the battle madness that had fallen over him. He backed away from the line and turned to Keiran O'Duinne, raising his bloody axe in salute

"Good lad!" he shouted. Kiernan plucked his sword from the ground and returned the salute.

In the brief respite granted by O'Neill's spearmen, the clansmen of the Cenél Eoghain slowly fell back, with O'Neill and Seamus O'Cahan bellowing at them to stay together. The hail of spears had forced de Courcy's Irish troops to recoil, but the sight of their enemy retreating helped rally them. Over the crest of the hill they poured now, sensing the O'Neill men were breaking.

Roland watched as O'Neill and O'Cahan formed their men into shorter lines between the church and the abbey buildings on either side. The Cenél Eoghain clansmen locked shields as the men of Antrim and Down came howling across the hilltop and crashed into them. The lines staggered but held—for the moment.

Across the square, Roland could hear that the battle had been joined along the barricades blocking the western approaches. He turned and ran toward the barricade blocking the Dungannon Road where he'd last seen Declan. As he sprinted across the square, he saw Margaret standing at the foot of the high cross holding the bell shrine, but did not pause to speak. He reached into his quiver as he ran and found only three arrows left there.

When he turned the corner of the monk's dormitory, he saw Declan standing atop the barricade, a shield in one hand and his broadsword in the other. The shield had two crossbow bolts embedded in its face. He cursed. At close range, those bolts could penetrate mail. The crossbowmen had to be dealt with.

He looked for a vantage point where he could have a clear shot and settled on the roof of the dormitory. He darted through the door to find a hallway that ran the length of the interior with small, windowless cells for the monks along the outer wall. He turned left and hurried to the last cell. There were four straw pallets on the floor, marking the tiny space as home to four monks. Through the walls, Roland could hear the sounds of battle only a few feet away.

Above his head were pitched beams covered in thatch. He set aside his bow and drew his short sword. There was a tiny stone ledge against the western wall that held a candle and a crucifix. He used it like a step to hoist himself up and began hacking at the dense mass of straw. As it started to loosen, he set the sword aside and pulled handfuls of the thatch down into the cell until he could see grey sky through a hole.

He widened the opening enough for his shoulders to pass through then dropped back inside to take up his bow. As he turned to climb up, he was startled to see a face peering down at him. The man was squinting as his eyes tried to adjust to the dim light of the interior. He did not see the horn-tipped end of the longbow that took him under the chin and sent him tumbling backwards off the roof.

Roland hoisted himself back up and poked his head cautiously through the hole in the thatch. The roof of the dormitory was empty. Pulling himself halfway through the opening, he peered over the south edge of the roof. It was a chaotic scene, with a solid mass of English warriors jammed into the space between the dormitory and the stables. Scores of men were clambering up the outside of the barricade, though few were taking their chances at the centre where Declan stood. Roland counted five dead or wounded men draped across the barricades at the Irish knight's feet.

Two crossbowmen standing well to the rear did not have to face this Irishman's deadly sword to strike at him. One was trying to get a clear shot at Declan and the other was bent forward, hauling back on the string of his weapon to cock it. Roland scrambled onto the roof and tried to find firm footing on the wet straw. A slip here would send him sliding over the lip and into the midst of the English attack.

He went to one knee, his other foot braced against the far edge of the hole. He steadied his breathing and drew, taking aim at the man ready to discharge his bolt. It was an awkward angle, but the distance was short. It took over a hundred pounds of pull to draw his bow and when that stored power was released the bodkin head arrow drove through the Englishman's mail and deep into his chest. As the man pitched forward his hand closed on the crossbow tickler and his bolt buried itself in the back of one of his fellows a few yards to the front.

The other crossbowman looked up in alarm when he saw his comrade go down. He saw Roland on the dormitory roof drawing a second arrow and frantically tried to fit a bolt into the groove atop the crossbow stave. He was too slow.

Roland looked back to the barricade and saw Declan raise his sword in salute. He didn't linger to return the gesture as two spears whistled past his head. Below him, a man ignited a torch and plunged it into the thatch where the roof overhung the outer wall of the dormitory. The dry straw under the eaves caught instantly.

It was time to move.

***

The archer on the dormitory roof did not go unnoticed by Captain Oliver. He was standing no more than ten yards from his crossbowman when the man took an arrow to the chest. His second crossbowman tried desperately to get off a shot, but fumbled with his bolt for a heartbeat too long and fell beside his comrade. Oliver saw one of his men fire the thatch on the roof to drive off this nettlesome archer. As the bowman retreated, Oliver realized with a shock that he knew the man.

Inness…

It was the bastard who'd laid him low at Carrickfergus! A feeling of triumph swept over him. He'd hoped one day to avenge that stinging insult. Now fate had delivered Sir Roland Inness to Armagh—and that day was at hand. He might be a mercenary, but here was one man he would gladly kill for free.

***

Roland ran down the narrow hall of the dormitory as clumps of flaming thatch dropped around his head. He beat out smoking embers on his shoulders and sleeves as he burst through the door and onto the square. Turning the corner of the burning building, he saw that the O'Duinnes were hard-pressed, but still holding back the English onslaught.

Near Declan, he watched Cathal O'Duinne making efficient use of his long-handled axe. The heavy blade could not penetrate good mail, but not every man coming over the top could afford the best mail and those that could still risked fractured ribs or cracked skulls from the force of the man's blow.

He'd seen over a dozen English dead on the far side of the barricade, but the mercenaries had also drawn blood. On this side of the barrier, he saw five dead clansmen lying where they'd fallen, but for the moment, the barricade across the Dungannon Road was holding.

Past the barricade he now saw smoke rising from the thatch of the stable roof. Inside he heard a horse's shrill whinny of alarm, but there was no time now to think of horses. Beyond the stable he saw the small barrier thrown up between the stable and the small huts of the village was in danger of being overwhelmed. He ran past the burning stables and drew his sword. As he ran, he saw Brother Cyril among the defenders, wielding a short sword with surprising skill. It was well that he did, as more mercenaries were gaining the top of the barricade.

Ahead he saw an Englishman with a short sword in one hand and an axe in the other standing triumphantly atop the jumble of wood looking down at an Irish warrior bleeding on the ground. Roland dropped his sword and drew his final arrow as the man bent his knees to hop down from his perch. The shaft took the mercenary in the gut and he staggered backwards, crashing into a pair of his comrades trying to scale the barricade from the other side. Out of arrows, he laid down his bow, took up his sword and ran to fill the gap left by the fallen clansman. As he stepped into the hole in the line, he hailed the monk.

"Doing the Lord's work, Brother Cyril?"

The skinny monk's eyes lit up and his mouth split into a gap-toothed grin when he saw who had stepped in beside him.

"Not at the moment, lord!" he said, raising his bloody sword. "I'll do me penance later."

***

Charles Oliver watched Roland Inness disappear through the roof of the burning dormitory and rushed to the barricade at the Dungannon Road, forcing his way through the crush of his own men assaulting the Irish line. He clambered up the side, enough to see into the square, and was rewarded with a clear view of the man he sought.

Inness had escaped the burning dormitory and Oliver watched as the man turned and ran to the south, passing out of view behind the stables. The mercenary captain climbed down from the barricade and pushed his way back to the rear. He tapped a sergeant on the shoulder.

251

"Bring twenty men and follow me!" he ordered.

The sergeant began grabbing men and pushing them to the rear to follow their captain. Oliver led them south, past the burning stable.

***

Up the hill, the commander of de Courcy's Irish troops looked up as the rain that had bedevilled his men finally ended and the sun broke through the clouds. Now that his troops had gained the high ground, he'd reformed his own lines and resumed the assault. Behind him, the north slope of the hill was littered with the dead and dying. The men of Antrim and Down had paid a high price to climb that slick hillside, but O'Neill's men had suffered grievous losses as well. He looked at the thin line that now stood between him and the square of Armagh.

"Over soon," he said to no one in particular.

***

Charles Oliver's lungs and eyes were burning from the smoke of the blazing stable as he picked his way over the barricade, but he paid no mind to that. He had sent his score of fresh men over the barrier and they had driven the Irish back. He could see them giving ground slowly, forced back beyond the entrance to the stable. Oliver knew the outcome of battles hung on such moments. If his men could put this small group to flight, the entire O'Neill line holding the western approaches to the abbey square could be rolled up. Then de Courcy could have his massacre, but first, he would deal with a more personal matter.

Twenty yards away stood Sir Roland Inness. The commander of the Invalid Company was at the centre of the Irish line, trying to keep their withdrawal from turning into a rout. Fate had now given him the chance to wipe away the stain this man had inflicted on his reputation. He moved forward slowly and watched as Inness stepped inside the arc of a battle axe and drove his short blade in under his man's chin. As the man fell backwards, Oliver stepped in his place.

"Inness!" he shouted, holding the hilt of his broadsword in two hands and moving cautiously forward. "You surprised me at Carrickfergus, but no surprises today!"

252

***

In the swirling smoke, Roland did not recognize the mercenary leader for a moment, but his words were enough to mark him.

"Captain Oliver," he called back, "how is the knee?"

"Well enough," the man growled as he moved in closer. Behind him, dozens of English mercenaries were streaming over the abandoned barricade, but seeing their captain challenge this lone man in the Irish line, they hung back to watch. A few spread out and began to circle Roland.

"Stay back!" the captain snarled. "I'll kill 'im myself."

The roof of the stable was fully ablaze now and the grey smoke grew thick around the men on the ground as Oliver continued to move slowly toward Roland.

"Gut 'im, Cap'n!" a rough voice urged from behind the mercenary captain.

Other voices hurled insults at the lone man who stood waiting for Oliver's approach. The Englishman affected a relaxed manner as he held his sword almost casually in his right hand.

"I'm told you dropped from Lord de Courcy's privy to escape," he taunted, sniffing at the air and wrinkling his nose in distaste. "Like a turd."

Roland paid no attention to his words or his manner. He watched Oliver's midsection and his sword hand and when the Englishman suddenly uncoiled at him with a straight thrust of his long blade, he parried it easily. The English groaned at the miss as Oliver sprang back.

As the mercenary readied his next advance, Roland sprang at him, directing a thrust at Oliver's head that sent him lurching backwards, but not before the tip of Roland's short sword opened a gash in the man's chin. The mercenary captain stumbled into the ranks of his own men, blood streaming from the wound, his face pale.

Sir Alwyn Madawc had once told him that there comes a time in a fight when a man knows he's beaten. It might come after trading many blows, when the arms grow heavy and the breath grows ragged. Or it can come with blinding swiftness when a man realizes he is overmatched. As a breeze momentarily cleared the smoke, Roland saw the shaken look on the Englishman's face and knew that Charles Oliver was beaten. Beaten men sometimes fight on even when they know they will die. It is a point of honour for some men. Oliver, being a stranger to honour, did neither. He pointed his sword at Roland and screamed at his men.

"Kill the bastard!"

The men standing idly watching their Captain be bested needed no encouragement. They surged forward. They were ten paces from Roland and the Irish line when a dark shape came barrelling out of the billowing smoke. A horse had bolted out of the burning stables and burst right through the English line, bowling over three men and scattering the rest. Even in the thick haze, Roland recognized the familiar lines of the animal.

It was The Grey.

And there was no mistaking the boy who was perched on the big gelding's back. Having cut a swath through the mercenaries, Finn Mac Clure deftly swung The Grey's head around and charged back through the startled ranks of Englishmen a second time, reining in before the line of Irish defenders. The look on the boy's face showed something between terror and triumph, but he blanched when he saw the fury on Roland's face.

"Down!" the young knight screamed. The boy slid off The Grey's back, his face flushed. Roland slapped the horse on the rump and it trotted off toward the empty square. Finn started to speak, but Roland grabbed him by the arm and shoved him after The Grey.

"Get yourself to the cross and stay there!" he commanded.

Finn saw no profit in arguing and fled behind the horse. Roland turned to Cyril.

"Get to Sir Declan," he shouted over the roar of the fire as the English recovered and started to advance once more. "Tell him to fall back. We can't hold them here!"

Cyril nodded and sprinted to the rear. Captain Oliver had managed to regather his men after they'd been scattered by the unexpected arrival of the horse. Now he ordered them forward once more. When they saw the O'Neill men falling back, the English sprang after them like dogs let off their leash. Roland watched them come and knew that if the Irish broke now, they would be slaughtered like so many sheep.

"Steady!" he shouted down the line as the mercenaries pressed in on them.

***

Declan gritted his teeth and shoved the heel of his boot against the man's chest. The mercenary had made a bad investment in cheap mail and Declan's broadsword had pierced it, sinking deep into the man's ribcage. Now the blade stubbornly refused to be drawn out. He shoved with his boot and jerked at the hilt desperately as another Englishman, with proper mail, was nearly on top of him.

At last the blade slid free and he raised it in time to block the new man's vicious overhead slash. In the heat of battle, men tended to forget basic swordsmanship. An overhead slash carries great striking power—if the blow lands, but if it does not, the swordsman is overbalanced and exposed. It was one of the first lessons one learned. As their swords met, Declan slid to his left and tilted his blade, forcing the man's weapon to slide harmlessly past. As the Englishman lurched forward, Declan slammed the steel pommel of his broadsword into his temple, dropping the man like a poleaxed steer.

They'd lost eight men dead or wounded at the barricade and slain a score of mercenaries, but there were just too many English to kill. A new rush of thirty men scrambled up the barricade and the O'Duinne clansmen were forced back. They gave ground slowly, their line now anchored by the burning buildings on either side of the road.

Behind him he heard someone shout his name and glanced over his shoulder to see Brother Cyril running toward him. The monk was pointing back toward where he'd come, and Declan did not have to wait for his message, He saw the Irish line that had held the southern barricades falling back toward the square. He grabbed Cathal by the arm and pointed to the O'Neill men off to their left.

"Form on them!" he shouted.

***

Up the hill by the church, the weight of numbers had begun to break Hugh O'Neill's line. In the desperate fighting, quarter was neither asked nor given. The O'Neill men knew that defeat likely meant death, so they fought like cornered animals. Still, they were pushed back, a yard at a time, into the abbey square. O'Neill looked behind him and saw Meg standing forlornly beside the high cross holding the bell of Saint Patrick. He felt a wave of despair as he wondered if, by trying to save Armagh, he had destroyed the Cenél Eoghain.

Inside the church, Archbishop O'Connor knelt behind the locked door of the nave and prayed. If O'Neill went down to defeat, he knew the locked door would be to no avail. He wasn't afraid to die, but knowing that Saint Patrick's bell would fall back into de Courcy's hands and this church, the mother church of Ireland, would be desecrated, broke his heart. He wept as he prayed.

***

Declan parried a slash at his chest, bringing his own sword down in a short chopping stroke that shattered the Englishman's shoulder. As the man recoiled, he looked to his left and saw Roland among the men falling back from the southern barricades.

"Roland! To me!"

Quickly the two lines merged and the retreat slowed. Roland drew up next to Declan, breathing hard from the fighting and the choking smoke from the burning buildings. In the wake of their retreat, both men could see de Courcy's mercenaries tearing apart the barricades they'd just abandoned.

"Cavalry next!" Declan shouted, pointing toward the Dungannon Road.

"Aye," Roland shouted back. "Going to get bloody soon."

***

Sir John de Courcy, Prince of Ulster, had waited a long time for this moment. He watched as his men tore apart the barricade across the Dungannon Road. It had taken longer than he'd expected for his men to drive the defenders off that infernal barrier, but soon the way would be clear. He turned in his saddle and looked down the line of his heavy cavalry, the most feared fighting force north of Dublin.

"Make ready!" he shouted and drew his long broadsword, holding it high overhead.

All down the line men drew their own swords and gripped their reins tighter. De Courcy patted his great white warhorse on the neck and leaned forward to whisper in the animal's ear.

"Now is your time," he said. "You were born and bred for this!"

The big horse pawed the ground, its nostrils flaring. De Courcy lowered his sword and pointed it toward the new opening on the road. He kicked his horse into a trot and eighty men followed him.

***

Declan chanced a look over his shoulder and saw that O'Neill's lines up by the church had grown dangerously thin and were beginning to be breached in places. Soon they too would be forced back into the square. He started to turn back, but something else caught his eye. It was Margaret, standing at the foot of the high cross, cradling Saint Patrick's bell in her arms.

He cursed under his breath. The girl was maddening! When they'd met at dawn, she'd promised to take shelter in the church when the fighting began. He admired her courage, but as he'd come to learn, a promise from Margaret Maelchallain was a flimsy thing.

He was turning away when he saw movement behind the girl and realized Meg wasn't completely alone. Standing near the high cross was the skinny boy, Finn Mac Clure. He knew Roland had ordered the lad to get out of Armagh the night before, but here he was. He uttered another oath.

Will no one in this damned country do what they're told?

As he turned back to face the advancing English, a line of horses charged out of the smoke.

***

The heavy cavalry surged up the Dungannon Road like a dammed river unleashed. A few of the mounts were spooked by the raging fires on both sides of the road and bolted, but most held formation as they charged between the burning buildings toward the abbey square. It was a sight to make even the bravest man quail, but the clansmen of the Cenél Eoghain had nowhere left to run, so they stood and fought.

Declan saw a spear on the ground. Plucking it up, he braced the butt against his foot just as a man on a bay warhorse was whipping his mount straight at him. No matter how well trained, a horse will not mindlessly impale itself on a steel blade and this horse was no exception. As Declan raised the spear, the animal reared and twisted away. For an instant, the rider's side was exposed and Declan drove the spear in under the man's ribs. Only six inches of the spearpoint penetrated the mail, but it was enough to unhorse de Courcy's man.

With its rider on the ground, the big warhorse pranced about skittishly, unsure what to do. Declan did not hesitate. He grasped the pommel and hoisted himself up into the saddle. Seizing the reins, he steadied the horse, then drove his heels into its haunches. The warhorse needed no further encouragement as it bolted into the path of an oncoming wave of riders.

De Courcy's men did not recognize the threat. The Irish at Armagh had no cavalry and the mailed warhorse with a mail-clad warrior in the saddle looked to be one of their own. By the time they realized their mistake, it was too late. Declan stood in his stirrups and smashed his blade into one rider's helmet causing him to tumble over his mount's backside. Uncoiling back to his right, he took a second rider in the side with a vicious backhand slash of his broadsword, unhorsing the man. Before any could stop him, he'd cut his way through the formation and was in their rear.

As he jerked on the reins to bring the horse around, he saw that the element of surprise was now gone. Three of De Courcy's men had turned their mounts away from the Irish line to deal with this new threat. Before they could ride him down, Declan whipped the horse into a gallop. The animal thundered across the cobbles, cutting directly across the path of another wave of riders bearing down on the Irish line. Horses and riders veered away, thinking one of their own men had lost control of his mount. The Irish, seeing this rider sow chaos among the enemy horsemen parted their line to let him pass. He rode through the gap and into the middle of the square.

As the heavy cavalry milled about in confusion trying to reform, Declan saw de Courcy sitting still as a statue on his huge white stallion. The magnificent horse stood a good seventeen hands high and the man looked to be over six feet tall. Atop this huge horse the Prince looked like some giant out of legend. Declan thought back to what Sir Roger had said about this Prince of Ulster.

One of the most dangerous men in Christendom.

In his full battle array, De Courcy certainly looked dangerous. He was staring into the square, like a hawk searching for a hare. For a moment, the Prince's gaze lingered on Declan then it moved on, sweeping across open ground until it reached the high cross. De Courcy stiffened and leaned forward, staring intently at Meg Maelchallain. He bent down and seemed to speak into his horse's ear.

Declan watched this odd display, then patted his new mount on the neck and spoke quietly to the animal.

"Yer Prince is daft," he murmured.

***

De Courcy could not believe his luck. The girl was standing there unguarded in the centre of the square, with the bell of Saint Patrick in her hands. He'd expected the Irish to send their precious relic south on a fast horse once it had been used to whip up O'Neill's troops before the battle. He'd hardly dared hope O'Neill would keep the thing at Armagh, but these men of Tir Eoghain seemed incapable of prudence. Now he would make them pay once more!

He dug his boot heels into the stallion's flanks. The big horse lurched into motion, gaining speed with each stride as it charged toward the Irish line. A man flung a spear, which de Courcy turned aside with his shield as the warhorse smashed into the thin line of men south of the square. It was hardly a contest. Men went flying as horse and rider burst cleanly through the Irish line and into the open ground beyond.

De Courcy did not slacken his speed, whipping the horse with his reins as the animal barrelled toward the high cross, its hooves striking sparks on the cobbles. Margaret saw him coming and stood frozen to the spot. Declan kicked his own horse into motion. De Courcy saw the rider coming at him and veered away from the cross to meet him head-on. He raised his shield on his left side and drew back his broadsword. As the riders met, de Courcy thrust his shield forward, leaving Declan with no angle to employ his sword and almost unhorsing him. As de Courcy swept past, he twisted in the saddle and unleashed his longsword in a vicious slash that missed Declan's head by inches.

Both riders hauled in their reins and turned for another charge. At the high cross, Margaret could not bear to watch and closed her eyes tightly. Declan watched de Courcy whipping his big horse back into a gallop and realized that with no shield this fight would not end well for him. He slapped the bay warhorse on the rump and charged back toward the oncoming rider. With no more than spear's length between them, he jerked his horse's head to the left.

The bay swerved into the path of the white stallion, slamming into the larger horse with a sickening thud. The impact knocked the bay off its feet. As it fell, Declan went with it, striking the ground with stunning force and sliding across the cobbles. The big stallion, unable to stop its momentum stumbled over the fallen bay, pitching forward. John de Courcy flew over the horse's head and landed with a crash twenty feet past Declan.

For a moment, neither man moved, then Declan stirred and sat up. His head was swimming and there was blood in his eyes. He could feel his left arm was broken above the wrist, but everything else seemed intact. He saw his sword lying just out of reach and dragged himself over to grasp the hilt. His horse had managed to scramble to its feet and wandered unsteadily off across the square.

Beyond the Irish line, he could see the Prince's men gathering to come to de Courcy's aid. Using his sword as a crutch, he got shakily to his feet. Margaret Maelchallain, who'd opened her eyes at the sound of the collision between the two horses, thrust the bell into Finn's hands and ran to Declan's side, putting an arm around his waist to steady him and draping his good right arm across her shoulders.

"You're hurt," she said.

Declan looked down and saw that he was bleeding on her blue dress and stepped away from the girl. A few feet away he saw de Courcy jerk and raise his head. He pushed Margaret back toward the high cross.

"See to yer bell," he ordered and turned to face de Courcy in time to see the big man drag himself up on all fours and lift his head. He looked right by Declan as though he wasn't there and stared at Margaret and the bell. There was madness in his eyes.

***

In the chaos of battle, the orderly passage of time can seem to gather speed or slow to a crawl as events unfold. Roland watched Declan disrupt the cavalry charge and make his way back inside the Irish lines in what seemed the blink of an eye. But as John de Courcy broke through the Irish line and Declan swerved his stolen charger into the path of the man's huge stallion, time seemed to slow as though in a dream. He saw the horses collide and go down. He saw the riders flung from their saddles. His gut twisted into a knot as he saw Declan slam into the cobbles and slide across the stones.

Seeing Declan lying motionless on the ground, caused time to snap back to its normal pace. Roland picked up the shield of a dead clansman and turned away from the Irish line. He ran toward his fallen friend and felt a surge of relief when he saw Declan stir and get to his feet. Behind him, he heard a new uproar and turned to see three horsemen slam into the Irish defenders, punching a ten foot hole in their line. A dozen English mercenaries followed them on foot, charging through the gap and converging on their fallen leader.

Roland sprinted toward the high cross where Declan stood leaning on Meg. As the English mercenaries fanned out and moved toward them, Roland saw Finn backed up against the high cross, clutching the bell.

"Get to The Grey, boy!" he shouted, pointing to where the big gelding stood placidly a few yards away from the cross. "Watch for an opening, then ride and don't look back."

The Irish boy had tears in his eyes, but he did not protest. He thrust the bell back into Margaret's hands and ran to the horse. Declan stood on his own now, swaying slightly from side to side, waiting to face the approaching English.

"Yer bleeding," he said as Roland reached him..

Roland looked down and saw bright red blood seeping through the mail on his left side. In the heat of the battle he had not noticed the wound and had no memory of receiving it. He looked at Declan's own bloody face and laughed.

"Maybe we'll bleed to death before they kill us," he said.

***

John de Courcy jerked his arms away from the men lifting him to his feet. He reached down and picked up his steel helmet and jammed it on his head.

"My sword," he said, pointing to his weapon lying where it had fallen on the cobbles. One of his men ran to secure the blade and passed it to the Prince who grasped the hilt. Sword in hand, he strode across the cobbles and barked an order for the mercenaries to make way for him. They spread out to let the big nobleman pass, then closed ranks behind him. De Courcy stopped ten yards from the two men backed up to the high cross. He looked at them with utter disdain.

"Ranulf's men," he hissed. "I might have guessed."

"Earl Ranulf cares not a whit for yer shitty little kingdom," Declan declared."

De Courcy snorted.

"You lie! But when you two fail to return to Chester, perhaps he'll choose to tend to the Welsh Marches and leave Ireland to me!"

Roland held his arms out to his sides in exasperation.

"Are we going to get on with this—or do you plan to talk us to death?"

De Courcy's lip curled and he moved toward them, his long blade held ready. Roland moved to meet him, but Declan stopped him, slapping the flat of his broadsword blade against his friend's chest.

"Not with that." he said, nodding toward Roland's short sword. "And you know I'm the better man with a blade. Watch my flanks."

With that, he went forward to meet the Prince of Ulster.

***

Sitting atop The Grey, Finn Mac Clure looked out over the horror that was the abbey square of Armagh and felt heartsick. He'd disobeyed his master and if, by some miracle, both he and Sir Roland survived the day, he knew he would never be trusted to be the man's squire. But seeing men falling all around, he felt certain that there would be no miracle this day. He felt oddly unafraid, knowing he would likely die soon. He just hoped it wouldn't hurt too much. It was sad that his life was about to end before it had well begun, but he had long ago concluded that it was an unfair world.

Below him he saw Margaret Maelchallain standing alone at the base of the cross holding Saint Patrick's bell. The relic had been taken from the Irish, stolen back from the English and would soon be back in de Courcy's hands. He shook his head. If Saint Patrick was directing these events, he must be a fickle saint indeed!

Near at hand, he saw the Prince moving toward Sir Declan with a dozen men behind him. He felt with his hand for the hilt of the dagger Sir Roland had given him. If he could only get close enough, he would plunge that blade into de Courcy's black heart. But Sir Roland had given him an order and he was determined to follow it—this time.

He stood up in the stirrups and looked out across the raging fight that completely encircled the square now and saw no path through the battle lines. The Grey was standing so steadily amidst the clamour of the battle that the boy squirmed around and stood up in the saddle to get a better view.

The fire at the monk's dormitory had largely burned itself out and through the clearing smoke he saw something odd off to the west. He looked again, straining his eyes and his breath caught in his throat. He slid down the side of the horse and ran to the high cross. He tugged on Margaret's sleeve, pointing to the west.

"Horses!" he shouted.

The woman seemed not to understand.

"Horses are coming up the road!" he shouted again.

"It's de Courcy's cavalry, Finn," she shouted back.

The boy shook his head.

"No, miss. It's Irish horses. Hundreds of them!"

***

The riders came out of the west and charged up the Dungannon Road, four abreast on their shaggy Irish ponies. Near the head of the column a man carried a standard that whipped in the wind. It was the crescent moon banner of Clan Mac Lochlainn.

They did not slacken speed as they reached the smouldering buildings on either side of the road, plunging through the last of the smoke and into the abbey square. Every rider carried an iron-tipped throwing spear and as they drove in toward the English they launched them with deadly effect. Men on foot as well as those mounted went down in scores. The riders peeled off to the side so the next rank of horsemen could take their place.

This sudden hail of spears tore holes in the English line and forced men to turn away from the hard pressed Irish in the square to face this new threat. As each wave of Mac Lochlainn riders hurled their spears, they dismounted and fell on de Courcy's men with axes, swords and dirks.

The surprise was total and the English mercenaries, assailed now from front and rear, began to fall apart. In dozens, then in scores, men began to break and run. At the north end of the square, the Irish levies, so near to breaking through the O'Neill lines, saw the Irish horsemen strike de Courcy's cavalry and watched in alarm as the English mercenaries crumbled.

The men of Antrim and Down had no love for the Cenél Eoghain. Nor had they marched to Armagh out of love for John de Courcy. They fought because they had been compelled to do so, but seeing the English break and run, they needed no encouragement to do the same. They turned away from the O'Neill line and fled back down the hill they had fought and bled to take.

***

Near the centre of the abbey square, the men who had come to de Courcy's aid saw the disaster unfolding behind them. One rushed up to the nobleman and grabbed his arm, frantically pointing to the collapsing English lines. De Courcy jerked away and turned on the man.

"My bell, damnit!" he screamed, pointing at Margaret.

But the three riders who had followed him into the square were already mounting their horses. The mercenaries, who had no mounts, saw their comrades being cut down and knew there was no profit to be had by dying in this square. Two Englishmen were the first to turn and run. De Courcy swore at them, but his oaths had no effect on the others who rushed to join the deserters. Their panicked flight left the Prince standing alone in the square, with only his three loyal riders begging him to flee.

John de Courcy might be a madman, but he was not suicidal. He swore a final oath and spat on the ground. He looked for his mount and saw the big stallion had wandered to the far end of the square. With no time to retrieve the animal, he cursed again, and ordered one of his men to dismount. When the man hesitated, de Courcy dragged him from the saddle and mounted the riderless horse. In the chaos south of the square, the rest of his cavalry were fighting desperately to cut their way out of the trap, frantically whipping their horses toward the east, the only clear path out of the killing ground that was the abbey. With a last withering look at Margaret and the bell, de Courcy dug his heels into the horse's flanks and joined the desperate mob fleeing for their lives.

Having seen the English lines fall apart, Charles Oliver and a dozen of his men had already fled the abbey square and were running for a patch of woods only a half mile to the east. In the trees, they might hope to evade pursuers. As they ran, de Courcy, now flanked by a dozen of his precious cavalrymen

265

thundered past them without so much as a glance. Oliver cursed at his employer, but kept running. Slowed by their mail, they'd covered only half the distance to the trees when the Mac Lochlainn men appeared on the road. As the English ran, men riding bareback on Irish ponies swarmed around them.

None reached the trees.

Victory

*R*oland and Declan, too weary and injured to take up the pursuit, watched as de Courcy and his men were put to flight by the onslaught of the Mac Lochlainn clans. The wound in Roland's side was still bleeding and he was beginning to feel the pain. He put a hand over the mail, pressing down to staunch the flow. He felt a little light-headed as he sat down on the stone pedestal at the foot of Armagh's high cross. Declan plopped down beside him, cradling his broken forearm with his right hand. He looked over at his friend.

"You look awful," he said.

"As do you," Roland replied with a weak grin.

He started to say more, but Meg appeared beside them and began to fuss over their wounds. She sent Finn to fetch a slab of wood for a splint and began undoing the lacing at the back of Roland's mail hauberk.

"Need to see what's under there," she said pointing at the seepage staining the mail at Roland's side. She made him raise his arms and, grasping the end of the hauberk sleeves, she pulled the heavy mesh over his head. She dropped down on her haunches and examined Roland's wound.

"Deep," she said flatly, "but you'd be spittin' up blood now if it had struck any vitals."

Finn arrived with a small flat piece of wood he'd wrested from the back of a chair and Meg sent him back to find a clean cloth and water.

"Keep your hand pressed hard there," she ordered Roland as she turned her attention to Declan, gently sliding the sleeve of his hauberk up until she found the ridge on his forearm that marked the break.

"This will hurt," she said, as she grasped his elbow in one hand and applied a surprisingly strong pull to his wrist.

There was a faint grinding sound as the bone slid back into place. Declan gritted his teeth but did not flinch. The bone set, she laid the wood along the top of his arm and tore strips from her dress to bind the splint into place. When Finn came hurrying across the square with a small bucket of water and a piece of linen he'd filched from a trunk in the dormitory, she set about cleaning and bandaging Roland's wound. When the last knot was secure she stepped back to admire her handiwork.

"I think ye'll both live," she declared.

"Thank you, Meg," Declan said as he got to his feet and extended his good hand to Roland, who hauled himself upright. All around them, there were pockets of de Courcy's men surrendering, or still trying to fight their way out of Armagh. The dead and wounded lay everywhere and the Augustinian monks had already emerged from their hiding places in the village to minister to men of both sides.

The thatch roofs of the stable and the western dormitory had fallen in on themselves and the fire was dying, leaving a thin haze of smoke hanging above the abbey. An odd stillness fell over the place as men looked at each other in wonderment that they had survived such a bloodbath. Some sought out companions separated in the fighting and more than a few went down on their knees to thank the almighty for letting them live.

Then the strange stillness was broken as a young man rode back into the square from the east and leapt to the ground, his face flushed with the glow of victory. Men parted out of the way as Conor Mac Lochlainn walked up the gentle slope toward the church. He glanced at Meg standing by the high cross holding the bell and raised a bloodstained sword to her in salute. Behind him, a clansmen raised a bloody axe over his head and shouted.

"Mac Lochlainn!"

All around, men took up the chant as the young clan chief climbed the hill.

"Mac Lochlainn! Mac Lochlainn! Mac Lochlainn!" echoed from the surrounding buildings as Conor's men fell in behind him.

Near the entrance of the church, Hugh O'Neill heard the cheers and saw the young Mac Lochlainn chief marching up the hill in triumph. He slung his axe over his shoulder and marched down the hill to meet him. When the two bitter rivals reached the high cross in the centre of the square they stopped, facing each other. All around the square men fell silent as the two stared at each other without a word.

Then Conor Mac Lochlainn raised a bloody sword over his head. Men all around the square slid their hands toward their weapons. For a long, agonizing moment Mac Lochlainn stared at O'Neill, then he dropped to one knee and offered the hilt of his sword to the man who had blocked his path to the kingship. O'Neill took the weapon and dragged Mac Lochlainn to his feet, clenching him in a bear hug. When he was released, the chief of the Mac Lochlainns turned to his followers and raised a fist.

"O'Neill!" he shouted and all around the hilltop of Armagh the Cenél Eoghain took up the chant.

***

It was fifteen miles from the abbey at Armagh to the ford over the River Bann. For the first ten of those miles, the faster English-bred warhorses were able to keep a distance between them and their Irish pursuers, but in time, the greater stamina of the Irish ponies began to tell. Five miles from the river, they began to close on the slower riders fleeing to the east.

In a panic, de Courcy's men whipped their exhausted mounts toward the river until they were completely blown. Only four riders survived to splash across the Bann.

A mile beyond the river, Sir John de Courcy dismounted and led his knackered horse off the road and into dense woods. He and his three remaining men hid there for a day as Irish patrols scoured the roads for any English stragglers. For two more days, they followed farm paths first east and then south.

It was nearing midnight when the nightguard on the palisade wall of the motte north of Newry heard a pounding on the gate.

It was a dark night and he couldn't see who might be calling at such an odd hour, so he hurried down from the wall walk to the gate below and peered out through the spy hole.

"Open up, for God's sake!" croaked the Prince of Ulster.

***

It took two days for the smell of burnt wood and thatch to fade at Armagh abbey and for the bodies to be buried. Archbishop O'Connor consecrated a new graveyard on the western side of Saint Patrick's church where men from Tir Eoghain were laid to rest beside men from Antrim, Down and England.

The clans of the Cenél Eoghain held vigils for the dead, then one-by-one departed Armagh for their home raths. With the holy abbey town secure and the bell of Saint Patrick safe in the hands of the Maelchallains, their thoughts turned to spring crops that needed tending and cattle that needed to be moved to new pastures. They would gather again in a week for Hugh O'Neill's inauguration at the sacred hill at Tullyhogue.

O'Neill left a small garrison behind to keep watch over the abbey town and to patrol the fords over the Bann. Once he'd seen to the security of Armagh, the high chief of the O'Neills rode home to Dungannon to await the ceremony that would elevate him to King of Tir Eoghain.

On the day after the battle, Margaret Maelchallain sought out Declan at Cathal's tent.

"How is the arm?" she asked.

Declan held up his left forearm, still secured with her splint, and waved it around.

"Good as new!" he said with a grin. "I had a good leech."

That made her smile.

"And your friend, Sir Roland?"

"Oh, the wound's still oozing a bit, but I don't see any corruption. I think he'll live, my lady."

"Change the cloth every few days," she advised.

There was an awkward silence as the subject of wounds and injuries was exhausted. Margaret's face flushed a little.

"Come walk with me?" she asked.

Declan nodded and offered his good right arm. Together they walked up toward the church, passing through the old graveyard on the east side. The many fresh graves on the west side of the church were too melancholy a sight.

"You will be going home?" she asked when they reached the crest of the hill?

"Aye, I expect so."

"You must miss your pretty little fort by the River Dee," she said wistfully.

"I do, Meg. I wish you could see it."

She turned and looked at him, her pale blue eyes searching his face.

"I would like that," she said, in almost a whisper.

"You could, you know. Come with me, Meg. We could be at Shipbrook in a week. Ye've done yer duty as Keeper. Let your brother take up that burden."

She gave him a sad little smile.

"I am sore tempted…," she began, but stopped.

"Mac Lochlainn?" he asked, already sensing the answer.

She nodded.

"He needs me, Declan, more now than if he were king. More, I think, than you do. As you say, I will set aside my duties as Keeper of the bell soon, but I've grown used to having a voice in the counsels of the Cenél Eoghain. I will have that with Conor. That I know."

"And Conor?"

"He's asked me, of his own accord, to marry him. It seems he loves me, Declan."

Declan gave her a wistful smile.

"Then he is smarter—and braver than I took him to be, Meg."

Margaret smiled back at him, then leaned in and kissed his cheek.

"I'll not forget you, Sir Declan," she whispered to him.

Tullyhogue and Home

The sound of pipe music drifted through the trees as twilight fell on the fields and forests surrounding Tullyhogue, ancient inauguration site of the O'Neill chiefs. On paths older than the memory of man, riders converged there from every direction, come to see a new king made for the Cenél Eoghain. It seemed half of Tir Eoghain was gathering for this event—the first O'Neill king in a hundred years.

Beneath the inauguration hill, a boisterous crowd was gathered outside a large hall. Every man of any note in the land had come to pay respects to Hugh O'Neill on this day. Turlough O'Hagan, hereditary guardian of Tullyhogue, met each of the new arrivals and directed them to where O'Neill was greeting well-wishers at the back of the hall. The chief of the O'Neills was dressed in his finest clothes. He still looked nothing like one pictured a king, but he had more than proven his fitness to rule with the victory at Armagh.

Standing proudly beside O'Neill was Keiran O'Duinne who had been officially named as the new king's herald. The young man's face lit up when he saw his father coming through the crowd and he tapped Hugh on the shoulder to alert him. O'Neill tactfully saw off a long-winded supporter and opened his arms wide.

"Cathal, old friend! I've been wondering where ye were!" he roared as he grabbed the O'Duinne chief by the hand and pulled him in for a quick embrace. "My first command as king should be for ye to sire more sons," he proclaimed. "Keiran now claims he can scratch his backside with his left hand," he said with a laugh, "and I damned well know he can kill Englishmen with it. Saw it myself! As for yer youngest, I'm sorry Sir Declan could not stay for this. We owe him much. He stood with us in our hour of need and showed us how to fight the English."

Cathal nodded.

"His coming was a blessing to me and to the Cenél Eoghain, Hugh, but the lad was ready to go home. I think he found what he came to Ireland to find."

Others were lining up to meet O'Neill and Cathal took his leave. As he left the hall, a shout went up as a large troop of horsemen came galloping across the meadow. As the riders drew near, he saw the crescent moon banner held high by the lead horseman. The Mac Lochlainns had come to do homage to the new king of Tir Eoghain.

Riding beside Conor Mac Lochlainn was his bride, Margaret Maelchallain. Cathal watched the girl dismount and smiled to himself. He hadn't failed to see the looks that had passed between the beautiful Keeper and his son and wondered if the young chief of the Mac Lochlainns knew how close he'd come to losing his new wife. Meg looked up and saw him smiling at her. She smiled back and gave him a little English curtsey, then took the arm of her new husband.

***

It was sunset, when from somewhere up the hill, drums began a solemn, steady beat. At the sound, Rory O'Cahan and Turlough O'Hagan directed men to clear the hall. O'Hagan was the guardian of Tullyhogue, but the chief of the powerful O'Cahan clan would conduct the inauguration ceremony as was his hereditary right. As the two men exited the building, torches set at regular intervals along the path up the hill were lit, pushing back the gathering twilight. The torchlight gave a pagan feel to scene and, in truth, parts of the inauguration ceremony had roots in a time before Christianity came to Ireland.

Men of the O'Hagan clan pushed back the crowd to make a path for the dignitaries as Hugh O'Neill stepped out of the hall. Turlough O'Hagan lead the processional, flanked by two of his sons. He was followed by Rory O'Cahan, who carried a staff of office in one hand and a golden shoe in the other. Next came Archbishop Tomas O'Connor, his snow white robes reflecting the orange light of the torches. Then came Hugh O'Neill, looking a trifle nervous but resolute amidst all this formality.

Trailing O'Neill were the chiefs of the clans that had pledged their support to him. At the head of this group walked Conor Mac Lochlainn and a half step behind him came Margaret Maelchallain, the only woman in the group. She was dressed in a shimmering green dress with gold embroidery, her long black hair woven into a thick braid. Around her neck, suspended by a silver chain, she wore Saint Patrick's bell. Men in the crowd crossed themselves as the Keeper passed by.

Behind Margaret came the O'Shanes, the O'Carolans, the Mac Mahons, the O'Gormleys and many other clans of the Cenél Eoghain. Near the end of that parade came Cathal O'Duinne, marching proudly with the rest.

The torchlit path wound along the contours of the slope until it passed through cuts in two steep earthen berms that enclosed the hilltop. Carved pillars of oak were set along the outer berm and more torches blazed atop the inner mound, illuminating a circular expanse of green grass. In the centre of the circle sat a boulder with three slabs of flat stone affixed to the back and both sides. This was the Leac na Ri, the inauguration throne of the O'Neills.

Turlough O'Hagan gave a small hand signal and the drums abruptly fell silent. The guardian of Tullyhogue then withdrew from the circle, his duty done. A buzz of anticipation ran through the crowd, but the voices fell silent when Rory O'Cahan stepped into the centre of the ring and raised his arms heavenward. For what seemed an eternity, he stood there, letting the silence set the stage for what was to follow. Finally he lowered his arms and began to speak.

"From the time of Niall of the Nine Hostages," he intoned, his deep voice booming into the night, "we men of the Cenél Eoghain have gathered here at the sacred hill of Tullyhogue to witness the inauguration of kings and to do homage to the men chosen to rule over us. On this day, we freely submit to an unbroken line of blood-royal that has flowed in the veins of our princes for seven hundred years!"

There were murmurs of agreement from the crowd as O'Cahan paused and looked over the assembled multitudes.

"Many a High King of Ireland has shared that royal blood and many a Prince of Tir Eoghain. Today we acknowledge, we accept, we proclaim Hugh O'Neill our King! On the morrow, messengers will ride to the other kings of the Irish—in Connacht and Tir Connell and Munster—bringing them greetings from our new King. To the English, he has already made himself known—at Armagh!"

That brought a defiant roar from the crowd. O'Cahan let them have their moment. There were few among the gathered clansmen who had not lost comrades in that great victory. At length, he raised his arms to silence the uproar. When quiet prevailed once more, he led O'Neill to the Leac na Ri. O'Neill sat on the stone seat and looked slightly dwarfed there. It mattered not to the crowd as O'Cahan completed the ceremony.

"Hugh O'Neill is King by right of arms, King by blood, King by all here who proclaim it!" he intoned. He handed O'Neill the staff of office then tossed the golden shoe over the man's head, a symbol of submission.

The crowd cheered until hoarse.

***

The two men stood at the stern of the trading cog and watched as the sun sank out of sight behind the low green hills of Ireland.

"It's a beautiful country," Roland said, "but I don't think I'll be coming back."

That prompted a laugh from Declan as he held up his arm, still encased in a splint.

"You didn't enjoy your traditional Irish welcome, Roland?"

Roland stretched his left arm and felt the tug of the newly-forming scar on his side

"Imprisonment and wounding, you mean?"

"Exactly! It wouldn't be a proper Irish gathering without a few bandages to show for it."

Roland looked up to see the sky turning shades of gold and orange above the western horizon,

"They'll be making O'Neill king about now," he said.

Declan nodded.

"If anyone can keep the Cenél Eoghain free, it's Hugh O'Neill."

"We could have stayed for the ceremony."

Declan shrugged.

"I got what I came for. It was time to go."

Roland laid a hand on his friend's shoulder.

"I think maybe you got more than you came for, Dec. She was quite a woman."

Declan swung around and leaned against the rail, facing east now, toward the Irish Sea and England.

"She was that, Roland. I suppose she's married now and I wonder if Conor Mac Lochlainn knows what he's getting in the bargain! Still, I think she made the right choice. I suspect Shipbrook may have been too small a place for a woman like Meg Maelchallain. As for me, it's home and I miss it."

Roland turned to face east with him.

"You could have been an important man in Tir Eoghain if you'd stayed," he said. "O'Neill trusts you."

Declan did not answer for a bit as he looked out over the bow.

"So does Sir Roger," he said finally.

The cog rose on a large swell and plunged down into a trough sending a wave of spray over the bow. On the deck below, Brother Cyril scampered beneath the forecastle in time to escape the cascade, but Finn Mac Clure, having never taken ship before, was drenched.

"He's got a bit to learn, but he's a good lad I think," said Declan nodding toward the sodden boy below them.

"I'd not have brought him along if I didn't think so."

"So what do you intend to do with the lad?"

Roland laughed as he watched Finn squeezing the salt water out of his shirt.

"You said it yourself. Irish boys make the best squires."

Declan O'Duinne

Acknowledgements

This foray across the Irish Sea required me to divert from the rich vein of British history I've been mining for the past five years and dive into late 12th Century Ireland—a bloody time with sparse records. Most historians have had to rely on the Chronicles of the Four Masters and the journals of Giraldus Cambrensis as the primary surviving records of this tumultuous time when Anglo-Norman invaders were relentlessly expanding their domains and Irish kings were fighting among themselves. I have used the same basic sources, but have been helped mightily by some folks who have far more knowledge than I.

I wish to thank Mr. James Kane, an Executive Committee member of the Association of O'Neill Clans, for his generous help in understanding the political setting in the north of Ireland during the final decade of the 12th Century and the rise to power of Hugh O'Neill.

I'm also grateful for the assistance and information provided by the staff of Ranfurly House Arts & Visitor Centre during my research visit to Dungannon, Northern Ireland.

I also wish to thank Ms. Nessa O'Connor of the Irish Antiquities Division of the National Museum of Ireland for telling me how to open the shrine of St. Patrick's bell!

Finally, I wish to thank my editor, Mary Grant, who has diligently reviewed all my manuscripts, fussed at me about my overuse of dashes, pointed out that "the man" is a lazy way to reference a character, noted that no one can be in two places at once and told me when a beautifully written scene wasn't "working." The Saga of Roland Inness would not be nearly as good without her—nor would the rest of my life. Sorry about that dash…

Historical Note

Most of the events depicted in *Declan O'Duinne* are fictional, but this story was built around a core of documented history. It is a tale set amidst the struggle of the Gaelic Irish to resist the rising tide of Anglo-Norman expansion into Ireland. That was a struggle that lasted for over four hundred years, ending finally with the "Flight of the Earls" in 1607, when the last of the Gaelic Earls lost the Nine Years' War and fled to the continent seeking support. They never returned.

Along with my fictional characters, a number of real historical personages appear in this story:

- *Sir John de Courcy*—Prince of Ulster: John de Courcy was an obscure Anglo-Norman knight who served in the garrison in Dublin when King Henry II made his one visitation to Ireland in 1172. Henry is alleged to have made a jest with the young knight, telling him he could have as much of Ulster as he could capture, but de Courcy did not get the joke. He later gathered twenty-two other itinerant knights, along with three hundred foot soldiers and invaded the north. He captured Down and Antrim and ruled there until 1204, when, on King John's orders, he was deposed and captured by Earl Hugh de Lacy. They took him while he was unarmed and unarmoured, praying at Down Abbey on Good Friday. He is said to have torn the iron crucifix from the wall and killed thirteen men before he was subdued. He was imprisoned and later released, but never regained his lands in Ulster. He was extremely religious, though perhaps not quite the zealot portrayed in my story.

- *Muirchertach Mac Lochlainn*—King of Tyrone: Here I took a few liberties with the historical record. Muirchertach did die in 1196, but it was not in a battle with de Courcy as depicted. He was actually assassinated at the council in Armagh that year, allegedly by an O'Neill adherent. Perhaps the fact that at least four O'Neill claimants to the throne were killed by the Mac Lochlainns in the 12ᵗʰ century may have had something to do with this. The assailant was never brought to justice.

- ***Hugh O'Neill***—King of Tyrone: I took fewer liberties with Hugh. He was a dynamic leader and adept at guerrilla warfare. After 1196 he became King of Tir Eoghain and kept the Anglo-Normans at bay until his death in 1230. He was one of the few Gaelic Irish kings to keep his people free of Norman rule and his descendants did the same until his distant namesake Hugh O'Neill (Hugh is an Anglicized version of the Gaelic name, Aedh) joined other rebellious Irish nobles in the Flight of the Earls in 1607.

- ***The Maelchallain Clan***: This is an amazing story. The Maelchallain family was, in fact, charged with the safekeeping of Saint Patrick's bell in 1091. They retained unbroken possession of the bell for over seven hundred years. The last custodian, Henry Mulholland, died childless in 1819. Mulholland is the Anglicized version of Maelchallain. The bell and its ornate shrine are now displayed at the National Museum of Ireland. The pictures of the bell and its shrine that follow were taken by me at the Museum in Dublin. The story of its loss in battle and subsequent theft are fictional as is the character of Margaret Maelchallain.

The battle scenes in the book are fictional, but loosely based on actual battles between the men of Tir Eoghain and the English.

- The battle described in the prologue is based on the Battle of Downpatrick, fought in 1177/1178. In that battle the King of Tyrone led an army against John de Courcy with seven holy relics in the vanguard. The Irish were routed and the relics seized by de Courcy.

- The fight at the River Bann ford is based on the Battle of the Yellow Ford, which was actually fought in 1598. The Battle of the Yellow Ford took place near the Blackwater River where the Irish dug a deep trench by the ford to block the English advance.

• The climactic battle for Armagh Abbey in the story is an amalgam of various encounters around the abbey town in the late twelfth and early thirteenth centuries. Armagh was sacked over a dozen times during the medieval period.

I had the good fortune to visit many of the places described in the book.

• **Carrickfergus Castle** is one of the best preserved Norman castles in the world. The inner ward and keep are little changed from when they were first constructed in the 1180s. Roland's escape from the keep via the privy would have been difficult, though not impossible. There were a number of toilet facilities set into the western curtain wall of the castle and into the keep itself that emptied into the harbour. They were designed such that high tide would wash away the waste twice a day and they still exist today. Allegedly, King John used one of these during his progress through Ireland in 1210 AD and the folks who manage the castle site have installed a life-sized replica of the maligned king in the actual privy there. See my picture three pages on!

• **The Abbey at Down** is no longer there, but the cathedral church, rebuilt many times, is and Saint Patrick is reputed to be buried there. Saint Patrick's church in Armagh was destroyed and rebuilt seventeen times and is now a Church of Ireland cathedral.

• **Tullyhogue** is now referred to as Tullyhogue Fort and is a few miles outside of Dungannon. The inauguration ceremony described herein includes what is known about the procedure as well as a few fictional flourishes. The O'Hagans occupied the site through the 17th century and the O'Cahans did officiate at inaugurations. It is well-documented that a golden shoe was thrown over the O'Neill chief's head during the ceremony to signify submission.

Declan O'Duinne

The Shrine of Saint Patrick's Bell

Wayne Grant

Saint Patrick's Bell

Declan O'Duinne

Privy, Carrickfergus Castle

Wayne Grant

Carrickfergus Castle
1196

Books by Wayne Grant

The Saga of Roland Inness:
Longbow
Warbow
The Broken Realm
The Ransomed Crown
A Prince of Wales
Declan O'Duinne

About The Author

I grew up in a tiny cotton town in rural Louisiana where hunting, fishing and farming are a way of life. Between chopping cotton, dove hunting and Little League ball I developed a love of great adventure stories like *Call It Courage* and *Kidnapped.*

Like most southern boys, I saw the military as an honourable career, so it was a natural step for me to attend and graduate from West Point. I just missed Vietnam, but served in Germany and Korea. I found that life as a Captain in an army broken by Vietnam was not what I wanted and returned to Louisiana and civilian life. I later served for four years as a senior official in the Pentagon and had the honour of playing a small part in the rebuilding of a great U.S. Army.

Through it all, I kept my love for great adventure stories. When I had two sons, I began making up stories for them about a boy and his longbow. Those stories grew to become my first novel, *Longbow.*

I expect to write one more Roland Inness book to complete the Saga and hope to have the next one out by late summer, 2019.

To learn more about The Saga of Roland Inness, visit my website at www.waynegrantbooks.com or the Longbow Facebook page.

The picture was taken at Carrickfergus Castle in May, 2018.

Made in the USA
Middletown, DE
15 January 2019